DO OR DIE
COWBOY

JUNE FAVER

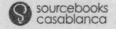

sourcebooks
casablanca

Published by Sourcebooks Casablanca, an imprint of Sourcebooks, Inc.
P.O. Box 4410, Naperville, Illinois 60567-4410
(630) 961-3900
Fax: (630) 961-2168
sourcebooks.com

Printed and bound in the United States of America.
OPM 10 9 8 7 6 5 4 3 2 1

Chapter 1

TYLER GARRETT DROVE AWAY WITHOUT LOOKING back. Truth was, he was afraid to even glance in the rearview mirror for fear he would turn his big Ford extended-cab truck around. Of course, he was hauling a trailer with the finest quarter horse ever bred, so turning around on that two-lane road might have given him a little trouble…but then, trouble was what he did best.

Ty was the middle son. The one who invented the word *trouble*, at least, according to his dad. No one could deny that "Big Jim" Garrett thought the world of his three sons, but somehow it was always Ty who inspired him to call out, "Here comes trouble."

Well, here goes trouble, Dad.

He placed a hand on Lucky's head. The two-year-old golden retriever regarded him with trusting eyes. "We're going to be fine, boy."

He reached the end of the farm-to-market road and idled, looking both ways for traffic, but of course, there was none. With a deep sigh, he hooked a wide right, allowing the trailer to arc out behind him as he pulled onto the interstate. He straightened his shoulders and thought about his destination.

Dallas.

Dallas, where Ty would take the first step in making his own dreams come true. Where he could polish his talent and live up to his mother's aspirations for him as well.

He frowned, his grip on the steering wheel tightening. *Too bad Mom didn't live to see this day. She always believed in me.*

A lump formed in his throat as he pictured her sweet face. She was the one who never failed to show up at the talent shows, looking pleased and applauding like crazy. Making her proud had been one of his prime motivators.

Big Jim, on the other hand, had just shaken his head and said, "That singin' stuff is nice and all, but you need to concentrate on your true callin', boy. You were born to be a rancher. It's in your blood."

Ty sucked in a deep breath and blew it out. Well, he'd done what he could to make that happen. He'd graduated from Texas Tech University with a degree in agricultural economics and range management. He'd devoted years of his life to making his dad proud of him, but ranching just wasn't in his heart.

His mother's last words to him were branded into his memory. She had placed her hand on his cheek and gazed up with love in her eyes. "Follow your heart, Ty. Not many people are blessed with the talent the good Lord gave you, so you need to make the most of it." She had lapsed into a coma and passed away the following day.

Ty owed it to her to make it big. And Dallas was just the launching pad. His friend Will had a recording studio and was going to cut a demo for him. Then, Ty was set to try out for the *Texas Country Star* television show. If he made it through to the state finals, he would go on to compete in the Nashville Idol contest. He was pretty sure he had a good shot.

Ty's departure was taking place a few days earlier than planned. Will had studio time available the beginning of the next week, but after the morning's blowup with Big Jim, Ty had decided to head for Dallas and just hang around at Will's.

He drove east, oblivious to the flat, northern Texas countryside. His head was someplace else, but without much effort, he filled the truck with his strong voice, singing one of his mother's favorite gospel tunes. He could see himself onstage, performing for the Nashville audience. For the world…

After a while, the town of Langston appeared on the horizon. He thought he should stop and grab lunch before the long drive to Big D. It was a fairly small town, so there weren't many choices. He passed a Dairy Queen and Tio's, a Mexican restaurant, before pulling in at Tiny's Diner. It was late, so the lunch crowd had already been and gone. Not too many cars outside. He parked where he could keep an eye on his rig and climbed down out of his truck, leaving the windows cracked for Lucky.

Funny to think he was really on his way. With all his dad's wealth, Ty had only taken what was important to him—his horse, his dog, his guitar, and a few clothes. *'Cause I'm sure not going back.*

A metal cowbell clanked against the glass door when he entered the restaurant. The aroma of good food hit him like a fist. He hadn't realized how hungry he was, since he had forgone breakfast in his rush to leave the sprawling Garrett ranch that morning. The Circle G, with its rambling, Spanish-style ranch house, the many barns, stables, and outbuildings; with thousands of acres of fenced pastureland for the beef cattle and horses; with the long heritage of the Garrett family steeped into the land. Not a problem. Surely his older brother, Colton, or his younger brother, Beau, would pick up the slack. They could take over running the spread when Big Jim was unable. They could provide for future generations of Garretts to carry on the tradition.

"Hello, Tyler," Crystal called out. She was a fixture here at Tiny's. A big lady with a big heart. "Table or booth?" She grabbed a menu and cocked her head, waiting for his answer.

"Table near the front window would be best." Removing his Stetson, he raked his hand through his thick, dark hair.

She walked him over to the window and placed the menu on a table for two. "Here you go. Iced tea?"

"That'll be good." He set the Stetson on the other side of the table and took a seat facing the door. When it opened, he had to check out the new arrival.

Man!

His breath caught as his gaze fell on one of the prettiest women he had ever seen. She wasn't exactly what one could call hot, but when she paused in the open doorway and took a look around, he felt like he'd been kicked in the gut.

Her large, wide-set brown eyes reminded him of a fawn, or perhaps it was her blondish-brown curls, swept up in an untidy gob at the crown of her head. Definitely had the air of a skittish animal, not quite tame. Her threadbare jeans had a rip on one thigh, and she wore a tank top with an oversize blue work shirt on top. She swept the room carefully, as though alert for something, then turned back in the open doorway and motioned someone through.

A young girl stepped forward, pausing when the woman's slender hand came to rest on her shoulder. The girl looked like a replica of the woman, with lighter blonde hair and a big cast on her forearm.

The kid had that same half-wild expression on her face, like she would turn and bolt from the restaurant if something spooked her.

Crystal came to slide Ty's iced tea on the table and then went to greet the newcomers. Apparently, the woman wanted to keep an eye on whatever was out there too, since Crystal seated them at the table next to Ty's, where she sat facing the parking lot. The girl was on her right, facing Ty.

He watched the woman carefully peruse the menu and then reach in her purse. She drew out a wallet and did a quick count of the bills inside. Ty felt a surge of pity, never in his life having to count his money before ordering.

When Crystal came to take his order, he ordered for three. "Just deliver the other two meals to that table," he said under his breath.

Crystal winked at him and went to turn in the orders. When she returned a few minutes later, she sat a salad on his table and also in front of his two guests.

"What? I haven't ordered yet." The woman pushed her chair back, gazing up at Crystal with a frown.

"The gentleman paid for your meal, ma'am." Crystal nodded to where Ty sat.

The woman regarded him icily, her soft mouth forming a straight line of disapproval.

"Pardon me for being so forward," he said, "but Tiny makes the best chicken-fried steak, and I thought you might like to enjoy it with me." She started to protest, but he cut her off. "It would be a shame to pass through Langston without experiencing the best chicken-fried steak in all of Texas." He grinned at her encouragingly.

She pressed her lips together again and nodded curtly. "Thanks." Her voice came out low and gravelly, and a blush tinged her cheeks.

"I'm Tyler Garrett, ma'am. Just showing some hospitality."

———w———

Leah Benson swallowed hard. The cowboy was grinning from ear to ear. *He must feel real proud of himself for springing for our meal.* "We appreciate it."

She glanced at Gracie, who was staring at her wide-eyed. When she nodded, Gracie picked up her fork and speared the cherry tomato on top of her salad. She popped it into her mouth and closed her eyes when she bit into it. Such a simple pleasure and yet one that had been denied them for a while.

The waitress came back with a carousel of bottled salad dressings.

"Oh, ranch!" Gracie said, as though that particular dressing was a rare treat. She grabbed the bottle and tried to open it, the cast getting in her way.

"Here, let me." Leah opened the cap and set the bottle in front of her daughter.

Gracie squirted a generous glob onto her salad and commenced eating like she'd been starved.

Leah exhaled. Well, it had been a long time since they had eaten in a restaurant of any kind, so this was a treat. She squirted the dressing on her salad and took a bite. The tangy dressing complemented the fresh and crispy salad. *Yes, this is good.* She and her daughter had run out of the sandwiches Leah packed before they left Oklahoma. She'd thought they could make it all the way to Gran's without having to stop for food. Lord knows the high cost of gasoline had devoured her small hoard of cash. But they were close now. Less than thirty miles to go, and then they would be safe.

The cowboy had stood and was walking toward her table. *No way! If he thinks he can buy us a meal and then come over here—*

"Pardon me, ladies," he said in a deep, mellow voice. "I could use a little of that ranch dressing, if you're done with it." He looked at Gracie, and she nudged it toward him. "Thank you," he said.

Leah tried to keep her eyes averted, but his clean, masculine scent seemed to wrap around her like an embrace. She watched him return to his table, noting the wide set of his shoulders and how they tapered down in a nice V shape to his well-filled-out Wranglers. When he took his seat, he met her gaze with a dimpled grin.

Oh no! I have no business noticing cute cowboys, not when I can't seem to get rid of the last one.

She picked up her fork and concentrated on her salad, studiously ignoring the attractive man at the next table.

When the waitress returned, she brought large platters, each filled with a huge portion of chicken-fried steak and mashed potatoes, all covered with creamy white gravy. There were small bowls of seasoned green beans on the side. A basket of golden-brown cloverleaf rolls completed the array.

Gracie was staring like it was Christmas, and Leah had to admit the aroma had her salivating. She cut some bites for Gracie, thinking the huge serving might make a good dinner as well.

The waitress placed the same meal in front of the cowboy. Some light banter passed between them, and then he set about enjoying his food.

Maybe his generosity was just a random act of kindness. Leah had heard about them but never experienced any firsthand.

As long as they made it to Gran's before nightfall, they would have a safe haven. A place for Leah and Gracie to recover from their wounds, both emotional and physical.

Leah glanced at the cast on Gracie's left arm. *A broken wrist.* Leah's stomach seized up with guilt, but she hadn't known Caine would be paroled and that he'd show up unannounced.

Heaving a sigh, she reflected that she should have left long ago, but they really hadn't had the money to relocate. Well, this latest disaster had set them on the road, ready or not.

She hurriedly gobbled everything on her plate, barely tasting the delicious food.

"Gracie, maybe you can eat that in the car," she said and hailed the waitress. "Do you think we could get this to go?"

When the waitress brought a Styrofoam container and a paper bag, Leah scooped the contents of Gracie's plate into the divided carton and snapped the lid on tight. After she slipped it into the bag, Gracie emptied the basket of rolls on top.

Leah went to the cowboy's table. "I want to thank you for your kindness, Mister—"

"Ty…Tyler Garrett," he supplied, rising to his feet. "Think nothing of it. It was my pleasure."

He had blue eyes, ringed by dark lashes. Dark like his hair. His eyes, blue as a summer sky, a sharp contrast to his deeply tanned face. He reached out to her and, without thinking, she found her hand enveloped in his much larger one. It was callused and warm. "You have a safe trip now."

"Um…thank you." Leah turned, but Gracie also extended her hand.

"Thanks for the meal, Mr. Tyler. It was delicious."

He bowed deeply over her hand. "You take care, little lady."

She smiled, the first real smile Leah had seen on Gracie's face since they had left Oklahoma. "My name is Gracie, and my mama is named Leah."

"Well, I'm happy to meet you, Gracie and Leah." He gave her another courtly bow.

Leah tried to quell the strangling sensation in her throat, hustling Gracie out of the restaurant and into their loaded vehicle. When her daughter was belted in and their small, terrier-type dog, Eddie, had calmed down, Leah pulled out onto the road.

Gracie continued to eat, and she shared a roll with Eddie, so they were content. Gracie's nose wrinkled up, and she made a face. "Ewww!" she shrieked. "Eddie!"

Leah sighed and opened the windows. "Honey, he can't help it. He's old. Every once in a while, he just has to…"

"He farts!" she exploded. "All the time."

Eddie, for his part, hung his head and thumped his tail on the floorboard.

"It's okay. The car is all aired out now."

"Eddie, please don't fart while I'm eating." Gracie gave him a stern look.

Leah had to laugh. Her daughter glowered, while her dog feigned innocence. If a flatulent dog was the worst obstacle they had to face, their future would be sublime.

The long, straight West Texas highway stretched out in front of them, like an arrow pointing the way to safety.

Leah heaved a deep sigh and tried to loosen her grip on the steering wheel, all the while thinking about the cowboy, whose blue eyes seemed to see all the way to her soul.

Tyler gazed out the window at the woman and child as they scrambled into the old beater of a car. He shook his head. Something about those big brown eyes. He could read the fear there. Someone somewhere had caused her a lot of pain. There was no trust in those eyes.

He watched her pull out onto the interstate and hoped they were headed someplace good. Someplace where somebody gave a damn about them.

Crystal came to refill his iced tea. "That was real nice, what you did for them, Ty."

He frowned, dipping his dinner roll in the cream gravy. "It wasn't a big deal."

Crystal snorted. "It was to them. That woman had bruises on her arms. When I was serving their plates, her shirt fell back, and it looked like handprints on her shoulders too. Somebody gave them a rough time." She set the tea pitcher on his table and went to clear the one so recently vacated.

Crystal's words stabbed into his consciousness. *What kind of man would hurt a woman?* No matter how controlling his father was, he would never have raised a hand to his wife. He had worshiped her, in fact. Since his mom died, it had seemed his father was even more driven to cement Ty to the ranch, to quash any hope he had of making it to the big time.

Ty heard his father's voice reverberating in his head. "Just forget all that music nonsense. This is your life, right here on the land."

He stared out the window in the direction the brown-eyed beauty had gone. It appeared they were headed in the same direction. He hoped her dreams would come true as well as his own.

—⁓—

"Now what?" Leah glanced at the gas tank, but there was over a quarter of a tank. That should get them to Gran's. But just then, the car took another lurch, sending her nerves into overdrive. "Why me?" she growled before looking over at Gracie, who sat biting her lower lip, her hands fisted in her lap. *Way too much burden for an eight-year-old.*

The car lurched again, and the motor cut out.

Leah managed to aim for the shoulder before the vehicle ground to a full stop. She leaned back against the headrest for several seconds and drew in a lungful of air. "Stay here," she ordered Gracie before climbing out to look under the hood.

Not that it mattered. Leah had no idea what she was looking at, but there did seem to be a lot of heat roiling up at her when she lifted the hood. She felt like giving up, but she couldn't, because Gracie was counting on her to get them to Gran's house. Counting on her to be the grown-up, even though she felt like sitting down on the ground and giving in to the ocean of regret threatening to rip loose.

Huffing out an exasperated sigh, she stepped back. *Stop it! You're better than this. Gracie needs you.*

She left the hood up and climbed back inside the car. "It's hot. I think if we just let it cool down for a while, I might be able to get it to start again."

Gracie stared at her with a frightened expression.

"Don't worry, honey. I'm sure it will be okay." Leah sucked in a breath and plastered a totally insincere smile across her face. "Really."

Eddie gazed up at her from the floorboards under Gracie's feet. He thumped his tail as if to agree with her. *Thanks, buddy.*

She hadn't seen much traffic since they'd left Langston, although it was a pretty well-traveled highway. On the one hand, she hoped someone would come along to help them. On the other hand, she hoped no one would come along to murder them.

A huge semi came barreling down the highway but didn't even slow down. The speed with which it zoomed by shook the car and its passengers as if to say, *Get out of my way. I'm coming through.*

A few more vehicles passed, but none even slowed down. Leah's throat ached with despair. How would she be able to get her daughter to Gran's house?

Leah was beginning to think they might have to start walking back to Langston, but that prospect frightened her as well. *Way too vulnerable.*

There seemed to be very little traffic on this highway. Maybe it was the time of day. Maybe there would be more cars and trucks as the day wore on. She just needed to be patient and not reveal any of the near-panic gathering in her chest. She gave Gracie a confident smile.

In her rearview mirror, she saw a truck. It was an old truck, but it was slowing down. "Oh, please, please, please…"

Leah held her breath, waiting to see who climbed out…but no one emerged. The doors remained closed. The motor idled roughly, emitting a deep growl-like roar.

Her heart fluttered. It felt as though a feather pillow had exploded in her chest. She noticed the truck's windows had been tinted dark. She couldn't see who was inside.

Maybe the driver expected her to get out.

"Mommy?" Gracie's eyes were wide with fear.

"It's okay, baby. Just relax." Leah sucked in a breath and reached for her purse. Cautiously, she reached inside, her fingers curling around the Beretta knock-off she had purchased at the pawnshop across the street from the diner. The pawnbroker showed her that it was loaded with a clip full of .25-caliber hollow points. He had assured her this would get someone's attention.

She had hoped never to have to actually wrap her fingers around it, but there was no way she would risk her daughter's life. The smooth metal seemed to warm in her hand. Taking a few seconds to gather her courage, she stared at the truck in the rearview mirror.

The driver of the truck revved the motor several times. It sounded like a monster growling.

Come on out, Mr. Invisible. If you think you can hurt us, you're mistaken.

She gazed at the truck in the mirror, mentally daring the driver to emerge. Out of the corner of her eye, she glimpsed something big and red. It was slowing down.

"Look, Mommy. Another truck is stopping."

A red extended-cab pickup slowed down and pulled off the highway onto the shoulder, rolling to a stop in front of her. There was a horse trailer behind the truck.

Now her small car was sandwiched between the two larger vehicles. Swallowing her claustrophobia, she kept a tight grip on the weapon in her purse.

The old truck behind her shifted into reverse, and the driver did a sharp U-turn, speeding off in the direction of Langston.

Leah expelled the breath she'd been holding. Her fingers still clutched the gun. She released them and withdrew her hand, shoving the purse under her seat.

The driver's side door of the red pickup opened, and someone was stepping out.

Her fingers tightened on the steering wheel. *Oh, please let it be someone nice.*

"It's Tyler!" Gracie shouted gleefully, as though that were a good thing.

Leah's stomach did a flip-flop when the big cowboy from the restaurant got out and headed back toward them.

He leaned down to peer in the window at them. "Hey, it's you. What seems to be the trouble?"

"I—I don't know. It just shuddered and came to a stop." She felt completely inadequate to deal with this situation. At least she didn't think the big cowboy would feed them and then murder them on the side of the road.

"Well, let me take a look." He went to peer under the

hood, and she got out to join him, aware of how big he was, of how he could snap her neck in a single blow.

"Um…what do you think?" She gazed at him doubtfully.

"Well, here's your problem. Your serpentine belt broke. Can't go anywhere without one."

While she appeared to be looking at the direction he was pointing, her eyes were blurred with tears. Blinking rapidly, she hoped to stanch the flow, but twin rivulets rolled down her cheeks. "I see. Well, you don't have a spare on you, or would that be too much to hope for?"

He took off the Stetson and ran his fingers through his hair. "Well, no, ma'am. I don't happen to have a serpentine belt on me, and we're right out here in the middle of nowhere. I don't suppose you belong to Triple A, do you?"

This struck Leah as funny, and she began to laugh amid all the tears. When she turned to face him, he frowned and reached in his pocket, unfurling a large, white handkerchief.

He flapped it in the air to open it before extending it to her. "Aw, you don't need to cry about it. I wouldn't leave you out here all by yourself."

Leah reached for the handkerchief and dabbed at her eyes.

He put his big paw on her shoulder and gave a couple of ineffectual pats. "Where were you headed anyway?"

She pasted on a decidedly fake smile and tried to retrieve her usual good humor. "To my grandmother's ranch. It's not much farther. I just wish we could have made it there."

He nodded. "Okay, I'm going to give you a tow. It's not far, you say?"

A bubble of hope welled up in her chest. "No, it's not far at all."

He nodded and went to open the passenger door of her car. "Come on out, young lady. I'm going to give you a ride to your great-grandma's house." He held out his hand to Gracie, and Eddie jumped up on the seat. The big cowboy picked up the small dog and tucked him under one arm while holding Gracie's hand with the other. He led them to the passenger side of his shiny red truck and opened the back door. He put Eddie inside and hoisted Gracie onto the seat. There was a large dog on the rear seat already, but he appeared to be friendly, wagging his tail. Closing the door, the cowboy turned to Leah, expectantly. "Ready?"

She nodded. "Oh yes." He handed her up onto the passenger seat and closed the door. She heard him in the back of the vehicles, and then he climbed up into the driver's seat and backed up a little. He left the motor idling while he hooked up her car, and then he slowly pulled out onto the highway. "You tell me where to turn."

"I will. Thank you so much. I don't know what we would have done without you."

"Somebody else would have stopped to help you, I reckon."

Yeah, somebody spooky in a dusty old truck. No telling what Mr. Invisible would have done to us. She shivered. *Or what I would have had to do to him.* "I was really worried. Just let me thank you for stopping."

He frowned and shrugged it off. He didn't seem to accept thanks well, so she pressed her lips together. "Where are you headed?"

He seemed to brighten. "I'm on my way to Dallas." He sent her a dimpled grin. "I've got plans there."

———

They chatted in little bits and pieces. He managed to drag from her that she was an Oklahoma girl. She told him her grandpa had passed away and she was moving back to help her grandmother with the ranch. *That should be good for her. Give her a fresh start.*

She smiled once, and it was like the sunshine breaking through on a rainy day. He just hadn't thought one woman could be so very pretty.

"That's the turn!" She sounded excited and pointed to a farm-to-market road cutting off to the right.

Ty slowed and made a wide arc, managing to get the truck, the trailer, and her car going in the right direction. He drove for almost ten miles when she directed him onto another side road. This one wasn't paved, but at least it was graded smooth. When he pulled up to the small house, he felt a sinking sensation in his chest. *This is not a ranch. This is a disaster.*

He could tell by her face that she thought so too. She gazed out the side window at the weed-infested fields and the run-down house and outbuildings. Everything was in disrepair.

"Um, are they expecting you?" he asked.

She bit her lip. "I think so. Let me just go inside. Would you wait here with Gracie for a moment?" She climbed down and approached the house.

He watched her step up onto the porch and knock on the screen door. She turned around while she waited, surveying the dismal prospects. Her face registered every emotion she was experiencing. Not a very good place for a woman to make a fresh start. He wondered how the people who lived here eked out a living at all.

There was a barn to the rear of the property. Also a stable and a long metal building, maybe a shed of some sort.

When the door was answered, a small, elderly woman came out onto the porch to throw her arms around Leah. It was nice to see Leah getting some affection from someone. She seemed to be wrapped much too tight, but he suspected she had her reasons.

The two women engaged in a rapid conversation in which Leah pointed to the truck.

Ty lifted a hand in greeting, and the old woman grinned and waved in return. More words were exchanged, and then Leah made her way back to the truck. He rolled down the window when she approached.

"My grandma wants to meet you. I told her how you helped us out." Her eyes were the color of aged whiskey in the late-afternoon sunlight. Her full lips curved up in a smile. Whatever this little place had to offer, it seemed to be enough to make her happy.

"Sure." He unfastened his seat belt and stepped out, then opened the back door for Gracie. He lifted her down, and the scruffy little mutt scrambled out as well. "All present and accounted for."

Leah flashed him a much more heartfelt grin and led the way to the house.

He had to duck when he stepped up onto the porch, because the roof was sagging in the middle, and he noted the rotten wood on the porch itself. Luckily it held his weight.

Leah pulled the screen open and motioned him to the open doorway. "This is my grandmother, Fern Davis. Gran, this is Tyler Garrett. He pretty much saved Gracie and me."

The elderly woman held out both hands to him. "Thank you so much for delivering my granddaughter and great-granddaughter to me safe and sound."

"Think nothing of it, ma'am," he said.

Her eyes crinkled up as a broad grin spread across her face. She threw both of her frail arms around him to deliver a fierce hug. "You're just an angel straight from heaven."

"No, ma'am," he protested, but she was dragging him into the house.

"I been cookin' all day. Surely you'll stay and have a bite with us." She gazed up at him with bright, birdlike eyes.

A small hand grabbed his. "Please, Tyler." It was Gracie adding her two cents.

Ty glanced from Gracie to her great-grandmother and finally settled on Leah.

She smiled. "I would really like it if you could stay for supper." Her voice was low-pitched and husky, sending vibrations to his libido.

"Well, I…uh…I guess I could stay. A man's gotta eat. Right?"

It was something about Leah's expression and how pretty she looked when she wasn't running on pure fear. Something that made him set aside his urgency to reach Dallas. He could just as well arrive late tonight. *Heck, Will's not expecting me until next week. Not a problem.*

While the three delighted females went to the kitchen, Ty headed outside to the truck and let Lucky out. He detached Leah's vehicle from the back of the horse trailer, then pulled out the ramp and walked his champion quarter horse, Prince of Darkness. The stallion was antsy and danced sideways, unsure of his surroundings.

"Easy, Prince," he said, soothing the stallion. Holding both reins, he began to walk the horse along the narrow road leading to the back of the property.

Gracie ran out to join him.

"Your horse is very pretty," she said, her eyes shining.

"Thank you, Gracie. Do you like to ride?"

"I've never been on a horse before. I'm only eight."

He laughed. "And how old do you have to be to ride a horse?"

She shrugged.

"I can't remember a time when I didn't ride," he said. "If I were going to be here longer, I'd give you a ride."

"That's okay," she said. "I might be scared."

He let that sink in as he looked around the property. The barn door had a broken hinge and stood ajar. Taking a look inside, he saw a decent store of baled hay stacked along one side. He wondered how much livestock there was to feed. An old model John Deere tractor was housed inside, but it was covered with a layer of dust. Whoever had stored it here hadn't used it recently. He'd noticed the fields they had driven past had not been cultivated and were left to lie fallow.

He gave his horse water and the high-grade feed he had brought with him.

When he and Gracie returned to the house, the table was set, and Leah was waiting for him.

Chapter 2

LEAH KEPT STEALING GLANCES AT TY DURING THE meal. He had removed his Stetson the minute he came inside the house, and he was polite to Gran. That was what she cared about most.

She had been shocked by how run-down the whole place appeared. *It's all my fault. I should have come home sooner.* Poor Grandpa must not have been able to keep up with things the last few years, and with all her troubles, Leah hadn't been thinking of her grandparents so much.

But this Ty wasn't treating Gran like some poor little lady living out a threadbare existence. He listened to her politely and laughed when she made a joke.

Leah wasn't willing to call him a nice guy, but she was coming around. Not every man was a complete jerk like Caine. Not every man was quick-tempered and brutal. Just her luck, she had been taken in by a handsome face without knowing what lay behind the mask. But she had been so very young…too young for sure.

She pressed her lips together and reached to help Gracie cut her food.

"How do you like the chicken, Gracie?" Gran asked. "She was one of my young'uns, so she's nice and tender."

Gracie's eyes grew round, and she set her fork down by her plate.

Leah sent her grandmother a frown. "Gran's kidding, aren't you? Go ahead and eat up."

Gracie glanced from her mother to Gran and back again.

"Oh, uh—" Gran stared at Gracie. "That's right. I was just kidding."

Reluctantly, Gracie picked up her fork and poked at the lima beans.

Ty smiled at her encouragingly. "This is life on a farm, Gracie. We raise what we eat, and we provide food for others too. That's our job." He gestured to her plate. "So eat up, and after dinner, maybe I can take you for a ride."

Gracie's eyes lit up, and she leaned toward him. "Really?"

"Sure," he said. "I'll have time before I hit the road."

Leah was relieved to see her daughter pick up her fork and dig right into her food.

"What do you do for a living, young man?" Gran asked.

Ty grinned. "Well, ma'am, I guess you could say I'm unemployed at the moment…but I'm expecting to get something going once I get to Dallas."

"Just passing through, then?" Gran cocked her head to one side. "I was thinking maybe I could hire you to do a couple of chores for me before you take off, maybe give you a little pocket money?"

Ty's grin widened. "That's mighty nice, ma'am, but I better be heading on to the city."

Gran shrugged. "Well, I had to ask."

Leah saw her grandmother's disappointment. "What is it you need done, Gran? I'm pretty sure I can help you."

Gran smiled and patted her on the arm. "A skinny little thing like you? Not hardly. Maybe I can find someone around here willing to do a little work."

Ty gave her a long gaze and heaved a sigh. "Well,

maybe I can stay until tomorrow. I saw a few things that needed mending when I was exercising my horse."

Gran looked as excited as Gracie at this announcement. "Oh, that would be grand!"

They finished the meal, and Leah helped clear the table. She put the dishes to soak before slipping out to see what Ty and Gracie were up to. Thinking it would make her spy mission less obvious, she fastened the leash to Eddie's collar. When she stepped off the porch, she saw Ty saddling his beautiful black horse.

A whisper of fear kissed her neck as she watched the interaction between her child and this stranger.

Gracie stroked the horse's nose and seemed to be confident around the big animal…and the big, gentle man.

Leah approached timidly. "Hey, you two. What are you doing?"

Ty turned to her, a wide grin on his face. "I'm pretty sure we're going to take a little ride around the property."

Leah glanced at the stallion. He snorted and danced sideways as far as his tether would allow. She swallowed hard and shook her head. "Really? Is it safe for her to be on such a…a big horse?"

Ty seemed to be appraising her reaction. "Sure. Prince is a registered quarter horse. He's a complete gentleman."

She nodded. "I just came out to give Eddie a walk… and to see Gracie."

He flashed another killer grin. "Well, let's get after it, then." Holding his arms out to Gracie, he lifted her onto the saddle. He placed her hands on the saddle horn and adjusted the length of the stirrups to fit her. "Ready?"

A wave of fear washed over Leah. The sight of her

small daughter sitting atop such a large animal constricted her breathing. She watched as Ty set off walking toward the barns, leading the horse by the reins. She fell into step beside him, hurrying to match his long stride.

"Glad you decided to join us," he said.

"I—I want to make sure Gracie doesn't fall off."

"That's not going to happen," Ty said. "It's not a good idea to plant ideas of failure in her head."

She let out a breath. "No, I suppose not."

"How did she break her arm?" he asked.

A vision of Caine's angry face flashed through her brain, and she winced. "Um...it was..." She bit her lip. "It's her wrist. She fell."

"I see," he said. "Well, she's not going to fall today."

They walked in silence, rounding toward the barn. Leah was aware of how bad the ranch looked. So much had fallen into disrepair since the last time she had visited. Her grandfather's passing had taken a huge toll on the property. She didn't know if her grandmother had the money to pay for the repairs. But she had offered to pay Ty for his services. Maybe she had some savings, because it didn't look like there had been a recent crop in the fields that surrounded them.

"I'll try to repair the barn door tomorrow," he said, as if reading her mind. "You should be able to secure it. What else do you think is most important?"

"I don't know." She hesitated. "It's been a long time since I've been here."

"Not a problem." His voice rolled out smooth as warm syrup, comforting her in ways she hadn't known needed comforting. "I'm pretty sure your grandma has a list for me." He gave her a wink, which also sent messages to parts of her anatomy that hadn't been visited in a while.

—⁂—

Ty could almost feel the fear radiating from Leah, like barbed wire setting her perimeter. He had no idea what caused this woman to be so terrified, but he was pretty sure it had nothing to do with him. Something bad had happened to her in the past…something really bad.

The little girl too. But Gracie was more open to him. She was looking for something good to happen.

He checked her expression, and she was relaxed in the saddle. She held on to the saddle horn with her good hand but wasn't gripping it in a panic.

"You doing okay, Gracie?"

She flashed a big smile that warmed his heart. "I like to ride this horse. He's nice."

He was glad this little ride was giving her so much pleasure. "I think you have the makings of a great rider," he told her.

Leah flashed a dark look in his direction.

He raised his brows, sending a silent question, but she shook her head. Obviously not something she wished to share in front of her daughter. He shrugged and cast about for another topic of conversation. "Were you raised around here?"

Leah shook her head. "No, but we visited quite often. I spent many summers here with Gran and Grandpa. The ranch was so much greener then. It seemed as if everything was growing, and there were animals…all kinds of them." She glanced up at him. "How about you?"

He hesitated. "Um, yeah. I was raised here in Dimsdale County."

She shrugged. "I didn't even know that's where we are."

"West of here. The other side of Langston."

Leah surprised him with a genuine smile. "What's west of here?"

"My dad's ranch."

She digested this fact. "Is it a place like this?" She spread her hands to include their surroundings.

"Yeah," he said. *About a thousand times bigger and more productive.*

"That's nice. I'm glad to know you grew up on a working ranch."

He chuckled. "Does that make me not as scary?" *There, I said it. Maybe I'll get a straight answer.* He watched as a series of emotions played out on her face.

"I don't know what you mean." She pressed her lips together in a firm line.

"If you say so, but I promise you, I'm not a bad guy." He tried to give her a reassuring smile, but she wouldn't even look at him. It was as though she had closed down completely. *None of my business. I get the message.*

She turned her attention to Gracie, falling back to walk beside her. Leah remained wrapped in her silent prison, sheltered from his prying questions.

With the setting sun behind it, the barn loomed ahead, large and gloomy like a hulking giant with a gaping maw. Ty resolved to repair the barn door first thing in the morning. After that, he could have a look around to see what else he could do in the short amount of time he had to spare.

Frowning, Leah stopped walking. "Am I crazy, or

does it look like that back corner of the barn is charred? It looks like there was a fire."

"You're not crazy." He pointed to the wooden pen situated behind the barn. "It looks like the fence back there has also burned." He wondered how a fire started in an area that didn't have much to sustain a fire. The fenced-in area may have been a pen for small livestock, such as pigs or goats. Ty took a few steps toward the barn, making a mental note to ask Fern about it.

Lucky ran ahead to check out the cavernous space. Ty whistled for him, and he made a U-turn to come right back by Ty's side. "Good boy!"

"Lucky sure is a good dog," Gracie called.

Ty grinned at her. "He knows it." He caught sight of Leah's face, and it was still troubled. "What kind of stock does your grandma have now? She mentioned chickens."

"I—I'm not sure. When my grandpa was alive, there were cattle and horses…maybe a few goats." She paused, gazing around. "Now, I don't know."

"Don't worry. We'll figure it out."

Leah gnawed her lip as she walked along beside Gracie.

He hadn't meant to cause her more worry. She looked so troubled he wanted to take her in his arms to comfort her, but he figured that wouldn't go over well. He blew out a frustrated breath. "Look, I just wanted to make sure any stock was taken care of for the night."

He heard the sound of a strangled sob, and when he got closer, he saw tears rolling down her cheeks. "Aww, come here." He opened his arms and almost fell over in surprise when she collapsed against his chest.

"I don't know what I was thinking," she gasped. "I

wanted to help Gran, but I have no idea what to do. She's probably going to have to take care of me too." Her last words morphed into an elongated moan.

"Mommy?" Gracie asked, her concern evident.

Ty placed a gentle hand on Leah's shoulder as she leaned against his chest. He reached up to Gracie, laying his other hand atop hers as she gripped the saddle horn, offering what comfort he could to these two very unhappy females.

Leah raised her head, fixing her sorrowful gaze on her daughter. "I'm just—" She seemed to gather her courage, visibly straightening her spine.

Ty swallowed hard. "Don't worry. Everything's going to be okay."

Gracie gripped his hand, her eyes wide with fear.

"Your mom's going to be fine. She's just...stressed."

Leah drew back. "I'm so sorry." She shook her head. "I didn't mean to do that. I don't know what's the matter with me." She tried to pull away, but Ty held her firmly in the protective circle of his arm.

"Hey, it's all right." He felt her relax against him, some of the tension evaporating at his words. "Look, I don't know what's going on, but if it would help, I can stay a couple of days to help you get things squared away. I can spare that much."

She sniffled. "Really?"

He gazed down into her beautiful whiskey-colored eyes. It was as though he stood at the edge of a deep gorge, contemplating the leap. His music career was going to take off once he hit Dallas, but Will wasn't expecting him until next week. He could afford to lend a hand to these three females in need.

Her lower lip trembled. "That would be so kind of you. I—I can't tell you how much it would mean to me."

And he jumped headfirst into the deep, stormy depths of her need. "Well, a couple of days won't make a difference. Maybe I can get a few things repaired around here."

Leah had no idea why, but standing in her grandmother's weed-infested backyard, with Ty's arm wrapped around her, was the first time she had felt safe in... *Oh hell. I can't even remember safe.* Her heart beat out a rhythm like a bass drum, and her stomach felt queasy, but even lower in her anatomy, something was stirring big time. *Oh, those killer blue eyes. Damn! I could believe anything he says when he looks at me like that.*

It wasn't as though he was going to be around long enough to break her heart. He said he would be leaving in a couple of days. She pressed her face against his western shirt. It was the expensive kind and had been starched and ironed, nice as anything.

He smelled great too. Not anything girly. Sort of like fresh citrus and something spicy mixed in. She wondered if he knew the effect he was having on her. *Yeah, it's a good thing he's going to be moving on.*

Eddie put a paw against her calf. His too-long toenails made her wince. Something else that needed doing, but she had left the clippers behind when she had departed in such haste. No time to think things through.

She wondered what would happen to the rest of their belongings. The landlady would probably take what she wanted and haul the rest to the trash bin. Maybe she would donate it. *Probably not.*

Sad to think everything of value was still crammed
into her old beater of a car. Not much to show for her
life. *Maybe I can make a fresh start. Lord knows I can't
do much worse than the first time out.* She glanced up
at Gracie, sitting so proudly in the saddle. *At least I did
one thing well.*

"You ready?" Ty asked Gracie. When she nodded, he
continued his walk around the property. They passed the
barns and outbuildings.

"The chicken coop needs to be closed up for the
night," Ty said, indicating the sad-looking structure.

"I can do that." Leah handed Eddie's leash to Ty.
She unlatched the gate and stepped through to the wire-
enclosed yard. It hadn't been cleaned in a while. That
was something she could do to help Gran. Taking a
quick head count, she could locate nine hens inside the
coop. *Not enough. And Gran harvested one of the girls
for dinner. Can't afford to do that again.*

Leah latched the door to the coop and stepped out of
the run. The gate was flimsy, but she secured it as best
she could. At least this was a small task she could do
for Gran.

When Leah turned around, her heart did a flip-flop
in her chest. The last rays of the sun cast a golden glow
on the scene, illuminating Gracie atop the black stallion, a wide grin on her face; Ty standing beside her,
holding the reins; Eddie on his leash, waggling his tail
furiously; and Lucky, the beautiful golden retriever that
sat patiently beside Ty.

It was one of those Hallmark moments that made
her ache all over. Everything looked so beautiful. She
wanted it to last forever.

She gave herself a mental head slap. *Not forever. Ty is just passing through.* But, she admitted to herself, deep in her heart of hearts, she wanted something that made her feel this same way. Happy…secure…a part of something, even though it was just a moment in this case.

They continued their stroll around Gran's big yard, most of the time in silence. The clip-clop of the horse's hooves seemed to give cadence to their steps.

Gracie sat atop the horse, looking like a small princess. Leah realized Gracie was proud of the fact she was staying in the saddle. Leah hoped there would be more satisfying moments for this little one. Those moments had been few and far between up until now.

"What crops did your grandpa usually grow in these fields?" Ty asked.

Leah shrugged. "Mostly wheat, some cotton. I seem to remember rye grass in the winter."

Ty frowned as he gazed out at the barren fields. "It's not too late to get a crop in."

"Sorry," she said. "I know nothing about farming. I'm not even sure why I'm here. I thought I could help my grandma, but now it seems I'm going to be more of a burden for her."

He frowned again, giving her a sideways glance under the brim of his hat. "I'm pretty certain she's really happy to have you."

Leah swallowed, willing herself not to give way to another emotional break. She drew a deep breath. "I hope so. She always told me, when times get tough, that's when families pull together."

Ty felt a whisper of doubt kiss the back of his neck.
Families? He thought of his own family, or what was
left of it after his mother's death.

Big Jim's scowling face came to mind. Although he
knew his dad would help him out in an emergency,
he couldn't imagine any circumstances under which he
would go running home with his tail tucked between his
legs. If he were starving, he would play guitar and sing
on the sidewalk for spare change rather than going home
in defeat. It was not an option.

Ty's brothers were following the right path, according
to Big Jim. Ty was going to miss them all right, but they
couldn't understand his need to express himself through
music. They didn't understand his "special gift," or so
his mother had called it. Whatever it was that drove him,
he'd come this far, and he couldn't back down now.

He gazed around the mangy-looking spread. Leah's
family seemed to be barely scraping by, yet she was glad
to be here. Whatever she was running away from, this
place appeared to be her safe haven. There was no doubt
the old woman adored Leah and Gracie. He hoped they
could survive here. Sucking in a deep breath, he made a
silent vow to do all he could the next day to give them
a head start.

Her hand on his sleeve pulled him back to reality.

"What are you thinking?" she asked.

Still frowning, he gazed down into her big, dark eyes.
"I was just thinking about things I need to do for your
grandma tomorrow." He shrugged. "Making a list."

She smiled, like the sun peeking through the clouds.
"You looked so intense. I thought maybe you were mad
at me."

"No, nothing like that."

"Good. I would hate that." She ducked her head.

He reached out to lift her chin. "Leah, I don't know what's going on with you, but whatever it is…I'm not that guy."

"Um. I—I…" She faltered. "I know."

"Okay, just so you know." He gave her a wink and moved on in his trek, leading Prince by the reins with Gracie astride. He hooked an arm around Leah's neck and brought her with him. She laced her fingers with his and kept in step. The two dogs trotted along beside him. Something about this parade gave him a sense of well-being. Leah looked as content as he felt. *I know this is only for now, but maybe I can do some good here.* He glanced down at her again. *I think I'm going to miss her a lot when I leave.*

Fern Davis put away the leftovers and did her best to tidy up her house. She had been thrilled when her granddaughter called to ask if she could move in. Leah hadn't spelled out what the problem was, but it couldn't be as bad as the events Fern had been experiencing.

If only her husband, Albert, were still alive. She knew he would have put his foot down and gotten to the bottom of all the devilment going on.

She didn't want to put Leah and Gracie in danger, but she also knew for sure she would die to protect them. Fern dried her hands on a dish towel and peeked behind the sofa where she had stashed her fully loaded shotgun. *Just let them Carter boys show their smarmy faces around here. I'll put 'em in the ground.*

She glanced out the front and smiled when she saw the big cowboy walking along with Leah and Gracie up on the horse. *What a purty picture.*

———∿∿∿———

They made a bed for Ty on the lumpy sofa. He'd insisted he could sleep in the truck but gave in when Gran insisted.

"In the old days, the hands used to stay in the bunk-house," Gran said. "There are beds and a kitchen. It used to be real comfortable."

"Yes, ma'am," Ty said dutifully.

"But it's not clean out there. You just make yourself comfy right here." She patted the sofa invitingly.

Leah cast a last glance at Ty and headed for Gran's spare room, Gracie in tow. She found their nightclothes among the hurriedly packed bags and dressed Gracie for bed. Tucking her in, Leah gave her a kiss on the forehead. Eddie jumped on the foot of the bed and curled up too.

Gracie mumbled a hurried prayer, ending with "an' God bless Mommy, an' Gran, an' Ty. Amen."

Leah's breath caught in her throat. How could this big cowboy come to mean so much to them both in so few hours? *How is Gracie going to feel when he's gone?* She swallowed hard. *How am I going to feel?*

She leaned down to brush a kiss on her daughter's forehead and pulled the covers up under her chin. "You go to sleep now."

Dutifully, Gracie snuggled down beneath the quilt and closed her eyes, her angelic expression the picture of peace and contentment.

Gazing at her child's sweet face, a knot formed in

Leah's chest. *This is the best place for us. I haven't been able to give Gracie much up until now, but that will change. Things will get better.*

Leah thought about her options. Maybe she could get a job back in Langston. It was the closest town and where Gracie would be enrolled in school come September. She wasn't quite sure what she might be able to do, but she was used to hard work, so surely someone would give her a chance.

The house was quiet. Tiptoeing out of their room, Leah padded down the hall toward the kitchen in her bare feet. Silently, she took a glass out of the cupboard and filled it with water from the tap. Moonlight spilled in through the window, bathing her in a soft glow as she lifted the glass to her lips. When she'd finished, she set the empty glass in the sink.

Turning, she almost stumbled over Lucky. The dog had been so quiet she hadn't heard him approach. Leaning down, she stroked his head. "Hey there, stealth doggy. You snuck up on me." She spoke in hushed tones, barely above a whisper.

The dog swished his tail from side to side.

"Do you need some water too? I put a big bowl right over here." She checked the corner of the kitchen where she had left one of Gran's mixing bowls earlier but found it empty. "Oh, thirsty doggy. Let me give you a refill." She held the bowl under the tap and set it on the floor, tucked in the corner so no one would run into it. "There you go."

The dog began to lap noisily. Leah knelt down beside him to run her hand over the silky fur. "Good boy," she whispered and rose from her crouch. When she turned, she ran smack into a brick wall. A warm, muscled brick wall with arms. She stifled a scream as she pushed off the wall and was gathered into a rough embrace.

"Easy, Leah."

"Oh, Ty! You scared me." Swallowing hard, she braced her hands against his powerful bare chest. The sensation sent her heart into a flutter. Longing surged through her. Longing for what, she wasn't quite certain, but longing nonetheless.

"Sorry," he murmured, his voice deep and raspy. "I thought Lucky was getting into something." He held her firmly against his warm torso.

She swallowed again. "N-no. I'm sorry I woke you." Gazing up, she couldn't read his expression in the darkness.

He expelled a breath, staring down at her moon-washed face. "You are just too pretty for my own good."

A rage of desire swirled low in her belly. Her pulse pounded in her ears. With no direction, she rose on her tiptoes and lifted her chin.

He made a sort of growl back in his throat before his arms tightened around her and he lowered his head. His kiss was soft, tentative at first, and then deepened. Lifting her off her feet, he devoured her mouth with hungry kisses. Heat from his bare flesh infiltrated her thin gown, setting fire to her desire.

His hunger seemed to fuel hers as the kiss continued to escalate.

Passion bloomed in her chest, sending a flush of plea-sure throughout her being. When she came up for air, she had wrapped both arms around his neck. Gasping, she shivered. Everything was happening too fast. The room seemed to be spinning, or was it just her head?

Heat emanating from his warm skin sent a spiral of lust to her core. She stroked her fingertips against the side of his face. The rough stubble of his beard rasped against her cheek, her neck, her shoulder.

"I'm sorry," he whispered. Holding her tight, he gave her a squeeze before setting her on her feet. "I had no business doing that."

Stunned, Leah stepped back, "No, I...I mean..."

Ty rubbed her cheek with the back of his fingers. "I'm sorry." He stepped away, and giving one rueful glance at her, he strode from the kitchen, leaving Leah leaning against the cabinet, tingling in the aftermath of their encounter.

———

Ty watched Leah glide silently to the back of the house. He stared after her for a moment, then threw himself down on the sofa and pulled the coverlet over his head. His heart pounded against his ribs like a wild animal straining to be freed from its cage.

He had never wanted a woman more than he wanted Leah. He could still taste her kisses. He could still feel her arms clinging to him. It was all he could do to keep from taking her right there on the countertop.

He swallowed hard and took a deep breath. If only he had met Leah under different circumstances, at a different time in his life, things might have been different. He felt a momentary pang of regret. But he couldn't let anything stand in the way of his music career. This was his one chance to make it, a golden opportunity he would be a fool to pass up.

Heaving a sigh, he tossed back the cover and stood

up. He strained to hear if anyone else was moving about in the darkness, but the only sound was that of his own pulse drumming in his ears.

Noiselessly, he twisted the knob on the front door. He stepped out on the front porch, allowing Lucky to slip out with him. The moon bathed everything in bright contrasts. It looked like an old black-and-white movie. The shadows were ebony-black, and all the other surfaces ranged from bright white through a full spectrum of grays.

Ty sucked in a deep breath. The air tasted of rain nearby. A clean, earthy scent. Rubbing his face with both hands, he tried to clear his head. Tried to erase the soft scent of Leah from his senses. He struggled to focus on what he needed to do.

Tomorrow, he would fulfill his promise to these unfortunate females and spend the day making as many repairs as he could around this godforsaken place. At most, he could give them two days, but that was absolutely all he could spare. Then, he would hightail it to Dallas. There was the gateway to his future. Not here on a broken-down ranch with a whisper-thin old lady, a young girl in a cast, and a beautiful, frightened woman with whiskey-colored eyes and lips that tasted like "stay."

Ty listened to the night sounds. A cricket chirped. The breeze stirred the high grasses. The old house creaked. *Just keep breathing in and out. Don't try to be a savior.* He raked his fingers through his dark, unruly hair. *Gotta keep my focus.*

—⁓—

Fern woke up before sunrise. She lay for a few moments, staring up into the darkness. Some sound…some infinitesimal noise outside. She forced herself to take a deep breath, letting it out silently. On alert, her hearing seemed to be heightened. A slight rustling sent spirals of fear fluttering through her chest.

She slipped out of bed. Without making a sound, she opened the drawer of her bedside table and withdrew the .45-caliber revolver that had been her husband's. Fully loaded, it was heavy but comforting. "Don't you worry, Albert," she whispered. "I won't let them weasels hurt our girls." She held it close to her chest as she quietly twisted the knob on her bedroom door.

The whole house was sleeping. The door to the room where Leah and Gracie slept was closed as Fern crept down the hallway. Once in the front room, she saw the big lump of cowboy curled up on her sofa, the blanket pulled up almost over his head. Noiselessly, she slipped past him, glad he didn't snore. Just the soft sound of his regular breathing.

Tyler's dog, Lucky, stood by the door. It looked like he was on alert too. He glanced at her and then back to staring at the door, his tail wagging slightly as though eager to go outside.

Fern opened the front door a crack, peering out into the darkness. She heard nothing out of the ordinary and slipped through to stand on the porch, the dog coming with her.

The air was cool, whispering across her flesh like a spiderweb, setting all her senses into overdrive. The moon was just a sliver in the black sky.

She jumped at the sound of someone running across the dirt.

She heard a low growl from Lucky before he took off, racing toward the road.

Her throat closed up. She couldn't breathe but stood clutching the gun, listening in the darkness. As she stood, on alert for the slightest sound, the silence was broken by the slam of a vehicle door and the roar of a badly tuned motor as it sped away.

Her jaw tight, she peered into the darkness, relaxing as Lucky came loping toward her, tail wagging. He looked satisfied with himself as though he knew he had chased the enemy from her door. "Good boy," she whispered, stroking his head. "Let's you an' me git back inside."

Turning, she stopped dead in her tracks. There was something dark stuck to the front door.

Her hand shook as she reached out to touch it. It was wet and cold with short fur. Shrinking backward, she stifled the scream raging in her throat.

A dead rat.

Swallowing hard, she gathered her courage and pulled the rodent off the door. She felt like screaming, not in fear, but in anger. How dare they come onto her property to leave this mess? If they thought they could frighten an old lady off her land, they had another think coming.

Outraged, Fern marched to the place behind the barn where she burned trash. She put the rat in the metal barrel, moving some trash to cover it.

Lucky sat waiting for her.

"No sense letting something like this scare the girls. They have enough problems without any of mine adding to them."

She walked back to the house, entering and securing the door behind her. Lucky settled on the floor beside his sleeping master.

———∿∿∿———

The next morning, Ty awoke with a start. He was disoriented at first, not remembering how he had come to be curled up on a lumpy sofa. He smelled bacon and heard kitchen sounds. He sat up, anxious to see Leah again. Then his resolutions from the night before hit him like a truck. Pressing his lips together, he exhaled. *Distance. I have to keep my distance.*

He groped in his duffel for a T-shirt and his worn jeans. These would do for working around this little ranch. He carried them in a bundle to the kitchen, where he found Fern Davis managing a stove and two cast-iron skillets. Bacon sizzled in one, and sliced potatoes were browning in the other. He felt a pang, recalling his mother preparing big breakfasts for her men.

She smiled when she saw him. "Howdy, young feller. I can't tell you how glad I am you decided to stay for a while. We sure can use the help."

"Uh…well, I'm glad to help out, ma'am." He had wanted to clean up before putting on his clean but ragged-out jeans and faded tee, but at the moment, he felt the need to be wearing more clothes. Clutching his soon-to-be-donned garments to his bare chest, he backed toward the hallway. "Just heading to the bathroom."

Fern nodded. "Second door on the left."

Ty turned and made a break for it. When he put his hand on the doorknob, Leah was just coming out. He swallowed hard.

Looking as though she had just stepped out of the shower, she wore a terry bathrobe, and her hair was still damp. Glancing away, she ducked her head and whispered a greeting. "G'morning, Ty."

"Ah, good morning, Leah." The thought of her nakedness underneath the robe hit him like a freight train. He held up his bundle of clothing, plastering on a fake smile. "Getting ready to do some work." *Stupid, stupid, stupid*.

She glanced up. "I see. I hope there's some hot water left for you." Her voice sounded soft and wistful.

He stared at her mouth, harnessing the desire to haul her closer for another taste of her kisses. "I…uh…I'll make do."

She nodded and turned away, padding down the hall in worn scuffs.

He watched her retreating backside as he tried to contain the ache in his chest. *What's wrong with me? I know what I have to do…so I better get after it*. He stepped into the still-steamy bathroom and closed the door firmly behind himself.

Chapter 3

LEAH DRESSED HURRIEDLY. SHE'D BEEN EMBARRASSED BY her earlier encounter with Ty. She hadn't even bothered to dry her hair. He probably thought she looked like a drowned rat. She expelled a pent-up breath. *Who cares what he thinks? He's not interested in me at all.*

He looked even more attractive in the morning. The dark stubble of beard around his jawline was sexy as hell, and the expression in his eyes was smoking hot. His body could best be described as *ripped*. An involuntary smile teased her lips. He'd looked so cute holding his bundle in front of himself, as though he could hide his broad bare chest behind a little wad of clothing.

She concentrated on helping Gracie get dressed. Holding her shirt, she guided the cast through the arm-hole. "There you go. Let's see if we can help Gran with breakfast."

Gracie's smile lit up her whole face, reminding Leah of what was really important in her life. *This is all about my daughter. I'm here to protect her and give her a better life.*

When they stepped out into the hall, the scent of bacon wrapped around them and buoyed them toward the kitchen. Eddie ran out and headed to the kitchen ahead of them.

Gran was expertly juggling skillets on the old gas stove, but she looked up and grinned when they entered. "Good morning, my sweethearts. I hope you slept well."

"Great." Leah snapped her fingers to get Eddie's attention. "Gracie is going to take Eddie out for a walk, and I'm here to help with breakfast." She smiled as her daughter fastened the leash and led the dog out the front door. "Come right back. We're almost ready to eat."

Gran waved the spatula at her. "Help yourself to some coffee if you want."

Leah poured the dark liquid into a mug and inhaled the delicious fragrance. She replaced the battered coffeepot on the trivet and took a sip. *Strong*.

In a short time, Gracie returned from the walk, Eddie close on her heels.

Leah motioned her to the table. Seating Gracie, she gave her hair a stroke. "Love you, baby." She turned to her grandmother. "What can I do to help?"

"You can set the table for me and pour milk for Gracie." Gran nodded toward the old refrigerator.

Leah poured milk into a jelly glass and set it in front of Gracie, who picked it up with both hands and began drinking.

Satisfied that her child was being nourished, Leah picked up her coffee cup. The aroma filled her senses, offering strength and renewal. *A new day. A new life. Here I am, ready to meet you head-on.*

Smiling, she turned to see Ty. He had been standing in the doorway, staring at her. She felt a flush creep up from her neck but managed a smile. She held up her coffee cup with raised brows, and he nodded.

"Sit right down, young man," Gran said. "Breakfast is a-comin' right up."

Ty grinned and took a seat beside Gracie. They

had an exchange in low voices, and something he said caused Gracie to giggle.

Leah wondered why he had to go to Dallas. What could be so all-fired important in the big city? She took down a cup for him and poured from the battered metal coffeepot. When she turned, she felt a little clutch in her chest. He looked so natural, chatting with Gracie. They were both grinning. Why couldn't there be a man like this in her daughter's life? *Or in mine, for that matter?*

The thought hit her that he might be going to meet a woman in Dallas. It made sense that he would have a girlfriend. In fact, she couldn't imagine that he didn't have to peel women off him. He was handsome and very masculine…and exuded some kind of sexy vibe, wrapped in a blanket of caring. Of course, he couldn't really care. He was probably just a nice guy, and she had mistaken his normal niceness for something else.

Leah sucked in a breath, realizing she had been staring at him while his coffee was getting cold. Giving herself a nudge, she propelled her feet forward and placed the cup in front of him. He reached for it, his hand closing around hers before she had a chance to let go. A spark of electricity shimmied up her arm from where their fingers had met. He must have felt it too, because his gaze riveted on hers, intense and smoldering. She flashed a smile and turned back to the stove.

Gran was filling plates with eggs, bacon, and fried potatoes. She thrust two plates into Leah's hands. "For Gracie and Ty."

Leah followed orders, delivering the plates to the table and placing them in front of the appropriate diners.

"That looks great," Ty said.

Gracie nodded her approval.

Leah brought the two remaining plates to the table as Gran directed her to be seated. She chose to sit beside Gracie, leaving the seat beside Ty for Gran.

"I got your biscuits right here," Gran called. She dumped an iron skillet filled with golden-brown biscuits into a napkin-lined basket and placed it in the center of the table.

"Everything looks great, Miz Fern," Ty said.

"Have some of my blackberry jam," she invited. "I put it up last summer. It was a 'specially sweet crop."

Ty complied, scooping a spoonful of the jam onto his plate.

"Gracie, maybe you can help me feed the chickens after we get done?"

Gracie's eyes opened wide. "Me? I get to help you?"

"Sure," Gran said. "In fact, if you do a good job, maybe that can be your chore."

Leah chuckled. "Feeding the chickens was my special chore when I spent my summers here as a child. I really got to know those hens."

Gracie grinned and wiggled in her chair. "How about the cows? Can we feed the cows too?"

"Them cows is sittin' on easy street," Gran said. "I got 'em in the east pasture for grazin', and they got the stream right there for drinkin'. When it gets to be winter, we got lots of hay stored up in the barn." She gave a wink. "Them cows is doin' good."

Leah picked up a slice of bacon and munched it. This was all too comfortable. She just had to keep breathing, and he would be gone in the blink of an eye. *Gone to his girlfriend in Dallas.*

"Miz Fern," Ty said. "Last night, when we were out walking, I noticed there was a charred section at the rear of the barn. It looked like some of the fence behind it got burned pretty badly." He set his fork on the table and stared at her earnestly. "I was just wondering how something like that got started."

Gran's forehead furrowed, and her lips tightened. "It was them danged Carter boys. They keep messin' with me."

"Carter boys?" Leah asked. "You mean some children are giving you trouble?"

Gran made a scornful noise. "Not hardly. Them boys is older'n either one of you two." She picked up her biscuit and bit into it. "Don't let your food get cold."

"Yes, ma'am," Ty replied, dutifully picking up his fork again. "There are a lot of Carters around here, but you're saying these particular Carter boys are adults?"

A small muscle in the side of her face twitched. "Aw, it ain't nothin' to worry about. Not a big deal at all."

"You're certain about that?" Leah held her napkin, gripped in her hand.

"Yeah, it's nothin' at all." She made a big show of buttering her biscuit.

"If you say so," Ty said, but his expression remained skeptical. "I'm going to drive in to Langston first thing," Ty announced. "I'm going to get a new serpentine belt and try to get Leah's car running, so if anybody needs anything, I'll be happy to pick it up."

Gran rolled her eyes and made a humming noise. "We could use a couple of things. Maybe Leah can ride along with you and do a little shopping."

Panic clawed at Leah's insides. The last thing she

needed to do was spend any more alone time with
Mr. Hot 'n' Unavailable. She cast about for some
reason she couldn't ride into Langston with Ty, but
of course, she was the obvious choice.

Leah took a biscuit and broke it open before slathering
it with butter. The aroma offered comfort to her miser-
able psyche, but not enough...not near enough. She ate
in silence, becoming a bystander to the blur of babble.

The conversation swirled around her. Oblivious to
her discomfort, Gran and Ty chatted about the ranch and
what needed fixing. Gracie chimed in, her voice floating
above the rest.

Even Leah's subdued mood couldn't cancel out the
effects of Gran's delicious breakfast. Slowly, her taste
buds asserted themselves, making her aware of the food
she was eating. Better than most anything she had eaten
in a while. She idly wondered if she would become one
of those fat little farm girls, chowing down on Gran's
great cooking.

As soon as the meal was over, she rose to clear the
dishes, but Gran waved her off. "You go on with Ty. Get
your car fixed. I'll jot down a list for you."

"Sure, Gran." Leah gave Gracie a kiss and settled her
at the table with a book while Gran cleaned the kitchen.

"After I tidy things up, Gracie, you an' me will tend
to those chickens."

When Leah turned, Ty was standing by the door,
gazing at her. His frame seemed to fill the doorway, yet
he didn't frighten her the way Caine had. She thought
Ty was a gentle giant, more likely to break her heart
than her bones. She tucked Gran's shopping list in her
pocket along with the ten-dollar bill she'd been given.

"You two stay out of trouble," Leah called, the note of false gaiety sounding flat to her ears.

Ty held the door open for her, and when she stepped out onto the porch, he took her arm, as though she were incapable of navigating the steps by herself. Opening the big diesel truck with his remote, he gave her a boost up onto the passenger seat, his touch scalding her like a hot iron.

He rounded the front of the cab and climbed in beside her. "We'll get your car fixed, and you can be running the roads in no time."

"That will be great," she said stiffly. "I mean, I really appreciate it."

"No problem. I kind of enjoy working on old cars."

She exhaled heavily. "Well, you should have a great time with my old heap."

He glanced at her, suddenly serious. "I didn't mean—"

"It's okay." She shrugged. "I know how old it is. How did you learn to work on cars?"

He grinned. "Around our place, there was always something breaking down. Lots of equipment and vehicles. My dad is pretty handy with all things mechanical. My brothers and I were usually hanging around learning from him."

"That's nice. It sounds like you have a good family."

"Yeah, I do. Things have been different since my mom passed away. Dad's always angry about something or another. It seems like he's always yelling, and mostly at me."

This declaration brought Ty's mood way down. His fingers tightened around the steering wheel, and he frowned at the road ahead.

"Tell me about your brothers," she said, anxious to change the subject.

"Colton is the oldest, and Beau is the baby of the family. I was stuck in the middle. Colt was the big football star in high school. Now, he's totally focused on the ranch, so he's my dad's clone. Beau just graduated last summer from his studies at Texas Tech. He majored in agriculture."

"I'm sensing a theme here."

He gave out a snort. "Yeah, somehow, I got left out of the farmer genetic cycle."

Leah turned to assess him. "I think you have it. At least you know a lot about farming and ranching. Otherwise, you wouldn't have stored up so much knowledge about horses and cattle and crops. You wouldn't care."

"I guess. I've got a degree in ag too, but it's not my everything, like it is theirs. I swear they wake up in the morning thinking about the ranch, the herd, the crops."

"What do you wake up in the morning thinking about?" She steeled herself for the answer. *The woman who waits for you in Dallas?*

"Music."

She must have given him a surprised look, because he laughed.

"I'm all about the music. I hear it in my head all the time. I write it. I play it. I sing it. It's all I've ever wanted to do."

Leah's chest felt tight. It was as though he had shared something of himself with her…something important. "I think that's nice. Are you any good?"

He grinned, giving her a sideways glance. "I'll let you be the judge of that."

His words brushed over her skin, intimate as a

caress, setting off little tingles of anticipation along the way. Did that mean he was going to sing for her? That sounded promising. "You must be talented."

"A few people have told me so." He was grinning as he gazed out the windshield.

She held her breath a moment, then blurted out, "What are you going to do in Dallas?"

He glanced at her, and she responded with a blush.

"I—I mean," she stammered, "you seem to be on some kind of deadline. I thought you might have someone…special waiting for you."

His grin widened. "Nothing like that. I'm just meeting up with an old bud from college. He's got a sound studio, and he's going to record some of the songs I've written."

A rush of unreasonable joy swirled through her insides. *Nothing like that.* She smiled.

He pointed over the steering wheel. "There's Langston up ahead. Put your number in here, and you can shop while I'm getting the things I need." He handed his phone to her. "Just call me when you're ready."

She stared at the device in her hands. "I—I don't have a cell phone."

Ty glanced at her, seemed to bite off a response, and reached for the phone. "You should have one in case of emergency, at least."

Leah nodded, gnawing her lip.

"Not a problem. I'll just get that belt for your car, and then we can do a little shopping." He pulled into an auto supply store and jumped out, leaving the diesel motor idling.

She watched him enter the shop, thinking the whole situation was feeling entirely too comfortable. In a matter of four days, she had gone from a total hellish disaster to sitting in a big, air-conditioned truck, waiting for the nicest guy she had ever met. She did a mental tally of the little she knew about Ty.

He must be from some kind of well-off ranching family, or he wouldn't be driving this truck, wouldn't have a beautiful Arabian horse, wouldn't feel like he could follow his dreams without a backup plan.

She hoped he would be able to make it in the entertainment industry...but she really hoped he would decide to stick around for a while. The more time they spent together, the more reasons she found to like him.

Ty pushed out of the glass door and climbed into the truck. "Out of luck. They've got an order coming in from their store in Amarillo and managed to get the serpentine belt on the truck. It will be here in a few hours." He backed out onto the street and shifted gears. "I have another stop, and then I'm all yours."

Leah swallowed hard. *All mine? That would be nice.*

Ty drove to a hardware store that was part of a national chain. "This is the last stop for me. Want to come in or wait here?"

Flustered, Leah decided to wait. Again, she watched him walk away with longing in her heart. She sat alone, wrapped in her private thoughts, an ache in her chest for the mistakes she had made...for the things she could never hope to have.

After about twenty minutes, she spotted Ty pushing a cart toward the truck. He disappeared to the rear, and she heard the sound of something heavy and hard hitting the bed of the truck.

A few seconds later, he was leaping onto the driver's

seat and backing out again. "My list is complete. Where to next?"

Leah gave him a tight little smile. "I only have ten bucks and Gran's grocery list. Where do people shop for food around here?"

"That would be the Bag 'n' Save. But I think we have a little more time to waste if we want to get that serpentine belt today. Let me show you around Langston."

She took a deep breath and expelled it forcefully. "Sure. That sounds okay."

"And we can grab lunch somewhere. Would you like to go back to Tiny's Diner? Or there's a great Mexican restaurant. How do you feel about Mexican food?"

She had to laugh. He looked so cute and enthusiastic. "Whatever you want is fine with me." *Beggars can't be choosers.*

"Well, I haven't had Mexican food in a long time. How about it?"

"I'm willing," she said.

He drove to the west side of town and pulled into the parking area of a restaurant. Only a few cars were clustered close to the entrance.

"It looks like nobody else thinks this is a good place," she said.

"It's just barely eleven. It will fill up," he said. "Let's grab a table and chow down." He swung out of the pickup and came around to open her door. He reached to help her alight, his hands at her waist. For just one long second, he held on to her, gazing into her eyes with an expression that seemed to match her own state of longing. She thought for a moment that perhaps he too wanted something he couldn't have.

—◆—

Inside, the hostess seated them in a high-backed booth and handed out menus with the day's specials handwritten on a sticky note.

"Everything's good here," Ty announced. He gazed across the table, noting her hesitation.

"I…uh…I only have the ten my grandmother gave me," Leah said. "I shouldn't spend it on food."

"Order whatever you want," he said. "My treat, of course."

She pressed her lips together for a moment. "I don't feel right about you paying for me." She laid the menu down as though that settled the matter.

"Look, Leah, I wouldn't have invited you to lunch if I wasn't paying. Don't worry about it." He reached over to open the menu for her. "Now figure out what you want, or I'll have to order for you."

She gazed at him and then, as though coming to some decision, picked up the menu again. "Thanks, Ty," she said under her breath.

"I can afford to pay," he said. "I've worked for my dad since I was in grade school. My brothers too, and Dad always paid us for our work. He said we needed to learn the value of hard work, and believe me, we worked. I still have a healthy bank balance, so don't think it will be anything but a pleasure to take a pretty woman to lunch."

He noted the slight flush that tinged her cheeks, but she smiled, even though she couldn't meet his eyes.

When the waitress returned, they ordered, but conversation seemed to be hard to come by.

"I'm going to work on your car when we get back to your grandmother's. Then, maybe I can repair the barn door and start mending fences."

"I can't tell you how much I appreciate all that you're doing, Ty." She leaned forward. "Maybe I can get a job to help my grandmother." She glanced around the restaurant. "I could be a waitress."

He smiled. "I'm sure you could. What kind of work have you done in the past?"

She shrugged, lifting and dropping her shoulders in a singularly defeated manner. "I worked in a veterinarian's office once. Not with the animals but just answering the phone and keeping the records straight."

"There's a veterinarian here in Langston," he said. "But she works out of her house and makes personal visits to all the ranches around here. What else have you done?"

"I worked in a Family Dollar for a while and as a file clerk and receptionist." Her brows knit. "Not very exciting, but I'm not afraid of hard work."

"I'm sure you'll find something," he said. "After we eat, we can stop by the newspaper office and grab a copy of the weekly paper. Check out the want ads."

She nodded and brightened a bit. "I just need to do something to help Gran out. I can't be mooching off her."

He smiled encouragingly. "You'll be fine. I know your grandmother loves having you here."

Their food arrived, and they ate heartily. He noted that Leah made short work of the large platter of food. He admired her spirit and hated that she seemed to have fallen on hard times. Whatever had caused her to leave Oklahoma and come to North Texas with only her daughter, a scruffy dog, and their few belongings, he hoped they would have a better life from here on out.

If only...

He quickly reined in his thoughts. He couldn't go imagining there might be something between them. Nothing romantic. There was no time, and it wouldn't be fair...to either of them.

But still, her kisses the night before had been earth-shaking. Every time he glanced at her pretty, soft lips, he was jerked back to the moment when he held her tight, when she clung to him and returned his kisses. It would be so easy to give in to the temptation those lips promised. *So easy...*

After they had eaten, he drove to the newspaper office and paid for the latest edition. He spread the paper open on the countertop and turned to the want ads. "Let's see what we have here."

"You looking for a job?" the lady behind the counter asked.

"My friend here is." He indicated Leah.

"I just took an ad from Mr. Ryan. He's the lawyer here. His secretary just ran off to get married."

Ty saw Leah perk up. "I know Mr. Ryan. He's my dad's attorney. Maybe we can drop by his office this afternoon."

Leah looked horrified. "Oh no. I'm not properly dressed to go on a job interview. Look at my hair."

He grinned and reached out a hand to touch her mop of curls. "Your hair looks fine."

"It's horrible. I don't have any makeup on. I'm a mess."

"How about if we just go by and pick up an application?"

She looked stricken but then nodded. "That would be okay."

Ty folded the paper and handed it to her. "You can check out the other jobs later and call about them."

When he pulled up in front of the office of Breckenridge T. Ryan, Esquire, Leah appeared to have turned into a statue. She stared out the window at the storefront office with something akin to horror etched on her fine features.

"I can go in for you, if you want," Ty said.

She shook herself out of her stupor. "No, I can do this." She reached for the door handle and was out of the truck before he could stop her.

"Wait for me," he said. "I can introduce you." He thought she looked relieved. Opening the door for her, he found Breckenridge Ryan, known as "Breck," rummaging around in a desk in the front office.

He looked up, frowning. "What can I do for you?"

"I don't know if you remember me, Mr. Ryan. I'm Tyler Garrett. You know my dad."

Breck pointed a finger at him, his frown abating. "Yes, one of Big Jim's sons. You're the middle boy, right?"

Ty nodded. "Yes, sir. And this is Leah Benson. I understand you need some office help, and my friend here is experienced."

Breck narrowed his gaze, giving Leah a once-over. "You type?"

"Um, yes, I can type real well."

"You don't need to be fast, just accurate." He spread his hands, indicating the mess on the desk. "How about filing? I can't find a damned thing."

Leah grinned, overcoming her shyness. "I can organize your filing for you."

"You're hired," Breck said, extending a hand.

Leah flashed a big grin as her hand was pumped in a hearty shake.

Breck told her it would be strictly five days a week and offered her a sum that made her grin again. "Come in tomorrow morning at nine. I'll get you started and give you a set of keys."

Leah fairly floated out to the truck. "That was so awesome. I can't believe you got me a job just like that."

Ty shook his head. "I didn't do anything but introduce you." He opened the passenger door and gave her a boost inside.

"No, I know how these things work." She gazed down at him. "Because he knows your family, he assumes I'm okay. If I had gone in there alone, he would have wanted references. You made all the difference."

He closed the door on her and rounded to climb in on his side. He pondered her words. Perhaps he had lent her come credence. He was glad he had been able to support her. The lovely Leah certainly needed some validation.

Chapter 4

LEAH WAS THRILLED. *I'VE GOT A JOB! JUST LIKE THAT, I'VE got a job*. She could hardly breathe. Her hands were clasped so tight together in her lap her knuckles were turning white.

Ty started the truck, the diesel engine roaring to life. "Okay, let's go to the Bag 'n' Save, and then I imagine your serpentine belt will be here."

She turned on him with a breathless grin. "Thanks so much, Ty."

"You gotta stop that," he said with a grin of his own. "I'm just being neighborly."

"Whatever it is you're calling it, I thank you."

He reached over to grab her hand and give it a squeeze. "You make it real easy to be nice to you, Leah." Then, as if he caught himself doing something he shouldn't, he drew his hand away.

Leah rode the few blocks to the grocery store, an uncomfortable silence suffocating her.

Once inside, Ty commandeered a cart, while Leah groped for Gran's list.

"Let me see that," he said, and she passed it to him with a sigh. He glanced over it quickly and tucked it in the pocket of his shirt. "How about some fresh stuff?" He headed for the produce section.

"Um, it's not on the list." She was painfully aware of the few items Gran had requested.

"Well, it's on my list. Let's see here. Does Gracie like fruit?" He proceeded to fill bags with apples, peaches, and grapes. He hefted a good-sized watermelon onto the carrier under the cart.

Leah kept quiet, nodding agreement whenever he asked her about some food item or another. He went up and down the aisles, filling the cart with all kinds of foodstuffs.

"Does your grandmother have enough ranch dressing? We better grab another bottle, because that seems to be the favorite." He tossed a large bottle in with his other gatherings. He got cases of dog food and treats too. By the time he was done, the grocery cart was piled high.

She cringed when they got to the checkout line and the total was rung up. She offered the ten-dollar bill, but Ty whipped out a plastic card and swiped it through the slot in front of him.

"You keep that for emergencies. You're starting your new job tomorrow, and you'll need to buy lunch."

The ache of impending tears stung her nose. *Not going to cry!* She bit the inside of her lips to keep her courage locked down. *It's all good.*

Ty stowed the groceries in the back seat and started the truck again. "One more stop, and we'll get that belt and take you home."

She nodded, feigning a smile.

He drove to a convenience store and left the motor idling while he went inside. He came back with a small bag and tossed it to her. "I got you a pay-as-you-go cell phone and some minutes. Be sure to plug it in when you get home. I don't want you out on the road without some means of calling for help."

That did it. She burst into tears, her shoulders shaking and her hands over her eyes.

"Oh, come on, baby girl. I didn't mean to make you cry." He reached over and hauled her to him, patting her shoulder while she bawled. He stroked her hair and held her closer.

"Everything has just been so hard," she said. "I mean—"

"Shh," he soothed. "You're here now, and everything is going to be all right."

"Well, yeah. You're being so damned kind to me. I don't ever remember anyone actually caring if I broke down by the side of the road or not or…or if there was food on the table." She sniffled loudly. "Or if Gracie liked apples or pears."

"I don't know why not. Somebody should care about you…a lot." He rested his cheek against her hair. "I care," he whispered.

She raised her chin, gazing into his eyes. Her heart thundered in her ears as he wiped the tears from her cheeks.

His expression melted any pretense of reserve she might have had. Softly, he brushed his lips against hers. And again, a little less softly. "Damn!" he muttered as her arms circled his neck. "I'm a goner." He laid a kiss on her that she felt all the way down to her toes. When they drew apart, he flashed a sudden smile. "Don't look so scared. We'll figure this out." He tousled her hair and put the truck in gear. "Buckle up, baby."

Leah nodded wordlessly, not sure what there was to figure out but willing to go along with it, whatever it was.

The last stop was the auto supply store where, once more, he left the truck idling and went inside to emerge with another bag he tossed in the back seat. "Now we're done. Let's get you home so I can start to work on your car."

They made the trip back to Gran's with their fingers interlaced.

Ty sang along with the radio, and he did, indeed, have an incredible voice. His rich baritone was right on key, and he seemed to know the words to every song the disc jockey played.

Leah's thoughts were jumbled. She was afraid to even try examining her feelings too deeply. She only knew this was the happiest she could ever remember being, and Ty had done it with his kindness and a few kisses.

When Ty pulled up in front of the little farmhouse, he saw Gracie outside playing with Lucky and Eddie. She dropped the stick she'd been throwing and ran up to greet them with a grin. The cast on her arm looked ungainly on her slender form. "Hi, Mommy! Hi, Ty!"

He got out and picked Gracie up, swinging her around a few times before setting her back on her feet. "Hi, Gracie. Are you keeping the dogs in line?"

She laughed and nodded. "Eddie likes to run around with Lucky. I throw the stick, and they bring it back to me. They're best friends now." She pointed to the unlikely duo. Lucky, a big, silky-coated purebred retriever, and Eddie, a small, black-and-white mixed breed with curly fur and bright, shiny eyes.

Eddie sat down and scratched behind his ear. Ty figured he would need to treat both dogs for fleas since they had become "best friends."

He opened the driver's side back door and loaded his

arms with plastic grocery bags. He looked back to see Leah gathering more and trailing behind him. Gracie ran ahead and held the screen door open, and he carried his load to the kitchen, setting everything in the middle of the floor. "I'll get the rest and leave you to put stuff away." He spoke to Leah, who nodded at him.

Returning to the truck, he contemplated the turn of events. He wasn't sure what had happened, but he could no longer pretend he was indifferent to the lovely Leah. He had felt the attraction from the moment she walked into Tiny's Diner with Gracie in tow. They'd both looked scared to death, like the boogeyman was hot on their trail.

He wrenched the truck door open again, grabbing the rest of the groceries and the bag from the auto supply store. He dropped the latter on the porch and hauled the rest into the house.

Leah and Gracie were gleefully going through the bags. Just the sight of their faces made his chest feel like it was full of feathers. "Where's your grandmother?"

Leah stared hard as he slipped the nicely starched western shirt off and arranged it over the back of a kitchen chair. Now he was wearing just a white T-shirt. "Gracie tells me she's out cleaning up the bunkhouse in your honor."

"That's mighty nice of her, but she didn't need to go to all that trouble." He raked his fingers through his hair and set his Stetson back on his head.

Leah laughed. "Well, you didn't look too comfortable crunched up on the couch. She must have thought you needed a little room to stretch out."

"Maybe she's right. I'll be outside if you need me."

He strode out the door, grabbing the bag he'd left on the porch and his tools out of the truck. He inserted a favorite CD and opened the windows so he could hear music while he worked before heading to Leah's car.

Popping the hood, he stared into the guts of the aged vehicle. He sang along with the CD as both dogs came to lie in the dirt near him. "Thanks, my buds." Eddie cocked his head, but Lucky just lowered his head onto his paws and prepared to go to sleep.

Ty opened the store bag and took out a plastic drain pan, then slid it under the oil reservoir and drained the dirtiest, sludgiest-looking oil he had ever seen. *Damn! I bet she hasn't had an oil change in a year.* He shook his head, a muscle tightening in his cheek. *Hasn't anyone ever taken care of you, Leah?*

It irked him that she was so grateful for any little thing he did to help her out. It shouldn't be that way. A woman as sweet and pretty as Leah should have someone by her side, happy to do all the things a man is supposed to do for a woman. He could see the shredded remains of the serpentine belt coiled around the various parts it was supposed to keep moving. Expelling a disgusted breath, he set to work, hoping his little contribution would help her stay safe on the road and help her start a better life.

Leah and Gracie finished putting away the groceries.

Gracie told her she had never seen so much food in her life. That made Leah feel happy and sad at the same time.

"Well, now we have it all put away safe, so let's go help Gran clean the bunkhouse and tell her about our windfall." Leah held out her hand to Gracie, who grinned and clasped it with her good hand.

They pushed their way out of the front screen, and Gracie called a greeting to Ty, thus affording a great display of rippling muscles as he straightened from under the hood of Leah's car and raised a hand to wave. He had ditched the T-shirt and looked like he belonged on the cover of a fitness magazine.

Dang! How hot is that? Leah swallowed and tried out a fake casual finger waggle while waves of lust roiled through her insides. He turned back to his task, and Gracie half dragged her around to the bunkhouse at the rear of the homestead.

She could hear Gran humming before they entered. All the windows were open, and the door stood ajar. When she stepped inside, Leah spotted Gran with a scarf tied around her head, turban-fashion. "Hey, Gran," Leah called. "Reinforcements have arrived. What can we do to help?"

Gran was washing something in the sink. She rinsed some sort of glassware under the running water. "Hello, you two."

Gracie broke free of Leah's hand, running to Gran's side. "Guess what Ty did?" she demanded. Without waiting for a reply, she went on, "Ty bought a whole bunch of food for us. Mommy and I put it all away."

Gran frowned and then looked at Leah for confirmation.

Leah shrugged. "He sure did. When we went to the store, he just went up and down the aisles and filled the cart. Nothing I could do to stop him." She picked up a tea towel and began to dry off the glass globes Gran had placed on the drain board.

"Well, he shouldn't spend his money like that. Nice young fellow, but surely he doesn't think we're some sort of charity case."

"Oh no," Leah said. "I'm certain he doesn't think that. He took me to lunch too."

Gran smiled at that. "I think that boy is sweet on you, Leah. Yes, I do."

Leah felt her face heat up. "He was just being nice… but guess what?"

Gracie and Gran said "What?" at the same time.

"I got a job. Ty took me to see a man, and he hired me on the spot."

"Yay, Mommy!" Gracie danced around with her good arm waving over her head.

Gran's eyes almost popped out of her head. "Doin' what? It ain't nothin' unrespectable, is it?"

Leah shook her head. "Nothing like that. I'll be working for a Mr. Ryan who is a lawyer there in Langston. He told me to come in and start tomorrow. It was because he knew Ty's papa."

"Well, I suppose that's all right then. I heard of Mr. Ryan. He's supposed to be a pretty good man." Gran pursed her lips. "Sounds like Ty is a fine, upstanding young man. Maybe you ought to set your cap for him."

Yeah right. Leah gnawed her bottom lip. "I don't think so. He'll be leaving soon, but I'm glad to have a job. I really appreciate what he did for me."

"You could do a lot worse." Gran gave her an amused look.

"Listen, Gran, what about those guys who set fire to your barn? Are they still giving you trouble?"

Gran's entire appearance morphed from pleasant to grim. "Just forget about 'em. They's the scum of the earth."

"You said they were messing with you. What did you mean by that?"

Her grandmother heaved a huge sigh. "They ain't important. Don't you worry. I can hold my own with those two."

Alarmed, Leah moved closer, lowering her voice to a whisper. "I don't think you're being truthful. What's really going on?"

"I got into it with their old man. Now he's sendin' his weaselly boys to give me a hard time."

"Tell me the truth. Did they set fire to the barn?" Leah's stomach was clenched like a fist.

"No tellin', but I'm pretty sure they did. I caught it early on and got it put out real quick."

"Oh no. What if they try something like that again?" Leah worried about bringing her daughter into such a dangerous situation.

Her grandmother spat out a derisive sound. "I'll blast them boys all the way back to their papa's place. Don't you worry one little bit."

Gracie came closer, tugging on Leah's sleeve. "Mommy, what can I do to help?"

Leah spied a glass container that looked like it would hold water or juice. "Here, honey. Why don't I fill this with water, and you can put it in the refrigerator so Ty will have something cold to drink?" She handed Gracie the filled jug and watched as she crossed the room to put it on a shelf in the old avocado-green refrigerator.

Gran was quite tight-lipped, so Leah did not bring up the topic of the vandalism again.

She finished drying the glass and glanced around. "It looks great in here, Gran."

"I've put fresh sheets on the one bed, and I plugged in the refrigerator in case he wants to keep something in it." She waved her hands around. "I cleaned up the kitchen and tried to tidy things a bit." She picked up one of the glass objects. "I even washed the light fixtures. They were a mite dusty."

In a flash, Leah realized her grandmother had stood on a rickety chair to take the glass globes down. She shuddered to think what might have happened. "Let me put those back up for you." She took the globes and arranged them on the small dinette table and chose a sturdier chair to stand on.

From her vantage point, she kept an eye on her daughter and Gran as they worked around the room, making things nice for Ty. When she had the light fixtures rearranged, Leah climbed down from her perch. "This place looks real homey. I'm sure Ty will appreciate your efforts."

Gran beamed, and Gracie twirled around in a circle.

With a pang, Leah realized she wasn't the only one who had become dangerously attached to Tyler Garrett.

He grinned and leaned his forearms on the fender. The new serpentine belt snaked its way through all the machinations it was supposed to keep moving, just as it should, and he was feeling pretty smug about it. The oil change must have helped, because the engine, while not exactly purring, was at least not chugging as it had done previously.

Ty straightened and wiped his hands on a rag he kept in his toolbox. He closed the hood and turned to find Leah standing behind him. "Whoa! I almost stepped on you."

She was smiling now, but it was a sad little smile. "It wouldn't be the first time I've been stepped on."

Ouch! He managed to get hold of his sharp retort before it left his lips. She needed to stop thinking of herself as a doormat, but maybe she had been stepped on too many times to know how to be anything else. "Want to try 'er out?"

"Sure," she said, and then her smile faded. "Maybe I better save the gas for tomorrow. The tank was pretty low when—when you found us."

He slid into the driver's seat and noted the level of the gas gauge. *Running on fumes.* "Well, I'm going to give it a quick spin. Jump in."

Her big brown eyes opened wide, but she hurried to get in on the passenger side. She fumbled for the seat belt as he revved the motor. "That sounds a lot better than before. It reminded me of a coffee grinder."

Ty drove to the end of the lane and then out onto the highway. The windows were open, and Leah's hair was blowing away from her face, showing off the sharp angles of her cheekbones.

He found a side road and turned around.

Leah was still grinning when he returned to the farm and shut off the motor. "Ty, you've been so great—"

He cut her off by pulling her across the seat toward him.

She stared at him, her eyes wide and her mouth an undeniable invitation.

He couldn't hold back any longer, capturing her luscious lips with his own.

The kiss was soft at first but quickly deepened. Her hand stroked his bare arm and reached to embrace him. Such a small gesture, but it set off a storm of lust raging in his core.

She pressed against him, the thin fabric of her shirt doing nothing to disguise the soft, warm woman beneath.

He heard a groan, surprised that it came from him. Tearing his lips away, he buried them in her windblown curls. How could he have fallen so far, so fast? And why now?

Holding her close, he felt his own heart throbbing in his chest. The timing couldn't be worse. Why hadn't he met her before, or better yet, after he had made it big in Nashville? He swallowed hard and pressed another kiss into her hair. "You can make it into Langston, but I'm going to get you some gas tomorrow so you can drive to your new job all week." His voice came out husky and rough. Cradling her head in his hand, he kissed her forehead and drew back to gaze into her eyes.

She grinned breathlessly and nodded. "Thanks, Ty. Thank you so very much."

He made a growling sound and raised an eyebrow at her.

"I mean, well…what else can I say but thanks?"

"That's plenty." He held her face in both hands and dropped a kiss on her nose. "Now, let me get back to work while there's still some light left." He climbed out and walked toward his truck.

~~~

Leah sat for a moment, relishing the warm comfort of his caring. She had no idea what tomorrow might bring, but for now, she was soaking it up like sunshine.

Reluctantly, she emerged, watching Ty's retreating form as he moved with an athletic ease. He didn't seem to have any idea how hot he looked with or without a shirt, which she found even more endearing.

When she stepped inside the house, she found Gran grinning at her. "So, that's how it is, huh?"

Leah shrugged, trying to stifle an embarrassed grin of her own. "I'm not sure how it is, but I'm just going to see what happens. Ty is the one with an agenda, and he'll have to decide what he wants."

Gran gave her an appraising look. "Any fool can see that young man is mighty sweet on you. I think it would be a good idea to decide what you want, young lady."

Leah pressed her lips together. "I...I want to be happy. I want to take care of my daughter and never put her in danger again." She drew in a breath and blew it out forcefully. "I want us all to be safe...from...from..."

"We'll be fine," Gran spat out tersely. "Nobody better ever come around here intendin' to hurt you or my little Gracie again. They just better not is all I'm sayin'."

Leah spent the rest of the afternoon working around the house.

Gran had already surveyed the huge quantity of food now stored in her refrigerator and pantry. A large bowl of fresh fruit sat in the center of the table, washed and ready to be eaten.

Leah could almost see the thoughts whirling around her grandmother's head. Gran realized what a nice man Ty was, and she wanted there to be something lasting between him and Leah, but Leah wanted to be fair. As much as she would like to believe such a forever was possible, she knew Ty's dreams of a music career had to be respected, so she would remain quiet and let things play out as they should.

As the sunlight faded, Ty remained outside, working. He was nowhere to be seen, although Leah frequently cast a glance through the screen door.

She helped Gran with dinner, which was more elaborate than before. The aroma of a luscious meatloaf in the oven wafted through the air. And Gran had made biscuits and tomato gravy.

Leah made a big pot of creamy mashed potatoes and arranged a salad in a glass bowl. Finally, she placed the brand-new bottle of ranch dressing on the table next to the fruit bowl.

"You better go out and see what Ty's up to. Tell him dinner will be ready in about twenty minutes." Gran nodded her head toward the oven. "I made a cobbler with some of the peaches, so I'll pop it in when the meatloaf is done."

"I'll tell him." Leah started for the door.

"That young feller sure does know how to work hard. He ain't no slacker."

Leah stepped out onto the porch. The sun was low, streaking the blue sky with long fingers of purple and salmon. Glancing around, she didn't see Ty, so she headed to the back of the property.

A bubble of joy rose in her chest as she spied him atop his big, black stallion. The horse danced a little, but Ty held the reins and stroked its neck. "Easy there, boy. You're all right."

Leah heard the same soothing tone he used on her when she was upset.

He looked up and spotted her, giving a wave. "Hey there." Still bare-chested and wearing his Stetson, the sight of him set her pulses to racing.

"Hey, yourself." Her words came out all gravelly. She cleared her throat. "Are you about ready for dinner? Gran says everything will be ready in twenty minutes or so."

He flapped the stirrups against the horse's flanks and rode to where she stood. "That's about as perfect as perfect can be. Just enough time for me to take you for a ride." He leaned down to her, extending an arm for her to grab onto.

She reached up, the desire to be held overcoming her shyness.

Ty swung her up effortlessly, arranging her astride the saddle in front of him. "Here you go. You're okay." His hand was on her thigh, burning through the denim.

An involuntary smile spread across her face. *Yes, the same tone of voice he uses on the horse.*

He arranged her hands on the saddle horn and wrapped one arm around her, resting it at her waist.

Exhaling, she tried to calm her jitters. *I'm okay.* But when Ty clicked the reins and the big horse started forward, she gripped his arm for dear life.

The horse was moving at an easy gait, and she realized she was in no danger of falling off. She tried to relax, and Ty pulled her back to rest against his chest. When they drew even with the front of the house, he turned his mount to the west, facing into the blazing glory of the sunset. She let out a little bleat of pleasure.

"Sure is pretty, isn't it?" Ty's deep voice rumbled in his chest, vibrated through her spine, and annexed her as a part of him.

She mumbled an acknowledgment of sorts, happy to be in his embrace. Happy to be happy.

They rode all around the property, but he headed back within the twenty allotted minutes. He drew up beside the porch and swung her down out of the saddle with one arm, then climbed down himself. He patted Prince on the neck and tied the reins to the porch railing.

Leah felt a sense of loss, having been deposited on her own two feet and deprived of the warm, secure blanket of Ty. She wrapped her arms around herself for comfort and waited as he made sure the horse was secure. She heard a soft whine and turned to find both dogs staring at her. Lucky swished his long and magnificent feathered tail, and Eddie waggled his curly little one.

When Ty turned to her, he looped his arm around her, ushered her up onto the porch, and held the door for her.

The aroma of good food hit her like a truck. She was suddenly aware of how hungry she was.

Ty grabbed a clean shirt from his duffel. "Let me wash up, and I'll be right out."

He disappeared down the hall and returned shortly, looking tidy with his shirt tucked in and his hair damp. "Something smells mighty good."

Gran turned from the stove to give him a smile. "Well, after you brought all this food home, the least we can do is cook you up a good meal. Come right over here and fill your plate, young feller, and take your seat at the table."

Ty gave a bow to Gracie and Leah. "Ladies first."

Gracie pranced ahead of him, and he pulled Leah into place, bringing up the rear of the line.

Gran dished up the tasty food onto their plates and shooed them to the table. "I have peach cobbler in the oven, so save a little room for dessert."

"Yes, ma'am," Ty said. He took his plate and set it on the table but waited until Gran brought her own food, then held her chair before he seated himself.

Leah sucked in a breath. *No fair! This man is making me fall in love with him. He's going to break my heart when he leaves*. She reached for her napkin, but Gracie clasped her hands, resting her cast on the table.

"Can I say grace?"

Gran clasped her hands together and nodded. "Of course you can, precious."

Leah and Ty followed suit, bowing their heads.

Gracie's eyes were closed as she fervently gave thanks for being there, for all the food, and for Ty, who saved them.

"Amen," Gran said. "Now, dig in and enjoy, children. There's plenty for seconds."

Leah reached for the biscuits, took one, and passed the basket to Ty.

Gran leaned toward Ty. "How was your day, young man? I saw you workin' real hard on Leah's car."

"Yes, ma'am. I got it running and repaired the barn door. I closed it up for you and repaired some of the fence that was down."

"Land sakes! That's a blessing." Gran beamed across the table at him. "Them Carter boys have been cuttin' my fence faster'n I been able to fix it. At first, I hired a couple o' hands to help, but them Carters is a mean bunch, 'n they scared 'em off." She scooped a bite of meatloaf into her mouth and chewed with a vengeance.

Ty set his fork down. "They've been cutting your fences?" His brow furrowed with concern.

Gran snorted. "Ol' Man Carter's been tryin' to run me off this land since my husband passed." She shook her head. "They's all meaner'n the devil."

Ty's face looked grim. "Now that I think about it, I remember the Carter family. Ray and Dean were bullies when my oldest brother was in high school. Colt got into a few fights with the Carters."

"Did he win?" Gran asked.

Ty nodded curtly. "Yes, ma'am. My brother Colton is bigger than me. He's not one to start a fight, but he sure knew how to finish one."

Silence as every person gathered around the table considered these revelations.

Finally, Gran laughed. A cackle, really. "I would have paid good money to have seen them Carters get their tails whupped."

Another silence.

Leah tried to envision a man even bigger than Ty but couldn't. Gran's disclosure about the Carters had taken the general mood way down.

Ty picked up his fork. "Is this tomato gravy?" he asked. "I haven't had anything this good since my mom passed." He made sounds of appreciation.

"So sorry to hear that, Ty." Gran gazed across the table at him. "I'm sure she's up in heaven, lookin' down on you right now and feelin' proud as punch for raisin' such a good man."

He shook his head. "I don't know about that, but she

always encouraged me to go after my dreams of a singing career. She thought I had a voice worth listening to." He winked at Gracie and quickly changed the subject. "Man! This meatloaf hits the spot. Could you pass me another biscuit, please?"

———

After dinner, Ty asked Leah if she had charged up the prepaid phone he'd given her. When she produced it, he made a call on his cell to activate it for her. Then he put Gran's old rotary-dial phone number and his cell number into her contacts. He also added both numbers to his cell. "Now we'll all be able to stay connected."

Somehow, this gave Leah hope that he didn't plan to drive off and forget her in a couple of days. She thanked him, pressing her lips together to keep from saying too much.

"No big deal. I need to take care of Prince. I'll be back in a little while."

"I—I can help," Leah said.

"Miz Fern, Prince is enjoying his stall in your barn."

"That's good," she said. "There's plenty of fresh hay in the barn. One of them boys I hired to bale for me did a good job of gettin' it stored right…then them Carters scared the bejesus out of him, an' he never even come back to get his last paycheck." The grim set of her mouth revealed her negative memory of that event.

A shiver that must have registered on the Richter scale coiled around Leah's spine. She rubbed her arms, feeling guilty that her grandmother had gone through this bullying alone. She should have come to Langston after her grandfather passed. Maybe she could have deterred the Carters from their plan to intimidate the frail woman into selling off her land at a bargain price. And for sure, she would not have been so available when Caine got paroled. She gazed sorrowfully at her daughter managing to eat with the big cast on her arm.

She found Tyler staring hard. He looked almost as grim as Gran.

"Okay, you can come with me to say good night to my horse." He headed for the door, and she trailed behind him.

She watched as he untied Prince's reins from the porch railing and stroked the horse's head and neck. "Good boy," he crooned. He made a clicking noise and led Prince toward the back of the property. He held out his other hand to Leah who hurried to catch up. Somehow, placing her hand in Ty's chased away the demons tormenting her and gave her courage to stride confidently beside him.

The big black stallion walked behind, his shoes making a clip-clop sound on the hard-baked earth. She was acutely conscious of the big animal on the other end of the reins. She gazed into his dark eyes, feeling a bit overmatched.

The barn was dark, but Ty threw the doors open wide and strode inside. He found a single bare lightbulb hanging in the center of the barn and pulled the knotted string. The bulb sprang to life, momentarily blinding her. The horse started, but Ty quieted him.

As her eyes adjusted to the light, she realized only the middle of the barn was bathed in light. Deep black shadows ringed the periphery.

Ty led the horse to the line of stalls located on one side of the barn. He chose one and led Prince inside before removing the saddle and reins. Heaving the saddle over the edge of the stall, he removed Prince's reins and hung them on a nail by the stall door.

He proceeded to feed and water his horse as well as brush him with a curry brush. The horse's black coat gleamed in the harsh light.

"That's about it, big boy," Ty said, giving Prince's flank a final pat. He closed the door to the stall and turned to Leah. "Thanks."

She grinned self-consciously. "I didn't do anything."

"Maybe I just like having you around." He held out his arm.

"Well, in that case, you're welcome." She linked her arm through his and followed as he turned out the light and secured the barn door.

On the way back, Ty stopped to secure the chicken coop and the pen around the enclosure.

When they returned to the house, they found Gran and Grace had cleared the table, put away the food, and washed dishes. Gran was folding a dishcloth, which she hung over a rack inside the cabinet under the sink. "Ty, you get that horse put back in the barn?"

"Yes, Miz Fern. I fed him, and now he's locked up tight in his stall."

"Leah, why don't you help Ty get his things settled in the bunkhouse?" Gran smiled encouragingly. "I'll help Gracie with her bath and put her to bed."

Leah glanced from Gran to Ty to Gracie. "Are you sure?"

As if to clinch matters, Gracie threw her arms around

Leah's neck. "Good night, Mommy." Then she ran to give Ty the same treatment.

Given her earlier conversation with her grandmother, Leah suspected collusion.

"You sleep well, Gracie," he called as she disappeared down the hallway in the direction of the bathroom.

Gran gave a little wave and trekked after her, leaving Leah alone with Ty.

She sucked in a breath. "Well, let's get you settled, then."

He nodded and picked up his bag. When they were outside, he got a few more things out of the truck, including a guitar case and some western shirts on hangers. Then he turned and looked at her expectantly.

She tucked her hand in the crook of his arm, content to walk along beside him as they made their way in the dark. Clouds had obscured the moon, so it lent very little illumination for their footsteps. "I should have brought the flashlight," she said.

"Nah. We're fine."

"Are you always so sure of yourself?"

He chuckled in the darkness. "Well, I've survived this long. I have no reason to believe my time is up. Besides, I have things to do yet."

"I see," she said. "I suppose you think I should adopt your ridiculously positive attitude."

"That's the idea. Keep your chin up and your eyes on the prize. That's my motto." He made a kissy sound when Lucky veered off course to investigate something in the overgrowth beside the path, and the dog immediately fell in by his side.

"Here we are," Leah announced when they reached

the bunkhouse. Ty opened the door, and she reached inside to flip the light switch. "It's not much, but you should be comfortable."

Ty looked around and grinned. "Looks fine to me." He sat his bags and paraphernalia on the floor beside the bed that had been made up. "It was real nice of your grandmother to go to such trouble."

"Yeah, well, you've gone to a lot of trouble for us... for me."

He shot her a look that went straight to her heart and brought a rush of color to her cheeks.

"I know you don't want me to be all gushy with thanks, but everything you're doing here makes a world of difference." She ran her tongue over her lips. "For all of us, but especially for me."

He lifted her chin, holding her gaze. "Aw, Leah, you're about the sweetest thing I've ever come across. I wish I could do more."

"You're doing plenty," she breathed, her heart thumping so hard against her ribs she was pretty sure he could hear.

Ty leaned down and placed a gentle kiss on her mouth. The next kiss wasn't so gentle. Nor the one after that. He wrenched his lips away from hers. "I don't know what it is about you, but once I kiss you, I don't want to stop." His gaze seemed to impale her very soul.

Leah swallowed hard. "I—I don't want to stop either." She felt her cheeks burning under his scrutiny.

He leaned closer, his cheek pressed to hers. "Tell you what. Let me get some things in my life straightened out, and then we can take a good look at what we have here. You can tell me then if you want me to stop."

Her knees almost buckled beneath her. "Okay," she whispered.

He kissed her cheek and then her neck, just below her ear.

Shivers followed the trail his lips made.

"I think I better walk you back to the house. I can't have you falling down in the dark."

Leah sucked in a breath. "No, couldn't have that."

———

Leah climbed in her car the next morning. She tried to quell the butterflies flying relay races in her stomach. First day on her new job, and not just any job. Working for Breckenridge T. Ryan would be the best job she ever had. *I've got to make a good impression.* Sucking in a deep breath, she blew it out, puffing her cheeks in the process.

Her hand shook as she fumbled to insert the key in the ignition. The keys slipped and jangled to the floorboard. Heaving an impatient sigh, she scrunched down to search for them, her fingers scrabbling over the dusty floor mat.

"Good morning."

She straightened suddenly to find Ty leaning his forearms on her open window. "Oh, hi…I mean, good morning." Raking her fingers through her disheveled hair, she flashed him a nervous grin. "I was going to leave for my new job. Can't afford to be late the first day."

He reached in to pat her on the shoulder with his big paw. "Don't worry. You'll do fine."

Pressing her lips together, she nodded and stuck the key in the ignition again, this time with success.

The intensity of his gaze set her insides on fire. Then,

quick as anything, he swept off his Stetson and leaned in to kiss her lips.

Startled, she stared at him, then flashed a smile. A rush of joy surged through her insides. This was going to be a good day. At least it was starting off right. She put the car in reverse and backed up a ways, trying not to show how much his kiss affected her. When she could turn the car around, she headed toward the road leading to the main highway. Only then did she look back to see the big cowboy staring after her, his thumbs hooked in his belt loops. Somehow, just knowing Ty was watching her sent a rare glow of self-confidence throughout her being. "I can do this," she said aloud.

When she arrived in Langston, she found the attorney's office quite easily, there being only two or three main streets to contend with. She pulled into a parking space out front, beside a big truck reminiscent of Ty's behemoth on wheels.

Glancing at her face in the mirror, she heaved a sigh. The wind whipping through the open windows had done a number on her hair, and her cheeks were pink. She took a moment to sweep her hair into a ponytail and secure it with a scrunchie. *Not great but better*.

Taking a deep breath, she got out of the car, crossed the sidewalk, and stepped inside the office.

Her new boss was bending over a wastebasket beside the reception desk with his sleeves rolled up and his tie askew. "Good morning, Mr. Ryan," she called.

"Good morning, Leah. Please call me Breck." He sighed. "It will just make things easier."

She smiled and approached the reception desk. "Um, can I help you with that?"

He grinned up at her. "I was trying to make things easier on you by getting rid of a lot of crap. I don't want you to go running out the door on your first day."

"No chance of that," she said. "I'm tougher than I look."

Breck surveyed her, bringing a flush to her cheeks. "Good to know." He straightened and gestured to the roll-around chair. "This will be your guard post, where you will screen the few calls I receive every day and vet the even fewer visitors." He raised an eyebrow. "I'm a rancher, Leah. I divide my time between the ranches and this office. I do have a law practice that includes everything from the drawing up of wills and managing estates to arranging for the release of someone's teenage son who went on a spree. Not like in the big city."

She wasn't sure what she was supposed to say to that. "I'm sure I'll figure it all out."

He grinned broadly. "Just see what you can do with the files and answer the phone then. I'll be in my office." He strode into said office and closed the door.

Leah released the breath she had been holding. Sinking onto the chair, she inspected the desktop and opened drawers. *Clutter, clutter everywhere.*

Dragging the wastebasket closer, she disposed of a used lipstick, empty gum wrappers, and a few bobby pins. She got a damp paper towel from the restroom to wipe out the large file drawer on the side and then put her small handbag inside. Simply sliding the drawer closed gave her a great sense of accomplishment.

She went through the remaining drawers, one by one, and managed to separate the trash from the office supplies. Tackling the desktop was another matter. A scarred piece of glass protected the darkened wood beneath. Leah finally cleared off everything and spritzed it with glass cleaner she found in the restroom under the lavatory. It smelled nice. An aroma she identified with the word *clean*.

Knocking softly on the attorney's door, she heard him tell her to come in.

"Mr. Ryan, I mean Breck." She smiled at that. "Where do I dump the trash?"

He swiveled around and rose to his feet. "Here, let me show you." He took the wastebasket from her hands and strode rapidly through a door hidden between filing cabinets in the back of the building. He led her out into a narrow alleyway. "These are our trash cans. It gets picked up weekly whether we fill them or not." He lifted a lid and dumped the contents of the wastebasket before clanging the lid down on top of it.

"Oh, hey, Breck!"

Leah turned to see an attractive young woman stepping out of another doorway leading to the alleyway.

"Hey yourself, Sara Beth. This is Leah, my new secretary. Be nice to her." Breck grinned widely.

The woman giggled. "Well, I sure will do that. Hi, Leah. Come down and see me later. I've got some great homemade cookies I'm willing to share."

Leah grinned and waved shyly. Still, Sara Beth looked friendly, and she could use a friend.

She spent the rest of the morning trying to get a handle on the filing system and answered the phone twice. She felt a little better about her ability to handle this job. *Not so bad, and I get paid every week.*

Breck stepped out of his office with a black Stetson

in hand. He nodded at Leah and set the hat on his head. "I'm going to meet my wife for lunch. Take your break whenever you want. Just lock up and put the sign in the door."

Leah jumped to her feet. "Lock? Sign?" She glanced around frantically.

Breck shook his head. "My bad. So much for your orientation." He pointed to the old-fashioned coat-tree behind the door where a clockface sign with movable arms was hanging.

Leah nodded.

"Here you go." Breck fished a set of keys out of his pocket and slid it onto her desk. "I forgot to give these to you. If I'm not back by five sharp, just turn out the lights, close up, and lock the doors." He grinned at her and sauntered out the door.

Swallowing hard, Leah picked up the keys. Two darkened brass skeleton keys and several smaller shiny ones. *I can do this*.

She glanced at the big clock positioned above the file cabinets. *Early yet. Just a little after eleven*. She had made a sandwich and stuck it in a ziplock bag in her purse. Maybe she would just eat at her desk. There was a big water cooler in the corner and a sleeve of small cups lying sideways across the top. Leah took out the plastic bag and placed it reverently in front of her on the desk, then rose to get a cup of cold water. *This will do nicely*. Returning to her desk, she took her seat and removed the peanut butter and grape jelly sandwich from the bag. She quietly ate her lunch, glad she was able to keep the ten dollars safe in her purse. No telling what she might need it for.

Chapter 5

TY SPENT THE MORNING REPAIRING SOME DOWNED FENCE. At first, he had thought the barbed wire might have rusted through or been broken by animals, but now, he could see that the wire had been cut through with some kind of sharp shears. He could see the Carters being responsible for this kind of destruction, but he didn't know why they would bother with terrorizing an elderly woman. Were they just being creepy, or would they actually try to harm her? Whatever it was, he thought he should look into their activities before he left.

He counted the cattle and could only account for eleven in Gran's "herd." There were a couple of goats in the pasture with the cattle. The goats seemed to be functioning in lieu of a lawnmower. And the remaining chickens were happily scratching in the dirt for bugs.

His head entertained all kinds of thoughts, wondering how people managed to eke out a living with so few resources. He thought of his family ranch with thousands of acres, some under tillage but mostly fenced pasture or range with many thousand heads of cattle.

Ty twisted the wire he had patched into the broken fence line, making sure it was strung tight enough to contain the small herd. He drew off his work gloves and reached in his pocket for a handkerchief to mop his sweating brow.

He thought about Leah, wondering how her first day

on her new job was going. He knew she had been nervous earlier that morning, but he had a good idea his dad's attorney was a pretty decent guy. He hoped Breck Ryan would treat her well.

He stuck the rag back in his pocket and slipped the thick leather glove on again. He gave the wire a final twist and moved on to the next gap in the line of fencing. The sun beat down on his shoulders, not uncomfortably, but he was already thinking about stripping off and taking a nice long and cool shower before dinnertime. He used his wire cutters to lop off another length of barbed wire from the reel he had bought at the hardware store and set about twisting it into a figure-eight link with the damaged section. He glanced at the edges of the original wire, realizing it looked as though this too had been cut and not broken or worn through. He frowned, making a mental note to carefully inspect the next area of damaged fence.

"Hey, Ty," Gracie called.

He turned to see her walking hand in hand with her great-grandmother.

"Hello, ladies," he replied. "What brings you out this way on such a warm day?"

Gracie giggled. "We brought you some tea. Gran says you might get hy-trated out here working in the sun."

Gran held up a thermos and offered it to him. "That's a fact. When my Albert was alive, I would always make sure he had plenty of liquid to keep him going."

Ty grinned. Twisting the cap off the thermos, he poured out a cup full of strong tea. He drank it down gratefully. *Sweet. Very sweet.*

"We put plenty of sugar in it for you." Gran smiled at him as he finished it off.

"Mighty good. Thank you, ladies, for taking such good care of me." He screwed the cap back on, thinking it would be less sweet once the ice melted.

"I think you're going to like what we're having for supper. We're making potato salad." Gran held up Gracie's hand. "And this little one is helping me."

"I can't wait," he said. "Um, how long has this fence been down? It looks like it might have been cut in some places."

Gran's face twisted into a grimace. "Must have been them Carter boys. Old Man Carter has been trying to buy this place for years, but Albert didn't want to sell out. Carter probably thinks I'll be easy pickin's." She pressed her lips tightly together and shaded her eyes with her hand. "Them's a mean bunch."

Ty felt his jaw tighten. The thought that some men were putting pressure on this frail little lady didn't sit right with him. "You ladies get on inside, and I'll be there in a little while. Thanks for hydrating me." He pasted on a grin and returned Gracie's wave as she turned back toward the house.

Carters, huh? Maybe Breck Ryan can give me a little help. Resolutely, he set about mending the fence.

Leah finished her sandwich and was in the act of disposing of the empty plastic bag when the door of the office opened. Startled, she let out a yelp.

Sara Beth, the woman she had been introduced to earlier, stepped inside, and she had a baby on her hip. "It's just me. I was going to make sure you came down to sample some of my cookies. I'm pretty sure you get a lunch break."

Leah took a sip of water to help the last of the peanut butter sandwich go down. "Yes, yes, I do...but I ate at my desk. Mr. Ryan told me to take a lunch break, but I brought my lunch today."

"Well, I hope you have room for some cookies. Come on with me. My shop is just two doors down." She gestured out the open doorway.

Leah pushed her chair back and groped for her bag. "Okay, I can come for a little while." She stood and grabbed the keys off the desk. Following Sara Beth, she placed the sign on a hook and gave herself a return time of thirty minutes. The old lock on the door looked as though it would match one of the skeleton keys, and her guess was correct. The key she selected turned the lock with a metallic thunk. She twisted the handle, and the door rattled, causing the glass to shake. The thought ran through her mind that the security left a lot to be desired.

Sara Beth waited for her a little farther down the sidewalk. "I'm so glad you and Breck hooked up."

Leah swallowed hard. "Hooked up?" she asked.

"I mean, I'm glad you came to work for him. He's a very nice man."

Leah nodded as she walked alongside the woman and baby. "He seems to be. Your baby sure is cute. Is it a girl?"

Sara Beth stopped and jiggled the baby. "Yes. This is Cami Lynn. I named her Camryn after our doctor. She delivered my daughter." She reached to open the door to her shop and stood back for Leah to enter.

"That's nice. Must be some doctor." Leah crossed the threshold and smiled. The shop was filled with all kinds of items. Handmade quilts were displayed on most of the wall space, and antique furniture was placed in groupings. There were tables with all kinds of bric-a-brac on top, and other items were displayed on shelves and in old-fashioned armoires. The space was large and airy, with an embossed tin ceiling peeling paint. "Wow," she mouthed.

Sara Beth's face split into a grin. "Does that mean you like my shop?"

"Oh yes. I love it." Leah spun around gleefully. "I could live here."

"That's just the way I feel," Sara Beth agreed. "No matter how I'm feeling, when I walk inside, I get real happy. Maybe it's all the pretty things."

"Must be," Leah agreed. "My daughter would get lost in here." She inhaled deeply. "What is that great smell?"

Sara Beth giggled girlishly. "Lots of things. I just mixed together everything that smells good."

"Mmm. It's lovely."

"Have a seat." Sara Beth indicated one of the stools placed in front of a glass display case. She went around to the other side and lifted a glass dome off a plate of cookies. "I made these for my boyfriend, Frank, but I really made a lot of them, so I thought I would bring them with me." She nudged the tray closer to Leah. "How about a soda? I have some in the fridge."

"Oh, I'll have whatever you're having." Leah selected a cookie and bit into it, inhaling the scent of spices. "Heavenly. Your boyfriend is a lucky man."

Sara Beth looked pleased. "He's a real sweetheart. I think I'm the lucky girl to have snared him." She let out a little laugh and headed to the back of the store.

Leah nibbled her cookie, tasting cinnamon and cloves...maybe a little ginger.

Sara Beth reappeared with two canned drinks and slid one across the scarred glass to Leah before taking a seat on the other side of the counter. "So, where do you come from?"

Leah sighed. "I was living in Oklahoma, but my grandparents live not too far out of Langston." She shrugged. "Well, my grandpa passed away, and I came to be with my grandma." She left out the part about running away from Caine and hiding out on the farm.

"That's real nice of you." Sara Beth selected a cookie and broke off a piece for the baby. She placed the little one in a playpen situated behind the counter with several pieces of cookie to entertain her.

"I don't know how nice it was. I think my gran needs a lot of help. I hope I'm able to do what she needs done."

Sara Beth gazed at her earnestly. "I have a feeling you're the kind of person who follows through on whatever she sets out to do."

Leah took a deep breath and released it. "From your lips to God's ears."

She stayed to chat for a while, enjoying the cookies and soda, but she kept an eye on the clock. When she had been there close to thirty minutes, she slid off the stool. "I'd better be getting back to work. Don't want to be goofing off on my very first day." She turned to leave, but Sara Beth called her back.

"Here, let me wrap some of these cookies for your daughter." She went to the rear again, returning with a sheet of aluminum foil to wrap a generous number of cookies. "I hope she enjoys them."

"Oh, that's a lot of cookies. Don't you want to save them for your boyfriend?"

"I have plenty more at home." Sara Beth grinned and folded the edges of the foil around the bundle.

Leah gratefully accepted the gift, glad she would have a treat to present to Gracie at the end of the day. She walked back to the law office, but Breck failed to reappear for the rest of the day.

She delved into the files and tried to figure out what kind of system her predecessor had used to store these important papers. She finally discovered most things were filed according to the kind of work Mr. Ryan had done for the client. The criminal defense cases were filed alphabetically, as were the civil cases. The estate work was a jumble, but at least it was somewhat together.

She felt she had made some headway when five o'clock rolled around, and she was reluctant to stop, but her daughter would be expecting her. Gracie and Gran would worry if she didn't show up in a reasonable amount of time. And there was Ty…

A smile crept across her face. She had studiously tried not to think about him today. Not to picture his clear blue eyes gazing at her. Nor thought about how strong he was when he picked her up like she weighed nothing. Or the tingle of anticipation she felt when she relived one of his toe-curling kisses. She heaved a sigh. *Oh yeah…those kisses.*

Leah closed the file cabinet she had been working on, and grabbing her purse and the bundle of cookies, she headed for the door. It was still bright daylight, but it looked as though some of the other storekeepers were closing too. She heard someone call her name and turned to see Sara Beth waving at her. A tall young man in a cowboy hat and boots carried the baby and

gave her a wave. *This must be the boyfriend.* He led
Sara Beth to his truck and opened the door for her. His
gentlemanly gesture reminded Leah of Ty. She watched
as the young man helped secure the baby in a car seat
and then climbed in on the driver's side. The picture of
the three people in the truck caused an ache of yearning
deep inside Leah.

She pocketed the office keys and groped in her bag
for the keys to her car. When she turned around, she saw
Ty sitting casually on the fender of his truck, gazing at
her with an amused expression. Her heart rate quickened
just to see him there. "What are you doing?" Her voice
came out all raspy. "Have you been waiting very long?"

"Not long. I just wanted to make sure you got home
okay."

She swallowed and stepped off the curb toward him.
"That's mighty sweet of you, Tyler Garrett, but I do
know the way home."

"Yeah, but you might run out of gas on the way. I
thought I would take you to the gas station."

Nodding, Leah headed to her car, but Ty fell into step
beside her. He took the keys out of her hand and opened
her door. When she stepped closer, he circled an arm
around her waist and leaned in for a kiss. The melting
from the inside out feeling washed through her. Some
distant part of her wondered how he did that with just a
kiss, but the rest of her was fully engaged in the process.

His dark-lashed eyes seemed to stare right into her
soul. *So blue. So intense.*

He broke the spell by gesturing for her to get inside,
and he closed the door. "Follow me," he instructed,
handing her the keys.

Numbly, she nodded her head, still wrapped up in his kiss. She turned the key in the ignition and followed behind when he pulled out. A convenience store was only a couple of blocks ahead, and he turned in, pulling up to the forward pump. Leah slowed and nosed in behind him.

"Sit tight, Beautiful," he called and swiped a card through the self-serve pump to begin pumping gas into her car.

She dug out the ten dollars, waving it at him, but he shook his head. After he filled her tank with gas, he filled his own with diesel, which took much longer.

He pocketed his receipts and returned to her open window. "Do you mean to tell me you didn't use that money for lunch?"

"I—I brought a sandwich today." She bit her lower lip. "And I made a friend who owns a store close to the office. She gave me cookies."

He huffed out a sigh. "Glad you got something to keep you going." He smiled. "Let's get out of here. Gracie and your grandma are cookin' up a storm."

———

Fern Davis realized she was happy...really happy. This was the kind of everyday happy she had felt when Albert was alive. Not the edgy, frightened, and frustrated tension she had been living with since her husband's passing.

The only difference was that her granddaughter had come home. And she had brought her own daughter with her...as well as a very nice young man.

Now, this beautiful Tuesday, her beloved granddaughter had gone to her very first day of work at her brand-new job. A job she would never have landed without the reference from Ty.

A broad grin spread across her face. *A very nice, responsible young man.* Ty had done his chores and gotten cleaned up to go into town. His express purpose was to make sure Leah had enough gas in her car to make it home from work.

Fern glanced out the front door at her granddaughter, laughing and playing with the two dogs. Gracie was coming out of her shell too. She had been such a scared little thing when they had first arrived. Now she was settling in. *If only she can be happy about school.*

"This will be your place someday, Gracie. You an' your mama will always have this land. It's your birthright." Fern turned away from the doorway, returning to the kitchen to check on her preparations for supper. Cooking for her family gave her great pleasure. *So nice to have my girls home.*

Fern set a dinner plate on top of a saucepan of mixed vegetables. She had no idea where the lid had gone or if there had ever been a lid, but the dinner plate would keep the vegetables from cooling off too quickly. When her family gathered around the table, she could just turn up the heat for a few minutes, and everything would be ready.

She gave the old Formica countertops a quick wipe down and then folded the dishcloth over a rack under the sink. Straightening up, she smiled as she surveyed her feast. Providing meals for those she loved was one of her greatest pleasures…well, cooking the food Tyler actually provided.

All at once, she heard a loud commotion coming from outside the house. She rushed to the door and stepped out onto the porch.

From behind the house, she heard yelling and the sound of horse hooves pounding the baked earth.

A man rounded the corner of the house, his loose shirt flapping behind him. A straw cowboy hat fell off and was immediately trampled by a large black horse in hot pursuit.

"Prince!" Gracie screamed, and the dogs took off behind the horse.

The man veered toward the road, and Prince reared on his hind legs to lash out with his front hooves. The man yelled again, threw his arms up to protect his head, and stumbled, falling on one knee. He then righted himself and ran full tilt to the caliche road leading to the highway.

Gracie ran to Fern, clasping her around the middle, she buried her face against her great-grandmother's shoulder.

A vehicle motor cranked up, revved hard, and drove away with a squeal. As the vehicle disappeared in the distance, only the sound of horse hooves and barking dogs could be heard.

Gracie lifted her head, gazing anxiously toward the road. In a matter of minutes, they heard hooves clip-clopping at a slower pace.

Lucky and Eddie raced up to the porch, tails wagging, apparently satisfied with their part in the pursuit.

Prince appeared, wearing his outrage like a shroud. He danced a bit, lifting his hooves high and bringing them down hard. Nostrils flaring, he bobbed his head, sending his magnificent mane flying. He approached the porch, slowing, then pounding one hoof on the bottom step. His reins dangled loose.

"Prince," Gracie said, her voice soft. She raised one hand and took a couple of steps toward the horse. "It's all right, boy."

"Be careful," Fern whispered.

Gracie reached out to stroke the horse's nose. He nickered, and then she stroked his neck. "Good boy. You're okay."

Cautiously, Fern approached and grabbed the dangling ends of the reins. "Easy, boy," she whispered. Wrapping the reins around a post, she made sure they were securely fastened.

Gracie, however, was still rapturously stroking Prince and talking to him in loving tones.

Fern let out a little snicker. "I swear, Gracie. I think that horse is sweet on you."

Leah followed behind Ty in his big red truck.

Her gas gauge was pointing all the way over to the right, showing how very full it was, thanks to his generosity. She had never experienced such caring or kindness from any living creature, except perhaps her grandparents, and they never had anything tangible to give. Every time she considered this unrequested and probably undeserved outpouring of compassion and benevolence, she experienced a tearful tingle and had to blink fast to keep from drowning in her own waterworks. *Nope! Time to stop bawling and get my life together… for Gracie and for Ty.* She swallowed hard. *And for me. I need to grow a pair of big ones.*

When Ty turned onto the caliche road leading to her grandmother's little ranch, she realized she had accomplished something that day that hadn't happened in some time. She had done a day's work for a day's pay. She hadn't been able to work for a while, and it felt good to be back in the habit of earning a living, supporting her daughter, and now she would be pitching in to help Gran with finances. One day down, three more to go. It was Tuesday, so she would get paid for only four days on Friday, but a paycheck was a paycheck.

Her insides were soaring, like a helium balloon, but she immediately put a clamp on her inflated emotions. She knew she was falling in love with Tyler Garrett, and he would break her heart in just a short time. He had his own destiny to fulfill. Even though he was acting like her personal hero, she had to gut up and save herself...*for Gracie...for Gran*. She pressed her lips together. *For me*.

When they arrived at the house, Gracie was sitting in the old wicker rocker on the porch, flanked by Eddie and Lucky. Ty's big black stallion was tied to the porch railing. All four perked up and assumed an air of expectation as Leah and Ty parked and climbed out of their vehicles.

"Mommy!" Gracie shouted, and Eddie wagged his tail in greeting.

Leah pulled the scrunchie out of her hair as she approached the porch and rotated her shoulders to relieve the remaining tension.

Ty frowned and made an all-inclusive gesture as he strode to the porch. "What's all this? Did you take Prince out for a ride, young lady?"

Gracie laughed. "No, it was the man."

Leah felt her insides go cold. "What man?"

Gran stepped out onto the porch, wiping her hands on a dish towel. "I think we was almost the victims of a horse rustler."

Ty gave an incredulous look, shaking his head slightly. "Care to elaborate?"

"Gracie an' me heard this ruckus, an' a man come tearin' around the side of the house, runnin' for his life."

Grinning, Gracie clapped her hands. "And then Prince came running after him. The man was screaming, and he dropped his hat right over there." She pointed to where a straw hat lay crumpled in the dirt. "Prince was really mad. He chased the man away."

Gran's eyebrows rose up almost to her hairline. "I thought fer sure they wuz both gone, but then we heard a car or truck start up and go roarin' off down the road. Your horse chased him for a while."

Ty's brows almost met in the middle. Turning, he stomped to where the crushed hat lay. He picked it up and inspected it before bringing it back to the porch. He stroked his hand over Prince's back and flank. "So how did he get tied up here?"

Gracie's dimples were working overtime. "Prince came right back here, and Gran tied him up. We've been watching him so nobody comes to steal him again."

Ty shoved his Stetson back on his head, regarding Gracie with interest. "So that's how it is. You ladies did a good job of taking care of him." He turned to Gran. "Did you recognize the man? Was it one of the Carters?"

Gran shrugged. "Coulda been. He was about the right size, but I didn't see his face. An' he was wavin' his arms in the air, tryin' ta keep Prince from kicking him in the head."

A muscle in Ty's cheek twitched, revealing his inner turmoil.

Leah could barely breathe. "The man...he didn't hurt either of you?"

Gran let out a bleat of humor. "Hon, that man was

a-runnin' for his life. I don't think he was a-thinkin'
about nothin' else but gettin' outta here."

Ty untied the reins and led the horse toward the barn.
"I'm going to see what happened in the back. I don't
know if the barn is going to be secure."

Leah handed her purse to Gracie and hurried after
him. "I'll go with you."

His grim expression softened. "Sure. I'm just concerned that some thug came here when we were both
gone. It just doesn't feel right for Gracie and your grandmother to be here by themselves."

She slipped her hand into his. "I know. I was feeling
so good about starting my new job."

"I'm sorry. I didn't even ask you how your first day
on the job went." Ty reached out and hauled her closer,
managing to massage the muscles holding her head on
her shoulders.

Heavenly! She exhaled. "It was great. Nothing much
happened except for me trying to make heads or tails out
of a very weird filing system. Mr. Ryan is very nice. He
went to have lunch with his wife and never came back."

Ty flashed a wide grin. "His wife is the local doctor.
Between them, they own a lot of land around here."

"Really?" Leah considered this news. "Is she any
good?" She would have to use her first paycheck to take
Gracie in for a checkup and make sure her wrist was
healing properly.

"Yep. She's great. Trained in Houston at the big
medical center. Nice lady." Ty quit ministering to her
shoulders and gestured to the barn, its doors standing
ajar. "Well, so much for security."

Once inside, Leah could see nothing out of the

ordinary. She trailed behind Ty as he led Prince to
the open stall. He made a guttural sound in the back
of his throat. "What a mess. It looks like Prince put
up a fight."

The expensive saddle Ty had carefully arranged over
the side wall of the stall had been knocked to the ground.
Prince's feed and water were strewn about.

"Damn! I'm going to have to clean up this mess. Why
don't you go on back to the house and spend some time
with Gracie? I'll be there in a while."

"Can't I help you in some way?"

He leaned down to plant a kiss on her lips. "Let me
change clothes, and then I can work off the boiling in
my gut." He looped Prince's reins around a post and
gestured for her to turn around.

She nodded and retraced her steps back to the house.

Gracie was waiting for her on the porch and opened
her arms for an embrace. "I missed you, Mommy." Both
dogs huddled nearby, wriggling in ecstatic wags.

Leah felt a clutch in her chest. "Aww. Did you have
a good time here with Gran? I mean, before the man
came?" She squatted down to her daughter's level, amid
dogs wagging and panting gleefully. "I heard you had
been helping her cook."

Gracie's face split into a wide grin. "I helped Gran
make potato salad and coleslaw," she said and then
frowned. "I was just scared." She assumed a stage whisper. "That...you know who...that he might get you."
She glanced up, over Leah's head, and then blinked and
looked away. "I'm sorry, Mommy."

Leah hadn't heard Ty approach. Her chest felt as
though a boulder was crushing it. She couldn't look at

Ty. She was afraid he was judging her. What kind of mother lets her child be fearful of a real-life boogeyman? "Don't worry. We're safe here." She reached for the screen door and ushered Gracie inside without ever raising her gaze to meet Ty's.

He stood on the porch like a statue, glowering after her.

She observed him from the corner of her eye as she greeted her grandmother and said nice things about the aromas coming from the kitchen.

Ty remained standing on the porch, staring in through the screen, his hands fisted on his hips. It was difficult to ignore the force of his gaze.

———

Ty shook his head. *Who is this guy she's running away from? Could she be married?* The thought hit him like a semi barreling full speed down the highway.

He remembered how she looked when he first laid eyes on her. Like she was running from the devil himself. Gracie too. He'd never seen a kid look so downright scared.

He was already simmering with anger over the attempt on his horse. Now the festering kernel of anger roiled his gut.

Tyler Garrett didn't get mad very often, but when he did, he was a force to be reckoned with. His dad had always sent him off to do some major chore where he had to work off his anger.

"You'd best put that bad temper of yours to work, Son," Big Jim would say and set him to riding fence or slopping the hogs. Anything to work off the brewing maelstrom.

Now, he felt as if anger were about to choke the life out of him. He swallowed hard and tried to catch his breath.

What if Leah was married? Surely, she couldn't kiss him with such passion if she was bound to someone else? But she sure had Gracie carrying on the subterfuge. He recalled how the child had glanced up at him and then away, as though there was a big secret and he wasn't allowed to know it.

Well, all right, Little Missy. If you think you can keep your secrets, you're wrong. He considered his options. Somebody would tell him. Surely, all three females couldn't hold on to a secret long if he was determined to learn the truth.

Ty huffed out an irritated growl and unbuttoned his western shirt. He stripped it off and draped it over the back of the rocking chair on the porch. His T-shirt would serve as a work shirt while he was cleaning up Prince's stall.

He was aware, with every step he took, that he was more upset with Leah for keeping secrets from him than he was over the attempted theft of his horse.

With shovel and rake, he cleaned out the stall and spread fresh hay. Then he removed the reins before refilling the water trough and feeding Prince the pricey sweet feed. "Good boy," he muttered, giving the horse's neck a few pats. He closed the stall and lifted his saddle back onto the railing.

"Okay, now the next problem." He secured the barn and headed for the house.

His cell phone sounded. He pulled it out of his pocket and checked the caller ID. Huffing out a sigh, he felt a momentary irritation, but it was probably because he was already irritated with Leah. "Hello, Beau. What's going on?"

"Hey, Ty," his younger brother greeted him. "I was just wondering what was going on with you."

Ty walked to the far end of the porch and took a seat on a dusty wicker rocking chair. "Not much. How are things on your end?"

A silence hung heavy between them.

"I'm okay," Beau said finally. "I was just hoping you might be on your way back home."

Ty let out a snort. "Why would you be hoping that?"

"We're your family, man. You just can't walk away like that." Another silence. "I miss you. Dad—"

Ty let out another scornful snort. "Please, don't tell me Dad misses me. I'd think he would be glad I'm gone. We sure don't seem to be seeing eye to eye lately." Ty arranged his boot on the rickety porch railing. *Another thing that needs to be fixed.*

"Of course he misses you," Beau said. "He's not going to come out and say it, but he's pretty upset. I figure he's worried about you."

Ty laughed. "Don't lose any sleep over me. If I need bail money, I'll call."

There was a chuckle on the other end of the line.

"I'm going to cut a demo in Dallas and then try out for a country music show. Maybe you can catch me on television, if I'm lucky enough to make the cut. If not, I'll figure out something. You know I have to try."

"I know," Beau said. "It's just—"

"Don't worry. I'll be fine. Tell Dad not to fret. What's the worst that can happen? I can become a major

country-western star and ride around the good old US of
A in a big tour bus." He laughed as Beau let out a guffaw.

"Yeah right."

"How is Colton?" The image of his older, very serious brother came to mind.

Beau let out a groan. "Don't ask. He's griping that
he has double the work to do since you left, and he's
getting a lot of grief from Dad too."

Ty couldn't imagine that his father's clone would
ever do anything to displease the man. "You're kidding
me, right? Colton is the golden boy of the family." He
felt a tightness in his chest when he said the word *family*.
He wasn't quite sure what that meant anymore.

It was Beau's turn to issue a derisive snort. "Nope.
Colton's getting your share. He says Dad doesn't expect
as much out of me. He's still giving me grief for being,
as he says, the beloved baby boy." There was a pause.
"We sure could use your help."

"Colton got you to call me, right?"

Another silence.

"Look, Beau, this is my chance to do the one thing I'm
really good at. I was born to be a singer, so I've got to try."

"You're pretty good at ranching," Beau put in wistfully.

Ty sucked in a deep breath and released it slowly.
"I've learned how to be a rancher, but I was born to
sing. Just tell Colton and Dad to step back and let me
try, okay?"

"Yeah. I'll pass that word along. And from me, Ty, I
wish you the best. I hope you make it to the top. For Mom."

Ty swallowed what felt like a big tangle of barbed
wire at the back of his throat. "Thanks, Little Brother."
He disconnected, his jaw tight with warring emotions.

He knew he had been given so much in his lifetime, and it was time to pay it back, but there was more than one way of giving. Maybe his natural talents would take him someplace. Maybe they would lead him home. Tucking the phone in his pocket, he leaned back, gripping the wicker arms of the chair.

He stared out at the pitiful yard with rusted farm equipment off to one side like the skeletal remains of dinosaurs he had seen when his fifth-grade class went to the museum in Lubbock. The sun was setting, casting these relics into silhouette. He sat motionless, until Gracie came out looking for him.

"Ty?" she called.

"Right here, Gracie."

She approached warily. "Gran says you should come inside to eat now. The table's all set."

He heaved himself out of the chair. "That's mighty nice of you to come give me that message." He reached out to tousle her hair, and she grabbed his hand, leading him inside the small house.

He ate, letting the women converse and only responding to direct questions.

Leah cast several sidelong glances his way but, for the most part, kept her head down and poked food into her mouth. When the meal was finished, she jumped up and started clearing the table.

Ty pushed his chair back and picked up his empty plate and utensils.

Leah was furiously scraping the plates and placing them in a sink filled with warm, sudsy water. When she turned abruptly, she ran smack into him.

"Whoa!" he murmured.

"Oh, sorry," she gasped and took the dishes from his hands. Turning back to the water, she sucked in a breath when Ty laid his hands on her shoulders.

He leaned forward, speaking softly against her ear. "We need to talk."

She bit her lower lip and nodded, looking so distraught his heart went out to her.

"I—I'll come to the bunkhouse when everyone has gone to bed," she whispered.

He gave her shoulders a squeeze and released her. Stepping back, he almost collided with Gracie, who had come to stand behind him.

Gripping her plate and utensils with both hands, she gazed up at him with large, solemn eyes.

Ty tried to force a smile as he relieved her of her offering. "Thanks," he said.

Tight-lipped, Gran stood beside the table, scraping leftovers into recycled plastic margarine tubs and snapping on lids. She looked to be as brittle as a dried mesquite bean and about as easy to break.

"Thank you for another great meal," he said and made for the door.

Once on the porch, the darkness embraced him, like arms closing around him. Filling his lungs with the night air, he blew it out, trying consciously to relieve the tension crowding his chest. Guitar in hand, he whistled for Lucky and stood for a moment gazing up at the stars. He would go to the bunkhouse, and he would sing his songs with Lucky howling harmony. No matter where or when, at least some things were constant.

Leah dried her hands on a threadbare dish towel and wiped down the counter. Maybe she could buy Gran a couple of nice new ones once she started getting regular paychecks.

She gave herself a mental reality check.

Nice idea, but I better think about getting Gracie some clothes to wear to her new school. She's going to need shoes and a winter coat of some kind. Maybe a heavy sweater will do for a little while.

Leah folded the towel over the edge of the chipped porcelain sink and surveyed the kitchen. *Can't get it any cleaner than this.*

Gran had headed to bed straightaway, and Gracie followed close behind her.

Turning off the overhead light, Leah went into the room she now shared with Gracie and found her daughter already in bed with Eddie curled up near her feet. The bedside light was still on. Gracie's eyes were closed but fluttered open when Leah leaned close.

"I'm sorry, Mommy. I didn't mean to tell Ty about him." Her brows were knit into a worried frown.

"Not a problem, sweetie. Not a problem." When Eddie raised his head, Leah scratched the curly fur on his neck. She brushed a kiss over her daughter's forehead. "You get some sleep, and I'll be in shortly." She snuggled the covers up around Gracie and turned off the light before tiptoeing out of the room.

Leah ran her fingers through her hair and located the flashlight Gran kept near the front door. Stepping quietly out onto the porch, she pulled the door closed behind her. She turned, gazing about anxiously. *No. Caine isn't lurking around in the darkness waiting to grab me.* She released a pent-up breath and straightened her shoulders. The night sounds enveloped her. Crickets chirped, and the frogs they called "peepers" chimed in for counterpoint. *Nice, familiar noises.* Her footsteps sounded unnaturally loud on the wooden porch as she crossed and stepped off onto the soft dirt. Flicking on the flashlight, she sighed heavily and started toward the bunkhouse, reconciled to facing Ty's wrath.

Of course he'll be angry. He deserves to be angry. In spite of the temperature, she shivered, wondering how Ty would display his wrath. She couldn't imagine his handsome face twisted in rage. *Gut up, girl. He deserves to know.*

A soft light glowed inside the bunkhouse. Leah lifted her hand to knock softly on the door, then repeated the process when she received no answer. She twisted the knob and stepped inside. "Ty?" she called hesitantly.

The only light came from a small reading lamp beside the bed. Gran had made this room really cozy. The usual sleeping quarters were in a separate room, with bunk beds against the walls, but Gran had arranged an old metal bedstead in the large room that had served as the dining hall and living room of sorts. Now, it looked like an efficiency apartment with the bed, a small stool serving as a nightstand, a rudimentary kitchen in one corner, a small table and chairs nearby, and one single upholstered chair, quite worn in places but still comfortable looking.

Hearing movement in the bathroom, Leah resigned herself to her fate. She sat down in the chair to wait.

Momentarily, the door opened, and Ty stepped out. His hair was wet, and he wore only a towel slung low around his hips. He stood, still as a statue, regarding her steadily. "I had given up on you."

She sucked in a breath. "No, I'm here." Her voice sounded small to her own ears.

He gave her a little smile. "I thought maybe you chickened out."

"Maybe I should have." She straightened her shoulders and lifted her chin.

"I'm glad you didn't." He crossed to the bed and took a faded pair of jeans out of his duffel. "I'll be right back." He ducked into the bathroom and returned almost immediately with the denims in place, stretched over his muscular lower half, while his muscular upper half remained bare.

Undoubtedly, he had no idea how his hunky maleness affected her. She didn't recall ever being sent into a state of drooling lust by the mere sight of a broad chest rippling with well-defined muscles and tight six-pack abs. A tracing of dark chest hair swirled over his pecs and descended in the middle of his ribs like an arrow pointing down into his denims.

She swallowed hard, trying not to think of where that arrow ended.

"Hey, don't look so scared." His voice cut into her thoughts. "I just need you to level with me. Tell me what's going on." He held out a hand.

Nodding, she stood and reached out to grasp it. Large and warm, he enfolded her, drawing her against him. Her cheek pressed against his chest, her palms flat on his stomach. "I owe you an explanation."

"Just tell me one thing." His voice rumbled deep in his chest. "Are you married?"

That question hit her like a slap in the face. She drew back, frowning. "No! Of course I'm not married."

He looked relieved. The corners of his mouth turned up in a smile. "Good to know." He lifted her off her feet and swung her around in a circle.

A rush of joy infused with passion surged through Leah's being. Wrapping both arms around his neck, a gurgle of laughter escaped her lips. "Where did you get that crazy idea?"

He set her on her feet but didn't release her. He gazed down into her eyes with such intensity she felt as though he was stripping her soul bare. "I was afraid this guy you're running away from might not be an actual ex." He planted a kiss on her nose. "I'm just glad to know you're divorced."

She thought her heart would stop beating right then and there. "Um, I'm not...divorced, that is."

Ty's dark brows knit into a perplexed frown.

Leah heaved a deep sigh, not wanting to reveal her ugly secret. Not wanting to spoil this one perfect moment. "I was never married to the man who impregnated me." She gnawed her lower lip, trying to read the series of emotions playing out on Ty's face.

"Whoa!" he said. "I'm not judging, Leah."

She pressed her lips together as she looked away, not willing to let him see her dismay. "It—it wasn't like that. He...he forced me."

Chapter 6

Ty's stomach clenched up, and he couldn't breathe. He turned Leah toward him, her face an exquisite portrait of misery. "I'm sorry. I didn't mean to bring up anything that would hurt you."

She shook her head vehemently. "Not your fault. It is what it is. I—" She covered her face with both hands. "I'm over it."

He frowned. "I don't think so. If you can still get upset, it's still hurting you."

She stood rigidly, her lips pressed together, not looking at him.

"Sit down, and I'll get you some water." He filled a jelly glass with cold water from the refrigerator and returned to find her sitting slumped on the side of the bed. He dropped down on one knee beside her and offered her the glass.

She moistened her lips, whispering, "Thank you." Taking a few sips of water, she set the glass on the makeshift table.

Ty reached around her to turn off the lamp. "Just relax, Leah. Whatever happened, it's behind you now. You have a beautiful little girl, and you've started over with a brand-new page. Whatever you write on it is up to you."

He climbed onto the bed and pulled her back to rest against his chest. He held her with one arm and leaned down to place a kiss against her hair. "Everything is going to be all right."

She snorted and then made a half-hearted stab at laughter. "There you go again, being Mr. Sunshine."

Ty exhaled, trying to banish all the dark thoughts in his head. "I'll be whatever you need me to be."

His words hung in the air like a neon sign. He thought about what he'd just said, then backed it up. "I'm here for you, Leah...and for Gracie." It suddenly became clear to him how much the two of them had come to mean to him.

She turned to face him and reached for him, and he leaned into her embrace.

It felt good to be needed. Mostly, it felt good to be needed by someone he was growing to need just as much. He kissed her, and then he kissed her again. He pulled her closer, and she settled with her head on his shoulder.

"Tell me," he urged in the darkness. "Tell me what drove you here to me."

She sighed, gnawed her lower lip. "I—I had to leave Oklahoma. I had to take Gracie and run."

His lips grazed her temple. "That much I could gather. I've never seen two people look so scared."

"We were... We still are. I hate that Gracie is afraid. No kid should have to feel that way."

"Just tell me. Who is after you?"

"Caine Daniels." Her voice dropped to a raspy whisper. "He—we went to school together, but he was older. He was always looking at me, and I was flattered. I was only fourteen, and he played all the sports, so everyone idolized him." A shiver swept her entire body, but Ty pulled her closer. "Of course, my parents would never have let me go out on an actual date, but they did let me go to school events with my friends. One Friday night, my girlfriend's parents dropped us off at a football game, and afterward, we were going to walk a couple of blocks to the Dairy Barn with some other kids. Caine came to talk to us. Another boy drove up in a car, and Caine told us to get in. He said they would drive us to meet our friends." She broke off, looking small and vulnerable in his arms. "I didn't want to go, but my friend was already in the front seat beside the driver. I got in, and of course, they didn't take us to the Dairy Barn."

The silence hung long and heavy between them.

"I tried to fight him off, but I was…" Her voice trailed off.

Ty realized his jaw was clenched like a vise. He was barely breathing. The sound of his heart, pulsing fast and furious, throbbed in his ears.

"They dumped us close to town and drove away. A sheriff's deputy happened to be cruising the area and brought us in. We were both battered and near hysteria, so he took us to the hospital and called the sheriff. He questioned us and arrested Caine and the other boy."

Stroking his fingertips over her cheek, he realized she'd been crying. Tears rolled silently down onto his shoulder. "Sorry that happened to you. I hope the sheriff did the right thing."

She nodded, her hair soft against his skin. "He did the right thing. The other boy went to a juvenile facility, but Caine was of age, so he was charged with rape as an adult." She swallowed hard, a little mew-like sound escaping her throat. "The community was torn apart. My girlfriend and I were treated like sluts and blamed for everything from Caine being sent to prison to the losing football season. The sheriff lost his job in the next election." She heaved a huge sigh. "And I found I was pregnant."

Ty remained motionless but felt like he'd been body slammed. He tried to process all the jumbled thoughts and feelings raging inside him.

Leah cleared her throat. "My parents had to move, and they thought I should give up the baby once she was born and go on with my life, but I couldn't. They—they kicked us out."

Her tears had stopped, but Ty felt physical pain over her parent's actions. As much strife as he had caused his parents, they had never considered throwing him out. "What did you do?" His voice came out all husky.

"They sent us to a home for unwed mothers run by some Catholic sisters. I learned a few skills. Office stuff, mostly. The nuns helped me get a job as a receptionist, and that was okay. I was able to afford a small efficiency apartment and pay for a babysitter." She took a deep breath and went on. "I've had several jobs since then. I was waitressing at a truck stop when Caine found me. He got out on parole and came looking for me." She shivered again; this time, the tremor almost shook the bed. "He was very angry. He blames me for everything that happened to him."

Blame the victim? Ty's heart pounded, his chest rupturing with fury. "What happened to him? He was responsible for where he wound up." He heaved a deep breath. "So you left Oklahoma and came here?"

She nodded. "Caine must have followed me home from work, because he showed up at our apartment. The minute he saw Gracie, he knew." She paused, drew in a deep breath, and plunged on. "There was a fight. He was choking me, and Gracie got in the middle of it. He shoved her away, and her wrist was broken. Thankfully, someone called the police, because they got there and arrested him. They threw him in jail, since he violated his parole, and he's awaiting charges for the assault."

The ensuing silence crushed in on them.

"Well, you're safe here," he whispered against her hair. "You're both safe."

She splayed her fingers out on his chest, and he covered her small hand with his own. "I hope it's over. I hope he stops looking for us."

He lifted her chin and kissed her. "You're here now, with me. I won't let anything bad happen to you, Leah."

Her arms encircled his neck, and she snuggled closer.

Ty embraced her with one arm and ran his other hand down the length of her body, from her hair, down her back, stopping to caress her rear before traveling down her thigh. He rolled her onto her back and kissed her again, caressing her with his mouth and hands. Her soft voluptuousness aroused him even more. Cupping her breast, he heard her soft intake of breath. He had the desire to crush her to him but resisted the urge.

"Leah, I want to make love to you."

She emitted a nervous giggle. "I can tell."

He pressed her hand against his arousal. She stiffened, started to draw back, but then he felt her relax against him, her fingers curling around the bulge in his jeans. He released her hand, stroked his palm up her arm to her shoulder. "It's just me. Nothing to be afraid of." He nuzzled her cheek, her neck, her shoulder. "And, Leah, honey, we can stop. If you want to stop now, don't worry. It's okay."

She drew in a breath and then exhaled softly against his neck. "N-no. Don't stop." Her fingers fumbled at the waistband of his Wranglers. "I—I want you too."

All the fireworks from the Fourth of July seemed to burst in his head.

She managed to open the top button of his jeans, and he did the rest, sliding out of his Wranglers and tossing them beside the bed.

All he wanted to do was please her, to soothe her wounds and heal her heart. He slid his hand under her shirt and released the clasp on her bra. Slipping her top off along with the bra, he felt her warm skin melt against his chest.

He could have been content to hold her this way all night long, except that she chose that moment to squirm against him, her movement setting fire to his passion. He kissed her lips and traced a line with his tongue down to her breast, circling her nipple and teasing it into a taut peak. She made a soft moan of pleasure, and he delivered the same treatment to its twin, gently suckling as she arched toward him.

He ran his fingertips down over her ribs to her waist, unbuttoning her pants and sliding the zipper down. Gently stroking her flat stomach, he eased the pants and panties over her hips, stripping them all the way off. Now, she lay naked with only the soft glow of moonlight to give definition to her body. "You are so beautiful," he breathed. "You take my breath away."

She smiled self-consciously, ducking her head. "I've never been beautiful, but I'm glad you think so."

He made a scornful sound. How could she not know her true beauty? *Unbelievable!* He would make it his job to convince her. "Baby, you're a work of art. I'm just a simple musician, not a poet, but I'm pretty sure I'll be writing songs about you."

She grinned. "Really? A song?"

"Yes, about your big brown eyes and the dimples in your cheeks." He kissed her again, then traced her lips with his finger. "And your mouth. I know there's going to be a song about your lips."

She made a little purr of amusement.

He kissed his way down her body, stopping at her navel to explore with his tongue. She giggled and writhed. This pleased him. He kneed her legs apart and trailed kisses lower.

She went rigid, not even appearing to breathe.

"It's okay," he whispered. "I will never intentionally hurt you." He caressed her mound with his fingers before he continued with his tongue. A sharp intake of breath was his reward, followed by a couple of gasps in rapid succession. The *oohs* went on throughout his performance, ending with a low and sustained moan.

Locating a condom, he tore open the package.

"What's that?" she asked, her voice tinged with fear.

"Protection. I didn't know if we would get around to using them, but I grabbed some at the store yesterday." He held it out to her. "Do you want to put it on me?"

Her hand shook when she reached for it. "How does it go?" Her voice was just above a whisper.

It struck him that she hadn't done this before. Perhaps her only prior experience had been an act of violence. Perhaps this was the first time she had been part of a loving act between a man and woman. "I'll take care of it," he said, unrolling it over his erection. Once he had it in place, he took her hand, allowing her to explore. "Are you ready? We don't have to do this, Leah."

"I'm ready." She leaned toward him, and he gathered her in his arms.

He leaned her back onto the bed and entered as gently as possible. *Slow and easy.* She wrapped her thighs around him as he began to rhythmically stroke into her. Little gasps punctuated his thrusts, and slowly, she began to rise up to meet him. Her passion thrilled him. As their bodies fused, he lost himself in the moment, forgetting everything but the beautiful woman in his arms, everything but the sweetness of their coupling.

When at last they lay spent, limbs and sheets still twisted together, he couldn't bear to release her. He rolled onto his back and carried her with him. Kissing her damp temple, he grinned, sweeping one hand down to squeeze her bottom. "I'm gonna write a song about the dimples on your butt too."

Fern lay awake. She knew that Leah was with Tyler. He was such a nice young man, and it was hard for a single mother to find time to be courted. She also knew that the likelihood of Leah meeting another young man with so many fine qualities, given the crop of locals available, was not that promising.

The problem was, the front door was unlocked. And her innocent great-granddaughter lay sleeping in the front bedroom. She didn't want to go into the living room in case Leah returned and caught her waiting up. It would not do to embarrass the girl.

Maybe she could just check one more time. She

slipped out from under the covers and sat on the edge of the bed, feeling around for her house shoes. "Just give them tonight to be together. One night is all I ask."

Resolutely, she made her way to the front door. The house was quiet. Eerily quiet.

Leah's dog was sleeping in the room with Gracie, and the other dog, Lucky, was in the bunkhouse with Ty... and Leah.

Fern realized she was holding her breath. A tingling sensation played around her spine, spiraling up to kiss the back of her neck.

Cautiously, she twisted the doorknob and peered out through the screen. The night air was cool and crisp. It smelled like hay and earth and something else she couldn't place.

A slight breeze caused a rustling of tree branches, the only sound her straining ears heard. She reached for her flashlight, but it was missing. Her stomach caught, but she quickly realized that Leah must have taken it. Relief washed over her. Yes, she wouldn't want Leah to be walking around in the dark.

Fern opened the door a bit wider and stepped out onto the porch. There was enough moonlight for her to see well, but there was no movement. Silently, she scanned the entire area, staring at the two vehicles to see if anyone was hiding there.

Another gust of air and the odor again. It was nearby.

Reluctantly, Fern reached inside to turn on the porch light. It was then she saw it.

A wreath of dried flowers lay near her feet. Dead roses. A funeral wreath with a note on it.

Rest in Piece.

The next morning, after breakfast, Ty walked Leah out to her car and gave her a kiss. She looked happy and not like the terrified woman he had first met. "See you later," he called softly.

She waved and drove away, turning toward Langston when she reached the end of the lane.

He felt buoyant, like his insides were filled with feathers. Making love to Leah had moved them to a different place in their relationship. He knew he couldn't walk away from her. He would make the trip to Dallas and cut the demo with Will, but he would be back. He knew he wanted more of her. Just what, he couldn't say, but at least they could admit to what they had between them, and they could take their time to explore. He watched her until she disappeared from view and then spun back around to gaze at the run-down ranch.

He emitted a snort of laughter as he surveyed the place. He'd declared he wanted no part of the ranching life, turning his back on the prosperous, sprawling Garrett spread, only to find himself here on this pitiful excuse for a homestead, trying to do everything he could to make things easier for the three females trying to exist here.

Gracie came out onto the porch. Wrapping her good arm around one of the uprights supporting the roof overhang, she raised the cast in a sort of salute. She looked sad.

"What's the matter, Gracie?" he called, advancing toward her.

She shook her head, pressing her lips together.

"Come on, baby girl. What's up?" He drew even with her and took a seat on the step.

Gracie sat down beside him. "Gran said school was going to start soon, and I got scared."

He regarded her bowed head, her lashes shielding her big brown eyes. "I'll bet you'll have a good time this year. You'll make some new friends and learn a lot of things. Knowledge is power."

She nodded bleakly. "I guess."

"I'll bet all the boys will fall in love with you." He tweaked her ponytail.

This elicited a tiny hint of a smile.

"What grade will you be in?" he asked.

She held up three fingers.

"Third is a great grade. What's your favorite subject?"

"I like to read…and do art. Those are my favorites."

He ruffled her hair. "Those are good. I liked recess best of all."

She turned to him, wide-eyed. "Recess isn't a subject."

"It's not? Well, it was my favorite." He grinned at her. "I better get busy. Lots to do today." He set to work, aware that Gracie watched him from the porch.

He managed to get the little tractor running and used it to drag some debris to a clearing. Maybe a good bonfire would help with the cleanup, but it had been dry. Apparently, no recent rain had fallen here. If he wanted to burn trash, he would have to make sure there was a wide cleared area around it. A little spark could be disastrous.

Gran was delighted to see the tractor in use and asked if he could till up the place near the back door where she had grown vegetables in the past.

Ty was happy to comply, thinking of the first time his dad had taken him riding on a tractor. He had thought that was the grandest of rides. Of course, Big Jim's tractor was much larger, and the driver's seat was closed in and air-conditioned, but still.

He made short work of plowing up the garden plot and drove the tractor under a shed to keep it out of the elements. His cell rang, and he answered it before the second ring.

"Ty? Where the hell are you, buddy? I had to switch things around, but I made time for you this week. You should come right now, and we can have more studio time to work up your songs. Ticktock. Time is a-wasting."

"What? I thought you were booked up this week." Ty sucked in a deep breath and blew it out forcefully. "Sorry, Will. I've been…delayed."

"Ticktock! You need to fish or cut bait. I blocked out studio time for you, but the rest of this month's calendar is filled. You're going to be too late to audition for *Texas Country Star*."

"I'll be there. Just hold my spot." He climbed down off the tractor and started walking toward the house.

"Sure, man. But if you're not ready to cut the demo tomorrow morning, I'll have to mark you off the schedule. Maybe some other time."

"No, wait!" Ty frowned. "I'm on my way. I'll be there this evening."

"Great. Come to my place tonight, and we'll catch up. You can get some rest, and tomorrow morning, we'll make the magic happen."

Ty rang off, feeling strangled. It was as though he had been dropped from a great height and landed badly. How could he go from being high on Leah to being jerked back down so suddenly? He swallowed hard, needing to remember his music. Needing to remember why he had left home in the first place. *She will just have to understand.* He glanced back at the house, where Gracie still sat on the porch watching him. *They all will.*

———

Leah was getting the hang of her routine. *Nothing to it.* If the phone rang, she answered it and took a detailed message for Breck if he was out, and he was usually out. She was making headway on the filing mess and beginning to understand a little of the crazy system her predecessor had fashioned. However, she found files jammed into other files with no rhyme or reason she could discern. Today, she had managed to create a simpler and more logical way of ordering the many records.

Earlier, Breck had given her instructions for preparing a new will for one of the area ranchers. Said rancher had acquired more assets and wanted to make sure those were properly distributed when he passed on to that big pasture in the sky. Breck showed her the previous document and what changes to make in the new one. There was a standard will format stored on the desktop, and she used this plus the earlier version and Breck's hand-scrawled directions. With this bit of sketchy instruction, he departed, stating he was driving over to the county seat for a bail hearing.

Leah worked on the project until her stomach began to growl. Then, she hung the clockface sign, locked the front door with the big skeleton key, and walked down to Sara Beth's store to eat her sandwich and enjoy the company of someone her own age.

The metal cowbell clanked against the glass in the door to Sara Beth's shop as she entered.

"Howdy!" Sara Beth called. She held her baby on her shoulder and was rhythmically delivering a series of pats and jiggles. "Just fed her, and now she's making me work for her burp."

Leah grinned, remembering when Gracie had been so very small. She slid onto one of the stools in front of the counter just as Sara Beth was rewarded with a juicy belch.

"There we go!" she crowed. Arranging the baby in her carrier, she placed it on top of the counter and took the seat beside Leah. "How is it going? Are you liking your new job?"

"I'm learning," Leah replied. "Trying to figure out the filing system, if there is one."

"Eat your food," Sara Beth invited. "Would you watch Cami Lynn for a minute while I get mine?"

"Sure." Leah placed her hand on the plastic carrier and rocked it gently.

Sara Beth disappeared into the back and returned momentarily with a small bag and two sodas. "I was hoping you might come down for a visit." She opened the bag and drew out several containers and two forks. "I made chicken salad, so I packed some for you." She pushed one of the small dishes toward Leah.

"Wow! Thanks a lot. I love homemade chicken salad."

"So does my boyfriend, Frank. I always make a lot, because he could eat a ton of it."

Leah removed the plastic lid and took a bite, rolling her eyes as she tasted the contents. "Divine!" she proclaimed. "Your boyfriend is one lucky guy."

Sara Beth grinned at her. "It's me. I'm the lucky one. Frank has just been so good to me." Her color rose as she tilted her head to one side. "I'm going to marry him. He wants to adopt Cami Lynn too, so we'll be a real family."

Leah stroked a finger over the baby's arm. "He's not her biological father?"

Sara Beth shook her head. Her smile faded as she pressed her lips together. Heaving a sigh, she straightened her shoulders. "Her daddy is dead. He…he wasn't the man I thought he was. I mean, he wasn't a bad man, but he made some bad choices." She gave the baby a kiss on her cheek. "And just look what he gave me. I could never be sorry about marrying him."

"She's beautiful," Leah said.

"I'm ready to get on with my life. I want my daughter to have a regular family. I mean, I could be a single parent, but why would I want to when the best man on the planet is in love with me?" She giggled, dimpling prettily. "I can't imagine for the life of me what Frank loves about me, but I'm glad he does."

Leah felt a tightness in her chest. "I'm happy for you. I'm sure there are lots of things he loves about you."

"What about you? I saw you with that big cowboy. He's one of the Garretts, I think. Is he your boyfriend?"

Leah wanted to believe Ty was her boyfriend, that last night had brought them closer together, that her revelations about her past hadn't tainted his opinion of her. "I—I think so. We've just recently met. He's way too good for me." She stopped talking abruptly lest she say too much.

Sara Beth adjusted the baby on her shoulder, gazing at Leah with a question in her eyes.

"I mean, he's from a really rich family, and I'm not. I don't have anything except a really sweet little girl."

Sara Beth huffed out a loud sigh. "There are so many more important things in this world than money."

Leah let out a little laugh. "Tell that to someone who

doesn't have any. The struggle to keep my child fed has been tough. I'm so glad to have this good job now."

She returned to the law office and continued her work, finishing preparation of the will and making some headway with the files. Whenever she allowed her mind to wander, she imagined returning to Ty's arms for another round of passionate lovemaking.

———

Ty boarded the horse with the local veterinarian. He met her at her small ranch and watched as she stabled him. Stroking Prince on the nose, he promised to return in a few days.

The drive back to Langston seemed too quick. He needed time to figure out what he was going to say to Leah. He knew their actions the previous evening had taken their relationship to a whole new plateau, and he didn't want to do anything to hurt her.

Parking in front of the lawyer's office, he sat for a moment, gripping the steering wheel with both hands. What to say? How would he tell her goodbye? He knew their new intimacy had made her even more vulnerable than she was before.

He hauled himself out of the truck and shut the door harder than necessary. When he stepped through the door, he found her totally absorbed in her work of sorting papers. "Hey, Leah."

She looked up, startled and then pleased. A wide grin spread across her face as well as a slight flush. "Oh, Ty. I wasn't expecting you."

He swept the Stetson off and raked his fingers through his hair. "I just needed to talk to you, if you have a moment."

She pushed back from her desk, arranging the papers in neat stacks. "Sure. What can I do for you? I just learned how to draw up a will."

Emitting a halfhearted laugh, he spread his arms as she drew closer. Walking straight into his embrace, she seemed to fit just right, the top of her head barely grazing his jawline. He closed his arms around her, feeling a stab of real pain when her arms wrapped around his waist. *Damn! Damn! Damn! This just feels too good.* He kissed her temple, and when she raised her chin, he grazed her lips. "I've got something to tell you."

She grinned up at him expectantly. "Tell me anything," she said breathlessly.

"Oh, baby. This is going to be difficult." He swallowed hard. "I'm leaving. I'm on my way to Dallas, but I wanted to tell you goodbye."

Her face looked frozen. He could see the pain in her eyes, and he thought she had stopped breathing. "I'll be back, but I don't know when."

She gulped, and her lips turned up in a fake smile. "Oh well. I knew you were leaving. It was nice to have you around. I...uh..." She sucked in a breath. "I hope you have a great trip."

"Look, Leah...I...we..." He faltered, gripping her against him. "I don't want you to think you've seen the last of me, because I'll be back."

She nodded furiously. "Yes, I'm sure you will. I'll see you the next time you're in town."

A knot of anger festered in his chest. "Leah, stop it. You're acting like I'm about to disappear forever, and that's not the case. I—I care about you."

Pressing her lips together, she nodded again, but this time, she was blinking fast and not looking at him. "I know. It will be all right. Go on. Don't worry about me. I'll be fine." She blinked again and fixed him with a dazzling smile.

He leaned down for a kiss and then another. Her arms came around his neck, and the kiss deepened until he couldn't tell where he ended and she began.

She drew back, tears spangling her lashes. "Be safe." Stepping away, she turned and grabbed a sheaf of papers. "I better get back to work."

"I'll see you," he said softly. Jamming the Stetson back on his head, he strode to the door and made his exit. Outside, he drew a deep breath, standing for a moment with his hands fisted on his hips. *She doesn't believe me. She thinks this is goodbye.*

He climbed into the truck and started it, the diesel engine rumbling to life. For a moment, he considered rushing back inside and asking her to come with him, but only for a moment. Leah was just getting her life together. The job was probably the best she would ever find. He wanted to comfort her, but he also needed to get on the road. *She's just going to have to understand. This is something I've got to do.* Heaving out a sigh, he put the truck in gear and headed out of town.

Chapter 7

Leah stood as if frozen, gripping a handful of papers to her breast. She couldn't breathe. She couldn't think. She couldn't feel.

The sound of the diesel motor starting up ripped into her soul like a chainsaw. If her feet could move, she might have ran outside and begged Ty to stay, but that was not an option. He had already given his time and energy to helping her and her family in so many ways she couldn't keep track of them. Now, she had to be strong enough to let him go.

She willed her taut muscles to relax. To feel the flow of energy return to her extremities. To be able to breathe and think and move.

Sucking in a lungful of air, she blew it out forcefully. She didn't cry. No, that wouldn't do at all. She owed it to him to be more of a woman at his departure than she was when he had arrived in her life.

A strangled sound escaped her throat. She swallowed hard. *No. None of that. I will be strong.*

She swallowed again and fumbled with the documents she held. Her fingers felt clumsy and wooden, but she managed to place her papers on the desk. It was time to lock up and go home, but she slumped into her chair, staring off into the corner. She slipped away from her surroundings and relived every moment of her life that Ty had touched.

She recalled when he had first bought a meal for her and Gracie. How fearful and wary she had been. And then when he'd caught up to her on the road in the broken-down car. He never hesitated to do the right thing. To offer a hand. To be a hero.

She swiped at a tear that rolled down her cheek. "No!" she said aloud, startled at the sound of her own voice rebounding back from all the hard surfaces. "No," she whispered.

It was after five o'clock, and she could escape, but she was reluctant to return home and see the faces of both Gran and Gracie. What would they think? Did they know already?

Biting her lip, she groped for the keys and her small bag. She pushed her chair up tight to the desk and turned out the lights. She locked up, noting the sign in the window and a reflection in the glass gazing back at her. *A distraught woman. A victim.*

No! her voice shouted in her head. *I am not a victim.*

Straightening her spine, she stomped off to her car and threw herself inside. *Not a victim. Never again a victim.* Slamming the door, she stuck the key in the ignition and started the car, revving the motor too hard. People on the sidewalk turned to stare at her. Embarrassed, she backed out and quickly pulled into the street, wanting to escape the questioning gazes. By the time she reached the edge of town, she could almost breathe. The tightness in her chest was abating, only to be replaced by a hollow ache.

How could I fall in love with him when I knew he was just passing through? How could I be so stupid? She hammered herself with recriminations all the way

back to the ranch. She turned onto the caliche road and
slowed to turn into Gran's drive.

Her throat closed up when she saw the empty space
where Ty had parked his big red truck…and the horse
trailer was missing too. Of course he would take his prize
horse. She felt as if she were choking as she coasted to
a stop. She turned off the vehicle and sat for a moment,
gathering her courage. *Okay, I can do this. I can't let
Gracie see me this way.* She stepped out of the car just as
the screen door burst open and Gracie came running out.

Gracie threw herself at Leah, grabbing her neck with
both arms, the cast encircling her like a vise. "Mommy!
Mommy! Guess what?"

The screen door banged again, and two dogs came
running after Gracie.

"What?" Leah managed weakly.

"Ty had to go to Dallas."

Leah squatted down in the dirt to embrace her daughter. Eddie came up to lick her arm and jump up against
Gracie. Lucky came on the other side and sat beside her.

"And he said he thought I was responsible enough to
take care of Lucky, so I'm babysitting him."

The weight of this announcement hit her like a fist.
Leah blinked rapidly. "He left his dog?"

Gracie nodded furiously.

Leah glanced from Gracie to Lucky and back again.
"Oh," she whispered. "He's coming back! He's really
coming back." She collapsed in a heap, falling on her
rear in the dust and taking Gracie with her. Both dogs
clustered around, poking her with their cold noses and
giving her reassuring licks. She lay on her back, staring
up at the early evening sky with a big grin on her face,

tears of joy rolling into her hair. Just like that, everything changed.

"Mommy, what's wrong?" Gracie stared at her with concern.

"Nothing, baby. Nothing at all."

~~~

It was dark when Ty pulled in at Will's place. It was an old, converted brick building with the recording studio downstairs and living quarters above. Ty rang the bell and listened as footsteps sounded on the stairs. The door was flung open, and Will grabbed him in a big man hug.

"Glad to see you, buddy. Thought you were going to chicken out." He pounded Ty on the back. Will was as tall as Ty and twice as wide. He seemed to have sprouted a beard since Ty had last seen him and bore an uncanny resemblance to a grizzly bear.

"Good to see you too, my friend."

Will looked around. "Where's your dog?"

"I left him with a friend," Ty said.

Will snorted out a laugh. "I didn't think you went anywhere without Lucky."

Ty felt a pang of guilt, hoping he had made the right decision in leaving his dog in Gracie's care.

"Come on in. Bring your stuff." Will motioned to him.

Ty grabbed his guitar and duffel and stepped inside. He followed his friend up the stairs and found himself in a large, open space. Some of the walls had been removed, and the decor was definitely an ode to the music industry. Posters of country and rap artists adorned the walls, and nearly every horizontal surface was littered with CDs, most identified by scrawls of black permanent marker.

Will rounded on him. "Man, I'm glad to see you. You're looking good. What's going on at the Garrett homestead?"

Ty took a deep breath and expelled it. "There's this girl…two of them to be exact…"

Will let out a howl. "Two of 'em and you didn't call me? I thought you were my friend."

Ty grinned and shook his head. "One of them is eight years old." A picture of Gracie gazing up at him so trustingly flashed into his head. He swallowed and went on. "And the other one…" He paused, pressing his mouth into a straight line.

Will looked at him expectantly. "And? The other one was what?"

Ty heaved a deep sigh. "Just absolutely the most beautiful woman I've ever laid eyes on." His voice trailed off as he visualized Leah's sweet face.

Will punched him on the shoulder. "Man, you got it bad."

"Yeah, I guess I do."

Will pointed to a faded green futon. "That's where you can crash, so drop your bag over there. The bathroom is under the stairs. Have you eaten?"

"I grabbed a burger on the way."

Will pulled a couple of longnecks out of his refrigerator. "Time to unwind, man." He flipped the caps off and slapped one into Ty's open palm. "Let's go upstairs."

Ty followed him to an enclosed stairway leading to the roof. "Wow! What a great view." He gazed out over the rooftops at the panorama of downtown Dallas and, in the other direction, the lights of Fort Worth. He wished Leah and Gracie could see it. That thought cut him like a knife. How had his life changed so completely in such a short period of time? What if he hadn't stopped to eat at Tiny's? What if her car hadn't broken down? The intricacies of fate amazed him, but somehow, he knew this was meant to be. It just felt too right. He lifted the longneck to his lips and let the cold liquid roll down his throat.

Will dragged two lawn chairs into place and plopped into one of them.

"Excuse me a minute," Ty said. "I have to make a call." He walked to the other side of the roof and leaned against the ledge. He selected a number and pushed the button.

One ring. Two rings. Three rings.

And a breathless Leah answered. "Hello?"

He couldn't suppress a grin. "Hello."

"Oh my. I wasn't expecting you to call... I mean, how nice."

He could visualize her face.

"I wanted to let you know I arrived. I'm here at my buddy Will's place." He paused, not sure why he'd felt compelled to call. "I guess I just wanted to hear your voice."

She let out a little mew of pleasure. "I'm so glad. I miss you already."

"Me too." He felt satisfied but couldn't seem to hang up. Just knowing she was on the other end kept him grinning like an idiot. "Gracie is a little nervous about going to a new school. I tried to give her a pep talk, but you might want to help her get ready."

"Thanks. I will. What are you doing now?"

"Standing on a rooftop, looking at the Dallas skyline, and thinking about you."

"Oh, Ty. That is so sweet."

When he finally disconnected, he returned to where Will was sitting, a big grin on his face.

Will looked at him over the top of his glasses before tilting the bottle back to drain the last of his beer. "Ty's got it bad," he pronounced.

Leah stood gripping the cell phone with both hands. *He misses me.* A gurgle of laughter bubbled up from her chest. She twirled around twice and then collapsed onto the bed.

The bed…

Ty had apparently pulled the quilt into place before his hasty departure, but it was still *the bed* where they had made love.

Leah had slipped out to the bunkhouse after putting Gracie to bed. Somehow, just being here had made her feel a little better. Then Ty's call had lifted her spirits even further. Tucking the phone in her pocket, she stretched out on the bed.

Sweeping her palms over the fabric of the quilt, she laughed again. The texture of the joined scraps of cloth and the stitching on top was pleasing. *A crazy quilt, like my life*.

Sighing, she dared to let herself imagine a future with Ty. She felt as if she were dancing on the edge of a deep and dark abyss, where, if she fell, she might never again find herself.

She embraced his pillow, curling around it. Burying her face to inhale his scent, she imagined his arms holding her. She fell asleep this way, waking at dawn, somewhat disoriented and definitely feeling guilty.

Leah ran to the house and managed to throw herself in the shower before anyone else woke up. When she emerged, Gracie and Gran were in the kitchen. The smell of bacon enticed her. She threw on her clothes and ran a brush through her still-damp hair.

"Something smells good," she called as she made her way down the hall.

Gran turned from the stove, a grin on her face. "I figured I needed to get in the habit of fixing a good breakfast for my girls."

"That's very nice, Gran." Leah took her place at the table beside Gracie.

"I want you to have something solid to help you get started on your workday, and our Gracie is about to start school. Both you girls need some feed in your gullet."

Leah saw the look of fear cross Gracie's face. "Absolutely right, and we appreciate your efforts. Right, Gracie?"

Silently, Gracie pursed her lips but nodded.

Leah's heart went out to her daughter. She knew how it felt to be afraid at school. She did not want Gracie to ever have to face the scorn of her classmates. "When I get my check, I'm going to take you shopping for some school clothes. I know you need new shoes." She reached out to give Gracie's shoulder a squeeze. "It will be fun."

A half smile quirked the corners of Gracie's lips. "Yeah."

Gran cleared her throat. "I got a little something with your name on it right here in my pocket." She patted her apron pocket. "I've started lockin' the front door since we been havin' all this trouble, so I'm a-givin' you your grandfather's key. Albert carried it with him every single day." She reached in her pocket and extracted a key with some metallic items dangling from the ring.

"Oh, thanks, Gran. I'm sure you're right I'll need this." She dangled the key in front of her. "Is this a dog tag?"

Gran pursed her lips as though gathering strength. "That there is Albert's dog tag from when he served in Vietnam. That was a bad time."

Leah folded her grandmother in her arms. "I'll take good care of this." She tucked the key in her own pocket and reached for a biscuit, happy to enjoy a hearty breakfast with her daughter and grandmother.

She got to the office early and was hard at work trying to arrange the files in some sort of order when Breck walked in.

He smiled and tossed his black Stetson on the old-fashioned bentwood coatrack beside the door. "Good morning, Leah. How are the files coming along?"

She rolled her eyes. "Crazy, but I'm getting there. I'm making a bible of sorts with everything cross-referenced so it will be easy to find after I get finished."

He let out a snort. "That will be amazing. You're doing a great job."

She felt a glow of pride blooming in her chest. She couldn't recall ever getting this kind of compliment from a former employer. "Thanks," she murmured.

"Can you find the will for James Garrett? My previous secretary prepared it, but I'll be damned if I can find it. I want to look it over before he gets here."

She searched through the estate files she had yet to sort and laid her hands on it in a relatively short time. "Um, yes. It's right here." She handed him a folder with the documents inside.

Breck leafed through the papers, nodding as he went. "Have you met Big Jim before? He's Tyler's dad."

A shaft of fear shot through her, swift as a lightning bolt. She shook her head. "N-no, I've never had the pleasure." She gripped the edge of the desk, her knuckles turning white.

"Let me know when he gets here." Breck walked into his office with the file in his hands, leaving Leah to dissolve into a puddle of nerves in his wake.

Resolutely, she went to the filing cabinet where she found the entirety of the Garrett estate paperwork and ran her fingertips over the neatly arranged files. There were deeds and transfers and wills galore. Sucking in a deep breath, she pulled out the entire set of documents and took them to a table near the water cooler. She spread them out, determined to learn what she could about the man she had lost her heart to.

As she sifted through the array of papers, a knot the size of a fist formed in her stomach. The enormity of the Garrett holdings was spread before her, spelled out in detail and alluded to in generalizations that were beyond her imaginings. She tried to comprehend the vast amount of wealth Tyler Garrett would fall heir to at some point in time, and that realization hit her like a truck. A big truck.

She read the will where Mrs. Elizabeth Jane Garrett had assigned all her worldly goods and property to be disbursed equally among her three sons, Colton, Tyler, and Beauregard. The will had been probated less than a year ago. Leah's throat felt dry.

How could people have so much when others had so very little? And how could it not matter to Ty how little she had?

She leapt up to fill a tiny cup of water from the cooler, which made big *glug-glug* sounds. Her hands shook as she raised the cup to her lips. She managed to gulp it down and then crush the paper in her fist.

What if he's only interested in me for the sex? I certainly was easy enough. He never said anything about being madly in love with me. I'm so stupid!

Tossing the remains of the cup in the trash can, she hurried to return all the papers having to do with the huge Garrett estate back where they belonged. She slipped them safely into properly labeled folders, now residing in neatly arranged, easy to find, very orderly drawers in the equally logically labeled file cabinets.

Leah leaned against the cool metal and exhaled. *I'm such a total fool. Ty couldn't possibly want anything more from me than just handy sex. I'm truly not good enough for him.*

The door opened, and she steeled herself, terrified to turn around. She felt the man's presence without even seeing him.

She pressed her lips together and squared her shoulders before pivoting to face a man who seemed to fill the doorway.

He frowned at her, as though he knew she had defiled

his son. He removed the Stetson from his thick crop of silver hair and hung it on the coatrack. "Breck in?" he asked shortly.

Leah forced a smile. "Why yes, sir, he is. You must be Mr. Garrett."

At his nod, she went to the closed door and tapped before entering. "Mr. Garrett is here," she announced.

"Oh good." Breck swung around and took his boots off the top of his desk. "Send him right in."

Leah turned to find James Garrett right behind her, bigger than a Caterpillar combine and looking just as solid. Fierce brows knotted above crystal-blue eyes that seemed to be examining her in detail.

Breck had come out of his seat and hemmed her in on the other side, extending a hand to the behemoth. "Big Jim! Good to see you. Have you met Leah?"

The two men pumped hands while keeping Leah sandwiched between them and the door.

Big Jim's fierce gaze returned to her. "No, I don't believe I have." He offered a paw.

Leah put her hand in his with as much trepidation as one might approach a bear trap. "Pleased to meet you, Mr. Garrett," she croaked.

"Folks around here just call me Big Jim."

"Leah is a friend of your son Tyler's," Breck offered.

"I'm so glad he brought her to me. She's been a blessing."

The blue eyes hardened to ice. "Is that so?" Big Jim's mouth tightened, and a muscle in his jaw twitched. "Well...we'll have to talk more, young lady."

Leah nodded, willing him to release her hand, willing him to stop dissecting her with his gaze, willing her own feet to move. "Yes, sir," she whispered and slipped from the room. The door closed behind her, muffling the sound of deep voices in conversation.

Even though her legs felt like melted rubber, she managed to get to her desk before collapsing. She sat with her hands clasped together, the sound of her own heartbeat throbbing in her ears.

Oh no. Oh no. What does he want? What will I say to him?

In due time, the door opened, and Breck motioned to her. "Leah, can you step in, please?" He motioned her over to stand beside Big Jim. "I need you to witness his signature." He showed her where to sign as witness after Big Jim had signed.

She formed the letters to her name slowly and deliberately, making certain her hand didn't shake as she did so. Straightening, she laid the pen down. "Is that all, sir?"

Breck smiled. "That's just fine, Leah. Thanks."

She made it back to her desk, and in a short time, Big Jim emerged from Breck's office, pulling the door closed behind him. He came to stand in front of her desk. "You and me need to talk, little lady. How about lunch?"

Leah was certain her heart stopped beating in her chest. She looked up at the towering personage. "I... uh...I brought my lunch, Mr. Garrett."

A hint of a smile flickered across his lips, and his eyes crinkled. "I think it will be all right to leave it for another day. Come on. I won't bite you." He crossed to retrieve his hat from the coatrack beside the door.

She sucked in a breath and pushed back from the desk. "I'll just tell Breck that I'm leaving..." she began.

"He knows." Big Jim jammed the Stetson on his head and gestured to the front door.

Leah obeyed meekly.

Once outside, she was faced with another large diesel truck, this one silver, with an image on the side and the name Garrett emblazoned in black letters.

He opened the door for her and gave her a boost up.

As she sat on the high perch, she fumbled with the seat belt while she watched Big Jim round the truck and climb in on the driver's side.

"Any preference?"

She shook her head, and he drove to the Mexican restaurant. He parked and got out, reversing the process wherein he rounded the truck, opened her door, and assisted her descent. At least she knew where Ty got his manners.

Once inside, he asked the hostess for a corner booth. He tossed his Stetson on the seat and slid onto the smooth plastic beside it. When the waitress offered menus, he said, "We'll both have the grande platter and sweet tea. That okay with you, little lady?"

She nodded. "Yes, fine."

As soon as the waitress was out of earshot, he leaned across the table and spread his hands. "So, how much do you care about my boy?"

Leah felt her color rising. "A lot," she said, barely above a whisper.

He searched her face, as though he might find some truth there.

The waitress returned bearing two tall glasses of iced tea and set them on napkins, then went to take another order.

Big Jim watched her depart, his jaw tight, and then turned his attention back to Leah. "I don't know how much you know about the dustup between me and my son, but I gather you've seen him since I have."

She clasped her hands together, interweaving her fingers for courage. "Yes, sir."

"How is he?"

The look of concern on his face caused Leah to relax her shoulders, feeling some of the tension drain away. "He's great."

Big Jim's eyes narrowed. "Where has he been since he left the ranch?"

"Um, he's been staying with us at my grandmother's ranch. Fern Davis's place."

The gaze became a trifle less fierce. "Davis? I know that place." He seemed to be considering something. "Where is he now?"

"Right now, he's in Dallas cutting a demo. I'm not at all sure what that means, but he seems to be really excited about it."

Big Jim brushed his palms over his face and back through his silver hair. "Lord! I've made so many mistakes with that boy."

"Really? I couldn't tell," she said, suddenly courageous. "He seems to have turned out to be a very fine man."

Big Jim expelled a lungful of air. "That's good to hear." Shaking his head, he gazed into her eyes as though searching for some answer. "I know he's a grown man, but he's just so…so…"

Leah grinned in spite of herself. "Yes, he is."

Big Jim pulled his glass of tea closer, a slow smile spreading over his features. "I think you and me are gonna get along just fine, little lady."

The waitress brought them each a huge platter of Mexican food, with a stack of flour and corn tortillas on the side. Leah hadn't thought she could eat so much, but it was delicious, and Big Jim seemed inclined to linger and converse about her favorite cowboy.

By the time they had eaten, she'd learned much more about Ty's childhood and about his athletic prowess and high school honors. She learned he had graduated with a degree in agriculture from Texas Tech University in Lubbock and returned to the ranch, where his father had hoped he would forget about music and get serious about "digging in," as he called it.

"I just don't know," Big Jim said. "I wish he could appreciate everything he's been given."

Leah swallowed, not wanting to intrude but feeling the desire to defend Ty in his absence. "I'm sure he appreciates everything," she said. "He's just got a lot on his mind now, what with the audition and all."

"Audition? He's auditioning?" The fierce blue gaze skewered her again.

"I—I believe so," she stammered. "I mean, he's got such a wonderful voice. Don't you want him to find out for himself if he's got what it takes to make it to the big time?"

Big Jim's shoulders slumped. "You sound just like his mother." He heaved a sigh. "My dear, departed wife thought Tyler sang like the angels. I blame her for filling his head with all this nonsense." He waved his hand as though to stave off her objections. "I know he's got a great voice, but there are more serious things to attend to. Our land is his real future."

She took a gulp of her sweet tea, carefully setting the sweating glass down in the exact same ring it had imprinted on the soggy napkin. "I'm sorry you don't believe in him."

Big Jim gave her a measuring gaze. "And you do?"

"Why wouldn't I? He's got the talent. Somebody's going to make it, and why not Ty?"

The dark brows drew together, causing her stomach to catch. "That's for people who don't have as much going for them as my sons do. I worked my whole life to make sure the boys would have something…and he wants to throw it all away." He blew out a stream of air. "Sorry, I didn't mean to raise my voice. It's just such a waste."

Leah met his gaze, trying to gather her courage. "You make it sound like there's a time limit on whatever you think Ty's throwing away."

He drew back, scowling. "You don't understand. We've been through this before. This time, I told him if he left, it was over. I was writing him out of the will."

The reality of this statement slapped her in the face.

His eyes narrowed. "So, you see…it does make a difference." He leaned back in the seat and folded his arms across his broad chest.

The waitress came to clear their plates and slid the check on the table close to Big Jim's elbow.

Without glancing at it, he reached into his breast pocket and took out a plastic card, slapping it down on top of the check.

Leah smiled when she realized Ty kept his plastic in the same pocket.

"You think it's funny? I suppose now you're not interested in him since he's been cut off."

Leah's eyes opened wide. "No, actually, I like him even more."

They stared at each other for a moment, neither flinching.

"Mr. Garrett," she said finally. "I have a little girl." She watched this information sink in on him. "And I love her with every molecule of my being. I will never intentionally do anything to hurt her in any way, no matter what choices she may make." She picked up the tea and drained it. The only sound was the ice settling back into the glass as she set it down.

—⁓—

Ty spent the day with Will down in the studio. The acoustics were great, and he marveled at Will's ability to balance sound and enhance his voice.

He took off the headphones and grinned at Will, sitting in the recording booth. "Don't make me sound too good," he said. "I don't want to fool them into giving me a chance and then fall flat on my face."

Will made a scoffing noise. "Trust me. Everyone will be doing this much and more. You've got a great sound. I'm just giving you a bit of glamour." He stepped out of the recording booth, grinning as he pulled his collar up and gave an Elvis-style lip curl.

Ty howled with laughter. "I suppose you want me to wear a little eye shadow too."

"Not hardly," Will said. "You need to remember, if you make it onto the show, you'll have to depend on the voters to keep you there. A lot of the voters will be chicks. You're a reasonably good-looking guy, but you could use some sexing up."

Ty drew back, frowning. "What? That sounds disgusting. You're kidding me, right?"

Will shrugged. "Yeah, I'm kind of messing with you, but kinda not." He took the headphones and hung them on a rack behind Ty. "If you want to win this competition, you're going to have to work on your image." He made a circle around Ty, looking him over critically. "The hair's good, but don't get it cut before your first audition. Women like that disheveled look. You look clean as a choirboy right now, but you need a little sex appeal to sell the package."

Ty stood with his hands fisted at his waist. He shook his head. "I don't know about this."

"Just listen to me." Will tugged on the back of Ty's shirt, adjusting the fullness in the back so the shirt tapered down close to his sides in the front. "Let's send a few shirts to be fitted to show off your manly physique, and while we're at it, you need to open up a couple of buttons. It's okay to show a little chest hair."

Ty laughed. "Come on, man. That's not me."

Will stepped back, crossed his arms over his chest, and raised one eyebrow. "How much do you want this?"

Ty regarded him, noting the serious expression. "I want it a lot."

"Then you have to be willing to do whatever it takes to get there, and that means boosting your sex appeal. Whatever you do, don't mention your girlfriend to anyone. All the women out in TV land want you single…unattached…available. Understand?"

Ty huffed out a breath of air. "Yeah, I guess so."

Chapter 8

AFTER BIG JIM DROPPED LEAH OFF, SHE SPENT THE rest of the day working on the files, but her mind was whirling with all she had learned over lunch. She saw a lot of Big Jim in Ty, but Ty was much sweeter. *Must have gotten that from his mother's side.*

In her heart, she was certain she didn't care about Ty's inheritance, but she thought it was just plain mean of his father to disinherit him because he was trying to go after his dream. *Well, Ty can just stay with me on the ranch...with Gracie and Gran. We can be his family.*

She drove home that evening thinking over all that had happened that day. She felt both good and bad about meeting Big Jim Garrett. She wasn't sure why he had invited her to lunch. He had obviously been surprised when Breck introduced her as a friend of Ty's, but he seemed to have some deeper purpose. That was what she wasn't certain about. She wasn't sure Ty would want her talking to his father, but Big Jim hadn't been willing to take no for an answer.

She hoped Ty would understand and not feel betrayed. As she turned onto the caliche road leading to Gran's place, she considered her position.

Ty's father had assumed that she meant something to Ty...that she was his girlfriend. Good thing he didn't ask how long they had known each other.

And she recalled the look of surprise that crossed his

face when she told him she had a daughter. Maybe Ty wouldn't have wanted her to disclose that information. Maybe he would want to make that announcement himself…or maybe not. Maybe he wasn't serious enough about her to take her home to meet dear old Daddy.

She pulled up to the house and turned off the ignition. She saw Gracie standing inside the screen, watching for her. A flood of warmth filled her chest. *Yes! This is what it's all about. This is what makes it all worthwhile.*

She got out of the car and went to meet her daughter, who had been followed by the dog parade. It seemed that Ty's dog, Lucky, was as fond of Gracie as Eddie was. At least they were sharing her affections.

That night, after dinner, she sat with her arm around Gracie, watching a situation comedy on Gran's old television set. There was still a tall antenna affixed to the side of the house, so they had access to three major stations and a local one out of Lubbock, where they read the farm and ranch reports all day.

"Mommy," Gracie whispered. "Do you ever think we'll be like them?" She gestured with her cast toward the television where actors portrayed humorous family interactions.

"What do you mean, baby?" Leah asked.

"You know…a family? With a dad?"

Leah felt her throat tighten. "I don't know. Is that what you want?"

Gracie nodded. "Yeah. I want a dad."

Leah wasn't sure how to answer. "You know not every family is happy together. Sometimes, people don't get along." She heaved a sigh. "Sometimes, being a family isn't like it appears on TV."

"I know, but it can be good, can't it?"

"Yes, it can. Sometimes, everyone is happy."

"That's what I want. I want you to be happy too. I want Ty to be my dad."

Leah was stunned. "Oh, honey. I don't have any idea how that could happen. I mean, Ty is a very nice man, but I have no idea what he has in mind."

Gracie turned to gaze up at her mom, wide brown eyes demanding answers. "Well, can you ask him? Ask him if he would like to marry us."

Leah sat up straight. "No! Absolutely not, and I forbid you to even suggest such a thing to him. That is not open for discussion."

"But you like him, don't you?" Gracie's innocent question opened a floodgate of emotion in Leah's brain.

Yes, I think I'm in love with him. No, I don't know if I am. Maybe it's just that he's been so kind to us. Maybe I'm only grateful. An image of Ty's face gazing at her with his piercing blue eyes stirred her libido. *Maybe it's just sex.*

"Yes, I like him, but that's all there is to it right now. Let's not push it, and see how things go. We have plenty of time for relationships to develop naturally. Ty may be gone a long time. He's very talented, and we don't want to do anything to keep him from making his dreams come true."

Gracie seemed to consider this. "Mommy, do you have dreams?"

It was Leah's turn to consider. "I think my dreams are much simpler. I want to be able to provide a good life for my daughter. That will make me happy." She dodged the cast as Gracie threw her arms around her neck.

Later, after Gracie was asleep, Leah packed her lunch for the next day. She wasn't planning on eating the stale remains of the sandwich she hadn't consumed earlier today.

Her cell beeped that she had a text, and she hurried to check it.

Ty…

A huge sigh escaped her throat and brought with it a wide grin.

We worked late. You're probably asleep, but I just wanted you to know I'm thinking of you.

"Oh…oh…" Suddenly, her fatigue was gone, and her heart was aflutter. She thought about calling him back, but in her lonely state, she knew it wasn't a good idea. She had given his father grief for not supporting Ty. She couldn't very well say or do anything to undermine his efforts.

She concentrated on taking deep breaths, satisfied that he was thinking of her. Satisfied that she would compose an appropriate response tomorrow. As for now, she headed for bed with a smile on her face.

The next day was a Friday. Leah drove to her job with some sense of anticipation. Knowing she would be off work for two whole days, she wasn't sure what plans to make.

When Leah unlocked the door and entered the office, there was a sealed envelope on her desk with her name scrawled in Breck's handwriting. Her stomach tightened, and she couldn't seem to catch her breath. Her first thought was that he was firing her. She tried to push that idea aside as she reached for the envelope. Inside, she found a check, made out to her and paying her through that day. It was good to know her new boss would pay her on time, even though he seemed to be absent more than he was in his office.

At noon, she took a full hour for her lunch. First, she went to the bank to cash her check and, feeling rich, stuffed the envelope of cash inside her small purse. She gathered her lunch bag and walked to Sara Beth's store but spied her boyfriend's truck parked outside.

She halted and peeked inside, seeing Sara Beth in animated conversation with a tall man who was holding the baby. Her friend looked so very happy. This was the kind of family Gracie wanted. A family with a man included.

Leah turned quickly and walked back the way she had come. She was too wired to go back inside the office just yet. Continuing her walk in the opposite direction from Sara Beth's store, she passed a pharmacy and a liquor store and then a hardware store. She rounded the corner and in the next block saw a church and, just beyond it, a small park with a children's play area. Picnic tables and a couple of benches nestled under trees. She headed to one of the benches and seated herself.

Heaving a sigh, she inhaled the scent of something floral, heard the drone of bees. A beautiful late-summer day, and she was free to enjoy it.

She unwrapped her sandwich and ate it, drinking the tepid sweet tea she had brought to wash it down. Now was the time to compose a text to Ty. To tell him how crazy she was about him. How much she wanted to be a part of a family with him... *No, that would never do.*

I'm thinking of you too.

She stared at the simple message a long time before hitting send.

"Well, looky here." A gravelly voice interrupted her reverie.

Leah jerked her head up to see an old, faded blue truck idling nearby. The windows were rolled down, and two men stared at her from inside. They were older than her, and they looked rough.

"Come here, you pretty little thing." The one in the passenger seat leaned out, reaching toward her. He made kissing noises and called out to her. "Come show us what you got."

Fear coiled around her like a giant snake, constricting her airway and her ability to move. She stared back at the two, then glanced around. There was no one within sight except the two in the truck. She realized this was the truck that had pulled up behind her when her car had stalled…before Ty stopped to offer assistance.

The driver leaned out the open window. "Come on, pretty baby. We can show you a real good time."

Leah stood and began walking rapidly back the way she had come.

The driver threw the truck in reverse and backed up to the corner to block her passage. "You don't wanna be that way, do you? We just wanna get to know you."

The other one let out a loud guffaw. "Yeah. Real well."

Leah's heart pounded a rapid tattoo in her chest. *No, not again.* She would fight back. She would…

The one on the passenger side opened his door and stepped out.

Leah ran around the back of the truck and onto the sidewalk, sprinting for the main street. She heard the sound of footsteps pounding behind her, then the screech of tires and the rumble of a big diesel motor.

Suddenly, Breck was out of his truck and standing between her and her pursuer. "Ray Carter, you better stop right there." Breck had his fists cocked and a look on his face that said he meant business.

Leah collapsed against the brick wall of the building, gasping for breath.

The aforementioned Ray Carter stepped back. He glanced at Leah and then back at Breck. "Aw, we was just havin' a little fun, Mr. Ryan. We didn't mean nothin' by it." He continued to back up a few steps and then made a break for the truck that idled a short distance away. When he slammed the door, the driver took off with a skid of gravel.

Breck stepped back, relaxed his fists, and turned to look at Leah. "Are you all right?"

She nodded, unable to form a complete sentence.

"You need to stay away from the Carter boys. They're meaner than rattlesnakes. Get in, and I'll drive you back to the office."

Shakily, Leah climbed into Breck's truck and rode the short distance to the office. "Thank you so much for stepping in. I don't know what would have happened if you hadn't driven by."

Breck looked grim. "I have a good idea what would have happened, and it wouldn't have been pretty. Let's go inside, and I'm going to call the sheriff. I want this on the record."

Once inside, Breck stomped into his office and made the call. In a short time, the sheriff himself walked through the door. He looked Leah over and then, without a word, went to Breck's office. The two men conversed in low tones before Breck called her in.

"Leah, sit down, and tell the sheriff what happened."

She took a seat and folded her hands in her lap, recounting the incident with the Carters.

The sheriff made a few cryptic notes in a small book and then stood. "I'll have a talk with those boys and their pa." He went to the door and paused, directing a stern glare at Leah. "And you, young lady…you be careful. Don't go off somewhere by yourself."

A shiver wracked Leah's body as the sheriff left the building. She drew a shaky breath, and when she looked at Breck, he was frowning.

"I don't like those Carters. I've represented them in a couple of scrapes when they were younger, but they're getting out of control. You have to keep your distance."

She nodded. "My grandmother said the Carters had been trying to get her to sell her place after Grandpa died. She thinks they cut some fence, but…but my boyfriend repaired the damage."

"You're speaking of Tyler Garrett?" Breck appraised her from behind his desk.

Leah nodded.

"He's a good man from a good family. I hope things work out for you."

She nodded and scurried back to her desk.

The rest of the afternoon passed uneventfully, with Breck staying in his office until around four, when he announced that he was closing up early and for her to go home.

He saw her out to her car and watched as she drove away.

Glancing in her rearview mirror, Leah saw him standing by his truck with his hands fisted on his hips. He
looked grim. Something about his scrutiny let her know
she had a lot to fear.

—∿∿—

Ty had spent the entire day in the recording studio with
Will.

Late in the afternoon, Will admitted two men and
took them into the sound booth.

Ty could see them in conversation, but apparently,
they had some private business with Will, although
occasionally he waved a hand toward Ty, and they all
turned to look at him.

Ty finally decided to take a break and maybe give
Leah a call when Will spoke to him through the mic.
"Hey, Ty, let's go over that last one again."

Ty knew he must have looked puzzled, but he nodded
and put the headphones back on. He listened to the
recorded soundtrack and sang the lyrics, just as he had
done earlier, but this time, the two men were looking at
him speculatively. He had no idea why they were there
or if there was any significance to their presence, but he
sang anyway.

One of the men who had joined Will in the booth folded
his arms across his chest and stared at Ty through the
glass, barely breathing, it seemed. The other man jammed
an unlit cigar between his teeth. He also stared but rotated
the cigar with some movement of jaw and tongue.

Ty made every effort to ignore them, because Will
was grinning expansively. His face reminded Ty of the
way he'd felt when he was a kid showing his prize bull

at the livestock show in Lubbock. Whatever was going on, Will had a shit-eating grin plastered on his face.

When Ty finished the song, Will exchanged a few words with the men, and they all emerged from the booth.

Will waved him over and introduced him. The men nodded, shook hands, and departed.

"What was all that about?" Ty asked.

"Just a step in the right direction, my friend. Don't you worry your pretty head about it. Old Will is going to make sure you get to know the right people."

Ty frowned. "Who were those guys? They hardly spoke to me."

Will gave him a thump on the shoulder. "Just two guys who can give your career a big boost, if they've a mind to. Come on upstairs. Let's get cleaned up for a little clubbing tonight. It's Friday, and the babes are hot."

Ty drew back. "What? I'm really not interested in clubbing. Besides, I have a girlfriend."

Will snorted. "Of course you do, and you want to make her proud of you. Tonight, it's all about being seen in the right places. Tonight, you have a date with destiny."

Reluctantly, Ty followed Will up the stairs.

⁓

When Leah was driving home, she kept looking in her rearview mirror, on alert for the faded blue pickup. But there were so many trucks on the road in this part of Texas. Her nerves were shredded by the time she turned onto the lane leading to Gran's house. Drawing a deep breath and letting it out all in a huff, she wished for the millionth time that Ty were home.

A voice in her head reminded her this was not Ty's

home. Just a poor little farm he had chosen to visit. When she pulled to a stop in front of Gran's little house, she got out and leaned against the car. Looking around, she noted the many improvements Ty was responsible for in the short time he'd stayed with them. Even the front of the house looked more presentable since he had hauled off the debris.

She felt a pang when she realized Gracie wasn't waiting for her at her usual post by the door. Walking rapidly to the house, she opened the screen door and stepped inside. She didn't see Gracie or Gran. She didn't smell anything cooking for dinner. Her throat tightened. *Where are they?*

Running outside, she glanced around, her heart pounding against her ribs. "Gracie!" Fear embellished her voice. "Gracie, are you here?"

Leah turned when she heard footsteps running from behind the house.

Gracie rounded the corner, two dogs loping beside her. She ran straight at Leah, a wide grin in place. "Oh, Mommy, guess what?"

Relief flooded Leah's chest as she gathered her daughter in her arms.

"I'm helping Gran make a garden. We planted some seeds already." She grabbed Leah's hand and began to pull her toward the rear of the property.

When Gran came into view, she had a big straw hat on her head and what looked like a broom handle in her hand. She was intent upon poking regularly spaced holes in the soft dirt Ty had tilled. "Hey!" she called. "I think we can harvest some vegetables for fall canning before the first frost."

Gracie stepped carefully back into the garden area and picked up a small glass jar. "We're planting a whole row of bush beans," she said.

By that time, Leah could swallow the boulder in her throat. "I see. That will be great."

"I've got some broccoli and beet seed saved too." Gran pointed to some other small jars she had placed along the side of the garden plot.

"I got my first paycheck today," Leah announced. "I thought I could take Gracie to buy school clothes at the Walmart tomorrow. You might want to come along too, Gran. I'm pretty sure you can find some seedlings for sale in the garden department."

Gran straightened, her eyes alight under the big straw hat. "Oh, that sounds like great fun. Just the three girls out for a special day. I'll treat you both to a cone at the Dairy Queen."

Leah went inside, intent upon starting supper for the hardworking farmers. She tried to shake off her earlier fears and focus on spending the next day with Gran and Gracie. It would be fun to shop for her daughter. Although there wasn't a wide selection of stores to choose from, she figured she should be able to outfit her daughter for school over the next couple of weeks with a little judicious shopping.

When the sun started going down, a noisy entourage entered the house, stamping their feet at the doorstep.

"That was fun!" Gracie declared.

"We'll see what they have for us at the store tomorrow," Gran said. "Maybe we can stop by the feed store too."

"Sure thing," Leah called. "You two wash up, because I'm putting dinner on the table." She felt good about doing her part. Although she knew she was not nearly as good a cook as Gran, at least she had put together a decent meal.

In some area of her brain, she wished Ty were there to see her in action. She would love to set a plate of food she had lovingly prepared in front of him. Would love to see him grin appreciatively. Would love to make him dinner every night.

She swallowed. *Won't do to think that way. No telling what's going to happen when he gets back. He may just grab his dog and take off again.*

She turned as Gran and Gracie took their seats at the table.

"Well, isn't this nice?" Gran smiled her approval.

At least someone appreciated her efforts.

———— ∞ ————

Ty had no idea how to get around in Dallas, so he rode along with Will in his Honda. He had to push the seat all the way back and hold his Stetson in his lap.

Will's driving was alarming to say the least. He sped along the freeway, weaving in and out of traffic. Ty wondered briefly who would claim his body if—no, when—Will drove under a semi as he seemed determined to do.

When the Honda finally swerved across the freeway onto an off-ramp, Ty thought he might live long enough to kiss Leah's sweet lips again. But when Will crossed four lanes of traffic on the feeder road to veer onto a side street, he had his doubts.

After a few stoplights, Will turned into a strip center with a big country-western nightclub located at one end.

When he ground the car into park and turned off the motor, Ty heaved a sigh of relief.

"Whew! Scared me, Will. I wasn't sure we were going to make it." He unfastened his seat belt and unfolded himself from the compact vehicle.

Will made a scornful noise in the back of his throat as he rolled out of the car. "Don't be a puss, man! It's survival of the fittest here in the big city. Kill or be killed."

Ty set his Stetson on his head and adjusted it to the right angle. "Thanks for the warning."

There was a line of people waiting to be admitted to the club, but with Ty in tow, Will strode up to the doorman, who waved them through.

"So, you know that guy?" Ty asked as he followed Will into the darkened interior.

Will chortled. "No, but he knows who I am."

A pretty cocktail waitress grinned at Will and led him to a booth near a raised stage and right beside the dance floor. A tented sign declared this table to be reserved, but the waitress swept the sign onto her tray.

Will climbed into the round booth and gestured for Ty to be seated as he ordered a couple of longnecks.

Ty gazed around, his eyes becoming accustomed to the dim lighting. The raised dance floor had a string of low-level illumination around the edge, probably to keep people from falling on their faces when they stepped up onto it. The stage at the back, near their table, had some glow-in-the-dark lights flickering on and off in time to the beat of the music. It looked like something might happen there eventually.

Recorded music played through the sound system. A few couples were dancing already. The songs varied from two-steps to ballads to rap, and it was loud enough to make conversation difficult.

When the waitress returned with their beer, Will handed her a couple of shiny discs. "Give these to the DJ, honey. Tell him they're from Will." He pressed some cash into her hand.

"I know who you are." She leaned in to accept the bills, favoring him with a flash of dimples and a display of cleavage before she walked away with a swishy, hip-rolling gait.

Will grinned as he watched her make her way to the DJ booth. "See, you're out with the man tonight."

Ty chuckled. "Looks like it. How did you get to be so famous?"

Will rolled his eyes. "Everybody wants to be a star. The good news is, I'm the guy who's going to make you a star."

"Good to know."

Will's assessment of his own importance was apparently accurate. As the night wore on, quite a few people came to shake his hand. An array of hot-looking females dropped by to give him a hug and a kiss. Although Will looked more like a teddy bear than a celebrity, it seemed there were many people who viewed him as someone with clout.

A man came over to the table with two women on his arms. Will introduced the man as the club owner, along with his wife and daughter. Will invited them to sit down, and they crowded in, sliding onto the curved seat beside Ty. The owner's wife sat next to Ty, her thigh pressed against his and her breast rubbing against his arm. He attempted to give her more room, but every time he scooted over, she did too.

The club owner raised his hand, signaling to the DJ and the light technician. A baby spotlight flooded the table with bright light.

Momentarily blinded, Ty couldn't see anything beyond their table, but the owner waved to the crowd, and so did Will. The disc jockey's smooth voice introduced them both, and then he introduced Tyler Garrett as an up-and-coming country star.

To Ty's amazement, people were applauding. Will nudged him, and Ty raised his hand in acknowledgment. The applause grew louder. The DJ introduced one of the songs Ty had recorded earlier, and the sound of Ty's own voice was heard through the sound system. His throat grew tight as he realized he had really taken the first step to making his dreams a reality.

——∿∿∿——

Leah cleared the table and ran a sink full of sudsy water. She began to wash the dishes, placing the rinsed plates in the draining rack. There was something satisfying about seeing the clean dishes. It made her feel as though she had accomplished something.

This was the same way she felt about getting Breck's filing system in order. It was something else that gave her a sense of accomplishment. She was doing her job.

She dried her hands and joined Gran in the living room. Gran was reading her Bible, and Gracie was sitting on the floor in front of the television, Eddie on one side and Lucky on the other. Lucky's long face was leaning against Gracie's legs. Whenever Gracie spoke, Lucky's tail flailed the floor.

This is nice. Just the way a family should be. As the

word *family* formed in her brain, she pictured Ty's face and smiled.

She checked the phone he'd given her. No messages or texts. She wondered if he would call tonight. She sure hoped he would, because she was missing him like crazy. *Maybe I should call him. No, that's way too pushy. I'll wait for him to call.*

"Gran, I need to talk to you about the Carters."

Gran slammed the Bible closed. "Why?" she snapped. "What did you hear about them?"

Leah swallowed. "I sort of met the two Carter boys today…unofficially. They chased me in their truck."

A blaze of color appeared high on Gran's cheeks. "Those bastards!"

Gracie looked around sharply.

Gran apologized and then lowered her voice. "What happened?"

Leah shook her head. "I'm not sure what would have happened, but my boss drove up and stopped them from bothering me. He called the sheriff after we got to the office, and the sheriff said he would talk to them."

Gran frowned so hard her brows almost met in the middle. "That entire Carter clan is the scum of the earth. You stay far away from them. Do you understand?"

Leah nodded. "I plan to."

"Did they know who you are?" Gran persisted. "I mean, do they know you're my granddaughter?"

"I don't think so. We weren't exactly introduced."

Gran sat with her lips pursed, clutching the Bible to her bosom.

Chapter 9

TY COULDN'T BELIEVE HE WAS STANDING ON THE STAGE IN this huge nightclub. He had a mic and was singing to his own recorded voice. Somehow, it felt like he was lip-syncing, but Will and the club owner were nodding and grinning at him. Most patrons in the club were watching him and nodding or swaying in time to the beat. Some remained on the dance floor, moving to his melody.

It wasn't the first time he had sung onstage, but he felt naked without his guitar, and the overpowering strains from the sound system throbbed throughout his entire body.

He felt his cell vibrate, and while still singing, he reached for it. *Leah!* He pushed the talk button, holding the phone close to the mic as though he was singing just for her ears. He recalled her delight when he had first sung to her. He wished she were here with him. Somehow, it would be easier with her by his side.

The song ended, and there was a round of applause. He bowed and started to leave the stage, but Will made a "go on" gesture, furiously winding his hand in the air. He heard the beginning of another song he had recorded earlier that day. "Hang on, Leah," he shouted into the phone and began singing the next ballad. He hoped she would understand what was going on. Holding on to her this way felt like a lifeline to the real world.

At the end of the song, he raised his hand to

acknowledge the applause but determinedly stepped down from the stage. Glancing around, he made a break for a hallway to the rear, where he spied the restroom signs. He paused by the fire exit just past the restrooms.

"Are you still there?" he said, covering his other ear so he could hear her.

"Yes," she said. "You were wonderful."

Ty grinned, acknowledging that her approval had somehow achieved monumental importance. "I'm glad you liked it."

"Where are you? It's so loud."

He heaved a sigh. "I'm in a club here in Dallas. My friend got them to play some of the songs we recorded today."

"Oh, Ty. I'm so very proud of you." He heard her catch her breath. "I'm sorry to interrupt. I just wanted to…to…" She broke off.

"No, no," he assured her. "You can interrupt me anytime. I wish you were here."

"It's Tyler!" a female voice trilled from behind him.

He turned to find several young women crowding around him. They were all talking at once and taking pictures with their phones.

"Here, Tyler," one shouted. "Take a picture with me." She ducked under his arm, and her friend snapped the photo as she hugged him around his torso.

"Hang on," he said into his phone. "Maybe I better let you go. Things are getting complicated around here…"

―⁓⁓―

"Yes…goodbye," Leah said to the dead air. She swallowed hard. "Tyler…"

She had been unable to resist any longer and, when she hadn't heard from Ty, had gone to sit on a wicker rocking chair on the front porch to place the call.

Ty was in a nightclub where women were crushing on him. An ache in her chest caused her to feel even more alone. *And jealous*. She acknowledged that feeling right up front.

She couldn't be angry with him. This was what he had always wanted. The fame that came with his future celebrity would bring with it a ton of female admirers. They would be the ones to download his songs and request them on the radio.

Leah leaned back in the rocker and rested her bare feet on the rickety porch railing. She heaved a deep sigh and gazed up at the moon. She felt as though she were the only human being in the entire universe right now. Her eyes were attuned to the darkness, and she could see small movements. Something tiny, maybe a mouse, ran along in the tall grass growing up next to the barbed wire fence. Tree frogs croaked rhythmically, and crickets chirped in counterpoint. A whisper of breeze caused tree branches to stir.

Her earlier fear of the Carters had dissolved into apathy. She wasn't feeling important enough to bother with. If she hadn't called Ty tonight, she would never have known he was in a club, being mobbed by his adoring female fans.

She huffed out a derisive snort. *How could they resist?*

A single tear trickled down her cheek. She wiped it away and chided herself for being an idiot. *I'm not some starstruck fool. I'm a grown woman, and I fell in love with a real man. A man who is kind and loving and sexy as hell.* She hiccupped and wiped at another tear.

"Oh, Ty. Please let it be me."

The next day, Leah woke up with a different mind-set. She decided not to live her life waiting for any man, even one as wonderful as Tyler Garrett. No matter how much she loved him, she couldn't control the future, so she would focus on what she could control.

It was Saturday, and she had a purse full of cash... well, not full, but enough to make her feel rich by comparison with her previous state. She would have to make sure Gracie was outfitted for school and see what she could do to help Gran.

After breakfast, she made a quick survey of their pantry and determined that, although Ty had provided a good store of foodstuffs, there were a few things she could restock.

Gracie was taking her duties as dog-sitter very seriously. She had taken over Eddie's care as well, feeding both dogs and taking them out for a run together.

Leah washed dishes and got dressed for their outing. She loaded Gran and Gracie into her car and set out for Langston.

Gran was almost as excited as Gracie, chattering about the local school and what seedlings she hoped to find at the feed store.

Gracie was quiet, but when questioned, she said she hoped they could find some new shoes she could run in. That was most important to her.

Leah assured her they would find good shoes, hoping

they could find something Gracie would love and she could afford. At the far end of town, she pulled into the Walmart parking lot. It appeared everyone in the surrounding area had had the same idea, because there seemed to be a million cars parked outside. She let Gran and Gracie out near the entrance and went to park the car. When she got back to them, Gran had commandeered a shopping cart and appeared eager to shop. She announced her intentions of exploring the garden center and set off in the direction of the big overhead sign.

Leah took Gracie to the girls' department, and they made a thorough investigation of the available wares.

"We need to get you five good outfits to start with," Leah said. "Maybe some things you can mix and match."

Gracie reached out a hand to stroke a powder-blue cardigan folded on a table. She looked wistful, but since they had not been able to afford much in the way of new things and a lot of Leah's shopping had been at thrift stores, this was a brand-new experience for both of them.

"Do you like that sweater?" Leah asked. At Gracie's nod, she sorted around and found it in a size she thought would last Gracie through the winter. She unbuttoned it and held it open for Gracie. "Here, slip your arms into this."

Gracie complied, smiling as Leah tugged the sleeve down over her cast. Then she looked around nervously, coloring when she saw another girl watching her.

"I think that looks great on you. Let's put it in the cart." Leah folded it across her purse in the top section of the cart. She glanced at the pretty, dark-haired girl, who appeared to be about Gracie's age, and smiled at her, but the girl turned away. *Must be as shy as Gracie.*

She looked for jeans in Gracie's size and put some in the cart, along with several shirts and pullover sweaters. Then she went to paw through a rack of dresses. She held various ones up to Gracie, noting which appeared to please her. They headed for the dressing rooms and crammed into a small cubicle so Gracie could try them on.

"Which dress do you like best, Gracie?" she asked. "You'll need one for church."

"Church?" Gracie asked, looking puzzled. "Are we going to church?"

Leah felt a stab of conscience. "Yes, we can go to church now. I don't have to work on Sundays anymore."

They chose a pretty patterned dress with a white collar. It would look good with the blue cardigan too, so Leah added it to the stash in the cart. She would have one more paycheck before school started, so she helped Gracie choose three outfits as well as the dress for them to purchase. When they emerged from the dressing room, the woman who was with the other little girl was coming out of another cubicle. The woman was a pretty Hispanic woman with a wide smile.

"I saw you at the restaurant with Big Jim Garrett," she said.

Leah nodded, her stomach grabbing at the memory. "Yes. I was there."

The woman held out her hand. "I'm Milita Rios. My father owns the restaurant."

Leah clasped her hand and slipped her other arm around Gracie. "This is my daughter, Gracie. She's going to be in the third grade this year."

"That's great. She'll be in the same class with my

niece, Tina." She indicated the young girl standing nearby. "Tina, be sure and help Gracie get to know everyone."

Tina smiled shyly and raised a hand in greeting.

Leah hoped this encounter would blossom into a friendship. *Lord knows Gracie hasn't had much in the way of friends at school.*

The two girls moved off and began to chat in low tones.

Leah felt as though a weight had been lifted off her heart. "Thanks so much. It's hard to be the new one in school."

"We'll have to get them together to play before school starts. Just bring Gracie by the restaurant, and the girls can hang out. Poor Tina has been reading or drawing in a corner while I work."

Leah wondered where the girl's parents were but didn't feel comfortable in asking.

"My brother is a widower," Milita supplied as if reading her mind. "And he had to take a job out of state, so I'm keeping Tina for him. At least he can have peace of mind that my dad and I will care for her, and she can stay in the same school."

Leah nodded. "I'm sure that's for the best."

When they left the dressing room area, Leah added a package of underwear and socks to the cart, and then they set off to find Gran.

"I think she said she was going to the garden center," Gracie supplied, pulling the cart by the front toward that sign.

When Leah pushed the cart out into the garden area, she didn't see Gran at first. There were fruit trees and lots of houseplants arranged in row after row. Leah turned down one aisle and saw Gran at the other end. She appeared to be upset.

When they neared, she heard Gran's voice raised in anger. "You get away from me! Let go of my cart!"

Leah thrust Gracie behind her and barreled the cart down the aisle. "What's going on here?" Her heart nearly stopped when she reached the end and saw the two Carter brothers with smarmy grins on their faces. One held onto the front of Gran's cart and wouldn't let her pass. When they spied Leah, their grins widened.

"Look who it is, Dean. That pretty little thing from the park."

Ray gave a hard shove to the cart Gran was trying to wrest away from him, and she fell back onto the concrete.

"Stay here," Leah instructed Gracie and rushed to help Gran. She had a cut on her elbow and appeared to be quite shaken. "Gran, are you all right?"

The one named Ray cocked his brow at Leah. "You related to this old hag? Well, ain't that nice to know?"

She assisted her grandmother to her feet and glowered at the two brothers, who stood snickering at her. "You get away from us, or I'll call the security guard."

The brothers laughed even more. They mimicked her words and hooted. "Now that we know where you live, we'll have to come pay a visit," the other brother, Dean, said.

A burst of anger exploded in Leah's chest. She jerked Gran's metal shopping cart toward her and then rammed it back into them. The one named Dean fell down, landing on his side and halfway into a raised area with various evergreens and concrete blocks marking the border. He cursed and scrambled to rise. He stood glowering at her while rubbing his hand against his hip.

"Stay away from us," she ordered, "or I'll tell Mr. Ryan. He had me make a report to the sheriff."

More jeers, but they moved away, glaring at her and also eyeing Gracie. The tall, gaunt one made a lunge at Gracie, and when she jumped and screamed, he laughed derisively.

Gran stood, holding her elbow, her mouth pinched up tight. "Those are the meanest snakes in the grass in all creation. I wish I had my shotgun, and I would have blasted them to kingdom come."

Leah gathered Gracie tight against her and tried to soothe Gran's feelings. She ushered them inside and went to the front desk, where she told the person behind the counter her grandmother had been attacked by two men. The woman summoned the security guard, and when Leah told him it was the Carter brothers, he rolled his eyes. He offered to call the sheriff's office for her, but Gran was anxious to leave. She appeared to be exhausted after the ordeal, so Leah waited while the lady behind the counter offered a first-aid box to tend to Gran's elbow. Leah cleaned it as best she could with hydrogen peroxide and covered it with a big gauze bandage.

Gran looked better by that time, so they checked out and left the store.

"Mommy, who were those bad men?" Gracie asked. "They scared me."

"No one you need to be concerned with," Leah interjected. "We're all fine now." She got her family settled in the car and drove away, checking for the Carter brothers in their old blue truck. *Damn! Why did we have to run into those monsters?* She drove to the Dairy Queen and bought a round of chili dogs and milkshakes. It felt good to be able to provide even a little treat for her family.

When they were back in the car, Gran asked to be taken to the feed store. She still wanted to see if there were any seedlings of fall vegetables in stock. When they had all trooped inside, Gran drew her aside.

"I'll tell you, I was sure glad to see you comin' when those Carters had me cornered. You looked like the wrath of God a-comin' to smite 'em."

Leah grinned in spite of the seriousness of the situation. "I was so mad I could have smote them into the next county."

They cruised the area with fruit tree saplings and moved on to the counter with a selection of vegetable plants growing in small containers. Gran got a couple of green peppers, a couple of pumpkins, and some winter squash.

"How about you, Gracie?" Gran asked. "Do you see anything else we need to plant?"

"Peas and carrots are my favorites," Gracie responded.

"Well, we can get some seed for those." She led Gracie over to a rack of seed packets, and the two of them had a serious discussion about which to purchase.

"Hey, there," a masculine voice said.

Leah turned to see Sara Beth's boyfriend at the counter. "Hello," she called back.

"Frank," he said. "I'm Frank Wilson."

Leah grinned. "Yes, I remember you."

He signed a ticket the clerk presented. "I'm just pick-ing up some supplies and feed for my boss. What are you doing here today?"

Leah pointed to where Gran and Gracie stood with their heads together. "My grandmother and daughter are planting a fall garden."

"That's always a good thing." He stopped and looked at Gracie, then back at Leah. "You'll pardon me for saying, but you don't look old enough to have a daugh-ter that age."

Leah blew out a breath. "Well, I had her pretty young."

He nodded. "So did Sara Beth." He shrugged. "A bonus for me. We're getting married in the spring."

"That will be lovely," Leah said. "You're a lucky man."

Frank gave her another wide grin. "Don't I know it."

Gran and Gracie made their selection and checked out. When they went to the car, Frank pulled alongside and got out to help load the plants into Leah's vehicle. Leah introduced Gracie, and Gran said she had seen him around town.

Leah felt a little better after they started toward home but kept an eye out for the blue truck. The last words from the Carters continued to haunt her. *Now that we know where you live, we'll have to come pay a visit.*

───∿∿∿───

Ty had slept late. Not his usual routine. He lay on the futon thinking about everything he had left behind in Langston. His horse was being boarded with the veteri-narian. His dog was being cared for by Gracie, and the woman he cared for was missing him…he hoped.

He stretched and thought about Leah and how much

she had come to mean to him. He was just coming to terms with the depth of his feeling. Probably being encircled with so many strange women the night before reinforced how much he cared about the one he'd lost his heart to. Although Will had been very comfortable surrounded by the crowds and functioned well with the people he deemed to be the movers and shakers, the whole situation made Ty feel uncomfortable. He enjoyed performing onstage, but milling around in the crowd was definitely not his thing.

He wondered if he might have felt differently if Leah had been with him. If she had been sitting at the table beside him, he thought it would have been easier.

Ty sat up and began to rummage through his things. Just a simple line of melody ran through his head, and he wanted to capture it. He found a scrap of paper and made a note of the tune, then he started writing a lyric that seemed to fit it. *A song for Leah.*

Since Will was sacked out and snoring on the bed, Ty didn't grab his guitar and strum the tune. He was itching to play the song he'd just written, but he didn't want to wake his host. Instead, he busied himself with paper and pen, jotting down lyrics and musical notes.

A smile spread across his face when he imagined her reaction. He thought she would be pleased that he wrote this song for her. Ty worked until he realized his stomach was growling and Will was showing no signs of getting up. Carefully stowing his notes in his guitar case, he took a stroll to the kitchen area and opened the refrigerator door. *Pretty bleak.* Several cartons of beer sat on the lower shelves and in the door.

He closed the fridge and checked the pantry but

quickly closed the door again when an open box of cereal and a few roaches greeted him.

He thought of the delicious and pleasant breakfasts he had shared with Leah, Gracie, and Gran. Acknowledging it was more than the food he missed, he climbed into his clothes and carried his boots to the bottom of the stairs before putting them on. He left the building, hearing the lock tumble into place behind him.

Once in his truck, he circled around for a while looking for food. He drove through a fast-food restaurant and ordered enough food to satisfy his appetite and Will's as well. He ate a biscuit stuffed with sausage and scrambled egg on the way back to the recording studio and punched the number for Leah's cell phone as soon as he parked.

She answered quickly, bringing a grin to his face. "Hello, beautiful," he said.

"Oh, Ty!" She sounded pleased that he'd called, but there was something else. An edge to her voice he hadn't heard before.

"Are you okay?"

"Oh, uh…yes. Why do you ask?" She suddenly sounded cheery. *Way too cheery*.

"Come on. Tell me what's wrong."

"Nothing," she answered quickly. "I'm in the car with Gracie and Gran. I got my first paycheck, and we went into Langston to get Gracie some school clothes."

"Tell him about the bad men," Gracie urged.

An icy fear coiled around Ty's spine. "What bad men?" he asked.

"Oh, it was nothing."

"Yes, Mommy. Tell him," Gracie insisted.

"Let me talk to Gracie," Ty said, all thoughts of food forgotten. He heard Leah sigh and the phone being handed off.

"Ty! We were shopping, and two bad men were hurting Gran. They pushed her down, and she hurt her elbow. Mommy ran the shopping cart into them."

"Really?" Ty's fingers flexed on the steering wheel. "Are you all okay?"

"Yes, but Gran has this bandage on her elbow, and we were real scared."

Ty swallowed hard, rage gathering in his chest. *Who could hurt a little old lady?* "Let me speak to your mother, honey."

"Yes?" Leah answered, sounding anxious.

"I'll be there tonight. Lock yourselves inside the house, and don't hesitate to call the sheriff if there's any funny business."

"Oh, Ty," she said. "I don't want you to have to leave before your business is done."

"Don't worry about it. I'll see you in a while." He disconnected and got out of the truck. When he rang the bell and banged on the door, Will finally answered, squinting into the light.

"Oh, man! What are you doing?" He opened the door for Ty to enter and then followed him back up the stairs. "What time is it?"

"Late," Ty said. "I've got to go back to Langston." He thrust the bag of food into Will's hands and began tossing his things together. In a matter of minutes, he had his duffel and his guitar in hand.

"Whoa! Wait up! What's the rush?" Will located his glasses and shoved them onto his face.

"I just need to be there. What else do I need to do for the audition?" He stopped in mid-stride to gaze at Will, who shook his head.

"Lots of stuff. We need to get you out there. You need to be seen. We need to build some buzz."

Ty heaved a sigh. "I hope you can buzz without me. I'll call tomorrow. I have to leave now."

Will shrugged. "I'll do what I can. I'll submit your audition tape and see if I can get some of the local DJs to play your tracks…create a fan base ahead of time." He followed Ty to the stairs. "But you really should be here. This is important."

Ty was already down the stairs and halfway out the door. "Just do what you can." He tossed his bag and guitar on the seat beside him and pulled away, raising a hand to Will as he drove away. He didn't know who would injure Leah's grandmother, but he was sure going to find out and put a stop to it.

Once on the highway, his heart felt lighter with every mile that brought him closer to the three females he had left behind.

"No, you just rest." Leah settled her grandmother on the sofa in front of the newscast and propped her feet up. "You've been through a lot today, so take it easy."

Leah unloaded the car and settled Gracie to peel stickers off her new underwear and cut the tags off the new school clothes she'd bought.

Gran seemed to be perfectly happy inspecting the seeds and plants she'd bought, which were sitting on top of magazines spread out on the coffee table. Other than the big gauze pad taped to her bony little elbow, she appeared to be none the worse for wear. "We can plant these tomorrow," she said to Gracie.

Leah locked the front door after looking around carefully to make sure there were no signs that the Carters had made good on their promise to "visit."

She had mixed feelings about Ty's cutting his trip short to come back to Langston. She missed him like crazy, so of course she wanted to see him. But she also felt guilty for being the cause of his early return. Surely, she could manage to stand up for herself and her little family. Surely, she could.

She had a flash of the one named Dean when she pushed the cart into him. Pure hate radiated in his gaze after he crawled back up to a standing position. And the other one, Ray…he had terrified her when he'd chased her from the park. How could she avoid them in such a small town? And how could she keep them away from the farm? The menace was real.

No, she admitted they frightened her, but what was a woman to do? She couldn't walk around frightened all the time. And she hated to think she would have to constantly be on guard, always looking over her shoulder. But how could she leave Gran and Gracie when she went to work? How could she leave them alone when they were so defenseless?

Ty pulled in at the little farmhouse just as the sun was going down. There was a light on inside. He sat for a moment wondering why this felt like coming home when his real home was farther west, on the other side of Langston.

An image of his father's stern face leapt, unbidden, to his mind. He let out a sigh and pictured his brothers instead.

Fun-loving Beau, the baby of the family. Always so easygoing and ready to lend a hand.

Colton, the eldest, was more serious, but he also enjoyed a good laugh. Ty recalled the many good times they had enjoyed together. Mostly when their mother was alive. Lately, things had been more than a little tense.

He climbed out of the truck and stepped up onto the porch. Giving a knock, he tried the knob and found the door to be locked. *This is a first. It's always been open before.* He realized Leah had heeded his advice. A stirring in his gut told him these women were fearful.

"Who's there?" Leah called out from behind the door.

"It's me, Ty," he answered.

She threw the door open, a haunted expression on her face. "Oh, Ty!" she gasped.

When he pulled the screen open, she fell into his arms. He kissed her deeply, responding to the aching chasm in his chest, which suddenly seemed to be flooded with warmth. Lifting her off her feet, he swung her around. She buried her face against his chest and clung to him.

"Hey, baby. I'm here. Everything's going to be okay."

She nodded furiously but didn't seem to be breathing.

He kissed her hair and laid his cheek against it. Holding her was the most important thing he could be doing.

A bark interrupted their reunion as Lucky pushed out the door and jumped around excitedly.

Leah stepped back, wiping her eyes but grinning.

Ty squatted down to give Lucky some attention, and he heard Gracie's voice call out. "Oh, Gran! Ty's home."

The word *home* seemed to drill into his conscience. *Home? Where is home now?*

He stood in time to be clasped around the waist by an exuberant Gracie. "Ty! I'm so glad to see you. I knew you'd come back."

"Well, of course. Was there any doubt?"

She gazed up at him, her expression rapt, and shook her head.

"Land's sake!" Gran called. "Let the man come inside the door."

Gracie pulled him through the doorway, and Leah closed it behind them. He thought she looked around a little anxiously before securing it.

Gran was on the sofa, struggling to rise. "Let me get you something to eat. You must be starved."

"Gran, you stay right there," Leah ordered. "I'll make something for Ty. You just rest."

Ty watched Leah and Gracie hurry off to the kitchen, so he sank onto the sofa beside Gran. "How are you doing?" Lucky thrust his head in Ty's lap, begging for attention, which he was only too glad to supply.

"About as good as could be expected," Gran retorted with a wide grin in place.

He spied a large gauze bandage on her elbow where the blood had seeped through. "What happened here?" She tried to blow it off, but he managed to draw the entire story from her. His anger must have been evident, because when Leah came from the kitchen, she took one look at his face and pressed her lips together in a firm line.

"Why don't you come in to the table now, Ty? We heated up a little something for you."

He stood and followed her, taking a seat at the place

they had prepared for him. Blowing out a breath, he tried to release the knot of anger binding his chest. "Thanks. This looks great." He gestured to the chair next to him. "Why don't you sit down and tell me what's been going on while I've been gone?"

Tight-lipped, Leah sent Gracie in to watch television with Gran and slipped into the chair. "I'm really sorry you came back, Ty." Eyes wide, she covered her mouth with both hands. "No, I didn't mean that. I mean, I'm sorry all this happened."

He reached for her hand. "Don't worry about it. I'm here. I have every intention of solving this problem, one way or the other." He gave her hand a squeeze and reached for the fork. "This looks mighty nice to a hungry traveler."

This brought a smile to her face. "I hope you like my corn bread. I used the recipe on the box of cornmeal."

He ate the food and managed to avoid mentioning the Carter brothers until he pushed the plate away. "Now, let's talk about the Carters. I know they had been giving your grandmother a hard time. My big brother and I had some run-ins with them when we were in school. What's going on?"

She looked down at her hands and murmured something he didn't understand.

Ty leaned closer and lifted her chin. "What is it, baby? You can tell me anything."

She met his gaze and gave him a sad smile. "I know." She swallowed hard. "I've already told you my deepest secrets."

He kissed her nose. "So tell me what happened."

Leah poured out the story of how the Carter brothers

had chased her with their truck and how the one called Ray had pursued her on foot. She told him about Breck interceding and warning her to stay clear of them and how he had facilitated her making a report to the sheriff.

"And you didn't see them again until today?" he asked.

She shook her head. "When Gracie and I were in the girls' department, Gran wandered off by herself to the garden center. When we went looking for her, the Carters had her trapped in the far back corner past the fruit trees. The one pushed her down with her shopping cart, and she hit the concrete. That made me so mad I went and shoved the cart into them. One fell down against the concrete blocks, but they were both looking real mean at us, and they said they would be coming to visit us real soon."

"Did you report this to the sheriff too?"

"No, I did tell the security guard, but I wanted to get Gran and Gracie home."

He brushed a strand of hair away from her face. "I think you need to make an official report of today's incident too. Maybe take out a restraining order. That might get their attention."

She sucked in a deep breath and pressed her lips together.

It caused him physical pain to see her so frightened. "Honey, we can't let this go. Apparently, these guys have been running over your grandmother for a while, and they think they can get away with it."

"I know you're right," she said.

"We're going to stand up to them. Bullies usually back down when their victim lets them know they aren't going to take it any longer."

Chapter 10

TY HAD GONE OUTSIDE WITH LUCKY TO SIT ON THE front porch while Leah was getting Gracie ready for bed. She found him still sitting in the old wicker rocker, softly strumming his guitar and humming a little. Softly, he sang an old John Denver ballad, his voice deep and rich. Lucky raised his snout to the darkened sky and let out a mournful howl. Ty laughed and stroked Lucky's head. "Good boy. Sing along with me."

Then he sang another song, one she wasn't familiar with, but she loved the lyrics as much as the sound of Ty's voice.

She had turned off the lights inside except for one, and the house looked like it was resting. Standing just inside the screen, she listened to him sing, his voice embracing her as surely as did his strong arms. She leaned her head against the doorframe, filled with a mixture of longing and anticipation. Taking a deep breath, she stepped out onto the porch and pulled the door closed behind her.

Ty stood at her approach. He placed the guitar on the chair and silently wrapped his arms around her.

Somehow, being held in this manner made her feel weak. All the problems of the past few days seemed to crash in on her. She clung to him, letting her fears ease away.

He said the words she knew would be forthcoming. "Don't worry, Leah. Everything's going to be okay."

When he said it, she could almost believe it.

He turned back to get the guitar but kept an arm around her. "Let's go."

She knew what he meant. "Yes," she whispered softly and fell into step as they made their way arm in arm to the bunkhouse and to the bed where they would make love again.

Ty led her inside and secured the door behind them.

Lucky curled up on a pillow in the corner. Somehow, this all seemed normal.

Only a small lamp illuminated the space with a soft glow. "Don't be nervous."

"I'm not," she insisted.

He grinned and drew her into an embrace. "Liar." He kissed her and skimmed his hands down her sides. He slid the zipper open on her pants and let them fall down to her ankles.

"Oh!" She started and then laughed. "Anxious?"

"I just want to see you. I want to touch you." He unclasped her bra and pulled her shirt off, letting it fall to the floor.

She felt a wave of shyness standing before him wearing only her panties, and she was divested of those quickly.

Ty's gaze roamed hungrily over her body, sending a rush of warmth swirling low in her belly. She felt light, almost airborne.

"Would you unbutton my shirt?" His murmured request jarred her back to earth.

"Sure." She concentrated on working the buttons through his cuffs and then made her way down his shirtfront. Running her fingers over his skin, she drew the shirt over his shoulders and pulled it all the way off.

Smiling, she held it against her breasts. The smooth fabric still held the warmth of his flesh. Her gaze traveled over the muscular contours of his arms and chest, a total work of art.

He smiled encouragingly. "I sure could use some help with my Wranglers."

A grin spread across her face. "I guess I could help you out." She hung the shirt over one of the straight-back chairs and turned to face him. Hooking her fingers in his belt, she unclasped it and then the button at the waistband. The zipper came next, but the dense denim material resisted her efforts.

Ty put his hands over hers to guide the zipper down. The sound caused a whisper of gooseflesh to kiss the back of her neck.

She glanced up into his eyes and was rocked by the heat of passion. For a moment, Ty looked like a sleek jungle cat, holding himself in check, waiting for her to catch up. Her fingers fumbled, stalling at his unzipped Wranglers.

A smile played around his mouth. He took both of her hands and kissed her palms, drew her against him, held her soft body against his hard maleness. Bending to kiss her lips, he lifted her in his arms and carried her to the bed. He lowered her gently and then stepped back to shed the rest of his clothing. He pulled off his boots and the Wranglers, displaying his amazing form with no pretense.

Without further preamble, he climbed onto the bed and onto Leah, devouring her with ravenous kisses. A flash of panic seized her when he pressed her back onto the pillow but just as quickly evaporated as a wave of desire roiled up from her belly.

Ty's hands were stroking her skin, creating a raging need inside her, a need only he could satisfy.

She whispered his name, and that seemed to kick him into overdrive. Where he had been slow and languorous, he was now on fire, and he was igniting her from the inside out.

"Oh, hurry," Leah whispered. Without any conscious effort, her legs parted, willing him to find her need and fill it. And just like that, his fingers pressed into her wetness, massaging to the point where she could hardly breathe. She gripped him with both arms, pulling him closer, willing him to enter, to take possession of her body, to remove her fear and satisfy her longing.

He opened the condom and applied it quickly.

The fact that he was in a hurry pleased her. She wanted to think his haste had something to do with the fact that he desired her. That she had the power to seduce him. This made her smile, because she had never considered herself to be powerful in any way.

When he turned back to her, his shaft properly clad, he began again to touch and kiss her.

Impatient, Leah pulled him closer, wrapped her legs around him.

He chortled. "Who's anxious now?"

"Me," she ground out.

"Well, all right, then." He grinned and set to the task of bringing her pleasure.

This...this is the best...the closest...the best. Her mind and her body were filled with Ty, with how he moved inside her, with how he managed to touch all her nerve endings at once.

Leah felt electrified, as though she might explode

at any moment. She rose to meet his strokes, writhing against him to wrest the savage pleasure emanating from their joining. With every stroke, she was lifted higher and higher until he finally brought her to the peak of pleasure. Wave after wave pounded her with ecstasy until she lay spent, still holding him in a viselike grip.

"Oh, Ty," she whispered. "I love you so much." She froze. *Oh no! I said it.*

Ty stroked the side of her face tenderly, then kissed her lips. "I know. I love you more."

Leah giggled. "Impossible."

―――᠁―――

In the morning, Ty woke up early. He was glad to still have his arms around Leah. It was Sunday, and he thought he should set a good example for Gracie. "C'mon, sleepyhead. Let's get a move on and go to church."

She jerked awake and stared at him groggily. "Whut?"

"Church. You know, Sunday-go-to-meeting? It's the thing to do in a small town. I'm pretty sure your grandmother would like to go, and we should take Gracie."

She nodded. "Okay. We haven't been going. I usually had to work late Saturday night and sometimes worked Sunday too."

"Well, that was then, and this is now." He set his feet on the floor and stretched. "I'm going to walk you back to the house, and then I'll get cleaned up. C'mon." He extended a hand to her.

She put her hand in his, and he pulled her to her feet, grinning. "Okay, okay. I'm up."

After he walked her to the house and made her lock the door, he hurried back to shower and shave. He found his last starched jeans and shirt, slipped into those, and combed his still-damp hair. He gazed at his face in the bathroom mirror. "This will have to do."

He drove the three females into Langston and pulled up to the church he had attended since boyhood. They were early, but all the better to introduce Leah and Gracie to the preacher. He had a sneaking suspicion this day would get way more complicated, but he thought he should face it head-on.

Once inside, he ushered Gran to a pew, and she waved to some of her lady friends. He took Leah and Gracie by the hand and led them to the parson's office at the back of the church. When he introduced Leah and her daughter, Leah seemed ill at ease, but Gracie was smiling and appeared to be comfortable. The minister told Gracie about the Sunday school for her age group, which would take place after the early service and before the late one. Ty led them back to the church and seated them beside Gran.

"That wasn't so bad, was it?" he whispered to Leah.

She shook her head, a faint blush staining her cheeks. "No, it was okay. I guess I have to be respectable if I'm going to hang around with you."

He stretched his arm along the back of the pew, just encircling her and extending his hand to shield Gracie. He felt a sense of satisfaction, as though things were playing out as they should be.

Big Jim Garrett arrived at the church a few minutes before the services were to start. The organist was playing hymns when he and his two sons hustled in the back of the church. He glanced around, looking for a seat for the three of them. He saw Breckenridge T. Ryan, his attorney, sitting with his pretty wife. He met Breck's gaze, and he raised a hand in silent greeting as he slid onto the pew beside them. Beau and Colton slid in on the outside.

The organist came to a rousing crescendo and then segued right into another hymn as the choir began singing. This one was a hymn that had been a favorite of his wife, Elizabeth. In spite of the time elapsed since her passing, the music brought the sting of tears to his eyes. It wouldn't do at all for the boys to see him break down like a sissy, so he took out a handkerchief and blew his nose, managing to wipe his eyes in the process. *Whew!*

He settled back in the seat to listen as the minister began with announcements.

Beau was straining his neck, peering at someone sitting up front and across the aisle. Probably some girl he was infatuated with. But he jabbed Colton in the ribs and whispered something Big Jim couldn't hear. Both of them were straining and gawking now.

"Settle down," he hissed.

"But, Dad," Beau began, gesturing in the direction he'd been gaping. "It's Ty."

Big Jim felt his chest tighten up. He couldn't seem to suck in a breath as his gaze traveled to where Beau was pointing. Sure enough, right there two rows back from the very front, his rebellious middle son, Tyler Garrett, sat with his arm around that pretty little blonde thing who worked for Breck. He forced himself to take a breath as the sound of his own thunderous heart drowned out anything the preacher might have to say.

He kept his gaze fastened on Ty throughout the

service and noted that he looked good. He appeared to be happy. But what was he doing here? He was supposed to be in Dallas, or maybe Nashville. Someplace where singing was supposed to make you famous. Someplace where the responsibilities of owning a working ranch were secondary to the joy of having people clap while you were singing. He felt his jaw tighten.

The preacher called out the number of a song in the hymnal, and there was a scramble as everyone struggled to their feet and to shuffle through the pages, searching for the right one.

When the organist started again, Big Jim could hear his son's voice above all the others. The voice his wife had been so very proud of. He straightened his shoulders, admitting to himself that Ty's voice was good. *But is this the right thing for my boy? Shouldn't he be on the ranch with me and his brothers?*

He blew out a breath and tried to sing along with the others, not able to tear his attention from the tall, dark-haired young man and his party. He spotted Fern Davis sitting on the other side of Tyler, next to a young girl with blonde hair. This could be the daughter the woman mentioned. *Leah! That was her name.*

Beau was grinning ear to ear, and Colton looked amused. Big Jim didn't ever remember Tyler being girl crazy, but he seemed to be crazy about that one. Ty kept exchanging glances with her, and they looked all lovey-dovey. *Dang! How did that happen?*

After the service, Fern led the little girl off, perhaps to the Sunday school classes, but Ty and his girlfriend stood and looked around. Beau stood and waved.

The look that crossed Ty's face wasn't exactly

cordial. But he nodded and put his hand on his girl-friend's back to urge her toward where they were sitting.

She smiled when she spotted Breck and waved. "Hi, Breck."

He stood and introduced her to his wife, the doctor. They began conversing as though the Garretts were not right there in front of them.

Beau jumped on Ty, enveloping him in a big bear hug, and Colton followed suit.

Ty greeted Breck and then gazed at his father. "Hello, Dad."

"Son," Big Jim acknowledged.

Ty put his arm around Leah's shoulder and drew her closer. "This is my girlfriend, Leah Benson."

Big Jim reached over the back of the pew in front of him to take her hand.

"Mr. Garrett," she said. "I've met your father, Ty. At Mr. Ryan's office."

Ty turned back to face him, a wariness in his gaze. "That sounds about right." He heaved a sigh. "And these are my brothers, Colton and Beau." Both reached to shake her hand.

"Man, Ty. How did you find someone so pretty?" Beau asked, staring at Leah with open admiration.

She blushed prettily, and Big Jim had to like that. *Not the stuck-up sort*.

Ty grinned at Beau. "I grabbed my angel when she flew too close to the earth."

Beau rolled his eyes, grinning.

"Don't let go," Colton said.

"Don't plan to." Ty slipped his arm around her waist.

Breck cleared his throat. "Why don't we go to have

some refreshments? I know I need a little coffee after that stirring sermon."

Big Jim nodded. He didn't want to let Ty slip away too soon. He followed the procession and wound up in the activity center where the ladies were dispensing coffee and doughnuts. He hung back, watching Ty interact with his girlfriend. The look of caring on their faces when they looked at each other told Big Jim everything he needed to know.

Big Jim stood beside Breck and munched a doughnut, using it as an excuse not to chat.

"Tyler is really looking good," Breck commented. "He seems to have found a really sweet girl too."

Big Jim grunted. "Seems so."

Breck took a sip of his coffee. "Leah sure is doing a good job for me."

"Say, Breck," Big Jim said. "I'd like it if you could just tear up that last will I had you draw up. I think I may have...been a complete jackass."

"I can't destroy it," Breck said. "But if you come to my office, I can remove said document and place it in your hands. What you do with it is up to you."

Big Jim nodded. "Sounds like the best thing to do."

In a few minutes, the Sunday school classes let out, and Fern entered the activity center with the little blonde girl beside her.

"Mommy!" The girl gave a gleeful cry. She presented her mother with something she had drawn or colored. It looked like it had pieces of construction paper glued on top.

Big Jim remembered when his sons used to come out of Sunday school with Bible verses and bits of paper glued together for his wife to ooh and aah over.

Ty was admiring the girl's artwork. Damned if he didn't look like a father just now. Big Jim swallowed hard. *My boy has grown up*. He wanted to heal the chasm between them. He wanted to pull Ty close and tell him he was proud of the man he had become. But he stood apart, sipping his coffee and watching as his family and friends interacted. A lonely man, wrapped too tight in his own grief.

As unlikely as it seemed at the time, Big Jim invited them all to lunch after church. He insisted Leah's grandmother and Gracie ride with him, and the two brothers climbed in the back seat of Ty's truck.

Leah could see the reluctance in Ty's face, but he went along with it. He followed his dad's truck, a grim set to his mouth. She squeezed his forearm, trying to lighten the tension. "Well, that was nice of your dad to take Gran and Gracie with him."

Ty snorted under his breath. "He's holding them hostage to make sure I follow."

His brothers gave a laugh but apparently agreed with him.

"Trust me," Ty said. "He's pumping them for information right now."

The small entourage turned in at Tio's Mexican Restaurant and drew to a halt. Before Ty could make it around the truck, his brother Beau had jumped out to open Leah's door and offer a hand to assist her down.

"Thank you," she murmured, casting a glance at Ty.

Tight-lipped, Ty ducked around his father's truck and helped Gran alight and then Gracie. When all the helpless females were ushered to the restaurant, Leah received an effusive greeting from Milita Rios. Milita took charge of Gracie and seated her in a booth with her niece, Tina.

Leah saw how pleased Gracie was to be sitting with her new friend.

Milita showed the adult party to a table near enough to keep an eye on the girls but not close enough to intrude. She passed out menus and took the drink order before departing.

There was an uncomfortable silence while everyone perused their menus, no one offering to open the conversation.

After they ordered, Milita returned with their drinks and later to serve the table. Everyone dug into the delicious food.

Big Jim kept casting furtive glances at Ty as though wanting to speak but unwilling to make the first move.

Ty, for his part, kept up a conversation with his brothers, reaching to take Leah's hand every now and again.

Big Jim chose to strike up a conversation with Leah. "That sure is a pretty little girl you got there, Mrs. Benson."

Leah felt her color rising. "Oh, I'm not married," she hurried to say.

Ty shot his father a frown that all too clearly said *shut up*.

"Hey, Ty," Colton interrupted. "How did the audition go? Did you make it to *Texas Country Star*?"

Ty heaved a huge breath and switched his focus to his brother. "I don't know. My friend Will is submitting my audition tape."

"So you're just waiting?" Colton asked. "You could

come home and help out around the ranch. We could sure use an extra hand."

A complete silence followed.

Leah focused on dragging a crispy tortilla chip through the bowl of salsa Milita had set on the table. She poked it into her mouth, quickly washing it down with iced tea.

"I'm going to help Leah and her grandmother for a while." Ty's voice was dead calm. No one else spoke. Maybe no one else breathed.

Milita returned to the table and refilled the iced tea glasses at that moment. "How is everything? Do you need more warm tortillas?"

About that time, the front door clanked open, and three men came in.

Leah glanced up in time to recognize the two Carter brothers with a scrawny older man. She almost choked on the food in her mouth. Swallowing hurriedly, she reached for her tea. She shrank down beside Ty, hoping to avoid their notice.

"Well, don't that beat all?" Gran exclaimed. "It's them low-life Carters. You'd think they would stay away from the Sunday-go-to-meetin' folks." She eyed them scornfully.

Ty's head whipped around to stare at the newcomers. He wiped his mouth on his napkin and slapped it down on the table. "Stay here," he said in a low voice. He pushed back from the table and strode purposefully across the restaurant to where they stood by the front door. In a single move, he grabbed both of the Carter brothers by the arms and steered them out to the parking lot.

Every head in the restaurant turned, and people moved to the front windows to watch.

"'Bout time those Carter boys got their asses kicked," one of the diners said. Murmurs of assent resounded.

"Oh no!" Leah cried and pushed her chair back, but before she could rise, Beau grinned at Colton, and both of them sprinted for the front door.

Big Jim heaved a sigh and threw his napkin down beside his plate. "Be right back, ladies."

By the time Leah had gotten close enough to a window to see what was going on, she saw Beau laying into the one named Dean while Ray Carter was on the ground, getting his face pounded by Ty. Colton and Big Jim restrained the older Carter.

Leah's stomach was tied in knots. The recent heavy meal threatened to be tossed right there.

The scream of a siren split the air, and the sheriff's car pulled into the parking lot. The sheriff himself got out, along with one of his deputies. They ran to break up the fight.

Ty landed one last punch before being lifted off his target by Big Jim himself. Voices were raised, and a lot of finger-pointing was going on.

Leah realized her grandmother was peering out the big plateglass window right beside her.

"That Ty's got a helluva right cross," she observed pleasantly.

—⁓—

Ty felt a pair of powerful arms lift him like he weighed nothing. He was deposited on his feet, and his first reaction was to draw back his fist and round on whoever it was who had interrupted him in the midst of teaching Ray Carter not to mess with Leah or Gran.

He heaved a sigh and dropped his fist when he saw it was his father. Big Jim stood with his hands fisted at his waist, his gaze cool, but there was something else there. Could it be pride?

The tense muscles in Ty's shoulders relaxed a bit, and he turned back to the scene from which he had just been removed. Ray Carter was still stretched out on the ground, but he was moving. Dean Carter was yelling and being restrained by the deputy. He had a cut lip, and blood was streaming from his nose and down onto his shirt. *Good for you, Little Brother.*

Old Man Carter was jumping around in front of the sheriff, yelling and pointing, while the sheriff was red-faced and looked like he was about to deck him. Another deputy pulled up and got out of his car. The sheriff called him over and gave him some kind of order, which could not be heard over Old Man Carter's tirade. The sheriff turned and marched straight over to where Ty and Big Jim were standing.

The sheriff extended a hand and Big Jim clasped it. "What happened here? Mr. Carter claims your boys jumped his sons out of the blue. Is this true?"

Big Jim looked at Ty and cocked his head.

Ty sucked in a breath and blew it out. "Yesterday, the Carters attacked Fern Davis at Walmart and injured her. They threatened her and her granddaughter. I was in the process of explaining to them how they should stay away from the ladies, and Ray threw a punch at me."

Big Jim cracked a smile. "Whoo! Big mistake."

The sheriff looked amused but stifled his grin. "And then what happened?"

"I…uh…I hit him back and kept hitting him." Ty

shrugged. "Then Dean Carter tried to jump on me, but my little brother, Beau, pulled him off."

The sheriff's mouth twitched. "Fern Davis, huh? She probably don't weigh ninety pounds. Those assholes attacked her?"

"Yessir," Ty asserted. "Knocked her down, and she has a big, bloody bandage on her elbow."

The sheriff's brows drew together. "I'll need her to make a statement."

Ty looked around and saw Leah and Gran inside the restaurant. He waved for them to come out, and they pushed their way through the crowd of onlookers.

"Oh, Ty!" Leah rushed to his side and he drew her close. "You're hurt." She gazed up at him, a stricken expression on her face. Gently, she placed her finger near his eye, and he winced.

"Yeah, he got me a good one."

The sheriff gave her a knowing look. "You're the little gal who works for Breck Ryan. I took a report on these guys harassing you."

She nodded. "And yesterday, they knocked my grandmother down."

"I think we can sort this all out at my office." The sheriff turned to his deputies and told one to transport the two Carters to his office and the other to interview the witnesses. "Big Jim, if you and your family will follow me to my office, I can take your statements there."

Leah appeared to be frozen in place. "Oh no! What does that mean?"

Ty turned to put his arm around her. "We need to tell the sheriff everything that happened. He can decide what to do."

Concern etched her face as she gazed up at him. "Are you in trouble?"

"Probably." Ty grinned and only then realized he had a split lip. "But it won't be the first time."

Big Jim leaned closer. "Why don't you take your brothers in your truck, and I'll bring the ladies? I don't think that little girl needs to be in the middle of this."

Ty nodded. "Thanks, Dad." To Leah, he said, "Go with my father. You and your grandmother can file a report on the attack at the store yesterday."

Leah nodded wordlessly, her hand on his forearm. "I want Gracie to stay here at the restaurant with her friend. Milita will watch her until we're done. Please be careful."

He gave her a kiss, which made his lip hurt, but he didn't care. "Don't worry. Everything will be okay."

Leah gathered Gran and shepherded her back to where Big Jim Garrett stood waiting for them. He assisted Gran into the front seat and closed the door, then reached to take Leah's hand and assisted her into the back seat. "Thank you," she whispered.

She noted that he didn't appear as fearsome as when they had first met. The thread that united them was their mutual concern for Ty.

Gran's face clouded. "Is Ty going to be all right? I feel bad that your boy got in trouble while fightin' them Carters for me."

Leah was surprised when Big Jim turned to pat Gran's hand. "Of course he'll be fine, Miz Fern. Don't you worry."

When they arrived at the sheriff's office, Ty's truck was parked and empty. She presumed the three brothers had trooped inside.

As Big Jim was turning off the motor, Breck and his wife pulled alongside. He got out but left the truck idling, and his wife remained inside. When they met up in front of the office, Breck said, "I thought I better come along in case I'm needed."

Big Jim pounded him on the shoulder. "Glad we can count on you, Breck. No telling what my sons might say."

Breck made a motion toward the door and swung it wide for Leah and Gran to pass. The outer office seemed to be filled with people. Both the Carters were inside, with the deputies standing between them. Ty, Beau, and Colton leaned up against the opposite wall. If looks could kill, they would have all been goners.

Breck and Big Jim hailed the sheriff as he emerged from the back of the building.

"Breckenridge T. Ryan, Esquire, are you representing the Garrett boys?" the sheriff asked.

"I am," Breck assured him.

The Carters exchanged a baleful glance and then resumed their hate-filled glares across the room.

The sheriff directed his deputies to escort the Carter brothers to two separate offices to take their statements. Ray dragged himself to his feet, and Leah noted he was limping as he made his way down the hall. Dean followed behind him, but she saw the deputy pull him into a different room.

Leah wanted all this to be over with so she could take her small family back to Gran's farm and keep them safe. Now that Ty was with them, everything would be better.

The sheriff gestured for Leah and her grandmother to be seated in the outer office and then motioned for Ty and Breck to follow him and led them down the hall.

She drew a shaky breath and pressed her lips together. "Don't worry, Leah," Beau said. "We didn't throw the first punch. I'm sure the witnesses will bear that out."

Leah noted the bloodied knuckles on both his hands. He looked relatively unscathed otherwise.

"Those Carters have been devilin' me ever since my Albert passed on." Gran shook her head. "It sure done my heart good to see 'em take a poundin'."

Leah put her hand on Gran's arm. "Don't say anything like that to the sheriff. That might make it worse."

Gran nodded wisely.

Leah felt like she was under intense scrutiny as Big Jim and Ty's brothers kept glancing at her. She didn't know what they were expecting of her. What had Ty's previous girlfriends looked like? For certain they didn't have a child. They didn't have the baggage Leah brought with her.

She remained still, trying not to call attention to herself. Beau and Colton exchanged a few words, mostly light banter, but she sensed Big Jim was as concerned as she was. Leah stood up and went outside for a breath of fresh air. She made a conscious effort to smooth out her furrowed brow. Pacing back and forth, she tried to release the tension in her neck and shoulders. When Leah turned, she ran smack into Big Jim Garrett. "Oh, sorry!"

He steadied her with a hand on her arm. "Easy. Are you okay?"

She nodded. "I just had to step outside. I thought

I might explode in there…and I'm concerned about
Gracie. We've been through so much together. She's
not used to being separated from me for very long."

Big Jim released her. "Don't worry about your
daughter. I'm sure she's doing okay with Milita Rios.
She's a fine young woman." He fumbled for his cell
phone. "Why don't you call and check on her? She's
probably worried about you too."

Leah smiled. "That won't be necessary. She's with
her friend. I'm just being overprotective."

Big Jim's craggy face split into a grin. "You must be
very proud of your little girl."

She released a sigh. "That I am. I just want to make
sure she's safe. And my gran too. I'm worried these men
might come by the ranch when I'm at work."

Big Jim gave her an odd look. "Let's see what we can
do about that." He held the door open for her to return
to the waiting area.

After a while, Ty came out and thumped Beau on
the arm. "Your turn." He took the seat beside Leah that
Beau had vacated. He held out his hand to Leah, and
when she slipped her hand into his, he kissed her fingers. She noted that his knuckles also looked as if he had
shredded them against a rasp.

After Beau, the sheriff questioned Colton and then
asked Miz Fern Davis to step into his office. Leah
started to rise, but the sheriff waved her back to her seat.
It appeared he wanted to question Gran by herself.

"Don't worry," Colton said. "Breck Ryan is there,
and he won't let her say anything she shouldn't."

Leah swallowed, hoping he was right. She didn't
know where she would get the money to pay Mr. Ryan,

but perhaps he would just take it out of her paycheck... maybe a little at a time.

After Gran came out, looking somewhat smug, the sheriff motioned for Leah to follow him. She stood and took in a deep breath. *Just stick to what happened with the Carters.*

As she was being escorted to the sheriff's office, she noted that the rooms where the Carters had been taken were now empty. She imagined they had finished their statements when she was outside. But how had they gone? She hadn't seen them make an exit. Maybe there was a side door? When she entered the sheriff's office, she saw Breck leaning against the far wall. Just the sight of him strengthened her resolve.

"Sit down, Leah. This won't take long," he assured her. "Tell the sheriff what happened at Walmart yesterday when your grandmother was assaulted by Ray Carter."

"Assaulted? Oh, I guess she was." Leah sat in the wooden chair across from the sheriff, who turned on a small recorder.

He asked her to state her name and her relationship to Fern Davis. Then he asked her to relate the events of the morning when she and Fern Davis had encountered Ray and Dean Carter at the local Walmart.

Leah responded as well as she could, recounting the incident in question and the threat when Dean Carter had promised to pay them a visit.

The sheriff asked a few more questions and then shut the recorder off. "I think that will do it. Be sure to see the judge first thing Monday morning." He frowned, the set of his mouth grim. "Tell him to call me 'bout all this

trouble." The sheriff stood and reached out a hand to
Breck and then to Leah.

She allowed him to shake hands with her but wondered what she needed to meet with a judge about the
next day. She glanced at Breck uncertainly.

He ushered her through the door and down the hall.
"Tomorrow," he said, "we'll go see the judge about a
restraining order."

Once outside, Ty arranged Leah and Gran in his truck.
Breck and his wife took off for their ranch with a curt
nod.

Ty said goodbye to his brothers, and they piled into
his dad's truck. That only left one person to be dealt
with. He turned to his father.

"Thanks, Dad. I appreciate everything you've done
today." He offered his hand, which seemed oddly
formal after the big, back-slapping man hugs he'd been
exchanging with his brothers.

Big Jim took the hand and pumped it twice with a
firm grip. "I did nothing."

Ty held his gaze. "Thanks for being so nice to Leah
and her family. They mean a lot to me."

Big Jim nodded. "I can tell. You take care of yourself, boy. Don't go looking for any more fights."

"Can't promise that. I have to protect Leah and her
grandmother from the Carters."

Big Jim snorted out a derisive sound. "No, you don't.
Let the law take care of the Carter boys. You just stay
clear."

Ty shrugged. "I will if they will."

———

After an amorous night of lovemaking, wherein Ty proved beyond a shadow of a doubt that he had no serious injuries resulting from his encounter with the Carters, Leah drove into Langston the next morning.

She was surprised to find Breck had arrived before her. When she looked in on him, he was lolled back in his chair with his boots propped up on his desk. He grinned at her. "Ready?"

"Um, I guess. What am I ready for?"

He swung his boots off the desk. "We're going to see the judge."

Talons of fear clawed their way up her throat. "What? Now?"

He grabbed his Stetson and headed toward the doorway she was blocking. "Sure. We want it in place before the Carters get out of jail." He settled the hat on his head and gestured for her to precede him.

She was glad she hadn't bothered to put her purse in her desk yet. "They're in jail?"

"They started the fight at Tio's and assaulted your grandmother the previous day." Breck escorted her out the front, putting the closed sign in place before helping her up into his truck. "If we time this right, we might get to Judge Horton before court."

Leah buckled her seat belt as Breck started the truck and headed for the highway. They drove in silence to the county seat, where he parked in front of the courthouse. Leah scrambled out, clutching her small handbag under her arm.

After walking down a long corridor, Breck knocked

on a door marked *Private*. A stern voice called out, "Enter."

Breck leaned into the doorway. "Judge? Got a minute?"

The small man, decked out in cowboy regalia, turned with a grin on his face. "I've always got a minute for you, Breck. Who is this pretty little thing?"

Breck introduced Leah and very quickly produced copies of the statements she and Gran had made the previous day.

The judge scanned them over quickly, his brow furrowed. "I know the name Carter."

"They've been in trouble before, but it's escalating, Your Honor." Breck outlined the need for what he called a TRO for both brothers on behalf of Leah and her grandmother.

The judge picked up his phone and asked someone to step into his office. Almost immediately, a pleasant-looking woman entered through a different door. The judge outlined what he wished her to prepare, and when she had gone, he slipped into a black robe hanging on a rack. "Daisy will get the documents drawn up right away, and I'll sign them. You're welcome to wait right here." The judge took his leave after effusive thanks from Breck.

Leah was feeling a bit bewildered, having no idea what a TRO was. She sat down in one of the leather chairs and clasped her hands in her lap.

In a few minutes, the aforementioned Daisy returned for Breck to look over the papers she presented. He approved them, and she disappeared again. Breck leaned back in his chair, apparently satisfied that he had accomplished his objective.

The next time Daisy appeared, she presented Breck with a sheaf of papers in a folder. He looked them over and then thanked her. He turned to Leah and she stood, following him out the door. She heard Daisy turn the lock behind them.

"Well, you look mighty pleased with yourself, Breck," she said. They traced their way back down the long hallway, their shoes sounding loud on the polished granite floors.

He chuckled. "I just got the judge to sign temporary restraining orders against each of the Carters on behalf of you and your grandmother." He shrugged, setting the hat back on his head. "It's only a piece of paper, and it won't protect either of you, but if they violate the order, the consequences will have more teeth."

She sucked in a breath when they stepped out into the heat. The air was dry, like walking into an oven. Breck tucked her into the truck and went around. For a moment, the feeling of baking in a blast furnace overwhelmed her, but then Breck got in and turned on the air conditioner full force. As they headed back to Langston, Leah hoped the pieces of paper would be enough to keep the Carters from any further contact with her or her grandmother. It didn't matter to her that the Carters could be punished for violating the restraining order. It did matter that they probably would anyway.

Chapter 11

CELIA DIAZ LOOKED UP JUST AS A TALL AND BROAD-shouldered young man filled the doorway of her classroom. He was very neatly dressed in a nicely pressed western shirt, Wranglers, boots, and a belt with a big buckle. Of course, he topped it all off with the requisite white Stetson. *Can you say "cowboy"?*

He swept off his hat and smiled down at the little girl whose hand he held. Her other arm was in a cast.

"Can I help you?" Celia climbed off the step stool where she had been tacking decorations on the bulletin board.

"Yes, ma'am." The cowboy spoke in a deep voice. "The principal said you were in your classroom, so we just came down to meet you. This is Gracie Benson, and I'm Tyler Garrett."

Celia noted the different last names with interest. "I'm so happy to meet you." She extended a hand and found it enveloped in a big, warm grasp. "Garrett? I've heard that name. Isn't there a big Garrett ranch around here somewhere?"

"Yes, ma'am. That would be my father's spread."

She cleared her throat and glanced down at the little girl. *Totally opposite coloring. Can't be related.* "And how are you, Gracie?" Celia flashed a smile.

The girl beamed. "I'm fine, thank you."

Celia looked back at Tyler. "Are you her father... brother?"

He shook his head. "No, ma'am. We're not related. I'm a close friend of the family. Gracie's mother is working, so I got her registered today."

"Enrolled," Celia corrected automatically.

"Um, yes, ma'am. Well, Gracie is enrolled to start your class."

Celia smiled. "That was very nice of you."

Ty clasped both his hands around Gracie's good hand. "I have a favor to ask you, Miss Diaz," he said. "We've been having a little trouble with some local fellows. Could you make sure she gets on the bus safely after school?"

Celia glanced from man to child and back again. "Well, of course I will," she said rather explosively. Did he think she just threw them out the door? "Young man, I have taught elementary school students for sixteen years. I assure you that I take the safety of every single student very personally. Of course I will see to it that she is safely on the bus each day. No problem."

Tyler grinned. "We sure do appreciate it."

"So you won't be picking her up yourself?" Celia asked.

"Her mother works until five, but I might be picking her up if I'm in town."

Celia offered her hand again. "Well, between us then, we'll make sure she arrives home safely. I'll see you on the first day of school, Gracie." She noted that the little girl looked less anxious than she had when she first entered the room. Celia smiled and waved as they left.

When Leah pulled in at the doctor's parking lot, she saw that Ty's truck was already there. She went inside

and found him and Gracie grinning at her. "Sorry to
be late."

"It's okay," Ty said. "Gracie is the last patient of the
day. The nurse took her in for an X-ray of her wrist and sent
the image to some specialist over at the county hospital."

Leah sank into the chair beside him and heaved a
huge sigh. "Thanks so much for helping us out. Being
new on the job, I didn't want to ask for time off."

The receptionist pushed a pen and clipboard across
the counter at Leah. "You're the mother? You need to
fill out her information."

Leah procured the paperwork and went back to her
seat. She quickly added the missing information and
returned it to the desk. She produced Gracie's immuni-
zation records and sat back down.

When the nurse motioned for Gracie to follow her to
the back, Leah took her by the hand.

The doctor was Breck's wife, Cami, and she smiled a
greeting. "Hello again. Good to see you two."

"Hello, Dr. Ryan."

"I sent the images of Gracie's wrist to a pediatric
orthopedic surgeon over at County Hospital. He just
called to confirm that her cast can come off, and he
faxed a set of exercises for her to do. He'll want to see
her in person in a couple of weeks."

Leah glanced at Gracie, whose eyes widened. Leah's
throat constricted with anguish. She was so sorry she had
inadvertently brought this injury to her child. Mutely,
she nodded at the doctor.

"I'll remove it right now," Cami said. "School starts
next week, and I'm sure you would like to get rid of this
thing."

Gracie's face lit up.

"Yes, please," Leah said.

In a short time, Gracie had been divested of her cast. The arm looked thinner than its mate, and the skin was paler.

"You can do some simple exercises to strengthen your wrist, Gracie," Cami offered and handed a paper to Leah with instructions for the exercises on it. She checked in a drawer and found a squishy ball for Gracie. "Try to squeeze this a lot when you're watching television or reading. It will help."

Gracie rotated her wrist gingerly and breathed out a sigh. She was sent out the door with an apple instead of a lollipop.

When they got back to the waiting room, Ty stood grinning at her. "There you go! Now we can arm wrestle."

Leah snorted. "I think not! She has some exercises to do to strengthen her wrist."

"Aww, you're no fun." He ruffled her hair.

When they were outside, Ty tucked them both in Leah's car and leaned in the window. "We better get back to the house. I hated to leave your grandmother alone out there all day, but I told her to call me if there was any trouble."

Leah nodded, and he went to his truck. She started her car and pulled out into the street with Ty's big, red vehicle on her tail. Somehow, just having him as her shepherd chased away any fear she might have had hovering in the back of her mind.

Gracie chattered about her new teacher and about how she would work on the exercises every day.

When they reached Gran's, the door was flung open,

and both dogs raced out to greet them, while Gran waited on the porch, her brow furrowed. Gracie ran up to meet her, babbling about the events of her day.

Ty was just pulling in when Leah made it to the porch. Gracie had already gone inside. "What's wrong?" Leah whispered.

"I think your friend from Oklahoma came a-callin' today."

Ice-cold fear slashed through Leah's chest. A huge tremor wracked her body as she dropped her purse. "Oh!" she whispered, covering her mouth with both hands.

Gran's eyes were grim. "Big, tall, blondish feller? Rough lookin'? I told him I hadn't seen you in years." She shrugged. "I don't know if he believed me or not, but he left."

Leah leaned against the doorframe to keep from dropping to her knees. "Oh no. Not now."

"Come on," Gran said. "Here comes Ty. After everything that happened with them Carters, maybe you don't want to spring this on him."

Leah nodded. She picked up her purse and pushed through the door. *No! I can't believe Caine found us so quickly. I thought I was being really careful.* She sank onto the sofa and tried to compose herself.

"Look, Mommy," Gracie said. "I can squeeze the ball real hard."

Leah plastered a fake smile on her face. "Good girl."

The next morning, Ty woke up early with Leah in his arms. Somehow, this just felt right, as though he should awaken every morning with this sweet face on his shoulder.

It was first light, and he could barely discern her features. A slight smile graced her pretty mouth, and her long lashes rested on her cheeks. She appeared to be sleeping peacefully, a much-improved state from the night before. She had been closed up and quiet all through dinner, seemingly wrapped in her own thoughts until someone jostled her out of her trance with a direct question.

This puzzled him. She had been in a great mood after they left the doctor's office. What happened between Langston and her grandmother's place to bring her so far down?

Perhaps Gran had said something to her. Maybe about the fight? Ty hadn't intended to exchange blows with Ray Carter, but then, Ty hadn't thrown the first punch.

He flexed the fingers of his right hand. Still a little stiff and swollen around the knuckles. *Nothing damaged. Nothing permanent.* The bruise on his cheek had turned a nice purple, and his lower lip was healing. He remembered how Ray had looked after the fight. He'd definitely gotten the worse part of the exchange. Dean too. His little brother had served him up proud. Maybe it was enough to keep them from bothering Leah or Gran again. Somehow, he doubted it. If they had two brain cells to rub together, they might have gotten the message, but he had a feeling the Carters were running on pure instinct and they didn't know how to back down.

Well, I better stick around until they figure it out. If they come around here, they'll be sorry.

Leah sailed through work that day. She felt especially proficient in performing her simple duties. She tried not to think about Caine's visit to the farm. She tried not to think about the Carters or how angry they had looked after their losing battle with the Garretts.

She focused on sorting and filing, and when her brain had an idle moment, she thought about Gracie and how happy she'd been to be released from the cast, about how she had made a friend in Tina, Milita's niece, and how she seemed to have gotten over her dread of starting school.

"Everything is going to be fine," she said aloud, repeating Ty's mantra. It seemed to work for him.

She had left him with Gracie and Gran that morning, for once knowing they would be protected from any evil that might be out there.

When Breck came in, he told her he had hand delivered the paperwork on the restraining orders to the sheriff and that Ray Carter had been released yesterday evening, but Dean was being held for the assault on her grandmother.

Leah shuddered, remembering the scowling brothers and their bloody faces.

Breck cocked his head and grinned. "Don't worry. Ray Carter can take a licking and keep on ticking."

She nodded, trying to force a smile. It didn't make her happy to see anyone hurt, even men as despicable as the Carters. She considered confiding in Breck about her reason for leaving Oklahoma, but the entire story was just too painful, and she was afraid he would tell her, as a lawyer, that Caine might have some rights over her child, even though he had forced himself on her. That, she could not bear to hear.

She busied herself with the files until lunchtime. Just before noon, the phone rang, and when she answered it, using her professional voice, she was met with a giggle.

"Well, don't you sound all citified?" Sara Beth was always a welcome respite.

"Hey, that's my job." Leah grinned in spite of her concerns.

"C'mon down to the shop. Frank grilled some ribs last night, and I brought leftovers."

"Sure thing. I'm on my way." Leah put the clockface sign in the door and locked up quickly. She almost ran to the little shop and pushed through the glass-front door. The cowbell clanked to announce her.

"Grab a fork," Sara Beth called.

When Leah got close to the counter, she saw it was covered with paper towels, and two disposable plates were filled with food. Ribs swimming in barbecue sauce had already been piled on the plates along with a generous helping of coleslaw.

"Oh, mercy!" Leah gasped. "This all looks amazing."

"Dig in," Sara Beth invited, tearing off a couple of paper towels and handing them to her. "I'm expecting this to get real messy."

"Smells divine." Leah's stomach gave a loud growl. She slid onto the stool across the counter from Sara Beth and picked up a plastic fork to take a big scoop of the slaw. The crispy, grated cabbage was mixed with just the right amount of grated carrot, and the dressing was creamy and rich. "Mmmmm…" she intoned.

"Glad you like it." Sara Beth picked up a rib with her fingers and began to gnaw the meat from the bone, smearing enough barbecue sauce to decorate her mouth, her cheeks, and the tip of her nose. "My Frank made this sauce himself. I'm just crazy about it."

Leah enjoyed the repast as much as the developing

friendship. She couldn't recall the last time she had a real friend. She hoped she would be able to stay here and let her friendships ripen, as well as her romance with Ty.

———⁓———

Ty drove into Langston with Gracie. He planned to stop by the feed store and pick up feed for his horse as well as the dogs. He had offered to take Gran with him, but she declined.

"Someone needs to stay here and guard the place," she said.

Earlier, Gracie had proudly shown off her three new school outfits. This triggered his decision to make the trip to Langston. Maybe a little more shopping was in order. He stopped by the law office when they first arrived to tell Leah he had Gracie with him and just to see her face.

"What is this?" He made a swipe at a deep-orange smudge by her mouth.

"Oh!" She colored. "I ate some barbecue ribs with Sara Beth. Really delicious, but I got the sauce all over me."

He leaned over to steal a kiss and Gracie giggled. "Yep. Delicious."

He told her they might take a drive to Amarillo if he couldn't find what he needed in town, and she didn't object.

"Have a nice drive." She waved as they left the office.

Now, he and Gracie were in a shopping mall and he was helping her to find a comfortable pair of shoes. The store clerk checked the fit and Gracie stood up. "Oh, these are so springy."

"Good for running and jumping," Ty said. He also helped her find a pretty pair of shoes to go with her new Sunday dresses.

"I've never had two new pairs of shoes before," she said, delight apparent on her face.

He didn't reply to that but was glad he could make it happen for her. When they left the mall, Ty was laden with all kinds of bags. They had selected about a dozen new outfits for school and a warm winter coat from the various stores.

Gracie skipped along at his side, wearing a pair of her new shoes. "Mommy is going to be so surprised."

He tucked her in the truck and stowed the bags on the back seat.

When they returned to Langston, he did indeed pick up the items he needed at the feed store. He turned off the highway onto the farm-to-market road leading to Gran's place and noticed a group of turkey vultures circling overhead in the distance. He watched them as he made the turn onto the caliche road leading to the house and realized they were circling something in the field to the west of the house on Gran's property. *Probably a dead rabbit or raccoon. Maybe it got hit on the road and dragged itself off into the field to die.*

Ty had every intention of plowing that field and putting in some winter rye grass to feed the cattle. As he got closer to the house, he saw an old truck on the road with the driver's door open.

He slowed and peered inside as they crept slowly by. It was a faded blue, and the seats were torn. He didn't know who would be coming way out here to call on Leah's grandmother, but he got an uneasy feeling about it and sped up, not slowing until he reached Gran's house.

The minute he stopped the motor, Gracie leapt out and ran to the house, excited to show off her new shoes.

She was jumping up and down impatiently, waiting for Gran to get to the door.

Ty felt a wave of relief wash over him when Gran opened the door and the two dogs rushed out. Heaving a sigh, he grabbed the packages and followed Gracie into the house.

When he stepped inside, Gracie was clutched to Gran's chest, babbling about all the new clothes Ty had bought her. The expression on Gran's face could be described as grim at best.

Ty set the packages down on the sofa and told Gracie to take them to her room. When she had disappeared down the hall, he turned with a frown. "Miz Fern, did I do something wrong? I just wanted to make sure Gracie had enough clothes to start school."

She waved her hand. "No. No, that ain't it. I just got some bad news for Leah when she comes home." She wrapped both arms around her frail torso, seeming to fold in on herself.

"Well, tell me. Maybe I can help." The very last thing Leah needed was bad news when she was just barely getting on her feet. "Maybe it's not so bad."

She went into the kitchen and took a seat at the chrome-and-plastic dinette set, clasping her hands on the table in front of her. She shook her head. "It's the worst. That feller she run away from in Oklahoma. He was here lookin' for her. I don't think he's right in the head." She raised her gaze to meet Ty's. "He's got that sick animal look, like somethin' that needs to be put down."

The back of Ty's neck prickled with her words. "I thought he was in jail."

Gran nodded. "I did too, but he was here, bigger 'n' meaner lookin' than I ever thought a man could look."

Ty pulled out a chair across from her and collapsed into it. "Damn!"

"Exactly."

Leah left work, looking around for the Carters' old blue truck. Maybe the temporary restraining order had done the trick. Maybe the Carters would stay away from now on. Maybe being confronted by Ty had taught them a lesson.

Still, a lingering apprehension settled in the pit of her stomach, accompanying her all the way down the highway. When she turned off on the farm-to-market road heading to Gran's, she heaved a deep sigh. Probably nothing to worry about. Let the law take care of the Carter brothers. Since Dean Carter remained in jail, maybe that would keep the other from acting on his own. Charges of assaulting her grandmother might not amount to much since Gran wasn't seriously injured, but she might have been.

There was nothing Leah could do about it at this point. She just hoped the violence had come to an end. And there was nothing she wanted more than to forget about the Carters and concentrate on making a good life here with her family.

She smiled, knowing the word *family* also included Ty, at least in her own mind.

Leah was still smiling when she turned onto the caliche road that dead-ended at Gran's place. *Almost home*. She thought she would change into her old, beat-up jeans and a T-shirt to see if she could help Ty with anything or maybe just sit on the porch and listen to him sing.

With a sickening lurch to her stomach, she spied the blue truck just ahead. The breath seemed to be caught in her throat. "Oh no! Oh no!" she moaned over and over again. "Please don't let them cause any trouble." Realizing the truck was stopped and the door open, she stomped on the brake with both feet. *What are they up to?*

Making sure the doors were locked, she peered around anxiously. The truck's driver side door was open, as though someone had jumped out, intending to get back in hurriedly. She had a suspicion they were up to their usual tricks, or worse. They had cut the fences in the past. *What would they do this time?* The fields were fallow, overgrown with high weeds. It would be easy to start a fire with all the dry grasses growing by the side of the road and into the fields. She realized a fire would be impossible to stop, spreading rapidly to the barns and outbuildings…to the little farmhouse.

Leah's imagination played out worsening disasters. *No, not going to let them get away with it.* She sucked in a breath and clicked her seat belt open. The sound of the wind rustling through the high grass sent a prickle of fear along her skin. Stepping out, she heard something else and glanced up. *Birds…big ones.* They were flying overhead, circling around with their big wings spread. She saw where the dried grass had been parted. Yes, the fence had been cut, and someone had stomped right through into the field. She was frightened, but more than that, she was furious. Her heart pumped out righteous anger in a tempo she could hear in her ears. *I'm not going to let them get away with this. Not again.*

Her foot collided with a large rock and she stumbled. She swallowed hard, picking it up with both hands as she stepped through the same gap in the fence. Although she tried to move soundlessly, her approach through the tall rustling grass would be heard by anyone in the area. The path veered to the left and she followed it, hoping to avert any damage to her Gran's property. Gripping the rock, she mentally rehearsed how she would clobber any Carter if she found him up to no good. *What else could he be doing here?*

She tightened her grip on the large rock as she crept forward. One of the birds swooped down just ahead of her. She heard it scratching around in the grass. When she stepped into a clear space where the grass had been beaten down, she froze. The rock fell from her hand into a pool of blood.

A man lay sprawled before her, his face bloodied and a gaping wound slashed from his chest all the way down to his stomach. He appeared to have been eviscerated. Giant black birds were gathered around him, picking at his entrails.

A tremor seized her, shaking her from head to foot. She couldn't draw a breath. Her gag reflex went into overdrive as she choked back the bile rising in her throat. She thought she screamed, but it came out as a whimper.

She looked down at her feet and saw that she was standing in the blood. Turning, she ran blindly back through the brush to her car and started it with shaking hands. *I have to get away. I have to get away.*

She peeled out and around the blue truck, her tires skidding in the dry, dusty road. *What if whoever did this has been to the house? What if my family…* She wheeled in at Gran's place and threw the car into park. Looking up, she saw Ty come out onto the porch, his brows knit into a frown.

She covered her face with both hands, giving in to the horror she had just discovered. *How could something like this happen?*

"Honey? What's wrong?" Ty opened the car door and pulled her to her feet. She collapsed against him, and he lifted her in his arms. "Baby, what happened? Are you all right?" He carried her toward the house.

"No! Don't go in there," she whispered. "There's a dead man."

"No, there's not," he assured her. "Everyone is fine."

"Please listen to me," she moaned, her voice trailing down to a whine. "You have to call the sheriff. There's a dead man out in the field. I saw him."

Ty stopped in his tracks. "You found a dead man?"

"Yes, and I don't want to scare Gracie. It was awful. Just call the sheriff."

Ty set her on the porch, and she collapsed into the old wicker rocking chair. She heard him make the call as she stared blindly in front of her. *What would this mean to her grandmother? Did she know the dead man? What about the Carters' truck abandoned on the road? Could it be one of them?*

Her grandmother came out onto the porch, looking worried, but Ty put a hand on her shoulder. Speaking in a low tone, he brought her up to speed and asked her to keep Gracie distracted. She nodded and hurried inside.

In a short time, the scream of sirens split the air. As they drew closer, Leah's panic grew until she felt she was being strangled. Suddenly, the sound stopped as two cruisers from the sheriff's office careened into the yard. The sheriff and two deputies spilled out of the cars and came running onto the porch where Ty stood beside Leah.

"What's this about a body?" the sheriff demanded.

"Me. I found it." Leah raised her hand like a schoolgirl. "It's all chewed up. I mean there are birds…eating on him…" She gave in to a violent shudder.

Ty put his arm around her shoulder and squatted down beside her.

"Where?" the sheriff asked. "In the house?"

"No, no," she insisted. "By the truck."

Puzzled, the sheriff looked over at Ty's truck.

Ty frowned at her. "That old blue truck sitting down the road? I passed by that earlier."

She nodded. "Yes. That's the one. It belongs to the Carters. They went after me with their truck. I'll never forget." She rubbed her hands up and down her arms to chase away the gooseflesh.

"Dean Carter is still in custody." The sheriff cocked his head to one side. "Just exactly where is this body?"

"In the field. I saw the fence was cut. The Carters did that before, and Ty repaired it. When I saw the truck and the cut wire, I went to see…" She covered her mouth with both hands and stifled a shiver.

Ty squeezed her shoulder. "You knew it was the Carters' truck, and you went there anyway? What were you thinking? Those men are dangerous."

She nodded helplessly. "I know. I just wanted to see what they were doing. I followed their trail, and when I got to the end, I found this dead man, his insides spilled out all around him." This vision in her head caused her to flinch.

"You two stay here," the sheriff ordered and returned to his vehicle. He backed out, followed by the deputies in the other car.

She sat staring at the place where the flashing lights stopped.

Ty kissed her temple. "I can't believe you got out of your car to go after one of the Carters. Honey, that was just foolhardy."

"I know. But I was really angry they would come around here again, even with the restraining order in place."

He stroked his hand over her hair. "What did you hope to accomplish? Either one of them could have snapped your neck in a second."

She nodded, unable to comprehend that she had been in danger; she'd just wanted to protect her family. She sat and waited, not wanting to take her anguish inside the house, knowing the sheriff would be back with more questions, knowing he too would want to know what she had been thinking when she jumped out of her car to challenge the trespasser.

~~~

Ty was dumbfounded. *How could she do something like going alone to confront one of the Carters? Why didn't she come up to the house to get me?*

He huffed out a breath. Of course, he hadn't known whose truck it was. If he had, he might have done the same thing. He was a lot better equipped to deal with the scumbag Carters. But then, he'd had Gracie with him, so even had he known, he would have continued on to the house... but he would have gone right back to find out what was going on. He supposed he could see her perspective.

"Was it—" He cleared his suddenly husky throat. "Was it one of the Carters?"

She shrugged, continued to stare off into the distance. "Could be. I—I couldn't tell. His face was all bloody. Crushed really. And there was blood everywhere."

What a day. He recalled coming home to Gran looking distraught because she thought Leah's boogeyman had come to call. Could there be a connection between the arrival of this Caine guy and the death in the field? And if it wasn't one of the Carters, what was their truck doing abandoned by the side of the road?

The sun was starting to cast long shadows, and dusk was coming on strong.

Ty's cell phone sounded and he checked the caller. *Will.* He sucked in a deep breath and let it all out. He wasn't in the mood to take a big helping of guilt over returning to Langston. He glanced at Leah, but she was still staring off into space. He moved to the opposite end of the porch and squatted down.

"Hey," Ty said by way of greeting when he answered the call.

"Hey, man! Just got the call. You made it!"

For a moment, Ty sat back on his haunches with a puzzled expression on his face. "What are you talking about?"

"The show. The producer called, and you're in. You're on your way to being the next Country Idol."

This news rocked Ty. He rolled down to sit with his back against the front of the house. "Whoa! You don't mean it."

"Yep, I do. So get your ass back here to Dallas as soon as possible. We need to plan your launch. Every minute is precious. Ticktock, man…ticktock."

Stunned, Ty remained where he was after he had disconnected from Will. He was all at once thrilled and petrified. What would happen if he left Leah alone now? Too much could go wrong.

First, there was the entire Carter family, and now this Caine guy.

Ty thought about taking Leah with him, but that was insane. Gracie still had to go to school, and Gran needed protection too. He couldn't leave them alone and vulnerable. Will would have to understand.

Ty sat back down beside Leah as the sky darkened, enveloping them in a comforting late-summer world. Crickets chirped and frogs peeped. The air was heavy with the scent of impending rain. *That's what we need. A good rain to wash away the dust…and the blood.*

At dusk, the sheriff returned and told them the body was being removed to the medical examiner's office in Amarillo. He turned on his flashlight and asked them to stand up.

Ty climbed to his feet and held out a hand to Leah. She stood beside him, looking small and frightened.

The flashlight beam traveled over both of them. He asked them to turn around and examined their clothing in detail. "Young lady," his deep voice boomed. "I'm gonna need those shoes."

Leah looked down at her feet, and so did Ty. The white summer slip-ons had dark spatters on them and the same dark goo caked on the sides.

"Oh no!" she wailed.

The sheriff put her shoes in a plastic bag and returned to glare at them, a stern expression on his face. "Considering the history of bad feelings between the

Carters and the Davises and that dustup between Tyler and the Carter brothers, I'm gonna have to ask both of you not to leave town anytime soon."

Chapter 12

THE NEXT MORNING, LEAH RELATED THE ENTIRE story to Breck.

He frowned and asked lots of questions, things she had never considered. Had she touched anything? Could there have been anyone else there in the area? Did she pass any other vehicles on the road that might have been coming from the crime scene? Was there a weapon left behind? Describe the wound…

Breck's frown grew even more intense, especially when he learned the sheriff had confiscated her shoes. "You stay right here. I'll be back." He grabbed his Stetson and jammed it on his head before storming out the front door. He slammed it so hard the beveled glass panel rattled in his wake.

Leah sat behind her desk and clasped her hands together to keep them from shaking. *Now what?* She was almost through with the estate files. She went back to the sorting table and surveyed the array of somewhat controlled chaos strewn across it. At least this would keep her brain occupied so she didn't have a complete meltdown.

Breck returned about an hour later. He tossed his Stetson on the coatrack and came to sit across from her at the table she used for sorting files. He leaned back in his chair and propped his boots on the edge of the table. His expression was so grim it sucked the air right out of her lungs.

"What?" She wheezed out the breathy question.

"The body has been identified as that of Ray Carter."

Leah clasped her hands over her heart, as if that would keep it from jumping out of her chest.

"When the medical examiner's men removed the body, they found a pair of very sharp shears underneath him. It must have been what Ray was using to cut the fence line."

"Shears? Like scissors?" she asked.

"No, these were antique shears, like they used to cut sheep's wool before modern electric clippers were invented." A muscle in Breck's jaw twitched. "It was strong enough to go through twisted wire...or flesh. Someone used them to open him up from stem to stern."

Leah yelped. "Oh, how horrible!" Even someone as vicious as Ray Carter didn't deserve to be brutalized in such a manner.

"The ME hasn't returned his preliminary report yet, but the sheriff talked to him when I was there, and the doc is thinking maybe Ray was dead before he was cut open."

"Dead? How?"

"He had extensive facial injuries. He thinks Ray died from blunt force trauma, and the slashing was the aftermath."

Leah recalled Ray's face the last time she had seen him, bloody and swollen from the pounding Ty had given him. She swallowed against the bile at the back of her throat. "What kind of person could do something like that?"

Breck cocked his brow at her. "Well, your boyfriend, Tyler Garrett, was the first one who came to mind. He did just get through giving Ray quite a pounding this past Sunday."

Leah shook her head vigorously. "No way! Ty would never do something like that. He's the sweetest, most gentle man I've ever known. It's just not in him to be cruel."

"I hope you're right. Ray's father is telling anybody who will listen that it must have been Ty or maybe all the Garrett brothers. He's making Ty out to be the killer."

Her stomach twisted into a knot. "Surely no one will believe that. Not anyone who knows Ty."

Breck shook his head. "Hope not, but it's still worrisome." He swung his boots off the table and righted his chair. "Ty stated that he was in Amarillo yesterday. That he took your daughter to get some school clothes, and that he saw the truck but didn't know it belonged to the Carters."

Leah swallowed hard. "So it couldn't have been him. He was with Gracie all day. He stopped by here after lunch to let me know he was leaving town with her."

Breck stood, staring down at her and rubbing his chin. "Hope that will clear him. It all depends on the time of death. We just have to wait for the medical examiner to make his ruling."

Ty called Will to let him know he wouldn't be able to leave Langston. He had expected Will to be upset, but Will went ballistic.

"You're shittin' me!" Will yelled. "This is going to wreck any chance you have to make it on *Texas Country Star*. The other contestants have been building their fan bases for years. Now you're stuck there in Hicksville because some dude got killed. That just doesn't make any sense."

Ty listened to the tirade, knowing Will was right. He was scuttling any possibility of success on the show. "I know, but it can't be helped." The sheriff had told him to stay put, and he had no choice but to follow orders.

Will released a raspy groan. "You've gotta get with it. I mean, are you even on Twitter or Instagram?"

"Um, no."

"Surely you have a YouTube channel? How about Snapchat? Or something as old-school as Facebook? That's where you'll pick up the grandmas and grandpas."

"I'm not there," Ty admitted.

A loud sigh hissed through the phone. "Ty, Ty, Ty... What am I going to do with you?"

"Beats me," Ty said. "Look, if you want to back out of this, I understand."

There was a long silence. "No, I can't do that. Dammit, Ty. I'm going to make you a star in spite of yourself. Let me get started on building some social media platforms. Is there a decent photographer in that one-horse town?"

Ty raked his fingers through his hair. "Not that I recall. I can ask around."

"No, never mind. I'll send one from Dallas. That way, I'll know what I'm getting." Will disconnected abruptly, leaving Ty to stare at his cell, the dead air invading his senses like an ominous warning.

He silenced it and slipped it in his pocket. Grabbing his Stetson, he shoved it on his head and went outside. He had tuned up the tractor, and he intended to till at least one field today. Planting winter rye grass would be an easy and economical way for Gran to feed her small herd through the winter. He climbed up into the seat and started her up. *Purrs like a kitten…well, maybe more like a big old jungle cat…with the croup.* But it was running.

He put it in gear and headed for the pasture he had determined would be his first objective. The sheriff still hadn't allowed them back into the field where Ray Carter had been slaughtered.

The body had been released to the family, and there had been a small funeral in town. Not many people had actually liked the Carters, but they were all curious. Only Leah's family and the Garretts had stayed away. No point in causing a scene.

By noon, Ty had tilled the small field and returned to the house for a bite to eat. Gran made him a couple of ham and cheese sandwiches, which he washed down with a glass of milk. He thought she enjoyed her role in keeping the family fed.

She tucked a dishcloth in the waistband of her apron and took a seat opposite him. "I know you have feelings for my granddaughter, Ty."

He met her gaze. "I do."

"I hope you know she really cares for you."

Ty grinned. "Yes, I know that."

Gran sucked in a breath and nodded. "I just hope you don't go breakin' her heart. She hasn't had much experience, you know."

He smiled. "I know. I wouldn't hurt her for all the world."

Gran nodded. She looked satisfied that he would keep his word.

He was back on the tractor when his cell rang. He was half expecting another tirade from the pissed-off Will, but it was a strange number. He answered.

"Tyler Garrett?" It was a female voice.

"That's me," he said.

"Well, where the hell are you? I'm about thirty miles east of Langston right now, and Will promised me a bonus if I get some great shots of you back to him tonight."

"The photographer?" He hadn't thought Will would hustle up someone the same day, but then, knowing how impatient his friend was, he realized sooner was better than later. He gave her directions, and she said she would see him soon.

He drove the tractor back to the house and was just getting off when a woman with flame-red hair zoomed into the yard in a silver Audi with the top down. He reached for his shirt, intending to put it back on.

"No!" she shrieked and killed the motor. "Please tell me you're Tyler Garrett."

He froze in place and nodded. "I am."

"Then don't move," she commanded, climbing out of the car with a camera in hand. She pointed the long lens at him and clicked the shutter a few times. "Get rid of the shirt and climb back on the tractor."

He complied, and she walked around the entire machine, snapping off pictures.

"Okay, you can put the shirt on, but leave it open in front." She circled him again, taking more shots. In the next hour, she photographed him in his truck, beside his truck, with his guitar, with his horse, and astride Prince.

He stood watching the small vehicle race down the caliche road, raising a trail of dust behind it. He heaved a sigh, feeling as though he had just been processed in some manner in which he was totally ignorant. He would leave it all up to Will. If he could just get to

Dallas before the competition started, maybe there was still a chance for him.

———※———

The first day of school, Leah put Gracie on the big yellow bus and waved goodbye. Her heart felt like it had swelled to twice normal size as she watched the vehicle bounce and sway along the road. She stood staring after it even when it had disappeared from sight.

Leah heaved a huge sigh. "I can't believe my little girl is growing up so very fast."

Gran nodded. "I know how you feel. Seems like just yesterday you was that age."

Leah heaved a huge sigh. "I don't think I was ever that age."

Gran frowned. "Maybe you're right. It does seem you had to grow up way too fast." She reached out to pat Leah's arm. "But you turned out just fine. I'm real proud of the woman you growed up to be."

"Thanks, Gran. That means a lot to me." She climbed into her car and pulled out, trailing after the bus, sighting it in the distance as it turned onto the farm-to-market road. She wondered how Gracie was doing. She wondered if her daughter would make new friends that day.

The bus turned off on a side road to pick up another child, and Leah passed it by, staring long and hard down the road after it.

Once at work, she was busy with her sorting and getting on a bit of typing Breck had left for her. Nothing exciting happened until just before noon, when Colton and Beau came into Breck's office. She looked up, surprised by their appearance.

"Hi, Leah!" Beau called. "So this is where you work?"

She grinned at him. "Looks like it."

Colton commandeered the chair opposite hers. "What time do you take your lunch? We thought we would take you out to get some chow." He had the same coloring as Ty but was a bit taller and heavier. Not overweight, just stockier.

"What brought this on?" she asked.

Beau perched on the corner of her desk. "Dad sent us in to pick up some stuff, and we thought we could get to know you a little better, say over a steak?" He grinned at her hopefully. He had the same blue eyes as Ty, but his hair was lighter, more of a sandy brown.

"How can I refuse?" She pushed back her chair and reached for her purse and keys. "Your timing is excellent, gentlemen." She called Sara Beth to tell her she was going out for lunch.

"Oh, hot date?"

Leah burst into laughter, causing both brothers to give her a quizzical look. "Yeah, two of them."

They waited while she placed the clockface sign in the door and locked up.

Beau opened the door of the big silver truck for her.

"Is this your father's truck?" Leah asked.

Colton climbed into the driver's seat. "No, it's mine. Dad got us all matching trucks, but Ty had to have the red one."

She laughed, thinking she was glad she had fallen in love with the nonconformist.

They drove her to the steakhouse on the edge of town. She had passed by it but never eaten there before. When they entered the establishment, the aroma of grilled meat was tantalizing. She hadn't realized she was hungry until that moment.

The waitress seated them and passed out menus. They chatted about how they liked their steaks, and when the waitress returned, Colton ordered rib eyes all around. There was a salad bar, and the three of them made a circle around it, returning to the table with their selections.

Leah was having a wonderful time. She wondered why the brothers would choose to take her to lunch but didn't question this lavish meal. She figured they had an ulterior motive and was braced to be questioned about her past at the very least. But they told funny stories about their earlier years, and she spent most of the time laughing.

She cleared her throat. "How is your father?"

Colton and Beau exchanged a glance.

Beau poked food in his mouth, she thought to keep from having to answer. She turned her gaze to Colton.

"Dad's a little better since he met you." Colton used his fork to dig into his baked potato. "He needed to hear from Ty…to know he was okay." He blew out a breath. "Since Mom passed away, he's been pretty hard to live with. Somehow, after meeting you and your daughter, he kind of softened."

Beau reached for a roll. "I think it was seeing how happy Ty is with you. It must make him think of his early years with Mom. He really has lightened up a lot."

Colton shot her a sharp glance. "So is this serious with Ty, or are you just toying with him?"

"What?" she squeaked.

"Well, we're hoping it's serious. Beau and I decided we would like you as a sister-in-law. How about it?"

Leah set her fork down and stared at each man in

turn. Beau had the appeal of a big puppy while Colton gave her a serious expression. "Are you proposing to me on Ty's behalf?" She reached for her tea and took a sip.

Another glance exchanged between the brothers.

"Not exactly, but we do want you to think about it. We promise to be the best brothers-in-law you could ever want." Beau finished with a wide grin, and his cheeks were pink with a blush.

"Seriously," Colton said. "You'd like it on the ranch. There's a really big house and plenty of room for you and your daughter…maybe some more little ones."

Leah choked on the tea she'd been drinking and suffered a coughing fit. "I don't think we're there yet. There are a lot of things going on, you know. The thing with the Carter brothers."

Colton scowled. "That will pass. I know Ty didn't have anything to do with that."

She set her glass down carefully. "And what about Ty's audition for the *Texas Country Star* show? He's got his heart set on performing there."

Colton let out a disgruntled snort. "He'll get over that. It was just something Mom put in his head. She thought he was good enough to go pro."

Leah gazed at him thoughtfully. "And you don't?"

He played with the potatoes some more. "I didn't say that. It's just that—with the ranch and all, he really should be there with us. It's a cooperative effort."

"I see." She exhaled softly. *So this is the agenda they brought to the table with them.*

Beau leaned forward. "I think Ty's got a great voice, but there are so many singers out there, just barely hanging on, not making much of a living. Any one of them would trade in their music for a shot at what Ty has waiting for him."

He looked so earnest; she had to feel for him. On the one hand, she felt defensive about Ty, wanting him to succeed at the one thing he dreamed about, but on the other hand, she realized the brothers were right. The advantages Ty was born with would satisfy most men... but Ty wasn't most men.

———

When Gracie stepped off the bus, Ty was waiting for her with a big grin on his face. He was anxious to hear how her first day had gone in her new school.

Both dogs ran to greet her as she made her way up to the porch.

Her face crumpled, and she ran to his arms.

"Hey! What's the matter? Are you hurt?" He squatted down to gather her in his arms, giving her a hug and then drawing back to peer into her face anxiously.

The bus driver was turning around and pulling away.

Gracie looked back over her shoulder. "Those boys. They were mean to me. They tore my new backpack and said awful things to me." She buried her face against his shoulder.

A flash of anger went off inside him. Who would be so mean to this sweet little girl? "Who were they, honey? Do you know their names?"

She nodded her head mournfully. "One is named Deke Carter. He's in the sixth grade." She sniffled. "It was him and his friends." She wiped away a tear, but another quickly followed. "He pulled my hair too."

Lucky licked her cheek, offering comfort as only a dog can. Eddie sat by her feet, whining softly.

Carter. Hearing the name set off a chain reaction, not unlike setting a match to dry kindling. Ty felt as though an explosion had gone off in his chest. "Don't you worry, Gracie. I'll put a stop to that. You won't have to worry about them again."

As he spoke, he wasn't sure how he was going to protect her, but he vowed he would keep her safe. "How about you go change your clothes and I'll take you for a ride? Prince needs his Gracie fix."

She brightened at that and ran off to the house.

Ty saddled Prince and brought him to the front of the house, where he found Gran waiting with Gracie. He lifted Gracie into the saddle and handed her the reins this time. He showed her how to hold them and how to use them to give the horse directions. He knew that Prince would walk alongside him wherever he went, but he thought this little girl needed to feel like she was in control of something.

He turned to find Gran frowning at him, her lips pressed into a thin line. "I just don't know what this world is a-comin' to when a little girl can't even go to school without somethin' like this happenin' to her. I guess them Carters has evil steeped into their DNA."

Ty put his hand on her shoulder, stunned by how thin and frail she was. But the look in her eye confirmed that she had a strong spirit and didn't take it lightly that someone was threatening her kin. Neither did he.

Gracie's spirits were considerably improved by the ride. When he lifted her off the big horse, she was grinning, and as soon as her feet touched ground, she laid her head against Prince's neck and gave him a hug. "I love you, Prince. You're the best horse in the whole wide world."

"He thinks so too." Ty took the reins. "Maybe you can help me give him some grain while I clean out his stall?"

"Oh, can I? I mean may I?" She jumped up and down a few times before falling into step beside Ty.

When Leah got home, she was upset about the bus incident. They agreed, between them, to take Gracie to school and pick her up afterward.

"But what about while she's at school? Surely they won't let a sixth grader pick on a younger child." Her large brown eyes showed concern for her daughter. "I can't believe I moved us this far only to put my child in danger again."

"I think I'll drop by her school tomorrow morning. I'll get to the bottom of it."

She seemed to take comfort in his words. At the moment, he had no idea what would happen when he visited the elementary school, but he knew he was going to make some waves.

Later, after supper had been eaten and the kitchen cleaned, Ty retired to the bunkhouse to work on a song. His phone rang and it was Will.

Ty answered it on the first ring. "So, am I a big star yet?"

Will snorted. "Laugh all you want, funny boy. You'll be kissing my feet in a few weeks."

Ty laughed. "Better put on some clean socks then."

"Your pics are tha bomb! I just downloaded them, and man! Talk about sex appeal. You should see 'em."

"Yeah, that would be nice."

"Don't worry. I'll make sure they get spread around where they'll do the most good. I loaded them onto your website."

Ty swallowed hard. "I have a website?"

"Of course you do. And you're on Facebook, Instagram, and Twitter too. I set you up with one of the shirtless images on your profile, and you're sending tweets twenty-four/seven."

"Hah! I don't have any idea how to tweet."

"Not a problem. I hired a personal assistant, and she's taking care of your tweets. Hell, you're even on Pinterest. On any of these sites, people can click on a link and go straight to one of your songs. The hits have been coming in like crazy."

Ty massaged the back of his neck. "That's good to know, I guess."

"By the time the show premiers, you will have a strong fan base. Crazed women begging for your autograph."

"Yeah, that sounds…awesome."

"It should. Our personal assistant is sending out auto-graphed pics by the armload."

"Autographed? I haven't even seen any pictures, much less autographed them."

Will laughed. "Well, I may have taken a little license with your autograph. You just keep practicing. Your voice should be in top form. Gargle or whatever."

Ty heaved a sigh. "You just go ahead and do what-ever you think is best, Will. I trust your judgment."

"Good man. Now, whose palm do I need to grease to get you sprung from that Podunk town? Is it the sheriff or someone else?"

"I don't know about that," Ty said. "Something else

has come up. I'm going to try and get it fixed tomorrow morning. I'll get back to you."

"See that you do. Time's a-wasting. Ticktock, man. Ticktock."

Early the next morning, Ty drove Gracie to school. He walked her inside, her hand feeling very small in his. He escorted her to her classroom and found the teacher, Miss Diaz, already at her desk.

She looked up and gave him a bright smile. "Well, hello there, Tyler…and Gracie. What are you two up to so early this morning?" She pushed back from her desk and came to stand right in front of him, gazing up into his eyes with interest.

"There's a problem," he said. "Some boys are bullying Gracie, and they've only had the first day. I want to put a stop to it right now."

Her eyes widened in disbelief. "Oh, good gracious. The boys in my class?"

Ty shook his head. "No, these are sixth graders. They ganged up on her on the bus ride home yesterday. From now on, either her mother or I will be bringing Gracie to school and picking her up. Please don't let anyone else pick her up but the two of us." He handed her a note that Leah had written out and signed that morning.

Miss Diaz looked at the note and nodded. "I'll make a copy of this and stick the original in her folder. The other one will go in the office." She leaned down to Gracie, gently placing her hand on the girl's shoulder. "Do you know the boys?"

Gracie shook her head. "No, but one is named Deke

Carter. Someone said they were in sixth grade." She glanced down, reddening. "I was afraid."

Miss Diaz patted Gracie's arm and sent her to put her things in her desk. She turned back to Ty, her face suddenly serious. "Everyone in that Carter family is just plain mean. The kids are constantly in trouble. I want you to go to the principal's office and make a report right now, before class starts. He needs to know what's going on."

She directed him down the hall and to another corridor.

Ty followed her directions. The halls were beginning to fill with children now, generally behaving well. Some teachers stood in their open classroom doorways, giving oversight to the students' passage.

When Ty stepped into the outer office, the school secretary came to the front to help him. He told her he needed to see the principal about a bullying incident, and her mouth formed a small O. She slipped into an adjacent office and returned quickly, motioning him inside.

Ty related his story to the principal, a man named Mr. Blanchard. He appeared to be stressed but made notes on a pad and asked the secretary to have the Carter boy brought out of class. He gestured for Ty to take a seat.

In a short time, the secretary escorted a tall, gangly boy into the principal's office. He eyed Ty, a sullen expression on his face.

Mr. Blanchard told him that bullying would not be tolerated and explained the boy's parents would have to come up to the school to discuss the incident. He also asked for the names of the other boys involved, but Deke hung his head, a muscle in his jaw working.

"I ain't no snitch," he mumbled.

"I can find out from the bus driver," Mr. Blanchard said, glaring him down.

The boy huffed. "Tom Rivers 'n' Albert Folsom. We was just havin' some fun." His gaze kept returning to Ty as though wondering why he was there.

Mr. Blanchard stepped to the door to ask the secretary to have the other boys brought to the office.

Deke gazed at Ty contemptuously. "Whut are you lookin' at?"

Frowning, Ty narrowed his gaze. "I'm looking at someone who's in trouble for bullying a little girl. Don't you feel proud of yourself?"

"Aw hell," Deke said. "Someone in her family done kilt my cousin Ray. We wuz just givin' her a little payback."

"That's not true!" Ty fixed him with a stern look. "No one in her family killed your cousin. His body was found on her grandmother's land, but they didn't kill him."

"How do you know?" The boy's mouth pinched up tight.

"Because I was there. Let the sheriff handle it, and just back off." Ty got to his feet and almost ran over the principal as he was making his way back into the room. "I have to go now," he said. "I hope you can stop this from happening again." He stormed out to his truck.

Leah timidly knocked on Breck's office door. When she peeked inside, he waved her in and pointed to a chair. He was on the phone, so she sat and fidgeted.

Apparently, the business of being a lawyer required one to argue incessantly and raise your voice. Oddly, even though Breck had appeared to be angry and he pounded on his desk for emphasis, when he hung up the phone, he turned a smiling face to her. "Good morning, Leah."

"Um, good morning, Breck." She paused, wondering how to begin. "I need to start taking my lunch break at a few minutes before three." She said it so fast, even she wasn't sure what she'd said.

Breck stared at her, a puzzled expression on his face. "What did you say?"

"It's my daughter. I have to pick her up right after school and—" She broke off abruptly, sucked in a breath, blew it out before starting again. "She was bullied on the bus. It was some relative of the Carters. I need to pick her up after school and…"

He leaned forward encouragingly. "And?"

"And I need to bring her over here until I get off work. She's a nice, quiet little girl…really. She can read or draw until my quitting time."

Frowning, Breck continued to gaze at her, his dark brows knit into a fierce frown. "That's all? Just go pick up your daughter and bring her here?"

Leah nodded miserably.

"That's nothing. Of course you can go pick her up. Not on your lunch hour though. The school is just a few blocks away. Just put the sign in the window and go get her. It won't take you any time at all."

Leah felt as though a tight band had been cut from around her chest. "Oh, Breck! I appreciate it so much. She was so scared this morning. Ty took her to school, and he was going to talk to her teacher or the principal or whoever could make it right." She stopped abruptly.

"Take it easy. I'm sorry the Carter boy is giving her a hard time. Damn! Poor kid. What a way to start off the school year." He drummed his fingers on the desk, frowning. "Unfortunately, we can't ask for a restraining order against a schoolkid. More's the pity."

She nodded solemnly. "So it's okay if I go pick her up every afternoon? I know it's an imposition."

Breck rubbed both hands over his face. "No matter what else is going on, whether I'm here or not, just go get her. Gracie's safety is more important than anything else."

―――∿∿∿―――

Ty had shared the events at the school with Leah, but she still looked worried. "I hope the principal will talk to the boys' families. I hope it makes a difference."

"Yeah, me too."

"In the meantime, I appreciate your help in getting her to school."

He frowned down at her. "About that—I talked to Will, and he wants me to come back to Dallas for a few days. He called the sheriff, and he agreed to allow me to travel that far. Will said it was because the sheriff's a fan of *Country Idol*…and he knows my dad and all… Anyway, are you going to be okay if I take off for a couple of days?"

"Sure," she said brightly…too brightly. "We'll be fine. Breck was really nice about me picking Gracie up in the afternoons. He said to just bring her back to the office and keep her with me right there. Nice as anything." Her smile looked a little tight.

He drew her into his arms and kissed her. "I won't go if you're worried. I don't want you to be afraid."

"Oh, we'll be fine."

"I wouldn't be going except Will said the *Texas Country*

Star producers are flying in and want to shoot some film of me singing in a club…you know, for promotions."

She nodded a little too enthusiastically. "Sounds like fun. You'll do great."

Ty was torn. He knew she was scared, and he was scared for her. There didn't seem to be a solution to this problem.

The next morning, he saw her off, driving toward Langston with Gracie in the passenger seat. Gracie looked back and waved.

Ty waved, feeling like a major rat. He wasn't happy about hanging them out to dry. He climbed into his truck and started her up. The diesel engine rumbled to life. He sat inside for a minute, gripping the steering wheel and looking around the little farm. It looked better for his having been there. He had cleaned up the rubble. Tilled a vegetable patch for Gran, which now bore row after row of sprouting seeds. He repaired the fence line where the Carters had cut it and planted two small fields with winter rye to use for cattle feed.

He put the truck in gear and headed out.

Still, it didn't feel right to be leaving them. But what if this was his only chance? What if he spent the rest of his life not stretching to make his dream come true?

As Ty turned onto the highway and headed toward Dallas, he reached for his phone. Only one way to make sure things stayed under control.

Leah picked up Gracie, and she spent the rest of the workday tucked in a corner of the long sorting table with a book. She had her crayons and a big legal pad if she got tired of reading but so far seemed content to bury her nose in the book.

Leah waited a good fifteen minutes after five to lock up, mindful of the time she had taken off to pick up her daughter and not wanting to take advantage of Breck's good nature. When she had Gracie in the car, Leah went through a drive-through to order a milkshake for Gracie.

In the back of her mind, she acknowledged that she was avoiding returning to the farm, because she knew Ty wouldn't be there. She felt sad, once again abandoned by someone she had come to love. She determinedly made conversation with Gracie about her classmates and her teacher.

"Miss Diaz is real pretty," Gracie declared. "She has real shiny black hair, and her lipstick matches her fingernails." She paused as if considering. "And she always smells good too."

"That's nice," Leah said automatically.

"I was kind of afraid to go out for recess, but Miss Diaz said the big kids have recess at a different time than us little kids. Well, we're not the really little kids. The first and second graders go out at a different time. My grade goes out at the same time as the fourth graders, and the big kids in fifth and sixth go out together."

Leah nodded intermittently, fixing a smile on her face. As she turned in at the little road to Gran's house, her stomach was in a knot. She hoped she wouldn't cry when she got home and Ty's big red truck was gone. She had to hold it together for Gracie. She could always mope later.

When she pulled up in front of Gran's house, she could hardly breathe. The big, shiny red truck was missing…but two big, shiny silver trucks were lined up side by side.

Gracie slipped out of her seat belt, peering over the dashboard. "Look, Mommy! It's Colton…and Beau."

Gran came out on the porch, shaking her head. She motioned for Leah and Gracie to join her.

Dazed, Leah climbed out and followed Gracie. Her daughter ran straight up to Beau, who hoisted her into the air like she was a toddler. Leah's heart did a flip-flop as she saw her daughter airborne, fearing her wrist might be reinjured. A scream died in her throat as Beau placed Gracie firmly on her feet.

Colton had set up a barbecue grill to the side of the house and seemed to be involved with some activity in which smoke was roiling up into his face. He looked hot, and not in a good way.

Both brothers greeted her, Colton waving a pair of long-handled tongs at her.

"Would you just look at that?" Gran exclaimed. "Ty sent both his brothers to babysit us while he's gone. Seems to think we need tending."

A rush of emotion choked Leah's airway, clouded her vision. "What?"

Gran snickered. "Yep, they just showed up and moved into the bunkhouse. The older one brought the grill in back of his truck and seems to think burnin' meat is better than fryin' it up in the skillet." She winked at Leah.

Beau gave a wink. "Nah, it's that rascal dog of his. Ty said Gracie would need some help taking care of Lucky. You know, opening bags of dog food."

Leah started to giggle. Suddenly, everything seemed funny. She laughed and laughed until she had to collapse into the old wicker rocking chair. She laughed until her sides hurt. Both brothers eyed her from a safe distance, and Gracie came to sit in her lap.

"Are you okay, Mommy?"

"Yes, honey. I'm absolutely fine. Everything is fine."

Chapter 13

"Tyler Garrett, ma'am." He reached across the table to shake hands with an attractive woman in her early thirties and then the man sitting beside her. The man had hardly spoken, but then again, there was little room to get a word in edgewise between Will and the woman. The two of them had exchanged a barrage of words in some rapid-speak only the two of them seemed to understand.

The woman swiveled her attention back to Ty. "You just look like a Country Idol. I mean, you have the right image." She turned to the man beside her, and he nodded. "Just perfect."

Will was grinning expansively. "And he can sing too."

"Of course he can," she agreed. "We heard the demo and saw the videos. He's perfect."

The foursome sat in a darkened corner of a Dallas bar. This one wasn't open to the public yet, but Will had wrangled an early entry due to his important guests. The visitors from Nashville had also brought a videographer with them, but he had yet to arrive.

Ty wasn't certain what the distinction was between a videographer and a photographer or cameraman, for that matter. He tried the word out, but it felt strange on his tongue.

The bartender brought drinks over himself, since it appeared to be too early for the waitstaff to be on duty. The owner hovered near the bar, chatting with the bartender while glancing frequently at those seated at the table.

Ty wondered what Will had promised him to be given access this way but figured he would make good on it. Will had a way of charming people into doing whatever he wanted them to do, and they seemed to be grateful for having been a part of his schemes.

Will and the woman were still yammering away while Ty quietly sipped from his longneck and the other man knocked back a few rounds of Jack and Coke.

Soon, the videographer arrived, a camera mounted on a tripod balanced on one shoulder and the strap of a huge canvas bag thrown over the other. He grinned and pushed his sunglasses up on his head. "Hi, everyone. This is a great setting." His gaze fell on Ty. "And this is our star. Pretty boy. The camera will love him."

Ty almost choked on his beer. *Pretty boy?*

"Can we get a barstool up on the stage?" the woman asked.

Will went to converse with the owner, and immediately, the bartender hoisted a barstool onto the stage along with a stand microphone.

Ty wasn't sure if this was part of the audition or what. Will had told him he had already been selected as a contestant. Will motioned him to the stage. He noticed the bar owner had disappeared but was apparently now running the lighting, as Ty was hit with a baby spotlight. Momentarily blinded, he groped for the stool and climbed onto it before setting his guitar on his knee. He began to strum the strings. Will walked up to the edge of the stage and told him to sing an old classic country song.

As Ty sang, the videographer moved around, apparently capturing him from different angles. He went through the list of several songs he had recorded, and the lighting changed each time. Now a series of strobe lights made it appear he was in a crowded club. A couple of the waitresses came in and moved to the edge of the stage, seemingly spellbound. The video guy captured their expressions too.

When Ty had finished his recently recorded repertoire, he stepped down off the stage. Will slapped a fresh, cold beer in his hand and thumped him on the opposite shoulder. "Dude! You were awesome!"

"I hope so," Ty muttered.

~~~

After dinner, Leah washed dishes and put them away. The meal had been delicious, and now Gran was sitting in the living room between Gracie and Beau. They were watching some situation comedy and laughing intermittently.

Colton sat at the table, enjoying a cup of coffee while he observed Leah as she worked.

When she had wiped down the countertops, she turned to find Colton still gazing at her. She felt her cheeks flame as she draped the dishcloth over the edge of the sink.

"Come sit down for a minute. You've been busy all night."

She sank onto a chair opposite him and folded her hands on top of the table. "What's on your mind?" she asked.

He smiled and set his cup down. "Ah, the direct approach. I like that."

Leah shrugged. "I don't know any other way to be."

"I like that even more." He gazed at her across the table as though weighing his words. "It seems my little brother has been quite busy here."

She nodded, suddenly uncomfortable. "Tyler has been a great blessing to us."

"All the improvements he's made must have been costly."

She cleared her throat. "Are you asking me if Ty has paid for these improvements?"

"Ouch!" Colton cringed. "I just can't be subtle with you, can I?"

"I'm not an idiot," she said. "I didn't ask Ty to spend a nickel on anything, but he did anyway." She sucked in a deep breath and let it out. "He even took it upon himself to buy Gracie some more school clothes." She watched as her words sank in on Ty's older brother. "He's a really good person."

Colton nodded. "Yes, he is."

"Mommy!" Gracie shrieked. "Come here. It's Ty!"

Leah ran in to the living room in response to Gracie's cries and almost stumbled when she saw where her daughter was pointing. Ty was on the television screen. He was singing on a stage. She couldn't really hear his voice, because an announcer was talking over him. It was an advertisement for the upcoming premier of *Texas Country Star*, the regional contest leading to *Country Idol*.

"Well, dang!" Beau exclaimed. "Looks like old Ty is gonna be a star after all."

A rush of warmth filled Leah's chest. He looked so happy and natural singing in the spotlight. He looked as though he belonged there and not on this little farm, no matter how much he cared for her. She mopped at her eyes as the image faded and the next advertisement came on. She turned away, seeing the expression on Colton's face.

He caught her eye and raised his brows. "I hope he knows what he's getting into. Dad is never going to understand if Ty walks away from the ranch."

⁓⁓⁓

The next day, Leah drove away from the little farm feeling confident at least that her grandmother would be safe with Colton and Beau there. They had outlined chores for themselves, and it appeared that they planned to keep busy.

She dropped Gracie off at school and watched as she walked up to the building. Tina had been waiting for her and fell into step beside her. That alone was enough to make Leah's day.

She was still stunned over seeing Ty on television. He hadn't called her last night, but perhaps he'd been too busy. She tried not to fret about it, but still, it seemed to remind her of all the differences between them and how he could just as easily forget about a simple person such as herself. She heaved a sigh and parked her car in front of the law office.

The day progressed as expected. Breck called in to say he would be in court most of the day and probably wouldn't be in at all. She had pretty much cleared up all the filing and didn't relish an entire day of sitting on her rear waiting for the phone to ring.

She enjoyed her lunch break with Sara Beth in the

quaint shop. Sara Beth was planning her wedding to Frank and had purchased a bridal magazine. Together, they turned pages and commented on the various gowns.

Sara Beth looked wistful. "Of course, I just want a simple wedding. I can't wear white, because I've been married before."

Leah shrugged. "I think nowadays you can wear any color you want."

Sara Beth frowned. "Really? I don't know. If you and your boyfriend get married, are you going to wear white?"

Leah caught her breath. "Oh, we're not thinking about getting married anytime soon. He's got a lot on his mind." She recalled that his brothers had proposed at least.

"Oh, I'm sorry. I just thought…" Sara Beth broke off.

Leah smiled. "It's okay. We just haven't figured it out yet."

She returned to the law office and tried to make herself useful while waiting for the time to pass.

It was just after two o'clock when her cell rang. Her heart did a little somersault in her chest when she saw it was Ty. "Hello," she answered breathlessly.

"Hey," he said. "Did I catch you at a bad time? Are you busy?"

"No. Breck has gone to the courthouse, and I've run out of things to do. I was just waiting until a little before three to run and pick up Gracie."

"Did my brothers get there okay?"

A wide grin spread across her face. "Oh yes. That was so sweet of you to send them."

"I didn't think both would want to go, but they both volunteered. One or the other will probably be going back to help Dad pretty soon, but maybe I'll be back before long."

"We saw you on television. It was so exciting." She heaved a sigh. "Ty, I think this is the right thing for you. I just wanted you to know how proud I am of you."

"Really?" She heard the pleasure in his voice. "Well, that makes me feel real good. I hope to make you even prouder, because I'm planning on winning this contest."

The front door opened and two deputies came in. She thought they must be looking for Breck. "Can I help you?" she asked.

"Leah Benson?" one of the deputies asked.

A cold chill spiraled around her spine. "Y-yes, that's me."

"Leah? What's going on?" Ty's voice sounded through the phone.

"Leah Benson, you are under arrest for suspicion of murdering Ray Carter. Keep your hands where we can see them." The deputy produced a pair of handcuffs.

"No!" she shrieked. "I didn't murder anyone. There has to be some mistake."

"I'm going to read you your rights, and we will be taking you to the county lockup."

"No, you can't," she protested. "I have to pick up my little girl at school."

"Leah!" Ty shouted.

"Ty! They're arresting me," she shouted into the phone. "They think I murdered Ray Carter. Please call the school. Gracie—"

"That's enough, ma'am." The deputy took the cell out of her hand and disconnected. "You'll have to come along with us now."

Tears streamed down her face. "Please," she implored him. "My little girl has no one to pick her up."

"You can make a phone call after you're processed." He fastened the handcuffs around her wrists and motioned for her to stand.

"I have to lock up."

"We'll do that for you," he said. They marched her outside and secured her in the back seat of a county vehicle.

As though in a trance, she stared out the window, unseeing, as the cruiser rolled quietly out of town, past the school, and out onto the highway.

———~~~———

Celia Diaz stood outside the school. It was a quarter after four, and all the other cars were gone from the parking area. The buses had long since rolled out with their loads of kids, but she was stuck here with the one child who didn't seem to have anyone else.

She looked at Gracie Benson. The little girl was terrified. Her big brown eyes scanned the street, looking both ways for whichever person was supposed to be coming for her.

"Why don't we go inside and wait for your mother?" Celia suggested.

The child nodded, gnawing her lower lip. "My mommy should be here soon."

"I'm sure she will be. Probably got hung up at work." Celia strode purposefully back to her classroom and sat down at her desk. She searched her class roster and located the phone number for the mother. There was a work number, so she dialed it first. *No answer.* A recorded message came on, the metallic voice announcing it was the law office of Breckenridge T. Ryan, Esquire, and that someone would return her call. Celia left a terse message, in case someone returned. She tried to keep the irritation out of her voice so as not to alarm the child.

Celia gave Gracie a smile and tried the other number, Leah Benson's cell. It rang and rang and finally went to message. Celia disconnected. She knew there was something going on. The cowboy had given her a note from the mother telling her to only release the child to her personally or to the cowboy and that Gracie's safety was involved.

Celia heaved a sigh. She had been planning on going home to sink into a bubble bath and then don her pajamas for a night of mindless television while grading tests. She fiddled with her pen, considering what to do if neither of the approved drivers came to pick Gracie up.

"Excuse me." There was a tall, older man standing in the open doorway of her classroom. He had piercing blue eyes, silver hair, and a rugged physique. She looked over his clothing. *Rough*. He wore a faded plaid work shirt, and his boots had seen better days. She noted the rip in his faded Wranglers. A working cowboy.

"Yes?" she said.

"I'm here to pick up Gracie Benson."

Alarm spread throughout her being. It suddenly occurred to Celia that, other than the janitor, they were the only ones in the building. Gaping at the man in the doorway, she judged him to be well over six feet tall, and he had the shoulders of a linebacker. He was probably in his early fifties, and even though she, at thirty-eight, was in excellent condition, she thought this big guy could easily overpower her. *Not gonna let that happen*. She pushed back from her desk, narrowing her eyes. "I think not. I have specific instructions as to who is allowed to pick Gracie up, and you're not on the list."

He walked closer and had the nerve to grin down at her. "Well, there's been a—" He stopped short, glanced at Gracie. "It's sort of an emergency," he whispered to her.

She stood up, glaring at him, while trying to appear as tall as possible. "Doesn't matter. I cannot release her to you. If you were the president of the United States, I wouldn't release her to you." She fisted her hands on her hips.

The big man regarded her. "Well, the people on that list are not coming. What do you propose to do?" He too fisted his big hands at his waist, now appearing to be twice as big.

"I'll just—" She suddenly lost steam. Huffing out a big sigh, Celia took her handbag out of the bottom drawer of her desk. "I will be taking Gracie home with me." She motioned to Gracie. "Come on, honey. We're leaving now."

Gracie stood, and when she reached the desk, Celia put her body between the man and the child. She would be damned if she would let some cowboy come in here and kidnap one of her pupils. Shooting him a fierce gaze, she slipped a protective arm around Gracie's shoulder and shepherded her toward the door. "You can close the door when you leave." She sailed out of the room, her young charge tucked safely under her wing.

~~~

Big Jim Garrett stared after the little spitfire who had just told him off. A slow grin lifted one corner of his mouth. Damned if she hadn't just nicely told him to go to hell…and he liked it. It had been a long time since a woman had caused that kind of reaction in him. *A long damned time*.

Well, at least the teacher was taking charge of Gracie. She would be safe with that little wildcat; he'd bet his shirt on it. Of course, the shirt he was wearing wouldn't be worth much. He'd worn his oldest clothing to do some extremely messy work. He'd been with the local veterinarian castrating bull calves when his son Tyler had called. Normally, it wouldn't have fallen to him to assist the vet, but considering that both of his other sons had traipsed off to Fern Davis's place, he had no other choice. With Colton and Beau helping Fern around the farm while trying to protect her, Leah, and the little girl, Big Jim had to take up the slack around his own ranch. He wondered where the boys were when Ty had been frantically trying to reach them.

Big Jim raked his fingers through his thick head of hair. He knew he hadn't been Tyler's first choice, but when he had received the call, he dropped everything to rush to Gracie's aid. Not that she needed it. The grin took over his face again. *Damned attractive woman… and sassy too*. Yes, he liked that.

He glanced around the classroom, searching for some clue as to who had the nerve to challenge Big Jim Garrett. His gaze settled on handprinted chalk letters tucked neatly in an upper corner of the blackboard. They were set off by a neat little box around them. *Miss Diaz. Well, a fine-looking little lady you are, Miss Diaz*.

Big Jim wrote his name and phone number on the note pad on her desk. At least she would know who he was, even if he wasn't the president of the United States.

He made his way out of the schoolhouse, remembering to close the classroom door per Miss Diaz's instructions. He grinned again when he recalled her expression. *Yes, a little spitfire.*

He left the school building and climbed into his truck. He was troubled over the situation with the girl he thought would be his future daughter-in-law. At least, Tyler had never shown this much interest in anyone in the past. And how had she bewitched his middle boy into spending his inheritance on her? He rested his hands on the steering wheel, thinking about the loving expressions he had witnessed on both their faces whenever they exchanged a glance. That warmed his heart. All he had ever wanted was for his boys to find the kind of deep and abiding love he had enjoyed with their mother. Yes, Leah was a keeper.

But she had been arrested for murder.

He shook his head and started the powerful diesel engine. The satisfying rumble centered him, helped him to regain his sense of balance. No way that little Leah girl could have murdered anyone, let alone a big, strapping asshole like Ray Carter. He reached for his cell phone and found the number for Breck Ryan. He was probably already on the job, but Big Jim just wanted to make sure. When Breck answered, it became apparent he had not been made privy to the information about Leah's predicament.

"What?" Breck's voice sounded like cannon fire. He uttered a curse.

Big Jim heard the squeal of tires and a growl from deep in Breck's throat. "Those idiots! Damn!" He explained he had been in court all day and had almost reached his own ranch but was on his way back to the county seat. "Let me call my wife to let her know I won't be home for a while." He rang off.

Big Jim tucked the phone in his shirt pocket. *Good.*

Maybe Breck can get to the bottom of this. Leah must be
scared to death right about now.

To be accurate, Leah was in more of a daze. She had
been petrified, but now she stared vacantly, unaware of
her surroundings.

Most of her worry was focused on Gracie. Who
would pick her up at the school? What if no one did?
She tried to picture what her shy and insecure daughter
would do in this situation.

Leah rubbed her wrists. The handcuffs had been
removed, and she now sat in what had been termed a
"holding cell." She had no idea of the time or how much
had passed since she had been arrested.

She had been transported to the county facility where
she had been told she would go before the judge the next
morning.

Her rights had been read to her, and she said she
understood them, but now, she wasn't sure she really did.
She had asked for an attorney and named Breckenridge
T. Ryan.

Now, she was decomposing in some kind of sterile-
smelling purgatory, wondering how long she would be
incarcerated before they would realize there was no possible way she would have been capable of murdering
Ray Carter.

She had been told she couldn't be questioned until
her attorney was present and he hadn't been located.
She vividly recalled the recent statement she made
regarding the assault upon her grandmother and how
Breck had stood by to ensure her rights were not

infringed upon and that the correct words came out of her mouth. She was exhausted and confused. It seemed she should be crying right about now, but she was too worried about her daughter to be concerned over her own state.

After many hours had passed and she was stiff from sitting in one place for so long, one of the deputies unlocked her cell and motioned for her to follow him.

A wave of fear paralyzed her. "But where are you taking me?"

Holding the door to the cell, he ignored her question, instead gesturing impatiently.

Leah was surprised she could even stand. Her legs felt like jelly as she took a tentative step forward. She swayed as though she might pass out but took a wider stance to steady herself.

Sucking in a deep breath, she released it slowly. *I can do this.*

She took a few steps and passed through the barred doorway. The surly deputy motioned for her to precede him down the narrow passageway. She glimpsed a couple of other prisoners, noting their seeming indifference to her passing. The hallway turned, and she had to wait for another door to be opened for her.

Her heart hammered against her rib cage as though trying to make a break from her chest. She had no idea where she was being taken, but this was different from when she had been brought into this maze. Her escort opened another door and said, "Wait here."

She stepped into a small room with a table and several chairs. *Oh no! They're not supposed to question me until Breck gets here.* Just then, a door on the other side of the small room opened, and another guard motioned for her to step through.

Every muscle in her body was coiled tight. She wasn't even breathing. Forcing her feet to propel her forward, she stepped into the next room and almost fell over.

"Oh my!" She clasped both hands over her mouth as a tightness in her chest suddenly melted away. "Oh my!"

She gazed around the room. Breck Ryan stood closest, his eyebrows drawn into a frown. And next to him was Big Jim Garrett. He had his burly arms wrapped around his torso as though giving himself a hug.

Beau and Colton Garrett stood close together, Colton's forearm resting on Beau's shoulder. Beau flashed a smile.

"Well, finally!" Frowning, Gran shook her head. "There's my girl."

And standing in the corner, looking at her with the most loving expression, was Tyler Garrett.

The ache in her chest expanded to the point of bursting. Her knees felt as though they were about to buckle. She swayed, but Ty rushed forward to grab her before she crumpled.

Strong arms wrapped around her and supported her. "Take it easy," he said. "Everything is going to be fine."

She reached out, her arms trembling. Holding Ty close, she finally let go of all the pain and fear she had kept inside. Sobs wracked her body as she clung to him.

"It's okay, honey. Don't cry."

She swiped ineffectively at her tears until Gran dug a tissue out of her purse and offered it to her. "I'm so glad to see all of you. But where is Gracie?"

"Her teacher, Miss Diaz, took her to her home." Big

Jim rubbed the back of his neck. "When Tyler called me this afternoon, I went by the school to pick her up, but that little teacher is fierce. She would only release her to you or Tyler."

"It was so late, we decided not to drag her along," Gran said. "And we didn't want her to be worried. I called Miss Diaz and talked to Gracie. She's fine."

Leah felt as though a huge weight had been lifted off her shoulders. "Thank God! I've been so very worried." If she hadn't been clinging to Ty, she might have collapsed.

Breck stepped closer. "Leah, you have to know, we had to pull in some favors to get you released. Big Jim here put up a half-million-dollar bond to guarantee your appearance tomorrow."

She sucked in a breath. *Half a million dollars?* Leah couldn't even fathom such an amount, let alone why someone would post it for her. Frowning, she asked, "What does that mean?"

Breck cocked his head to one side. "By filing a bail bond with the court, the defendant will usually be released from imprisonment pending a trial or plea." He raked a hand through his hair, a sure sign he was stressed. "I had to strong-arm a judge at a dinner party to get him to agree to it. So you and Miz Fern will be staying at the Garrett Ranch overnight."

Leah glanced at Gran, but she blinked and shrugged, indicating she was okay with it. "Um, sure. That's great. I thank you, Mr. Garrett. I don't know how to repay your kindness...or your generosity."

Big Jim waved off her thanks, but she noticed a muscle in Ty's jaw working. She hoped he wasn't upset with his father. She didn't want to be the cause of any more strife in the Garrett family.

"Let's get out of here." Big Jim gestured toward the door and they all trooped out.

Leah had to sign for her property at the desk, which only consisted of her purse, keys, and cell phone.

Once they were headed out of the city and on the road, it looked like a parade of pickups in formation moving toward Langston. Leah rode in Breck's truck so he could talk to her about the case on the way. Ty trailed close behind with Gran buckled up in the front seat. Big Jim was next, and Colton and Beau were riding together in one of their identical, big silver vehicles.

Leah turned to Breck. "So, how much trouble am I in?"

"I did some digging, and they seem to think they have some kind of circumstantial evidence to incriminate you. That, plus the run-ins you had with the Carters." He shook his head. "Bad history. I think the district attorney just wanted to wrap this case up fast and doesn't care who he nails for it."

Her throat was dry, and her voice sounded raspy when she spoke. "I can't imagine why they would think I could kill a man, even if there was bad history. I mean, I didn't cause any of those run-ins. The Carters were the ones who chased me, and it was Ray who knocked my grandmother down with the shopping cart."

"We'll find out tomorrow morning. I suggest you get a good night's sleep. I'll pick you up at 7:00 a.m., so we'll be at the courthouse first thing. We want to get it over with."

Breck turned onto the road leading to the Garrett homestead, driving through a big, horseshoe-shaped

archway with the name *Garrett* emblazoned over the
top. He crossed over a cattle guard, jarring the truck
in passing. The entire procession rumbled through the
entrance behind them.

Leah gazed around. Fenced pastures lined both sides
of the road, with cattle grazing on lush grasses. This
was Ty's home turf. This was what he was used to. She
pressed her lips together, silently comparing her current
surroundings with the small, run-down ranch owned by
her grandmother.

When Breck stopped the truck, it was in front of a
large, rambling, Spanish-style ranch house with red
tiles on the roof. The front was landscaped with flowering bougainvillea in a deep-purple color and lots of
vibrant-pink crape myrtle. The effect was quite lovely.
Leah could see at once this place had been groomed with
loving hands.

"I'll see you tomorrow morning, Leah. Be ready."

"Yes, sir. I'll be prepared." She unbuckled her seat
belt and was in the process of climbing down when Ty
appeared to offer a hand. Just the sight of him made her
feel warm all over.

He grinned, his hands lingering at her waist. "Here
you are."

Eddie ran up to greet her, barking his welcome.
Lucky followed, waving his tail from side to side.

"I'm okay, at least for the moment. It was sure nice of
your dad to pay so much to get me out of there."

Ty frowned. "Yeah, I'll have to thank him for that."

The other trucks pulled in around them, and Breck
took his leave, backing out and then zooming back the
way he had come.

Leah gazed around, overcome with shyness. "Wow! This is quite a place."

Ty nodded. "My dad's empire. It was...different when Mom was alive."

She slipped her arms around his waist and looked up at him. "Different? How?"

He shrugged. "It felt like a home. Now, it's just an enterprise." He patted her arms. "Come on. Let's go inside."

Holding her hand, he led her toward the house, first walking through a shady pergola with some sort of stone floor. It immediately felt cooler, as though they had entered a leafy tunnel. Flowering vines grew up on the sides, letting the last rays of sunlight filter in to touch her as she passed.

Ty held the massive front door open and quickly stepped inside behind her. He wrapped his arms around her, pulled her back against him, kissed the side of her neck. "I was so worried about you."

The tension that had held Leah in its talons for the past two days slowly drained away. For the moment, she felt safe, protected. "I was really worried too, but mostly about Gracie. That was very nice of you to get your dad to go check on her."

He huffed out a snort. "He wasn't my first choice. I tried Colton and Beau first but couldn't reach either one of them. Finally, I called Dad, and he was willing to drive to the school to pick her up."

Leah gnawed her lower lip. "I need to talk to her. She must be worried sick. I've never been away from her overnight."

"I'm sure your grandmother or my dad has the teacher's number."

She nodded, somewhat comforted.

Beau and Colton entered through the front door, and Leah stiffened, but Ty didn't release her. She sighed, glad he wasn't ashamed of caring for her, glad he hadn't stepped away from her when faced with his brothers' scrutiny.

"Where's Dad?" Ty asked.

Colton grinned, tossing his hat on a rack beside the front door. "I believe he's taking Miz Fern on a grand tour of the ranch."

She felt Ty's arms tighten around her. She patted his forearms. "That was nice of him."

"Come on, Leah," Ty growled. "Let's get something to eat. You must be starved."

Colton nodded. "Hey, we're all hungry. Let's rustle up some grub." He thumped Beau on the chest, and the two raced ahead of Leah and Ty.

She glanced at him, but he rolled his eyes and gestured for her to follow in the direction his brothers had gone.

When they arrived in the kitchen, Leah was amazed at the layout. The Garrett kitchen seemed as big as Gran's entire house. There was a cavernous eating space with a table and a dozen chairs. It was situated in a corner with a lot of glass looking out on a deck with another lush garden. There was also a long bar with seating on the outside and a preparation area lined with shiny stainless-steel appliances on the inside.

Beau and Colton were peering into a large, brushed-steel refrigerator that appeared to be very well stocked. Between the two of them, they were pulling items out and setting them on the granite countertop.

"We can grill," Colton said. "Here are a couple of chickens and some steaks."

"And a salad." Beau tossed all manner of fresh

vegetables on the counter. "And baked potatoes." He set a half dozen large potatoes near the sink.

"You just relax, Leah," Colton called over his shoulder. "We'll take care of everything."

"Oh my goodness," Leah said. "I'm not used to being waited on."

Colton raised an eyebrow, fixing her with an amused stare. "You mean my little brother Tyler hasn't shown you what a great cook he is?"

Leah smiled, glancing from Colton to Ty.

Ty gave a one-sided grin, looking a bit sheepish. "I haven't had occasion to cook lately."

Colton made a grunting noise. "Slacker! You've been making this lovely lady cook for you? You weasel."

Beau pounded Ty on the shoulder, laughing. "Just chill, Big Brother. Colton and I will throw supper together. Fire up the grill, Colt. I'll make the salad." He took a big colander and put all the vegetables in it, then set it in the sink and turned on the tap.

Ty kissed Leah's fingers and seated her at the counter across from where Beau was working. "You sit here and keep an eye on my baby bro, and I'll go out to make sure Colt doesn't drop the steaks in the dirt."

She watched him trail after Colton out onto the back patio. He finally seemed to be regaining some of his usual good humor.

Leah turned her attention to Beau, who was studiously laying the rinsed salad ingredients out on paper towels. "Do you want some help?" she offered.

Beau shook his head. "I couldn't very well accept your help after giving Tyler a hard time for not cooking." He glanced at her, his blue eyes as penetrating as

Ty's. "It's just that our mother made it a point of teaching the three of us to cook. She said Dad was a disaster in the kitchen, and she didn't want any of her sons to be so helpless."

Leah folded her hands on the cool countertop. "She sounds like quite a lady."

Beau sobered. "She was. Dad may have been the brains of the ranch, but Mom was the heart and soul of it."

Leah pressed her lips together. It sounded like the Garrett brothers had been very fortunate in the parents they drew. Lucky indeed.

Chapter 14

TY TRIED TO RELAX. HE OPENED THE BEER COLTON handed him and let the icy liquid roll down his throat.

Colton opened the hood of the grill and turned the meat over, spearing it with a long fork. Beau had brought out potatoes seasoned and wrapped in foil to line up on the sides of the grill. The meal would be a typical Garrett production with beef from their own ranch.

Colton had been making small talk up to this point. He glanced at Ty and heaved a sigh. "Leah seems like a really nice girl."

Ty nodded, took another sip of beer. "That she is."

"Any…uh…plans I should know about?"

"Plans?"

"Don't play dumb, jackass. You know what I'm talking about. Are you planning on making Leah a part of this family?"

Ty felt the muscles in his neck tighten up, and his shoulders wanted to crawl up to his ears. "Why would I want to make the poor girl suffer? I could just roll her in poison oak. That would be about as pleasant."

"Hey, we're not so bad." Colton glared at Ty, squinting through the smoke rising off the grill. "Don't tell me you're not in love with her. I can read you like a book, Little Brother. Large print edition."

"I love her," he said. "I'm just not sure I want to subject her to all this manipulation."

Colton closed the top of the grill with a bang. "What's the matter with you anyway? There are many thousands of acres here. You can pick your own little section and build your honeymoon cabin there. You don't have to live in Dad's back pocket, you know."

Ty released a deep breath. "I know. I just don't want Leah or her daughter to feel like they have to live up to some role Dad will write for them. I want them to enjoy being who they are without having to dance to his tune."

Colton shook his head, frowning. "Man, you sound angry. Do you hate Dad that much?"

Ty reeled as though Colt had punched him in the face. "I don't hate him. He's my dad. But without really knowing how, I seem to have completely disappointed him. I just can't be some little paper cutout like he wants me to be." He finished his beer and rooted around in the cooler for another.

Colton pointed to the large outdoor preparation area. "Bring me that platter, Little Brother. Let's plate up this meat."

Ty straightened, staring at Colton for a moment before complying. He hoped his dad didn't think he hated him. He sucked in a breath and blew it out before reaching for the platter. He set it close to Colton and backed away. It had been so very difficult to break out from under his father's thumb. Now, he felt trapped again, and worse still, he had brought the woman he loved into it. She didn't even realize what she was in for.

He stared up at the night sky, a thousand stars glittering overhead. Considering Colton's words, he wondered if Leah would be content to live here. Would there be enough room for them to live as a couple without his dad interfering? Was there enough room in all of Texas for that to happen?

—∿∿—

After dinner, Leah was surprised when Ty drew her away from the others. She felt his father's and brothers' eyes following them.

Ty escorted her to his truck, stating he wanted to take her for a ride. She got in, and he went around to climb up on the driver's side. "Just thought a little moonlight drive was in order."

She flashed a grin. "That sounds romantic." Scooting closer, she leaned against his shoulder and softly laid her hand on his thigh.

Ty started the truck and headed out to what he described as one of his favorite places on the ranch. When they had driven to the end of the paved road, he turned onto one of the dirt roads that crisscrossed the property. Finally, he came to a stop at a little draw with a group of trees and a creek running through it. He lifted her hand and kissed her fingertips. "Come on out. We can talk."

A ripple of fear spread through her. That sounded ominous. What did he want to talk about? He stepped down and held out his arms to her.

Sliding under the steering wheel, she leaned down and into his embrace.

"Oh, Leah," he said, gathering her close. "I don't have any idea what my future holds."

She pulled back, gazing up at him. "Well, that makes two of us. Tomorrow, I may be thrown back in jail and stay there forever."

Softly, he kissed her lips and then again, not as softly. "C'mon," he said abruptly. He led her to one side of the clearing where several large boulders were nestled together. He climbed up on the biggest one and held out his arms, pulling her up beside him.

She laughed nervously. "What are we doing here?"

"This," he said. He leaned back and indicated he wanted her to join him.

Although the rock was not exactly comfy, when she curled up next to Ty and he offered his cushy shoulder for a pillow, it wasn't so bad. Gazing up at the heavens, she drew in a breath. The clear night sky overhead looked as though an enchanted jeweler had thrown a zillion diamonds out onto black velvet. The moon glowed white, giving everything an ethereal radiance. "Oh my!"

"Exactly."

She could hear the smile in his voice. "This is beautiful."

"It is. I wanted to ask you if you would like to have this view every night for the rest of your life."

"Well, sure. It's gorgeous."

He leaned toward her, grinning. "I mean, would you like to live here with me for the rest of your life?"

Her heart did a flip-flop in her chest. "Like, married?" Her voice broke.

"Yeah, that's the deal. I don't have any idea what's going to happen in the next couple of months. I don't know if I'm going to get kicked off the Idol show the first week or go on to the finals. I don't know if I'm good enough to make a living at it."

"I think you are, Ty," she said softly.

"But this"—he gestured around to the clearing—"this is what I can offer you right now. If I stop trying to chase a dream and move back here, I can give you and Gracie a secure place right here. We can grow to be old people and have our bones buried right here."

She stroked the side of his face with her fingertips. "Ty, you know I'm in love with you."

"Yes, I do."

"I have no idea what's going to happen tomorrow. I may get thrown in jail and never come out, so I can't make any plans…and then there's Caine. He's bound to come back into my life and screw things up again."

"Doesn't matter. I will spend every nickel I own for your defense. There is no way this murder can be pinned on you." He planted a kiss against her temple. "And so far as this Caine goes, he has no place in our lives."

"But I can't be the cause of you giving up your dream. For your information, I would follow you anywhere you want to go. If we live in the back of your truck while you're singing in bars, I could do that. But I couldn't make Gracie go through that with me. She needs something stable. If I can make it through tomorrow, and Breck clears up this mess, the best thing I can do for Gracie is just return to Gran's and go to work every day…and take care of her. Let her have a normal life where she goes to school and graduates and has a fair shot."

He nuzzled her cheek. "You mean give her all the support you never had?"

How come he always hits the nail right smack-dab on the head? She sighed, nodding vigorously.

"That's what I want for her too." He leaned back and stretched, gazing up at the starry night.

"This is a beautiful place, Ty. When things get straightened out for both of us, can we talk about it again?"

He chuckled and rolled up to a sitting position. He leaned over and kissed her nose. "Sure we can. I'm just glad to know you would live in the truck with me."

———∞———

Leah was a basket case the next morning. Although the bed in the guest room was quite comfortable, she had slept fitfully. In her dreams, she had entertained the Carter brothers, including Ray, with his face caved in, as well as Caine. She was running, not sure who was chasing her, but when she looked back, her shadowy pursuers were gaining on her.

Waking before the alarm sounded, she sat up on the edge of the bed and pulled on her previous day's clothing. She dropped her head into her hands and let the fatigue and tension wash over her.

There had seemed to be an endless number of guest rooms in the Garrett household. Gran had been shown to a very nice room. She had run her hand over the satin comforter and said, "This is real nice. I'll sleep like a baby right here."

Ty, however, had led Leah to his former room and told her to let him know if she needed anything. She had a pretty good idea of what he needed, and she probably did too. She just wasn't comfortable giving it to him in the house where his father and brothers slept...not to mention her grandmother.

Resolutely, she stood and made her way to the bathroom, cleaned herself somewhat, and ran her damp fingers through her unruly hair. She gathered it in the scrunchie she had worn the day before and surveyed the results. *Not good, but relatively clean.*

She tidied the bathroom after herself and opened the door to find Ty standing in the hallway, leaning against the doorjamb.

"Good morning, beautiful," he whispered.

She smiled, feeling instantly better. "Good morning. You didn't have to get up this early to see me off."

"I didn't," he said pleasantly. "I got up this early to accompany you. I'm not going to let you go without me."

"Oh, Ty. That's so sweet."

He insisted he wanted to make her something for breakfast, but she refused. Her stomach was tied up in a knot, and she feared she wouldn't be able to keep anything down.

When Breck Ryan came roaring down the private road in his pickup, Leah was waiting with Tyler standing by her side. She had the feeling that this was what she could count on her whole life through if things worked out with Ty. *If I don't go to jail on some trumped-up charges. If I don't screw up the best thing that has ever happened to me...other than Gracie. Can't screw that up either.*

Breck drew to a stop beside them. The passenger side window came rolling down silently. "Hop in," he said. "We can talk on the way over."

Leah looked up at Ty, and he gave her a kiss before helping her up into the truck. "I'll be right behind you."

When they were on their way, Breck gave her a stern look. "Pretty serious between you and young Garrett?"

"I think so. Everything is just such a mess right now."

"I understand that. Now, you're going to be deposed. You need to tell the truth, because you will be under oath. I've found that sometimes, omitting some tiny little bit of information can really trip you up in the long run, so just answer the questions truthfully. If I feel a question is not appropriate, I'll interrupt." He glanced at her again, concern written on his face. "Do you understand?"

Leah sucked in a deep breath and let it out. "Yes, I'm to answer all questions truthfully, unless you interrupt, and then I'm not to answer."

"Right." He straightened his shoulders. "I just hope we can bring this mess to an end. I know you want to get home to your little girl, and I would sure as hell like to see my wife with her eyes open."

"Breck, I will pay you for representing me. You may have to take it out of my pay for the next hundred years, but I intend to pay you back." She paused, gnawing her lower lip. "And Mr. Garrett too. I can't think why he was willing to put up so much money for me."

Breck glanced at her again, a crooked smile on his lips. "I'm pretty sure it's because of Tyler's great affection for you. Big Jim is dead certain you're going to be his daughter-in-law...and he likes you. Besides, he didn't have to come up with half a million dollars. He only had to put up ten percent. Fifty thousand is a drop in the bucket for him. Don't worry. He can afford it." He clicked his tongue. "Of course, if you skip out, he would have to forfeit the entire amount."

"Well, I would never do that," she hastened to assure him.

"I never for a moment thought you would. Now, tell me one more time about how you found the body in the field."

As they drove, the sun continued to rise, bathing the landscape with an early morning glow. Sunlight glistening through the dew likened the passing landscape to a field of pearls.

Leah sighted buildings in the distance, standing like silent sentinels against this flat landscape. They drove past miles and miles of pastures and open range, most populated with clumps of beef cattle and a few mesquite and cacti. Each species of vegetation lent its own austere beauty to this rugged countryside.

By the time they arrived at the county seat, Leah's nerves were fried. She kept her palms gripped together in a sort of silent supplication. In her brain, the word *please* replayed over and over again. When they were parked and out of the truck, she found Ty by her side, his ever-present smile a haven for her storm-tossed soul.

Breck led the way into the DA's office and placed his card on the secretary's desk. The three of them were led to the back where Breck shook hands with a Lieutenant Clemmons. He introduced Leah and Ty.

Lieutenant Clemmons took a hard look at Ty and pointed to a chair. "You'll have to wait over there."

Ty glanced at Breck, who nodded. Ty squeezed Leah's hand. "I'll be right here."

Clemmons then waved Breck and Leah toward an open office and, on the way, spoke to another officer. "Tell Bradshaw they're here."

Leah's stomach felt like it was in a vise. Breck gave her a reassuring nod, but it didn't help much.

In a few minutes, a man in a suit came into the small room and closed the door behind him. He sat across the table from Leah and Breck, passing a sheaf of papers to Clemmons, who rifled through them and then leaned back to stare across at Leah.

Bradshaw set a small recording device on the table halfway between himself and Leah. He stated the date and his name, then asked her to state her name.

He asked her to recount the events leading up to her discovery of the body of Ray Carter.

Leah glanced at Breck, who nodded, and then began to tell how she saw the truck and noticed that the fence had been cut. She said she went to see what the Carters were doing on her grandmother's property.

"Did it not occur to you that this was a dangerous course of action, given the previous encounters with Ray and Dean Carter?"

"I suppose so," she said. "But at the time, I thought maybe they were starting a fire in all the dry brush."

"And if this had proven to be true, what would you have done?"

Breck raised his hand to silence her. "My client will not comment on 'what ifs.' Stick to the facts."

Bradshaw's mouth tightened, and he reshuffled his papers. "How about this, then? Miss Benson, if you did not kill Ray Carter, how did your fingerprints wind up on the murder weapon?"

Leah stared at him without speaking. She felt a cold prickle on her skin as though someone had spritzed her with ice water. "I—I have no idea."

"You have a murder weapon?" Breck asked.

"Yes, there was a rock lying close to the body, and the medical examiner's office has positively established that this object was used to bludgeon Mr. Carter to death." He nodded to Leah. "There were several smudged prints, but those belonging to Miss Benson were clearly identified."

"Oh no! Not the rock." Leah began to tremble violently. "I picked it up on the road before I went into the field. I thought—I thought—"

"You thought you needed a weapon to confront Mr. Carter. This is called a weapon of opportunity."

"Wait a minute," Breck demanded. "You actually think Miss Benson is strong enough to have overpowered someone as big as Ray Carter with a rock?"

Bradshaw's lower jaw jutted out as he glared at Breck. "This was a crime of passion. Whoever killed Carter was acting out of pure hatred. After he was dead or dying, his killer sliced and diced him with a pair of rusted antique shears. That was overkill."

Leah covered her mouth with both of her shaking hands. She couldn't grasp how this man thought she was capable of such a despicable act.

There was a knock at the door, and a uniformed officer came in to slide another folder to Clemmons and exited quickly.

Clemmons scanned the papers and frowned. "That will be all, Miss Benson."

Breck gazed at him intently. "Is there a further development in the case? Is that why you're dismissing Miss Benson?"

Clemmons let out a huff of air. "The ME has determined that the individual who crushed in Mr. Carter's face had to be over six feet tall and have a much greater body mass than Miss Benson. She is free to go." He leaned to whisper something to Bradshaw, who nodded. "However, we would like to talk to the young man who was accompanying Miss Benson. His stature corresponds to that of the perpetrator."

"You're way off base there, Clemmons," Breck said. "Mr. Garrett has a rock-solid alibi."

"Yes," Leah nodded furiously. "He spent the day with my daughter in Amarillo buying school clothes."

It seemed there was a glaring battle going on between Breck and the two men sitting across the table. Breck pushed his chair back abruptly. "If that will be all, gentlemen, we will be on our way." He put his hand on Leah's shoulder, and she managed to stand upright. Breck took her arm and led her from the room.

Ty got to his feet when he saw them, and Breck motioned for him to join them as he made a beeline for the exit. Once outside, he turned on Leah. "You never mentioned anything about a rock."

She stopped in her tracks, nervous in the face of Breck's indignation. "I completely forgot about it. I think I must have dropped it when I came upon the body."

Breck let out a frustrated grunt. "Well, it's a good thing the medical examiner decided it took someone a lot bigger and stronger than you to crush Ray Carter's head in, because otherwise, you would be looking at murder one."

Leah nodded vigorously. "I understand. I'm so sorry. I didn't even remember picking up the rock."

Ty circled his arm around her shoulders in a protective gesture. "I'm pretty sure she wasn't expecting to come upon a bloody nightmare."

Breck turned on him. "And you better watch your step, because you were already mentioned as a possible suspect, based on your height and build." He took a step back and blew out a breath. "But I wouldn't be too worried. If it came down to it, I'm sure with time and date stamps on your receipts from shopping in Amarillo and store security cameras, we could prove your innocence." He raked his fingers through his hair and jammed the Stetson back on his head. "Let's get back. Leah, if you can go into the office this afternoon, we can try to construct some semblance of normalcy today."

Leah heaved a sigh of relief. At least she still had a job. "I will get there as soon as I can."

Breck drove off, leaving Leah and Ty to follow. Ty opened the passenger door of his truck but pulled her into his arms for a passionate kiss when they were tucked inside the shelter of the door.

She wrapped both arms around his torso, imprisoning him in a fierce embrace. "I'll be so glad when this is all over. I hate having something so awful hanging over us."

Ty gazed down at her. "Breck doesn't seem to think we have a lot to worry about."

"But whoever killed Ray Carter on my grandmother's property is still out there. I won't be able to relax until that person is caught."

"Baby, you don't know the Carters. They're the scum of the earth. I'm sure whatever else was going on with Ray, he had to have made a bunch of enemies. Any one of them could have caught up with him, and it just happened to be at your grandmother's place. Don't let it worry you."

She nodded, filled with a sense of uncertainty laced with foreboding. She rode back to the Garrett ranch, her hand on Ty's thigh, with him singing along to the radio.

As they turned in at the big horseshoe-arched entrance, she considered how much her life had changed in such a short time. She had fled Oklahoma with her daughter and the bare essentials, not knowing what she would find but certain it had to be better than what she was leaving behind.

Now, she had the love of a very good man, the best job she'd ever held, and the prospect of providing some kind of security for her daughter's future. She tried to relax and enjoy the place she was in her life at that moment.

Ty was crooning along to an old Eagles tune, appearing to be perfectly content.

All she had to do was chill out, stop creating drama in his life, and let him attain the stardom he was born to reach. *I can't keep getting in his way.*

They pulled up in front of the Garrett ranch house. Big Jim and Gran came out to meet them.

"Oh, thank heavens," Gran exclaimed. "I was so scared for you."

Leah leaned down to embrace her. "It went surprisingly well. They decided it would take someone a lot bigger and stronger than me to have done the deed."

Big Jim scoffed. "Well, of course it would. I could have told them that."

"I need to go to work and get my car," Leah said. "I can collect Gracie after school and then come pick you up after I get off."

"Now, just wait a second." Big Jim held up both hands in protest. "Miz Fern and I have been talking, and we think we have a plan."

Leah felt Ty stiffen behind her.

Gran nodded her head wisely. "We was talking, and it

seems that whoever killed that Carter feller is still out there, and we don't know if he's through with killin' people."

"Yeah, I thought of that too." Leah swallowed hard.

"Well, Big Jim here offered to let us stay at his ranch until the killer is caught. It would be a lot safer than out at my place."

"But, Gran, what about your animals? The cattle and chickens? We would have to go over every day to feed them and look after the house." Leah frowned, wondering how they would manage the logistics.

Big Jim chuckled. "Don't you worry about your livestock, Miz Fern. The boys and I can make sure they're taken care of. We Garretts would never let an animal suffer."

Leah turned to Big Jim. "Are you sure? I hate to put you to so much trouble." She glanced from Big Jim to Ty.

"No trouble at all. If need be, we can bring your livestock here. There's plenty of grazing land. We can put the cattle in one of the small pastures, and the boys can clean out one of the sheds to use as a chicken coop. Your choice."

Gran was grinning ear to ear as she looked on. Everything seemed to be settled for her.

For his part, Ty looked grim. He stood with his boots planted and his hands fisted at his waist.

"Seriously, Son, you don't want these ladies to be at risk, especially if you're going back to Dallas." Big Jim addressed Ty, his voice persuasive.

Ty sucked in a deep breath and exhaled forcefully. "I suppose you're right. I don't want them to be in any danger. I...uh...I planted some winter rye for feed, and there's hay stored in the barn."

"Good for you, Son, but I have to know: Where is your horse?" Big Jim asked. "Colton said he wasn't at Fern's place."

"I boarded him with the veterinarian before I took off for Dallas. I didn't want the ladies to have to care for him." Ty was frowning now.

"You can bring him home. You know he'll get good care here while you're gone," Big Jim said. "And there's no need for you to go to that expense."

Ty sighed again. "I suppose you're right on that too, Dad."

"Great." Gran clapped her hands together. "So I can have all my chickens safe under one roof, so to speak."

Ty nodded. "For the short term." He and Big Jim gazed at each other intently. "At least until the killer is put away or I get kicked off *Country Idol*."

Leah let out a strangled laugh, tried to take some of the pressure off the situation. "Don't be silly, Ty. You're going all the way. I know it."

He ran his hands up and down her arms. "I appreciate your support, but we'll see how it goes. I'll take you to grab lunch in town and then drop you at Breck's office. I'll pick up my horse and meet you here after you get off work."

It suddenly seemed so simple. Everything was working out better than she could ever have imagined.

Ty took Leah to lunch and then to the law office. She looked really happy, so he tried not to let his misgivings color her expectations. He couldn't imagine how his father had suddenly backed off of his stance about the possibility of Ty having a career in music. They hadn't talked about it privately, but at least Big Jim was making a public showing of support.

He drove to the veterinarian's place, settled up with her, and hooked the horse trailer to the back of his truck. Prince nickered and waved his handsome head when he spotted Ty.

He rubbed Prince's neck. "Easy, boy. I'll have you home soon." The word *home* struck a chord with him. For a brief moment, the little run-down ranch owned by Leah's grandmother had felt more like home than his father's vast domain. He thought that might have had more to do with the people involved than any amenities.

He sighed and led Prince into the trailer. He seemed to be in high spirits, prancing up the ramp, as though he too was anxious to be going home. Probably anxious to see Gracie.

Once Ty secured the doors, he climbed in his truck and headed back to the Garrett ranch…his dad's ranch. The place where he'd sworn never to return.

"We'll see how it goes," he said aloud. The Garrett ranch was a place where Leah and her family could be safe while he was gone. It all made sense, and he could see that it was for the best. At least that's what he kept telling himself.

Leah opened the office as soon as Ty dropped her off. She had two hours to put in some work before she went to pick up Gracie at school. She'd missed her daughter so much her chest ached.

Leah checked the answering machine and made notes on the few calls, placing the messages on Breck's desk.

She was surprised when the door opened and Sara Beth popped in.

"Hey, you," she sang out, a wide grin on her face. "Where ya been, girl?"

"I just had some...business to take care of."

"Well, I'm glad you're here. I missed you." She gave her friend a wide grin.

Leah's chest flooded with warmth. Nice to have a real friend for a change.

"I'm taking a break from the store. It's been real quiet today. I thought I could run down here and at least say hello."

Leah pointed to the chair by her desk. "Well, sit down and tell me how things are going in your life. How is your boyfriend?"

"He's great! In fact, he's taking care of the baby today. His sister came to visit, and he wanted to introduce her to Cami Lynn. We're all going to have dinner tonight when he picks me up."

"That sounds so nice," Leah said. "I'm just so happy for—" She broke off suddenly when the door was thrown open so hard it banged against the coat-tree, sending it clattering to the floor.

"Well, isn't this cozy?"

Leah's worst nightmare stood framed in the open doorway. "Caine!" she gasped.

Sara Beth jumped to her feet. "Oh, land's sake. You scared me." She eyed him, her expression betraying her apprehension. "Well, if you folks will excuse me, I better be getting back to the store." She took a few steps toward the door, but Caine blocked her path.

He glared down at her, seemingly immense next to

her petite form. "Where do you think you're going, little one? It's just getting interesting."

Sara Beth swallowed hard, her gaze flicking to Leah and back to Caine. "Well, I have to—"

"No, you don't. We can have a party right here, just the three of us." He wrapped his sinewy fingers around Sara Beth's upper arm. "Now, you go back over there and sit down where I can keep an eye on you." He thrust her toward Leah's desk before twisting the lock in place.

"Listen, Caine," Leah began. "You don't have to involve Sara Beth. This is just between the two of us."

He turned, an amused expression on his face. "Y'think?" He crossed the room in three strides. "Because of you, I spent eight long years locked up in a hellhole with the sickest of animals."

Sara Beth's face contorted, as though she might burst into tears at any moment.

Leah's heart thrashed against her ribs like a wild animal trying to escape. She swallowed hard, recalling her last encounter with Caine, when he had beaten her and choked her until Gracie intervened. Leah straightened her shoulders. "Just how do you figure it was my fault? You served a part of your sentence for rape. That was all on you."

"No!" He slammed his fist down on her desk, scattering papers with his force. "You wanted it. You and that friend of yours, Maryanne. You were both ripe for it."

Angered, Leah stood up, drawing herself to her full height. "We were little girls. We did not ask to be raped." As she said the word, she saw Sara Beth flinch.

Something flared in Caine's eyes. He leaned across the desk and backhanded her with such force she landed against the metal filing cabinets and sank into a heap on the floor. Dazed, she raised her hand to her throbbing cheek.

Caine bent over Sara Beth. "What are you looking at, little one? You want some of this?"

"No," she whispered, shaking her head vigorously.

He stroked her cheek with the back of his hand. "Pretty little thing."

Leah's protective nature surged to the forefront. "How did you get out, Caine? I thought you were back in jail after you showed up at my apartment in Oklahoma."

He turned to her, skirting around the desk. "Funny you should ask. I have you to thank for that. When you split, you failed to make an official statement to the police, and they charged it off to a domestic disturbance." He loomed over her, his fingers rhythmically clenching into fists and straightening.

She vividly remembered those same fingers clasped around her throat. "How—how did you find me?"

"That was a bit more difficult. I couldn't find hide nor hair of you, so I looked up your girlfriend back in Hobart. Little Maryanne Harris grew up real nice. She was still living with her mama, but after we had us a little talk, she remembered you had grandparents with a ranch somewhere near Langston, Texas, and you used to go visit them every summer."

Leah stifled a shiver. "She told you that?"

"That she did." He leaned close, his breath falling on her face. "After a little persuasion," he said, his voice almost crooning. "And she gave me her car. That was real nice of her, 'specially since she had no use for it anymore."

"What do you mean? What did you do to Maryanne?"

Leah heard the ragged edge to her own voice and tried to control it. "Is she dead?"

He laughed, a loud guffaw that ricocheted off the hard surfaces like a gunshot. "Well, she might be, considering I buried her behind a little shed in her mama's yard. And I used her car and credit card to get me all the way here."

Sara Beth let out a squeak, covering her mouth with both hands.

Chapter 15

BIG JIM GARRETT GRABBED HIS PHONE THE SECOND time it rang. "Hello," he said.

"Is this the gentleman who came to my classroom to inquire about Gracie Benson?"

Big Jim could immediately envision the vibrant woman on the other end of the line. "Why, yes, Miss Diaz, it is. Is everything okay with Gracie?"

Miss Diaz huffed out a breath. "She's fine, only her mother didn't come to pick her up. She called and talked to Gracie last night and said she would be here right on time today…but she hasn't arrived."

A spiral of fear coiled down Big Jim's spine. "Well, her grandmother is here at my house. We can come get Gracie right now, if you'll release her to us."

Another deep sigh. "I couldn't reach her other contact either, Tyler Garrett. I suppose there's some relationship here?"

"My son."

"I'll release Grace to you and her grandmother, but I'm deeply concerned. If this continues, I'll have to contact the child protective services."

"No, I mean, yes. I understand. We'll be right there." He hung up and tried to reach Ty on his cell phone, but it went straight to message. *Damn! Where is that boy?*

Hurriedly, he located Fern Davis and loaded her into his truck. He may have exceeded the speed limit on the way to Langston, but he figured he had a damned good reason.

When he reached the town and headed to the school, he made another call to Tyler. This time, he answered.

"Where is everyone? I just got my horse in the stable and washed myself up."

By the time they reached the schoolhouse, Big Jim had brought him up to speed. He was striding down the hallway of the school, Fern Davis in his wake.

"You need to find out why Leah isn't here to pick Gracie up herself."

"Damn," Ty exclaimed. "Did you check the law offices? That's where I left her."

"Not yet," Big Jim said. "We're here for Gracie, and then I'll drive over there."

"Thanks, Dad. I'm on my way." Ty disconnected.

Big Jim stopped at the open doorway to the third-grade class. He reflected that this was the least-strained father-son conversation they had shared in months. He tucked the phone in his pocket. Fern Davis had caught up and scrambled around him.

"Where is my Gracie?" she demanded.

The pretty, little dark-haired teacher sat at her desk, and Gracie was right in front of her. *Good. Front row seat. Teacher's pet.* He nodded to the teacher. "Miss Diaz."

She looked him over from his face down to his boots. A smile spread across her face. "Mr. Garrett."

Yeah, I'm looking a little better than the last time you saw me. "Folks around here generally call me Big Jim."

Dimples flashed in her cheeks as she gave him an impudent grin. "They do, huh?"

Gran was busy gathering Gracie's things and fussing

over her. She hustled Gracie out, and they were walking down the hall toward the truck.

Big Jim took a moment to return Miss Diaz's thorough inspection. He liked what he saw.

Miss Diaz picked up her purse and keys and headed to where Big Jim was standing. "Well, Big Jim, folks around here"—she gestured to the empty seats in her classroom—"they call me Miss Diaz." She put her hand in the middle of his chest and backed him out into the hall. "But you can call me Celia."

Ty was in his truck and speeding toward Langston before he'd even disconnected from his dad's call. It felt as though his insides were clamped in a vise. There was no way Leah would have failed to be right there, waiting to pick Gracie up immediately after school, unless she was in some kind of trouble.

When he arrived at the law office, he found his dad's truck parked in front beside a sporty looking Mustang, but Leah's old beater was nowhere to be seen. He rolled to a stop and jumped out.

Big Jim climbed out of his vehicle, leaving Gran and Gracie inside. "I called Breck at home, and he said he thought Leah should still be here until five."

"Something's wrong," Ty said. "She wouldn't have left without good reason, and she wouldn't have failed to pick up Gracie."

Ty stepped to the door of the law office. The big beveled glass inset didn't boast the clock-face sign that was always in place after hours. He put his hands up to shade his eyes from the glare and peeked inside. There was still a light on, and it appeared to be business as usual. He twisted the knob, and the door opened inward.

A deep sense of foreboding washed over Ty. "Hello?" he called.

Big Jim pushed the door farther open.

There was a bentwood coat-tree behind the door that had been knocked down. The only other sign of disorder was a batch of papers scattered on the floor near Leah's desk.

"Leah?" Ty's voice sounded hollow within the confines of the tomb-like offices.

He heard a soft moan from the far side of the room and rushed toward the sound. Spying a form crumpled on the floor behind the table she used for sorting, he called out, "Leah."

Ty knelt and gently turned her over, seeing it wasn't Leah. He helped the young woman to sit up as she made little sputtering noises.

She touched her throat gingerly. "He…he choked me," she said in a raspy voice.

Ty noted the bruises on her face and throat. "Who?"

Big Jim called the sheriff and then fetched a cup of water from the water cooler against the wall. "Here, little lady. Drink this."

She accepted it gratefully, taking several tentative sips, "The man…he was someone Leah knew. Someone from Oklahoma." She swallowed hard as a rush of tears rolled down her cheeks. "Leah tried to help me escape, but he came after me and choked me. I thought I was going to die… I guess I passed out."

The sheriff and a deputy entered through the open door and took charge of the scene. Big Jim immediately took charge of the sheriff and told him what they had learned.

The sheriff called for an ambulance and then came to squat beside Ty. He regarded the victim, who was crying and holding her throat. "Sara Beth? Are you okay?"

Ty supported Sara Beth, who seemed likely to collapse again. "Where is Leah? Did the man take her?"

The young woman turned her horrified gaze to him. "Oh no! I hope not. He admitted to killing some woman in Oklahoma. Just matter-of-fact like. He said he had been in jail and it was because of Leah."

"Caine!" Ty said.

———~~~———

"Hurry up!"

Leah tightened her damp hands around the steering wheel, her fingers cramping with the effort. "I'm already going over the speed limit. You don't want me to get stopped by the highway patrol, do you?"

"Hah! I been up and down this road a dozen times and I never saw a cop car."

Leah said a silent prayer there was one coming to her rescue at that moment. "My friend…the woman who was in my office. Is she all right?"

"It depends on your definition of all right." His lips twitched in derision. "I would say she was resting peacefully when I left her."

"She's okay? You didn't hurt her?"

"Naw! She's just a little bit dead. I choked her until she turned blue."

"No!" Leah howled. "You didn't have to do that. She—she was my friend."

"It wasn't my fault. You were the one who was sittin' all cozy like, gossipin' with your girl. I couldn't leave her to tell the tale, now could I?"

Leah stared blindly out the windshield. Struggling with a combination of anger and terror, she cast about for some way to get free…to turn the tables on Caine, but other than running the car in the ditch, she came up blank.

"My boyfriend is going to come looking for me. He's expecting me to be home by now."

"Now don't you go lyin' again. I met up with your boyfriend this last week and I smashed his face in. Ugliest sumbitch I ever did see." Caine slouched back against the door, regarding her through half-closed eyes.

Leah swallowed against the bile rising in the back of her throat. She saw him shaking with laughter out of the corner of her eye but refused to look at him.

"An' then I took some rusty old shears he had on him and cut him good. He looks even uglier now."

She sucked in a shaky breath.

"Aww, what's the matter? Are you gonna cry for your poor dead boyfriend?"

"That was not my boyfriend," she said as calmly as possible.

"Liar," he said. "What would that guy be doing at your place? He was working on the fence when I come up on him."

"No, he was cutting the fence. He was someone who had been bothering my grandmother for a long time."

He tilted his head to one side as if he hadn't made up his mind whether to believe her or not.

"Turn off right up here," he directed, pointing to the farm-to-market road to her grandmother's house.

She slowed the vehicle. "Where are we going?"

He snorted. "Why, we're going home."

—∿∿∿—

Ty paced the length of the law office and back again. His dad and the sheriff were talking in low tones. Sara Beth had been removed by ambulance to the hospital over in Amarillo.

He couldn't believe this guy, Caine, had come out of the woodwork to kidnap Leah. Where would he take her? What would he do to her?

Colton and Beau came into the office, looking around. "What's going on?" Colton asked. "First there were messages from Ty and then Dad."

Ty glowered at them. "A little late to the party."

"Sorry, man," Beau said. "We got here as soon as we could. We went over to the school, but it was locked up tight, and we saw Gracie and her grandma out in Dad's truck."

"What's going on here?" Colton demanded.

Ty quickly brought them up to speed, but he was so anxious, their presence was more irritating than comforting.

"I want you boys to drive Miz Fern and Gracie back to the ranch and wait there with them." Big Jim pointed at Colton. "You make sure they're safe at the house."

Colton glanced from Big Jim to Ty but nodded and reached for his keys. "Sure thing."

Ty released the breath he'd been holding.

Big Jim called him over. "The sheriff just got an update on the Mustang outside. They ran the plates, and the car was stolen from a murder victim in Oklahoma." He shook his head. "At the murder scene, they matched fingerprints to a convict who violated his parole. The victim's credit cards have been used here in Langston too."

Ty reeled as a wave of nausea rose to choke him. He hadn't eaten since breakfast, but if there had been anything in his stomach, he would have hurled it right then. "I can't lose Leah, Dad."

Big Jim nodded. "The sheriff is on it."

Ty glanced at the sheriff, who appeared to be punching buttons on his phone. "I see."

"They're looking for her car." Big Jim placed his hand on Ty's shoulder. "If there's anything I can do, just let me know." He glanced down and then raised his eyes to meet Ty's. "I know I let you down in the past, when I didn't listen to what was important to you, but I'm trying to make it up to you, Son."

Ty released a breath he hadn't even been aware he was holding. "I know you are, Dad. Let's just get through with this. I need to get Leah back."

"Do you have any idea why this guy targeted Leah?"

Ty nodded. "Yeah. Leah told me about someone she went to school with back in Oklahoma. He—he assaulted her when she was just a kid and went to jail for it. Sara Beth said it was the same man, and he was blaming Leah because he served time. She said he sounded bitter and admitted to murder right in front of her."

Big Jim nodded. "Maybe that was the woman in Oklahoma. He sounds like a real nutcase."

Fear coiled around Ty's spine like a snake. *And he's got Leah.*

Leah drove down the road toward her grandmother's house. She had no idea what Caine had in mind, but it was clear to her he had no conscience at all.

Leah's throat was so tight she could hardly breathe. She slowed and turned in at Gran's drive. She ground the gears into park next to one of the big silver trucks and turned off the motor.

"Whoa!" Caine gazed around suspiciously. "Where did this truck come from?"

Leah had no idea which one of the Garretts it belonged to, nor where they might be situated. She wished they were ready to jump out and save her.

"It belongs to one of my boyfriend's brothers. He left it here when he went out of town."

Caine squinted at her, a wariness in his eyes. "Y'don't say? Well that's one sweet ride. I might be taking it with me when I leave."

She swallowed hard. "Now what?"

"Now me and you are going to have some fun." He pulled the keys out of the ignition and tossed them on the dash. "Get out."

Leah's pulse pounded in her ears. *I have to get away, but how?* She surveyed Caine's lean, muscular body. She might be able to outrun him, but he appeared to be in excellent shape, and he had overpowered Ray Carter, who had been well over six feet tall and strong as an ox.

Swallowing hard, she put her hand on the door handle and swung it open. She stepped out into the dry heat of an early dusk. Crickets chirped and cicadas sang. The air felt close and heavy, like walking into a damp blanket.

Caine unfolded himself from the passenger side, then sauntered close to where she stood.

"You must be hungry," she said.

He straightened his spine and gave her a hard look. "Yeah, I could eat."

She walked purposely to the house as though she had the right to. Marching up on the porch, she opened the door, letting it swing wide as she strode through. "Sit down. I'll see what's in the fridge."

He followed close behind her, grabbing her shoulder and whirling her to face him. "Okay, but no funny business."

Leah tried to maintain eye contact without flinching. "Sure." She turned back to the kitchen and opened the refrigerator. "Let me see. I have chicken and I have ground beef. I can whip you up some mashed potatoes."

"Yes," he snarled. "I want chicken. Haven't had any home cookin' since they took me to prison."

"Okay then." She took the ingredients out of the refrigerator and set them on the counter. "How do you want your chicken? I can bake it or I can fry it."

He sucked in an audible breath and sank onto one of the chairs to the dinette. "Fried chicken? Yes, fried."

Leah took out one of her grandmother's heavy cast-iron skillets and set it on one of the front burners of the stove. She opened the can of Crisco and scooped a generous portion into the pan before lighting the burner under it. She stopped breathing as she reached in a drawer and removed a large and very sharp knife. Without turning around, she began to cut the chicken into serving pieces. The legs and thighs first. Caine didn't move from the table, and she was afraid to look around lest she alert him. She opened a canister and scooped flour onto the counter, added salt and pepper, and rolled the four pieces in the mixture, then slipped them into the hot grease. She picked up the knife again, this time severing the breast bone. Deftly, she cut apart the rest of the chicken and dredged it in flour. *Just act natural. Don't look nervous.*

Leah grabbed several potatoes out of a basket and began to pare them, hoping her homely actions didn't raise any suspicions on Caine's part. Rinsing the potatoes in a colander, she placed them in a deep pot and covered them with water. She set the pot on a back burner and lit the flame under it.

The silence pressed in on her. The only sound was the sizzle of chicken frying in melted grease. She was afraid to look at Caine. Afraid to speak. Mostly, she needed a miracle right about now.

"Who would have thought?" Caine broke the silence.

She glanced quickly around, then continued to turn the chicken, using a long-handled fork with two sharp tines.

He was still sitting at the table, his hands splayed out on the surface in front of him.

She had surrounded herself with possible weapons, not knowing when she might get the opportunity to use any of them.

"I never thought you would be the little Suzy Homemaker type. With that body, I figured you would have become a stripper."

She didn't respond. Instead, she concentrated on spearing pieces of chicken with the long fork and turning them over, as though this task required all her concentration. All the while, she mentally rehearsed how she would stab him with the fork or the knife if he got up off the chair.

"I spent eight years thinking about what I would do

to you when I got out, but I never pictured this." The chair creaked as he leaned back in it. "I was just barely eighteen when I went to prison. Do you have any idea what they do to young guys in prison?"

Leah didn't answer, keeping her head averted.

He slammed his hand on the table, causing her to flinch. "Do you?"

Leah dropped the fork, sending it clattering to the floor. Swallowing hard, she leaned down slowly to pick it up, her hands trembling violently. She shook her head, finally daring to glance at him again.

"Let's just say them boys used me like—" He broke off, his voice low and deadly. "No man should be treated that way."

Her gag reflex was working overtime. "Tha—that's horrible," she said.

He let out a low growl, like an enraged animal. "You think so? I promised myself, when I got out, I would make sure to pay you back for doin' that to me."

A heavy silence followed.

She stole another glance at Caine. His face was like a marble sculpture of pure hatred.

———

A sheriff's department helicopter hovered over the scene, relaying images back to headquarters.

Ty stared at the video on the sheriff's monitor. His heart throbbed in his chest, resounded in his ears, quickened the blood pulsing through his veins. *There she is.*

"She may not be with Caine at all," the sheriff said, his tone reasonable. "I'll just send a couple of deputies out to the Davis place to make sure she's all right."

Yeah right. "You do that, Sheriff. In the meantime, I'll be checking on her myself." Ty made a break for the door.

"Now, hold on a minute, Son," Big Jim shouted.

"Wait!" the sheriff yelled.

"Damn!" Big Jim let out a disgusted snort and followed on Tyler's heels.

Ty was already halfway to his truck when Big Jim caught up with him. "Hang on." He laid a hand on Ty's shoulder.

Ty spun around, not willing to let anyone get in the way. "I can't stop, Dad. I have to find her."

"I know that," Big Jim said. "We better take my truck."

Ty let out an impatient sigh. "Why?"

Big Jim gave him a knowing look. "Because I have guns." He clicked his remote to unlock his vehicle.

"Okay," Ty said. "But I'm driving."

Big Jim tossed him the keys. "Knock yourself out." He climbed into his own truck on the passenger side and reached for the seat belt.

Ty was astonished. Was his father actually letting him take the lead on something? He quickly recovered and jumped into his dad's silver, extended-cab pickup, identical to his except in color. Well, with perhaps a few more bells and whistles. He turned the key in the ignition, taking in a huge lungful of air when the powerful diesel engine roared to life. He tore out and made it to the edge of town in no time at all. He glanced at his father. "Guns, Dad?"

Big Jim issued a huge sigh. "Of course." He opened the glove compartment and took out a large caliber handgun and a box of shotgun shells.

He reached behind the seat and pulled a shotgun in a case to the front seat. "I just figured we ought to be prepared for all eventualities."

A chill ran down Ty's spine. To hear his own father talk about the possibility of pointing a gun at someone was hard to take. "Well, I hope it doesn't come to that."

"Son, if this Caine fellow is with her, he's a dangerous son of a bitch. You can't go in there all 'let's talk this over and be friends.' That man killed a woman in Oklahoma and tried to kill Sara Beth Jessup. I'm pretty sure they're not having a tea party."

Ty nodded. "I know you're right. I just hope he hasn't hurt her."

He drove in silence, way faster than the law allowed. When he slowed to turn off the highway and onto the farm-to-market road, his palms were damp. This Caine had hurt Leah in the past. He had injured Gracie. A cold rage seethed in Ty's gut. He didn't need a gun. If Caine hurt Leah again, Tyler Garrett would kill him with his bare hands.

———— ❦ ————

Leah used Gran's ancient potato masher to pulverize the hot, boiled potatoes. The sound of the metal instrument against the stainless-steel bowl was enough to set her teeth on edge. She added butter, salt, pepper, and a little cream and continued the assault on the potatoes.

She had taken the last pieces of chicken out of the black cast-iron skillet and set them on a folded paper towel on a big Fiestaware platter. Now she had the two items ready with no more stalling. She was out of time. Taking a plate out of the cabinet, she loaded it up with a big serving of potatoes and placed three pieces of chicken alongside. She turned to Caine, approaching him warily with her offering.

"Right here," he growled, indicating the space in front of him.

She sat the plate down, but he grabbed her wrist when she tried to draw away. "Bring me a beer and some ketchup." He released her abruptly.

Leah was amazed her rubbery legs could transport her to the refrigerator. She opened it and peered inside, momentarily confused as to what she was looking for. Pressing her lips together to keep them from trembling, she found the ketchup in the door and removed a long-neck bottle of beer from the back of the top shelf.

"Hurry up!" Caine snapped.

"Coming," she sang out, trying to inject a cheery note into her voice.

She set both items on the table and stepped back.

"No, sit yourself right down here. I want you to tell me about my daughter."

All the air was sucked out of her lungs. Her heart stopped beating. Her brain flatlined. He had said the words she feared most. In her heart, she had never thought of Gracie as having any connection with Caine. Gracie belonged to Leah. Caine had no right to Gracie or any knowledge of her.

"Well?" He picked up a drumstick, tearing a bite of meat off with his teeth as he glowered at Leah.

"Um, she's eight now."

Caine snorted. "Well, I know that. Tell me something I don't know."

"She's in the third grade, and she's very smart." Leah

heard the sound of a vehicle approaching. *Maybe it's Ty. Maybe it's someone to help me.* She raised her voice and started talking faster. "She loves animals, and she has a dog named Eddie. She's only been in her new school a few days, but she already has a friend."

The screech of tires right outside was impossible to cover up.

Caine turned around to stare out through the screen and the open doorway. "Oh, hell no!" He jumped up and grabbed Leah, dragging her in front of him. He backed up to the counter where she'd been working and grabbed the knife she had used to cut up the chicken. When Ty burst through the door, Caine held the knife against her throat. "Easy now," he warned. "You need to back on out of here. Me and the little woman here was just settin' down to dinner."

"Put the knife down," Ty ordered.

"Well, you ain't in no position to be tellin' me what to do." Caine took a step backward, but Ty advanced toward him.

"You do not hurt her," Ty said. "You can walk away from this, but so help me, if you hurt her, I will take your life."

Caine laughed and loosened his grip on her. "This must be the boyfriend." He gestured with the knife, and she twisted away, reaching for the cast-iron skillet, still filled with smoking hot grease. When Caine grabbed at her again, she slung the grease on him, bashing him with the skillet in the process.

Cursing, Caine howled in anguish, dropping the knife and sinking to one knee.

Ty rushed him and threw a punch that took Caine

all the way down to the floor. Ty scooped Leah into his arms, crushing her against his chest. "Are you all right?"

Leah wrapped her arms around Ty's torso, but when she opened her eyes, she saw Caine reach for the knife as he struggled to his feet. She let out a scream, and Ty turned, thrusting her behind him.

At that moment, a shotgun blast exploded Caine's chest. He fell back, lying motionless on the floor, his eyes wide open, gazing at the ceiling.

Big Jim Garrett stood, holding a shotgun on the fallen man, a steely expression on his face.

Ty drew her back into his arms. "Everything is going to be fine."

Leah pressed her face against his shirt.

The sound of sirens could be heard in the distance.

Big Jim snorted. "'Bout damned time."

Chapter 16

LEAH'S EARS WERE STILL RINGING FROM THE SHOT-
gun explosion, and now the high-pitched sound of sirens
grew louder and louder.

A few minutes later, the sirens wound down as two
sheriff's department vehicles screeched to a stop in the
front yard. Two deputies came running into the house,
their hands on their holstered weapons.

Big Jim stood stoically to one side, his shotgun
broken over his forearm. He appeared to be remarkably
calm, considering that he had just shot a man dead.

The deputies shouted into their two-way radios, each
voice drowning out the other.

Ty held Leah, keeping her face averted from the
bloody remains strewn on her grandmother's kitchen
floor.

She was still shaking with fear, although the reason
for her terror lay dead beyond any doubt.

The deputies confiscated the knife and Big Jim's
shotgun before questioning him.

"My dad was only protecting us," Ty protested.

One of the deputies raised a hand to quiet him. "We'll
get to you in a minute."

Big Jim appeared to be completely relaxed and not
in the least bit concerned. He gazed at Ty, giving him
an almost imperceptible nod before turning his attention
back to the deputy.

Leah raised her face to gaze at Ty. "I'm so sorry I caused all this trouble." She heaved a sigh.

He brushed her hair back from her face. "Baby, nothing that happened here was your fault. You were the victim. I'm just glad you're safe. I couldn't let him hurt you again."

She pressed herself back against him, her head tucked under his chin. "I feel so relieved. Am I a bad person to be glad Caine is dead?"

Ty pressed his lips against her temple. "I don't think so. Caine needed to be put down like the rabid animal he was."

Ty told the deputies he was taking Leah to sit on the front porch and shepherded her outside. Temperatures were dropping, and the night sky was more black than purple. Stars were strewn across the heavens, and a chorus of frogs sang counterpoint to the crickets.

Apparently, all was right in the universe. In spite of the terror and violence Leah had experienced earlier, the images were being eased from her brain. Drained, she felt limp with fatigue. Suddenly, she jerked, alert to the real issue. "Gracie! I didn't get to the school to pick her up. I have to go."

Ty stopped her. "Don't worry. It's already taken care of. Gracie and your grandmother are safe with my brothers at the ranch."

Leah blew out a sigh of relief. "Thank God!" she said fervently.

Ty sank onto the wicker rocking chair and pulled her into his lap. "Just relax. This will be over with, and we can go home."

The word *home* resonated in her brain. She wasn't quite sure where home was anymore. She had thought it was here on her Gran's little farm, but apparently, Ty was referring to Big Jim's huge spread.

Leah rested her head against his shoulder, her tension suddenly melting from her taut muscles. She slipped her fingers inside his shirt, needing to feel closer to him. "Thank you for saving me."

He kissed her forehead. "You can't get rid of me that easily. I'm keeping you."

She laughed. "I want you to."

Another vehicle came roaring up to the house, red and blue lights flashing but no siren. The sheriff turned off the motor and stepped out, glaring at Ty and Leah as they sat cuddled together. "What's this about a shooting?"

Ty rolled to a standing position in one smooth move. He set Leah on her feet and stepped forward to meet the sheriff. "The man who got shot is the same one who tried to kill Sara Beth and kidnapped Leah. He had a knife and was threatening to kill Leah when my father blasted him with a shotgun. Dad saved both our lives."

The sheriff rubbed his jaw. "Well, Big Jim is a righteous man. I've never known him to do anything rash. I don't suppose he would shoot someone without a damned good reason." He nodded at Ty and went into the house without any further discussion.

Ty stared after the sheriff a moment, slowly shaking his head. "I'm always amazed at my father's sphere of influence. The man's got clout."

Leah stood on tiptoe to plant a kiss on his cheek. "Well, that's a good thing."

He resumed his seat in the rocker and pulled Leah into his arms. Wrapped so securely, she felt safe for the first time since she'd had to leave Oklahoma. No, she felt

valued for the first time in her life. Someone loved her.
Someone was willing to fight to protect her. It was even
more than Ty. It was his family who'd stood by her too.

The next vehicle to arrive was an ambulance, but
they weren't hurrying. Someone must have told them
their passenger wasn't in a rush. The ambulance pulled
close to the house, and the two attendants climbed out,
removed a gurney from the back, and rolled it through
the front door.

Leah was content to keep her eyes closed and her
face pressed against Ty's neck. Whatever was happening inside couldn't hurt her as long as she remained so.

Big Jim stepped out onto the porch. "The sheriff says
you kids can go home. I'll wait until everyone is gone
and secure Fern's house. I'm pretty sure the sheriff will
give me a ride home."

"We'll wait for you, Dad."

"Your little Leah looks plumb worn out. I'll be fine."

Leah roused herself at that. "We'll wait for you."

Big Jim's face split into a big grin. "That's real nice."

After quite some time, the ambulance rolled out with
Caine's remains in a black, zippered body bag. The
deputies exited the small house and climbed in their
vehicles, leaving in a much more sedate manner than
they had arrived.

Finally, the sheriff and Big Jim came out and shook
hands on the porch. The sheriff departed, and Big Jim
motioned to Ty and Leah. "Let's go home."

Ty and Leah climbed out of the chair. "Right behind
you, Dad."

The next morning, Leah woke up in Ty's bedroom at the Garrett ranch. Surprisingly, Ty was in bed with her. She didn't remember much of the ride home or how she had gotten out of the truck and into the house.

That they shared a bed was somewhat disturbing. She figured his brothers and father knew they were intimate, but she wasn't sure she wanted to rub their noses in it.

A few rays of the early-morning sunshine crept through the curtains.

She watched Ty as he slept, feeling nothing but love for him. Dark lashes shuttered his eyes. The planes of his face were sharply defined in this light, and his jaw was shadowed with a scruff of beard. She resisted the urge to run her fingertips over his cheek.

His blue eyes opened. "Good morning." His voice was rough with sleep.

"Good morning." She cuddled closer in his arms. "I better get up and get ready for work."

"No," he said. "With everything that happened, I think you can take a day off. Breck will understand."

"Do you think so?" She hated the idea of shirking her duty, but she would also love to remain in Ty's arms and be able to embrace her entire family, not allowing them out of her sight.

She was painfully aware of the danger she had been in the night before and how easily she could have become the victim. An even more tragic outcome could have resulted. "I'll call Breck."

He nuzzled her forehead. "I could have lost you yesterday."

Leah splayed her fingers over his chest just above his heart. "Maybe. I somehow knew you would find me."

"I need to ask you something."

"You can ask me anything." She leaned back to gaze into his eyes.

"Are you ready to marry me now? I don't want to wait any longer."

Her breath caught in her throat. "I love you like crazy, but I still have to take care of Gran and Gracie. I'm not sure it's fair to ask you to take on my responsibilities."

A slow grin spread across his features. "Don't be silly. They're a part of you, and I love you. The question is, will you take on my responsibilities? I have two crazy brothers and a father who thinks he rules the world and everyone in it."

Leah laughed. "Maybe he does. He sure came in at the right time last night."

Ty kissed her forehead. "Maybe."

"Seriously, Ty. Your dad is a great guy."

"I'm beginning to think so." A smile touched his mouth and crinkled his eyes.

When they made it to the breakfast table, Leah was clad in one of Ty's T-shirts and a pair of cutoff shorts. She embraced Gracie, who had spent the night in the room with Gran. She gazed around the kitchen, at the hum of activity and the morning bustle, at all the people she loved and had grown to care for. "Yes."

Ty spun around to face her. "Was that a yes?"

Leah giggled. "Yes. What more could I ever want than this?"

"Yahoo!" Ty grabbed her and lifted her in the air. "She's going to marry me!"

There was an uproar of voices in the Garrett kitchen. Beau grabbed a saucepan and beat on the bottom with a large ladle, while Colton hooted and made drumming noises on the table.

Gran clapped her hands and said, "Thank heavens!"

Big Jim folded his arms across his chest and beamed his pleasure.

Gracie ran over to throw her arms around Ty's legs. "Now you'll be my daddy."

Big Jim contacted a construction team out of Amarillo to build a home for his middle son and his bride. He claimed it was his wedding gift to them. He also gave them two sections of land.

Leah had asked what a section of land was, and Ty had whispered that it was six hundred and forty acres.

She swallowed hard. "You mean to tell me your father just gave us over twelve hundred acres? Just for us?"

"Just for us." Ty squeezed her hand. "And for Gracie and her brothers and sisters."

Leah laughed. "Just how many brothers and sisters did you have in mind?"

"Whatever happens is fine with me." He suddenly sobered. "I would like to formally adopt Gracie. I think it would be nice if we all shared the same last name."

"Oh, that would be wonderful. Gracie will finally have the daddy she's always wanted."

He stroked the side of her face. "Another thing...I thought we could build a little cottage for your grandmother, so she could be the queen of her own castle but still keep her close."

She couldn't stop grinning. "A cottage for Gran. She's going to love that...and I will too."

"And a chicken coop, of course."

"Of course." She felt as though a down pillow had exploded inside her chest. Everyone she loved would be gathered together. *Family...*

It seemed that Big Jim didn't want to take any chances that Ty might slip away from him again. He became much more supportive of Ty's musical career.

They hired a hand to live at the bunkhouse behind Gran's house to take care of the property and farm the land for her.

The wedding was simple. At least more simple than expected.

Leah had wanted to wait until Ty was through competing on *Texas Country Star*, but he wouldn't have any of it. She chose Sara Beth as her bridesmaid and Gran to give her away. Gracie, of course, led the procession down the aisle.

All the Garrett men were lined up and waiting for her at the altar. Ty was flanked by both brothers and his dad, and all wore enormous grins.

The most exciting moment of all was when Ty placed the wedding ring on her finger. It had belonged to his mother. Big Jim thought it should go to the next Garrett bride. Ty offered to buy her a brand-new engagement ring of her choice, but she was thrilled to wear the one his father had given his bride. She hoped Elizabeth Jane Garrett was looking on and that she would approve their union.

The wedding reception was held at the Eagles Hall in Langston, where a country band had been booked to entertain and the dance floor had been opened to the public after the reception.

Leah sat at a table with her new husband, her daughter and grandmother, plus her new in-laws. They were joined by Sara Beth and Frank and by Breck and his wife, Cami.

She couldn't remember ever being so very happy in her life. It appeared that all the guests were enjoying this event nearly as much as Leah herself. This day was a culmination of all her dreams coming true at one time. *Hitting the jackpot.*

Big Jim Garrett surprised everyone by bringing a date with him. Celia Diaz looked really good on his arm, and when he took her out onto the dance floor, Colton and Beau clinked their longnecks together and toasted them. "'Bout damned time," Colt murmured.

When the band took their first break, two strangers entered the hall. The woman had flame-red hair and a camera with a long lens clasped in her grip. The man who came behind her lugged some kind of tripod slung over one shoulder and a huge camera bag on the other.

Leah leaned over to Ty and whispered, "Are those people from around here?"

"The photographer is from Dallas. I don't know where the videographer is from."

She had no idea what a videographer was or what he was going to do, but he began to unpack his equipment and set up close to the stage.

The next arrival was a big, bearlike man with glasses and a beard. He entered, looked around, and made a beeline for the other new arrivals. There was hand shaking and back slapping, with the furry-looking man making gestures toward the stage.

Ty grinned broadly as the man strode across the

length of the hall with a wide grin of his own. Ty stood up to greet him and introduced him as his friend Will. Ty made room at the table, seating Will on the other side of Leah.

Will gazed at Leah with open admiration but addressed Ty. "I can see why you were in such a hurry to get back here." He gave a nod. "Man, she is an eleven on a ten-point scale."

Ty snugged an arm around her. "She's better than that."

Such glowing praise brought a flush she felt as heat rising from her neck.

When the musicians returned to the stage, the leader announced the addition of a local singer for the next set. He introduced Tyler Garrett as an emerging artist and a contestant on the upcoming *Texas Country Star* television program.

Grinning, Ty stood and sauntered to the stage amid applause and cheering.

Leah noted the photographer and videographer were on duty. She glanced at Ty's father and was glad to see Big Jim applauding and beaming from ear to ear. He looked very proud of his middle son.

Ty took the stage with a confidence that amazed Leah. She couldn't imagine how it would feel to be able to stand up in front of so many people without passing out from pure fright. Yet he grinned and adjusted the microphone to his height. He thanked everyone for their good wishes regarding his wedding earlier in the day and gestured to his "beautiful bride, Leah."

Will nudged her. "Smile. This is being recorded."

Leah sucked in a breath and froze as the crowd turned to her. The video guy and the camerawoman aimed their lenses in her direction. Leah bared her teeth in what she hoped passed for a smile, all the while expecting her heart to pop out of her chest at any moment.

Ty gave her a reassuring grin and patted his chest over his heart, a silent *I love you*. He sang a few songs made popular by other artists and then announced he was going to sing a song he had written for his bride. "Leah, you are the love of my life, and all my songs are dedicated to you."

Tears filled Leah's eyes as Ty sang a beautiful ballad he had written just for her. He sang about falling in love with her big brown eyes and sweet smile. He told the story of needing to leave but wanting to stay with her. His lyrics wrapped around her like a warm blanket.

For the first time in her life, Leah felt secure. She finally knew what love was and that it would endure through time, no matter what might lie ahead.

When he finished the song, he blew her a kiss, and everyone rose to their feet to applaud.

Gracie got out of her seat and threw her arms around Leah's neck. "Mommy, I'm so glad we married Ty."

Leah swallowed hard, her throat choked with emotion. "Me too, baby. Me too."

Ty sang one more song. When that number ended, he returned to the table. Standing beside Leah, he held out his hand. "May I have this dance?"

Leah grinned as she put both hands in his and he pulled her to her feet. "I'm not all that good at dancing," she protested.

He led her out to the middle of the dance floor, gently guiding her. "You're in luck, because I'm really good at dancing."

She giggled. "And modest too. I hope I don't stumble all over you."

Ty drew her close and led her around the floor in a two-step. He kissed her forehead and then her lips.

Leah relaxed against his chest, his arms tight around her.

"You worry too much," he said. "Trust me. Everything is going to be just fine."

Read on for an excerpt from the next book in the
Dark Horse Cowboys series by June Faver

HOT TARGET
COWBOY

Available January 2019
from Sourcebooks Casablanca

Chapter 1

COLTON GARRETT WAS LATE.

He hated to be late for anything, but most especially anything having to do with his father. He could already see the disapproval in "Big Jim" Garrett's eyes and hear his huff of impatience.

As the oldest of the Garrett sons, Colt was somehow expected to set a good example for the others. To be perfect, it seemed.

Colt heaved a sigh as he pulled his truck in at the auction barn and located a parking space. He knew his dad would already be there with his youngest brother, Beau.

Well, Colt's tardiness couldn't be helped. Just as he was preparing to leave the ranch and had barely climbed into his truck, his middle brother, Tyler, called, and he could hardly hang up on him.

Tyler, a rising country-western star, was on his first tour with his recently formed band. As a newlywed, Ty missed his bride, Leah, but since Leah's eight-year-old daughter, Gracie, attended the local elementary school, Leah couldn't exactly run off and join him on the road. Ty was lonesome and didn't want to make Leah feel bad, but getting everything off his chest to his big brother had apparently done him a lot of good...or at least that's what Ty had said.

Colt climbed out of his truck and stomped through the unpaved parking area, roiling up a layer of dust with his freshly polished boots. He frowned, realizing he would have to give them another shine if he planned to go to the weekly dance at the Eagles' Hall in Langston that evening.

He had hoped to enjoy a few beers at the bar and a few dances with some of the local talent. Friday nights were meant for dancing and an end to the seemingly endless toil of keeping up with the sprawling Garrett ranch.

Colt entered the auction barn, looking around for his dad and his youngest brother.

The smell of fresh hay and animals mingled with Texas dust. A familiar aroma to a working cowboy.

"Hey, Colt!" Evan Burke greeted him. "Going to be at the Eagles' tonight?"

"You betcha," Colt responded. "Hey, have you seen my dad?"

Evan rolled his eyes. "Hard to miss Big Jim. He's on the other side of the show barn, inspecting some stock. He was lookin' for you earlier."

"Yeah, I imagine he still is." He gave Evan a clap on the shoulder and strode off to meet his fate. Not that Big Jim was anyone for his sons to fear, but he had a way of expressing his displeasure that left the unfortunate offender with no doubt as to their shortcomings. Colton didn't like to be that person.

As the oldest of the three brothers, Colton was also the biggest. He was six foot four like his dad and had the shoulders of a linebacker. Making his way through the milling crowd was slow going, but at least he could see over most of them. He started when he heard a feminine yelp.

"Watch it!"

He had smacked into someone and turned just in time

to grab her before she rebounded onto the ground. He was staring into the face of the most beautiful female he had ever laid eyes on, much less held in his arms. "Um, sorry," he said.

She made a growl in the back of her throat. "Honestly! Colton Garrett, you need to watch where you're going. You could kill a girl just by stomping all over her."

Perplexed, he gazed into her dark eyes, seeking some recognition, but was unable to place this lovely young woman. "I didn't mean to step on you... Uh, do I know you?"

She huffed again. "Oh, for Pete's sake. Of course you do." She pushed away and gave him a scowl before tossing her long, dark hair and striding away.

Colt gazed after her, trying to place her in the long line of girls he had known over the course of his lifetime there in Langston. He was certain the long-legged beauty hadn't been in his graduating class in school. He would have surely remembered her.

She was tall, with legs up to her neck. Her butt was round, and Colt couldn't stop staring as her rear moved with each step in her faded Wranglers. She wore a sleeveless western shirt that snapped up the front and showed off her slim but well-toned arms to advantage. And her breasts...oh, yeah. She had 'em. *Dang!* Now he was standing in the milling throng of mostly male farmers and ranchers with a hard-on like a horny teenager.

Colt swept off his Stetson and held it waist high to cover his state while he raked his fingers through his hair.

But he couldn't tear his gaze from the unknown female.

Her long, straight hair had been topped with a white, straw cowboy hat, and she wore an attitude as though she had a permanent case of get-the-hell-away-from-me.

Colt sighed. Casting back in his memory, he couldn't think of any particular girl who had disliked him so openly. In fact, having been an all-star athlete in the local high school had made him pretty popular. Most of the local girls he knew had fallen all over themselves to make sure he was aware they found him attractive and totally desirable as a boyfriend. Of course, a lot of that had to do with the size of his father's ranch. Girls who grew up in farm and ranch territory knew that God wasn't making any more prime Texas real estate, and being a future heir to a considerable hunk of that land would have made him popular with the local female population even if he wore thick glasses and had buck teeth and a face full of zits.

Being a Garrett in this part of the world was generally thought to be a good thing. Why this particular girl didn't think so was a puzzle to Colt. But he had no time to figure it out.

He followed along in the direction the mystery girl had taken, all the while keeping an eye out for Big Jim or Beau.

The latter individual hailed him with the wave of a hand. "Hey Bubba."

Colt cringed at the nickname. "Don't call me that," he admonished.

His youngest brother gazed up at him, his intense blue eyes, a Garrett characteristic, twinkling with mischief. "How about Mud? That's what I'm thinking your name is. You better go make nice with Dad. He sent me to find you." He grinned. "Or, I should say, to 'see if you had gotten your lazy ass out of bed yet.'"

Colt drew in a deep breath and let it out, shaking his head as he did so. "I'm in trouble?"

"Not so much. Dad's got his eye on some horses. He wants you to take a look at the lot of 'em and give your opinion."

Colt gazed at Beau with an exaggerated look of surprise. "Me? He wants my opinion?" He placed his hand on his broad chest.

Beau gave him a shove. "Don't be an ass. Of course he does. The opinion of the lowly little brother counts for nothin'…but you…" He gave Colt another nudge. "You da big expert."

Colt grinned, emitting a wry chuckle. "And you da lil' bro who gets off easy."

Beau raised his brows. "You think it's been easy growing up in your shadow?"

Colt grunted. "You think it's been easy breaking ground and paving the way for you two losers?"

The brothers kept up their good-natured teasing as they strolled toward the show barn.

Colt put his Stetson back on his head and looked around. "Hey, do you know who that girl is up ahead? The one with the long, dark hair?"

"And that bodacious backside?"

They both stared at the aforementioned rear with due reverence and fascination.

"Yup, that's the one."

"That, big bro, is Joe Dalton's little sister. None other than the lovely Misty Dalton. What do you think? Pretty hot, huh?"

Colt felt as though he'd been sucker-punched. Joe's little sister... She couldn't be more than nineteen or twenty to his twenty-eight. *Too young. Way too young.* "Why haven't I seen her around before?"

"Roll your tongue back in your head, Colt. You're gonna trip on it."

Colt took a long look. "She knew who I was, but I couldn't place her."

"You had graduated and were off at college when she hit high school. No reason you would have noticed her as a freshman... Hell, she's a couple of years younger than me. For you, she would practically be jailbait."

"Shut up." Colt continued to fill his eyes with the rare beauty.

She walked with a certain graceful bearing that he found appealing, like a queen among her subjects. Head high, back straight. Her wide-set dark eyes flicked around the crowd as though she too searched for someone.

Colt felt a tug of something he was surprised to recognize as jealousy. He hoped she wasn't looking for her boyfriend...or, worse still, her husband. He cleared his throat. "Do you know if she's married or going with someone?"

Beau gave him a sharp glance. "Man, you're not kidding, are you? Is this a case of that 'love at first sight' thing I've heard about?"

Colt chuckled. "Well, it seems to have worked out for Ty."

Beau cocked his head to one side and stroked his chin. "Sure did," he muttered.

———

Misty Dalton scanned the churning crowd for either one of her brothers. Joe was dead set on selling off the Dalton stock, no matter what she or her little brother, Mark, thought about it. With their dad so very ill, she supposed they didn't have much choice, but it killed her to see the pain in Mark's eyes over losing his beloved Appaloosa stallion. He was only twelve years old and had raised the horse from a colt.

This was just too much misery for one so young to bear. At least she had gotten to enjoy a childhood with both parents.

When their mother was alive, things had been different. Her mom had been a cheerful, churchgoing woman, a "treasure above rubies," according to her dad.

But when her mom was killed, riding on the church bus to a women's retreat, everything changed. The remaining family members seemed to have stopped functioning when they buried their matriarch. They slogged through their days with no particular plan or ambition. Misty was only fifteen at the time, and somehow it had fallen to her, as the surviving female in the household, to shop for groceries and produce simple meals and to wash dishes and do laundry. At first, Joe shouldered a lot of the responsibility for the ranch, while their father had fallen into the bottle, deadening his pain with liquor to make it through the sleepless nights. Now, he was dying of liver disease and stomach cancer. *Not fair. The whole thing is just not fair.*

Misty pressed her lips together and swept the hall with her gaze again, searching for Mark or Joe. She blew out an exasperated breath when she spied the Garrett brothers. *Big assholes*. She compared the two, walking side by side.

Beau, the younger one, had gone to school with Joe. She guessed he was okay. Not bad to look at. Despite being tall and broad shouldered, he almost appeared downright puny standing next to the other one. *Colton. Mr. Everything at Langston High.*

She could see his eyes from where she stood. Bright blue, almost turquoise, set in his tanned face. Ringed with black lashes all around to match his dark, dark hair. He wore an expensive western shirt and Wranglers that fit just right, showing off his muscular thighs. Sitting on his head was a soft gray Stetson. *Absolutely freakin' perfect, Mr. "Check me out. I'm a hot cowboy."*

She knew her brother Joe had looked up to his friend Beau's big brother. Idolized him, in fact. Colton Garrett went out for all sports and seemed to do well in all of them, and like in all small towns, Langston citizens were very supportive of their athletes. She recalled all the games where her entire family had sat together on the sidelines, cheering on the local boys.

She pressed her lips together. Those had been good days, but then her family had fallen apart.

Yes, Colton Garrett had been everything Joe Dalton aspired to be. An athlete. A scholar. And rich.

Too bad Joe had never been any of those things, and if Fred Hamilton, the president of the bank, had anything to say about it, the Daltons would be penniless and tossed off their land soon enough.

Poor Dad. He hadn't been able to work much the past couple of years. Joe was doing his best, but it seemed to be too big a task for him to take on all the responsibility for the ranch by himself. Joe just wasn't cut out for ranching, much to the disappointment of their father.

Paco and Rosa Hernandez, the older couple who had lived on the ranch for as long as she could remember, helped out a lot. Paco would till the fields and tend the stock, but he was getting old too. She huffed out a sigh. The Hernandezes were drawing no salary for all their hard work, just food and a place to live… This was the situation since the Daltons had fallen on such hard times. They were indeed like family, and Misty loved them dearly.

Sadly, the one who loved the ranch the most was way too young to take over.

Mark had a deep and abiding kinship with the ranch and the stock. He seemed to have a natural affinity for all the animals and some kind of sixth sense about the crops. Too bad it would all be gone before long.

Misty spotted Mark leaning against the metal wall and motioned for him to join her.

He pushed away from the wall and approached, his gaze cast down and his lips tight with anger and sorrow.

She looped an arm around his neck, giving him an awkward hug. "Let's gut up and get this over with."

"I hate him. He didn't have to put my horse in with the others. He knows how much I love Sam."

"I know how you must feel, but I'm pretty sure Joe is trying to sell off everything we can while we still own it." She gave him a surreptitious kiss on his temple and pulled him along with her. "Be brave, honey. Let's go say goodbye and hope we get top dollar. We sure do need it."

Mark made a scoffing sound deep in his throat. "I wish I was dead."

"No you don't. I need you. Be strong now."

He fell into step beside her as they made their way into the big show barn where the auction would take place and then out the side door where the various lots of horses were grouped for the prospective bidders to inspect.

—⁓—

Although Colton's attention had been captured by the lovely Misty Dalton, the minute he entered the show barn, he was forced to pay homage to his father.

Big Jim stood by the railing with one eyebrow raised as his sons approached. "Well, good afternoon, Colt. Glad to see you could make it."

"It's barely 10 a.m., Dad. Gimme a break."

"Give me a break," Big Jim insisted. "I wanted you to take a look at the horses out back. I'm particularly interested in two different lots. Go check them out, and then tell me what you think."

"Sure." Colt thought he was getting off easy and wondered what it was about the horses that had his father so excited.

"Check out lots 236 and 211. Looks like some good stock there." Big Jim pounded him on the shoulder and moved away from the railing. "Beau and I are going to the cattle barn. I'm lookin' to add a little breeding stock to the herd." He put his hand on Beau's shoulder but kept his gaze fastened on Colton. "You might want to think about investing in some stock too, Son."

Beau laughed. "Yeah, you can afford it."

"I'll keep that in mind." Colt watched his father and

brother head out behind the show barn to the area where
cattle were being offered in lots for inspection before the
auction. He blew out a breath, headed for the area marked
Horses, and stepped outside where portable fences cor-
doned off the different lots of horses grouped for sale.

He found lot 236 and gave his approval. There were
six beautiful Arabs being offered. Just the kind of horse
to catch his dad's eye. One stallion and five fillies. The
stallion was antsy, dancing a little on his fine hooves, his
neck arched as he looked over the crowd. *Yes, perfect
for Big Jim Garrett.*

Colt moved down the line to locate the other horses
Big Jim had deemed worthy. At the very end of the
line, he found lot 211. This was a mixed lot with a
big Appaloosa stallion, a roan gelding, a couple of
Appaloosa fillies, and two sorrel fillies. Not a bad lot
at all.

A young boy was leaning against the fence, stroking
the stallion's neck. Silent tears were running down his
face, unchecked.

Cute kid. He had dark hair in need of a trim and a
few freckles scattered across his nose. His clothes were
worn, and his boots were scuffed.

"Hey, son," Colt said. "This looks like a good horse.
What can you tell me about him?" He reached to give
the horse's nose a stroke.

The boy sniffed. "He is a great horse. His name is
Sam. I raised him from the time he was a foal."

"Good job. And now you're selling him?"

"No," the boy moaned. "My big brother is. He says
we need the money and we can't afford the feed him
anymore."

Colt felt a tightness invade his chest. "That's too bad. What's your name, boy?"

"Mark," he answered. "Mark Dalton. I'm in the sixth grade. If I was older, I could get a job and pay for his feed."

At the name *Dalton*, Colt sucked in a breath. Mark had the same coloring as Misty. Maybe a younger sibling. "My name is Colton Garrett. You can call me Colt. Maybe we could work something out." He chatted with the boy for a bit and then returned to the auction barn.

From the entrance, he glanced back and saw Misty approaching her brother. She handed him a canned soft drink and gave him a hug.

Colt could see the pain on her face as well. He recalled the boy's words that they couldn't afford to buy feed for their stock. *Sad state for a family.*

"Well, hell," Big Jim exploded. "When I suggested you might want to buy some stock, I didn't mean for you to buy the lot I was interested in."

Colt grinned at him. "My mistake, Dad. I thought you would be satisfied with those fine Arabs and leave the other lot for me."

"Mistake, my ass!" Big Jim was grumbling, but he finally admitted he was glad Colton had invested in some horses on his own. Why this particular lot he couldn't explain.

"Dunno, Dad. That big Appaloosa looked like he could sire a few good foals, and the Appaloosa fillies are fine too."

"I'm glad you broke loose with some of that money

you've been sitting on forever." Big Jim shook his silvered head, piercing his son with the intensity of his blue eyes. "I've paid you for working on the ranch since you were in grade school. I've never seen a kid hoard cash the way you do. I'm just glad you finally found something to invest in."

"I have other horses," Colt said, a defensive note in his voice.

"Gifts. Every one of your horses has been a gift."

Colt grinned. "You can give me those Arabs anytime you want."

Big Jim snorted. "Not a chance. I'm going to the cattle auction now, unless you want to buy the lot I'm planning to bid on."

Colt slapped Big Jim on the shoulder. "No, you go ahead. Maybe Beau will bid on them." He watched as Big Jim shook his head and made his way to the cattle area.

"Colt?"

He turned to find Mark Dalton gazing up at him. "Hey, son."

"Did you mean what you said?" the boy asked.

Colt regarded him seriously. "Sure did. Are you agreeable?"

A grin split Mark's face. "Are you kidding? Yes." He stuck out his hand.

Colt shook it, somberly. "So, we're partners, right?"

The boy nodded.

"And you'll ride the bus out to the Garrett ranch after school to give Sam some exercise and do other jobs for me?"

Another gleeful nod.

"I'll drive you home after your work is done. I'm

going to pay you, and you can buy Sam back from me anytime you see fit."

"Yes!" Mark shook hands enthusiastically.

"Deal," Colt said. "See you Monday afternoon." He turned to watch Mark race out of the show barn, a grin plastered across his face.

"I don't know what you're planning, but you better not break my brother's heart."

Colton whirled around to find Misty Dalton gazing up at him. Not an ounce of trust in those dark eyes. "I assure you I had no such intentions."

"He's had enough pain and disappointment to last a lifetime. I won't let you hurt him again." Her lower lip trembled, and Colt had to stop himself from reaching out to stroke her cheek. Her skin was alabaster white, setting off the large, dark eyes to perfection.

He reached for her hand instead. "I understand how you feel about your little brother. I have two of them, and I feel the same way." Her hand felt small tucked inside his large one.

She lifted her chin slightly, still skewering him with her dark gaze. "But you're big enough to stop anyone who tried to hurt them." She wrested her hand from his grasp.

He nodded. "I am, but I respect your feelings, and I would never do anything to cause Mark any pain. I grew up on a ranch, and my dad paid me for my chores. I'll do the same for Mark. It will be good for him and good for me too."

"But why are you doing this?" she persisted.

He heaved a sigh. "Why not? Can't I just take an interest in Mark? He was so heartbroken at losing the horse. I wanted to help him."

Her expression softened. "Okay," she said reluctantly.

He was curious as to why this family was in financial trouble. Not being able to afford to feed one's stock was indeed a problem. "I'm sorry you had to sell your horses, but be secure in the knowledge that they will be well cared for at the Garrett Ranch."

She nodded, pressed her lips together, and suppressed a shiver. "Good to know… My father is ill, and it pained him to agree to sell, but my brother Joe convinced him it was for the best."

Colton considered the young woman in front of him. He had to admire her courage as well as her beauty. "I'm sorry your father is ill," he said. "I wish him a speedy recovery."

Her lips twitched. "He's on hospice."

The full weight of her pronouncement settled heavily on him. "Tough break. Will you and your brothers be okay?"

She shook her head. "I don't think so." She turned away, grimacing.

"Well, I hope to see you again sometime." Colton raised a hand, but she walked away from him, presumably so he wouldn't see her tears.

About the Author

June Faver loves Texas, from the Gulf Coast to the Panhandle, from the Mexican border to the Piney Woods. Her novels embrace the heart and soul of the state and the larger-than-life Texans who romp across her pages. A former teacher and healthcare professional, she lives and writes in the Texas Hill Country.

ROCKY MOUNTAIN COWBOY CHRISTMAS

Beloved author Katie Ruggle's new series brings
pulse-pounding contemporary romantic suspense
to a cowboy's Colorado Christmas

When single dad Steve Springfield moved his family to a
Colorado Christmas tree ranch, he meant it to be a safe
haven. He quickly finds himself fascinated by local folk
artist Camille Brandt—it's too bad trouble is on her trail.

It's not long before Camille is falling for the enigmatic
cowboy and his rambunctious children—he always seems
to be coming to her rescue. As attraction blooms and
danger intensifies, this Christmas romance may just prove
itself to be worth fighting for.

For more Katie Ruggle, visit:
sourcebooks.com

CAUGHT UP IN
A COWBOY

USA Today bestselling author Jennie Marts welcomes you to Creedence, Colorado, where the cowboys are hot on the ice

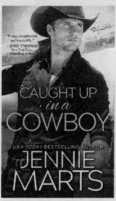

After an injury, NHL star Rockford James returns to his hometown ranch to find that a lot has changed. The one thing that hasn't? His feelings for Quinn Rivers, his high school sweetheart and girl next door.

Quinn had no choice but to get over Rock after he left. Teenaged and heartbroken, she had a rebound one-night stand that ended in single motherhood. Now that Rock's back—and clamoring for a second chance—Quinn will do anything to avoid getting caught up in this oh-so-tempting cowboy...

"Funny, complicated, and irresistible."

—Jodi Thomas, *New York Times* bestselling author

For more Jennie Marts, visit:
sourcebooks.com

TEXAS RODEO

A groundbreaking contemporary Western romance
series with real-life Texas rodeo action

By bestselling author Kari Lynn Dell

Reckless in Texas

Bullfighter Joe Cassidy is a hotshot in the ring...but falling in love with fierce single mom Violet Jacobs? That's a whole new rodeo.

Tangled in Texas

Injured bronc rider Delon Sanchez thinks things can't get worse...until he learns his physical therapist is his oh-so-perfect ex, Tori Patterson.

Tougher in Texas

When rodeo producer Cole Jacobs loses one of his cowboys and his cousin sends along a replacement, he expects a Texas good ol' boy. He gets longtime rival Shawnee Pickett.

Fearless in Texas

Rodeo bullfighter Wyatt Darrington can never let Melanie Brookman know the truth: that he's been crazy in love with her for years.

Mistletoe in Texas

Hank Brookman is ready to return home for the holidays and make amends. Most of all, he hopes Grace McKenna will give him a second chance at love so they can celebrate Christmas—Texas Rodeo style.

"A fun, wild ride!
You need to pick up a Kari Lynn Dell."

—B.J. Daniels, *New York Times* bestselling author

For more Kari Lynn Dell, visit:
sourcebooks.com

HOW TO WRANGLE A COWBOY

Fall in love with the Cowboys of Decker Ranch from RITA finalist Joanne Kennedy.

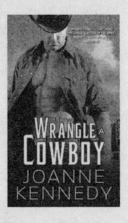

Ranch foreman Shane Lockhart fears his livelihood—and his young son's security—are threatened when the ranch is taken over by the late owner's granddaughter, the most beautiful, exasperating woman Shane has ever met…

For more Joanne Kennedy, visit:

sourcebooks.com